A CROSSFIRE OF POWER AND PASSION

BLUE HAWK. Born to a Cheyenne woman and raised with the Indians until tragedy swept him into the white man's world, he was Caleb Sax—a hero in war, a legend on the frontier, a man about to risk everything for love.

SARAH. As fiery as her Irish heritage, she pledged herself to a man she was forbidden to touch—and was sent away to marry another in shame.

WALKING GRASS. A darkly sensuous Indian maiden, she would belong to the brave courageous enough to undergo the Sun Dance ritual for her hand.

EMILY. The beautiful daughter of a fanatical preacher, she wanted a man who was heathen, wanton, shocking, and magnificently male.

BYRON CLAWSON. The degenerate son of a rich family, he desired a beautiful woman to advance his ambitions—even if he had to win her by treachery and violence.

Also by F. Rosanne Bittner

Frontier Fires

Forthcoming from
POPULAR LIBRARY

F. Rosanne Bittner

SAVAGE HORIZONS

POPULAR LIBRARY

An Imprint of Warner Books, Inc.

A Warner Communications Company

A special thank you to my agent, Denise Marcil.

POPULAR LIBRARY EDITION

Popular Library® is a registered trademark of Warner Books, Inc.

Cover illustration by Franco Acconero

Popular Library books are published by
Warner Books, Inc.
666 Fifth Avenue
New York, N.Y. 10103

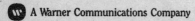 A Warner Communications Company

Printed in the United States of America

First Printing: February, 1987

10 9 8 7 6 5 4 3 2 1

In Memory . . .

For my grandmother, Florence Williams, whose American Indian blood gave her strength and spirit. She was a woman who lived today but belonged to yesterday. She is gone now, but her spirit lives on. My most cherished memories are of the days I spent with her as a child in her little house that had no running water and no modern conveniences; days spent listening to "The Lone Ranger" and "Gunsmoke" on the radio; nights spent sleeping on a feather mattress and listening to trains that passed by in the night, an old clock ticking away the time, ticking away the precious moments I had left with Grandma Williams. Perhaps it was being with her that instilled in me a love for the pioneer spirit, the thrill of listening to good stories and, later, a desire to write my own. I often feel her guidance as I write, and I know I owe much of my success to the things she taught me as a child. I can still hear her laughter, hear her playing the harmonica, feel her hugging me, smell her lilac scent. She was not wealthy in terms of money, yet she gave me gifts no money could buy.

Introduction

This novel contains references to historical characters and events that occurred during the time period covered. All such references are based on factual, printed matter available to the public. However, all primary characters in this novel are purely fictitious and a product of the author's imagination. Any resemblance of these characters to actual persons, living or dead, or of fictitious events to any events that may have occurred at the time of this story are purely coincidental.

This story takes place from the late 1700's through 1832, that growing time in America that was the beginning of the end for the American Indian, a time when the western border along the Missouri River bulged at the seams, soon to give way, spilling emigrants onto the prairies and over the Rockies in search of intangible dreams, shouts of "Manifest Destiny" on their lips. Some even went into Mexican territory to a place called Texas.

Within these pages lies the story not just of one man and the loves and losses destiny brings him, it is also the story of the growth of a nation—the first of a continuing saga that will carry you, the reader, from lands where no white man walked through the Civil War years and beyond. The major historical events of this novel and its sequels are true events. This first book begins in present-day Minnesota and moves to Fort Dearborn, which today is Chicago, Illinois. Other settings include "Unorganized Territory," which is most of the present-day Plains states, from Kansas all the way to North Dakota; "Indian Territory," which is now Oklahoma; and "Mexican Possessions," which include present-day Texas, New Mexico and Arizona, as well as California and parts of Utah and Colorado.

Prologue

There was a time in this land when the Indians west of the Mississippi knew little of the white man. They did not fear him then. They were much more curious than hostile, and most trusted the white man, for they had not been exposed to him long enough to understand that the white man could talk with two different tongues. This was a time when innocence prevailed among the native men of the deep forests and open plains, a time when game was abundant, the buffalo thick as a black sea, and the waters crystal clear. Those were glory days for the Indian, days of full stomachs and freedom.

But all of that would change, beginning with those first white men who came, the trappers and hunters. These first men were mostly French, and they befriended the Indian, some sincerely, some for personal gain. Through them were born sons and daughters of mixed blood, people who belonged to neither world; their lives were hard. This is the story of one such man, from his poignant birth through a life that moved in rythmic episodes between both worlds. The Indian called him Blue Hawk. To the white man he was Caleb Sax.

1

Chapter One

THE day was unusually warm for the season of the Moon of the Falling Leaves, and thirteen-year-old Little Flower swatted at a fly that buzzed relentlessly around her head. The branches of beach, maple, oak and pine hung limp from the humid air, and the sun created an eerie orange glow as it filtered through the thick woods that surrounded the small Cheyenne village.

Little Flower pulled open the laces of her tunic. The buckskin dress was all she wore, but perspiration still wet her long, black hair, making it cling to her neck. The day had been so hot that the women had done little work and the men chose not to hunt, even though winter skulked just to the north, waiting to bring its bitter cold down from Canada into the lands of many lakes where Little Flower and her family dwelled in mud and thatch huts.

The year was 1793, although Little Flower did not think in such terms. She knew nothing at all about white man's ways, his languages and cultures. In fact, at that very moment she stood staring at the first white man who had ever come to their village.

Little Flower was amazed by the man's pale skin and eyes as blue as the sky, as well as the hair on his face as thick as a bush. Actually, she thought him quite ugly. His eyes were set too close together, and his nose was large and hooked. His clothing was soiled, though he wore only buck-

3

skin pants because of the heat, revealing a massive chest covered with black hairs. His skin did not look clean and shiny like the skin of Cheyenne men; he had a different odor about him that made Little Flower wrinkle her nose.

The man had first come to their village two sunrises before, offering tobacco, food and amazing trinkets as signs of friendship. Little Flower could not help but be intrigued by the beautiful beads, pretty ribbons, fine black cooking utensils and the wonderful, bright object in which she could see herself. Yet all the gifts the *vehoe* had passed around did not change Little Flower's suspicion that there was something evil about him. It was not so much that he was ugly; it was more the way he looked at her. Several times she had caught him staring at her, licking his lips like a hungry wolf, and she wondered what he would do to her if he ever caught her alone.

The white man had won the friendship of the Indian men and the fascination of the women with his many wonderful gifts. Even today the women continued to pass around the bright object that reflected their images like the still waters. Sometimes they argued over it. A few, men and women alike, would have nothing to do with the white man and especially not with the magic object that could capture their image. Surely there was something evil about looking at one's own spirit face to face. Perhaps the *vehoe* himself was an evil spirit in the shape of a man. Most of the men, including Little Flower's father, White Bird, chose to accept him, for he had brought a gift more wonderful than any of the others, something in a brown bottle that brought happy feelings and great power when a man drank the fiery liquid inside.

The men were sitting in a circle, passing around the brown bottle and playing the hand game with the *vehoe*. Little Flower watched them in silence, peeking around the corner of her mud hut. Her brothers, Deer Man and Many Bears, along with four other Cheyenne, made bets as White Bird shuffled the walnut shells quickly. A bright red berry lay under one of them, and White Bird's hands moved so quickly it was almost impossible to keep track of the shell that hid the berry. Little Flower saw her father laugh when he again tricked them all. Frenchy, as the pale eyes called himself, scowled in disgust, handing White Bird another wad of tobacco in payment for his bet.

Little Flower wished she could make her father laugh the way he laughed now. But whenever he looked at her, she saw only scorn and dissatisfaction in his eyes. She seemed to be able to do nothing to please him. Old Grandmother, who also lived with them, had told her it was because White Bird's heart had broken when his wife had died giving birth to Little Flower.

"If you had been a son," the old woman explained, "it would have been easier for White Bird. Your mother had given him two sons. But then you were born, and she died. Ever since White Bird has been trying to decide why the Great Spirit cursed him by taking your mother and leaving behind a girl-child. A girl-child is just another mouth to feed, until she has her first flowing time and can bear sons. Then she becomes something of value to her father. You are very beautiful, and White Bird can get many gifts for you when a brave decides to make you his wife."

Little Flower was uncertain why her first flowing time would make her instantly a woman. One moon before she had had her time, a frightening and confusing experience. Her father had rejoiced and celebrated while Little Flower sat in the menstrual lodge, weeping over things she did not understand and wondering what would be expected of her when she became some brave's wife. She did not want to be a wife, not yet. She still liked to play with her stick dolls and help Old Grandmother, who was her only source of love and strength. Now that she had become a woman, she wore the chastity rope made of reeds, and she could not look upon her older brothers; nor could she look upon an unrelated boy who might become a suitor. It seemed that everything had suddenly become different and frightening since she had so abruptly changed from girl to woman.

The men playing the game suddenly laughed loudly, startling Little Flower out of her thoughts. Frenchy handed over three beads to White Bird, and Little Flower wondered if the *vehoe* had an endless supply of the colorful beads, the fiery water and the fists full of tobacco. The pale eyes had made the reasons for his generosity clear when he first arrived. He had shown the Cheyenne men his strange instruments called traps, made of a hard, cold material with cutting teeth that snapped when stepped on. In spite of the language barrier, Frenchy had managed to explain to the Cheyenne men that the traps were used to catch beaver, and that if the Cheyenne would help him catch many beaver, he would bring them even more gifts.

For some reason the *vehoe* liked beaver furs. Little Flower wondered what he could do with them, and she wondered, too, just how many more white men lived in that unknown world beyond the great woods. Did they all look like Frenchy, and did they all bear such splendid gifts?

Frenchy passed around the bottle again, and the Cheyenne men drank from it, their laughter growing louder. Before long, Frenchy's gambling luck began to change. Suddenly Deer Man stood up and threw down the last of his beads in anger. He had lost them all. Little Flower's eyes widened when her brother also removed the handsome blue quill necklace his wife had made for him only days earlier. He threw it at Frenchy and stalked away.

Little Flower's eyes teared. Surely the *vehoe* was evil to have made Deer Man give up such a prize. The necklace had been a love gift from Sweet Seed Woman, Deer Man's young wife. She had spent many hours making it for him, her hands pricked and bleeding badly from the sharp quills. Little Flower greatly admired the necklace, and envied Sweet Seed Woman her talent for making the most beautiful quill necklaces in the tribe. There were plenty of porcupine where they were camped, and Sweet Seed Woman could always make another necklace, but it was a painstaking chore that left a woman's hands very sore. Little Flower suspected Deer Man would not even have used the necklace in a bet if not for the strange water in the brown bottle. It made the men act strangely and do wild things, made them slur their words and made their eyes red and frightening. She was sure the bottle contained evil spirits, and she hated Frenchy for giving the fiery liquid to Deer Man.

Looking back, she saw Frenchy drink some of it, wiping his lips on his arm and handing the bottle to White Bird. Little Flower's father took another swallow and let out a war whoop, his eyes gleaming like a crazy man's. Little Flower was sure the evil water was something that got right into a man's blood and came out through his eyes and mouth, as though he was possessed by a demon.

The shell game grew more serious, and the *vehoe* was winning more than losing. Soon the other Cheyenne men had nothing left to bet, and the game was down to Frenchy and White Bird, who had lost most of the gifts Frenchy had given him, as well as a fine parfleche and a stone hatchet. He continued to drink the fiery water, becoming more daring and determined, for White Bird was known among the Cheyenne as the most skilled at the shell game. He gestured that he wanted to play again, but Frenchy threw up his hands to indicate White Bird had nothing of value left with which to gamble. The *vehoe* shook his head and started to rise, and White Bird growled at him to sit back down, motioning with his hand angrily.

Frenchy shook his head, frowning. He removed his hat and scratched his head, as though thinking a moment, and Little Flower made a face at the sight of his long, matted hair. It was not clean and combed like the Cheyenne men kept theirs. She frowned with curiosity as he held out his hand, indicating a small person, then pointed at White Bird. He held out both hands, making a motion to indicate the shape of a woman, then pointed to his private parts, making a copulating gesture. He held out his hand again to indicate someone short, and White Bird grinned. He turned to Many Bears, Little Flower's oldest brother, who had remained to watch.

"He wants me to use your sister as payment if I lose the next game," White Bird told his son, his words slurred.

Little Flower's heart pounded in horror. She cringed farther around the corner of the hut, wondering if she should run away. Her eyes filled with tears. Did her father hate her so much that he would give her away to the strange white man? Old Grandmother had said she was worthy of the finest brave, and now she could hear her brother arguing that very point.

"You know Black Antelope has eyes for her," Many Bears shouted angrily at her father. "He will give many blankets and horses for her."

But White Bird was full of the evil water and was thinking and acting foolishly. "If I win, the *vehoe* will give back all the things I have lost, plus corn and tobacco, as well as his fine hunting knife, in return for Little Flower. I would get gifts, and I would get a husband for my daughter."

"She is too young," Many Bears argued. "Cheyenne men should have a chance to ask for her, as well as Black Antelope. You know he is already preparing many gifts to offer for her. He will be very angry if you do this, Father."

Frenchy watched with a sly grin, unable to understand all that was said so heatedly in drunken Cheyenne, but aware of what the argument was about. But he wanted the pretty little Cheyenne virgin, and he would risk the Indians' anger to get her. White Bird waved his son off and spit, and Little Flower choked back tears. Not only was her father considering giving her to the white stranger, but this was the first time she had heard Black Antelope wanted her. Black Antelope was Sioux, an honored warrior, strong and handsome. She barely knew him, yet she knew he would make a much better and more honorable husband than the smelly white man with the narrow eyes and a hooked nose, whose language she did not even understand.

"I believe the pale eyes has magic powers," White Bird argued. "He is a man of wealth, with many gifts, and with fire sticks. He has the magic water that makes us happy. It would be good for my daughter to be married to him. He can bring us many more gifts than Black Antelope. He knows of another world, where there are great houses on water and where many white men gather together in stone buildings. He has told us this. He has brought us traps to catch beaver and will give us food and gifts for the furs. It is good that he has come here. We can learn many things from this man with pale skin." White Bird stood up, sticking out his chest proudly. "I, White Bird, will be the first Cheyenne to give a daughter in marriage to this man of great powers! It is a good bet. If he loses, I get everything back and more, and if he still wants Little Flower, I will demand much from him and get many good gifts in return."

"It is a foolish bet," Many Bears replied cautiously.

White Bird pushed at him. "Get away from me, my son. Do not argue with your father. It is a good bet."

Little Flower hurriedly snuck around the hut and darted inside, her wide, frightened eyes meeting Old Grandmother's. The old woman looked at her sadly. "My ears have heard," she told her granddaughter. "It is a bad thing your father does, but if you must go to the *vehoe*, you must go proudly. Do not shame your father by refusing to do his bidding. You wear the chastity rope, Little Flower. Do not be afraid. The *vehoe* must honor it and wait until you are ready to take a man, as any honorable Cheyenne would do."

Little Flower hurried to her side, huddling down beside the old woman who had been the only mother she had ever known. "But he is not Cheyenne," she whimpered. "He is not anything Indian. Maybe it is different with white men. I am afraid of him, grandmother."

The old woman put an arm around her. "I should chase your father out of this hut for what he is doing, but with my daughter dead, and your brothers having their own wives, your father is all I have to provide for me. I cannot help you, grandchild, except that I am here when you need me. I cannot undo your father's decision."

She rocked the girl gently, while outside the final game was played. An eerie silence hung in the air, broken suddenly by Frenchy's victorious laughter. Little Flower looked at her grandmother, and tears ran down her childlike cheeks. The old woman's heart ached for her grandchild, such a small girl expected to behave like a woman. Suddenly White Bird walked into the hut, his eyes wild from the whiskey. He looked at Old Grandmother boldly, as though to challenge her to argue with him. The old woman stiffened, holding her chin high.

"I have heard." She gave Little Flower a hug. "Your daughter is ready. She will make you proud. But the day will come when you, White Bird, feel no pride. You will regret this day, and you will know shame. My daughter would have cast you out for what you are doing."

"Be still, old woman, or I will cast *you* out, and your belly will be empty." He walked over and grasped Little Flower's arm. "Come! I have promised you to the *vehoe*."

Little Flower sniffed and swallowed, tossing her head and looking defiantly at her father. "You do not have to pull me," she told him proudly.

The man let her go, stepping back in surprise. He jerked his head then, indicating that she should leave the hut.

Little Flower walked out, her insides churning, her heart breaking over the fact that none of the normal customs had been followed. She had been won in a bet. There had been no courting, no romantic flute playing, no period of gift giving, and no one had bothered to ask if she *wanted* to marry the pale eyes. The *vehoe* stood before her, his eyes gleaming as he licked his lips again like a wolf. He handed a sack of corn and a strip of tobacco to White Bird, even though the Cheyenne had lost the bet, the gesture indicating he thought the little Cheyenne girl of great value.

Time moved too swiftly then, and Little Flower began to feel she was living in a dream—or a nightmare. She was far from ready for the reality of a woman's world, but it was crashing down around her, hitting her sharply with its stones of pain and fear. She had never heard of another Cheyenne woman marrying so quickly, out of force.

Frenchy's eyes moved over her hungrily, his whole body feeling hot and tingly at the thought of being the first to take the lovely woman-child. Her cries of pain would give him great pleasure. It had been a long time since he had been with a woman. Virgin or not, he wouldn't bother going easy with this one. His mind whirled with so many pleasurable fantasies that he could barely think straight.

White Bird pushed Little Flower closer to the *vehoe*, indicating that he gave her to Frenchy. Little Flower struggled not to turn her nose up at the white man's smell. Frenchy grinned even more, his face red as a berry, his yellow teeth reminding Little Flower of the fangs of a wild animal. He turned to his pack mule and handed another bottle of the fiery water to White Bird, indicating that he wanted to give yet another gift in return for his wonderful prize. Then he reached inside the pocket of his soiled buckskin pants and took out the blue quill necklace he had won from Deer Man. He handed it to Little Flower, demonstrating before the others his kindness and generosity toward his new young wife. For a brief moment, Little Flower felt a ray of hope that the man might be kind to her after all. She clung tightly to the necklace, happy that at least she had it now and could give it back to Sweet Seed Woman if she wished.

White Bird nodded his approval of Frenchy's kindness. Frenchy grasped Little Flower's arm firmly, pulling her toward the hut he had bribed some Cheyenne women into building for him in return for bright cloth and beads. He had enjoyed watching them, and wished he could bed some of them. But he had been cautious, not wanting to offend any of the men, because he wanted these savages for friends, not enemies. They could be a big help to him in the fur trade. Now he had won the prettiest girl in camp, fair and square. He did not have to worry about offending anyone. She was his wife.

He shoved Little Flower into the hut, closing the heavy, bearskin flap after them. It was close and smelly inside, and Little Flower stared in terror as the man with the ugly pale eyes stumbled closer, himself full of fire water. He grasped her tunic and ripped it down and off her so that she was suddenly naked. She felt ashamed and terrified.

Outside everyone else went back to their own affairs. It was done. Little Flower belonged to the French trapper and should feel honored to belong to a white man who had come from a distant, unknown land and brought such wondrous gifts.

"We will demand to see her." Many Bears sat arguing with his brother inside Deer Man's hut. Sweet Seed Woman sat quietly, interlacing quills for a new necklace for Deer Man to replace the one he had lost to the pale eyes. Her heart still burned with irritation at Deer Man for gambling away her gift.

"He is her husband," Deer Man replied dejectedly. "We can make no demands."

"And she is our sister. For four days we have not seen her. Why? Why does he not let her come out? And where does she relieve herself? Inside the hut? I tell you something is wrong. To let him marry her was wrong. I told our father that. When he is not full of the firewater he knows this and is sad. And to relieve his sadness, he drinks more firewater. Now he does nothing but lie around uselessly, moaning about how he could have gotten more gifts for his daughter from Black Antelope and about how stingy the pale eyes has become. Father will do nothing to help Little Flower. It is up to you and me, my brother."

Deer Man sighed. "I thought the *vehoe* would be more honorable. He brought us many gifts, things we have never seen before."

"He is full of tricks, and our sister did not want to go to

him. I think she needs our help. I think we should go to their hut and demand to see Little Flower. Why does she not come out when he does? And even he comes out only to get wood and to give us a few beads for more meat. Since he took our sister he has not even shown us how to use the traps, as he promised. He is lazy and is living off our food. And he smells like a skunk."

Deer Man looked over at his wife, watching her work the quills with fingers again painful with sores. Sweet Seed Woman looked back at him. Inside the privacy of their hut, she was free to speak her mind without disgracing her husband.

"I speak as a woman," she told him softly. "A woman knows about a man by his eyes. I did not like that pale eyes. He is not kind. I think he is cruel to all people, not just his enemy. We owe him nothing, for he was not first adopted into the tribe. Nothing about his marriage to Little Flower was done according to custom, and the spirits will not be pleased until it is made right. I fear the spirits will punish White Bird for what he has done, perhaps punish all of us unless we help Little Flower."

Deer Man looked at Many Bears and nodded. "I agree. In the morning when he comes out to relieve himself and borrow more food, we will demand that he bring our sister out also, or let us go inside and see her."

"And if he refuses?"

"We will get others to help us. He will be unable to refuse if he values his life."

Many Bears grinned and nodded. "Good. I am glad you agree."

Frenchy wiped grease from his mouth onto his soiled clothing, glancing over at Little Flower, who sat huddled in the corner of the hut wrapped in a bearskin. The days had cooled since that hot, terrible day she had been given to the pale eyes for a wife, but she was sure her heart was much colder than the coldest winter day—never had she known such revulsion and hatred.

"Time to tie you up and make sure you don't run off on me, bitch," he grumbled.

Little Flower knew by now what the words meant. She cringed further into the corner, wishing death would come to relieve her of the horrors of the pale eyes. He walked over to her, jerking her back to the bed and the stakes he had pounded into the dirt floor. He pushed her down, and the bearskin fell from her naked body. She shivered from the cold air, but he paid no heed. She had not been allowed to dress since the first night he had torn off her dress. Sometimes he forced the hated firewater down her throat to make her more submissive to his animalistic advances, but it did not work as he had hoped. It only made her struggle and fight him.

"You lay still, girl," he grumbled. "You get up and I'll beat the hell out of you." He grabbed a small spade and covered a hole he had dug for her to relieve herself.

"You're starting to stink," he mumbled. "I suppose I'll have to let you out of here eventually so you can wash. If you'd settle down and act like a good wife for Frenchy, he would trust you not to run away. Always I have to tie you. How many times must I get inside of you for you to understand that's the way it is and you should enjoy it, hmm? Maybe Frenchy is not big enough for you. Maybe you would look for a nice, big Indian buck to take Frenchy's place?"

He jerked her arm up to a stake and she whimpered. "You wild Indian bitches are all whores, but Frenchy's wife will not be one." He picked up a piece of rawhide and started to wrap it around the raw flesh of her wrists, stopped when he heard voices outside.

"Frenchy!"

The trapper recognized Many Bears' voice. Little Flower also recognized it, and she wanted to cry out to her brother but dared not. Frenchy glared at her, motioning for her to be still. He got up and quickly left the hut. Little Flower could hear him greeting her brother jovially, as though they were great friends. She heard Many Bears demand to see her. He had to repeat it several times, and she knew that at first Frenchy did not understand what Many Bears was saying. Then she heard Deer Man's voice as well, and her heart quickened with hope. She sat up and pulled the fur robe around herself, afraid someone would enter and find her naked.

Tears welled in her eyes at the realization of how dirty and smelly she was. She did not have the pretty looking glass and she was glad, for she would not want to look at herself now. She felt ugly and bad, and her body screamed with pain from her husband's continuous rapes and beatings. She had put up with the torture, for she did not want to shame her father. But she had shriveled down to bones in only five days, unable to eat because of her pain and unhappiness.

She heard scuffles then, and shouting. Frenchy was yelling, obviously cursing, although she did not truly understand everything he said. The next thing she knew, Many Bears jerked back the entrance flap and stepped inside. Her eyes widened and she scooted back more. She could see the shock in her brother's eyes, and his nose curled up at the smell.

"What has he done to you?" Many Bears looked appalled. He stepped closer, and Little Flower turned away, hanging her head and weeping. Many Bears knelt behind her and put his hands on her shoulders. "Tell me, Little Flower. Deer Man and I are here to help you if you want it. You did not choose this man. You have the right to leave him."

"He would only come after me . . . kill me."

"Then we shall kill him first. It is easily done."

She covered her face. "I would not weep for him," she whispered.

Many Bears knew the meaning of the words. He had her permission to get rid of the pale eyes. "He violated the chastity rope," he said quietly, his words more a statement than a question.

Little Flower nodded. "He ties me . . . beats me. If I could I would run away." She wiped at her eyes, smearing the dirt on her face. "He uses me . . . like a dog. And he makes me drink the fiery water. If I cannot be free of him soon, Many Bears, I will put a knife into my heart."

She bent over and wept harder, and part of the blanket fell away to reveal large welts on her thighs. Many Bears' anger knew no bounds as he also noticed the raw flesh on her ankles and wrists. He touched her hair gently.

"Our father will know what he has done and be ashamed. I, too, am ashamed. Today this husband of yours has seen his last sunrise. He will never again touch you, Little Flower."

His jaw tense with burning anger, he stalked out of the hut. Little Flower heard more cursing and shouting from the pale eyes. She could hear scuffling feet and struggling sounds, and then awful screams. She knew the Cheyenne men were using their knives and tomahawks on the *vehoe*, and his screams of pain and terror made her glad. Soon he no longer cried out, and after several minutes Old Grandmother appeared inside the doorway. The old woman looked around the hut and cursed, holding up her fist, then came over to Little Flower and enveloped the girl in her arms.

"Come, child. Come home."

"He is . . . dead?"

"*Ai*, granddaughter. That bad one is dead and will not hurt you again."

Little Flower wept. "I will not . . . mourn him," she sobbed. "Forgive me, Grandmother."

"There is nothing to forgive." The old woman stroked her hair gently. "It is White Bird who needs forgiving, for he greatly wronged his daughter. He knows he did a bad thing. You will not go to another man unless it is someone of your own choosing. I will chase out your father and starve to death before I let you go again unwillingly. May *Maheo* strike me dead if I do not keep this promise."

Chapter
Two

THE magnificent Sioux warrior rode proudly into White Bird's camp, carrying several blankets. Other braves walked behind him, carrying food and more gifts. Horses were still new to the Indian and not easily come by, but Black Antelope had stolen his from a camp of Red Coat soldiers farther north. His entrance on the animal made him appear even more grand and brave and handsome than usual. He led another horse alongside his own, and black flies buzzed mercilessly around them, despite the animals' swishing tails.

Black Antelope's dark skin glistened with sweat from the unusually hot, humid October day. The weather had again slyly turned warm, giving no hint of the cold winter to come. In spite of the heat, Black Antelope appeared clean and neat, his long hair plaited into two braids intertwined with colorful feathers, as well as three coup feathers at the base of one braid. A string of tiny bells with colorful scarves hanging from them was tied around each of his legs just below the knees. Other than that, he wore only a loincloth and a deerskin vest, with several strings of brilliant beads decorating his chest and a copper band around the bicep of each arm.

Black Antelope's grand entrance brought stares from the Cheyenne women, especially the available ones. They whispered and giggled as the man rode through camp, with dogs

17

barking at the heels of the horses. He went directly to see White Bird, who came out from his hut when he heard the commotion.

Little Flower followed her father, curious about the noise. When her eyes met Black Antelope's, she immediately looked away, remembering her brother's words with White Bird about Black Antelope wanting her in marriage. She felt suddenly hot with shame, afraid of what Black Antelope would think of her for being the woman of the ugly white man. She ducked back inside the hut, putting her hands to her cheeks to cool them.

"What is it, granddaughter?" Old Grandmother asked, noticing the girl's distress.

Little Flower sat down and returned to mending a pair of her father's moccasins. "It is Black Antelope."

The old woman's eyebrows arched, and a sly grin spread across her thin lips. "*Ai*? Has he come with horses and looking grand?"

Little Flower did not look at her, but nodded.

Old Grandmother chuckled. "I think Many Bears sent runners to Black Antelope some days ago. I think maybe Black Antelope was told about you and that bad white man. And I think Black Antelope is very angry with White Bird."

Little Flower frowned and looked at her grandmother. "Why?"

The old woman winked. "You do not know?"

Little Flower looked back at the moccasins, surprised that after her horrible experience with the pale eyes she should feel such a strange, wondrous movement deep in her body for the grand warrior who had just ridden into her father's village. She had seen Black Antelope before, had stared in awe at the accomplished Sioux warrior many talked about. But she hadn't known then the man had a desire for her. Now that she knew, and was aware of man, her emotions were mixed. Being Black Antelope's woman would be a great honor, and instinctively she knew he would be nothing like Frenchy. Yet the thought of being with any man that way now struck fear in her heart, a fear mixed with odd desires for Black Antelope that surprised her.

"What brings you to my camp on this hot day?" she heard White Bird asking just outside.

"You know what brings me," Black Antelope replied in a deep, commanding voice. "Little Flower was to be mine, and you gambled her away to a dirty white man who was cruel to her. I have come for her, White Bird. I do not ask for her—I *tell* you. You can no longer deny me." There was a moment of silence before he continued. "I have brought you a horse. With this horse and the horse and mule you kept from the pale eyes, you are a wealthy Cheyenne. Horses can carry heavy loads and relieve you of work. I also have blankets. I give you these things not because I beg for Little Flower. After what you have done, I no longer have to beg. I give them because I show you how much I value your daughter . . . more, I think, than you do."

Little Flower's eyes filled with tears, and her heart filled with the warmth of love.

"It is not up to me," White Bird replied. "I and Old Grandmother have promised that she need not marry again unless it is her choice."

"Then let me stay here and camp nearby. I will visit her every day and we will talk so she can know me better. Then she can decide. But it must be soon. Winter will soon be upon us, and it is far to my village."

White Bird ducked inside and motioned for Little Flower to come out. She stared at him a moment before quickly standing, smoothing her tunic and running a quill brush through her hair. She put a hand to the handsome blue quill necklace which Deer Man and Sweet Seed Woman had allowed her to keep. It seemed too big for her frail neck, but she thought it so beautiful that she wore it all the time. She hoped at this moment it made her a little prettier than usual. Her father motioned for her to make haste, and she walked outside on shaking legs. Raising her eyes to meet Black Antelope's, she felt sharp desires coursing through her at the gentleness she saw there, and at the power and grace she sensed in the man.

"You heard what was said," White Bird told her. "Do you wish for Black Antelope to stay so that you might consider him as a husband?"

She took a deep breath, wondering if he would still want her after she told him what she must tell him—that she carried the white man's baby. She walked closer to Black Antelope. She was a woman now, and she would behave as one, with courage and pride. She reached up. "Take me to another place, Black Antelope. There is something I must tell you."

He released the horses he had brought and reached down, grasping her hand. Something warm and wonderful moved through them both when they touched, and Black Antelope knew more than ever what he wanted. He leaned over and whisked her up onto his horse, setting her in front of him. Then he turned the animal and rode away from the village.

Little Flower felt beautiful and more alive than she had for weeks. Black Antelope's powerful, reassuring arm was wrapped around her from behind, and she felt dwarfed and small. He rode to a nearby river and halted his horse, staying on the mount as he breathed in the sweet scent of Little Flower's hair and enjoyed the feel of his arm over her body.

"What is it you wish to tell me?" he asked.

She hung her head, afraid he would throw her from the horse when she told him. "I . . . I am . . . with child," she managed to say. She squinted her eyes closed and swallowed, but nothing happened. He sat very quietly for several long seconds before replying.

"I regret that I did not have a hand in killing the pale eyes," he told her, his voice gruff with jealous anger. His grip on her tightened. "If you will be my wife, you will know only gentleness in my bed, honor as my woman. It will not be like it was with him. This I promise."

She raised her head, turning slightly to look at him. "But . . . I carry his child."

He studied her exquisite beauty. "Is that supposed to change how I feel for you? Remove my desire for you?"

She looked away, feeling warm again. "But I would want you to love it and treat it as your own."

"Does any Sioux or Cheyenne man turn away a little one? Our villages are full of adopted children captured from our enemies. When they are small, they are not enemies, just children. It will be your child. You will love it, and therefore I will also love it and provide for it."

She smiled at him for the first time. "Then you may stay and we will talk. The moon last night was only half a moon. When it is full, I will decide."

He forced back an urge to take her then and there, to pull her from the horse and lay her down in the grass and make her his woman. But this one was fragile. She had known brutality and he sensed her fear. He would do as she asked. "Very well," he said aloud. "I will take you back now." He turned the horse and returned to the village.

There followed two weeks of courtship. They spent time walking and talking, and Black Antelope brought her daily gifts and gave freshly killed game to White Bird.

"The winds grow colder now," the man told Little Flower on the fifteenth day of his stay. They stood beside the river, red and brown leaves floating by them. "Last night the moon was full. If you want to be my wife, I must know so that I can go back to my village and get the rest of my belongings, for you will want to stay here among your people for a while. Is this so?"

She turned and looked up at him. "*Ai*, I would like to stay with Old Grandmother a while longer." She looked down and shivered, wondering if it was from the cold or the wonderful feelings Black Antelope gave her. "The child grows inside of me, and I need a husband. But I would not take you for a husband just to be a father for my baby. I would take you because . . . because I desire you, and want to be your woman. But I am afraid. You must promise to wait until I am ready." She thought for a moment about the horror visited upon her by Frenchy, and the little girl in her sobbed. "If you touch me before I am ready I will sink a knife into your belly the moment you are sleeping," she blurted out.

She stood shivering a moment, then felt warm, strong arms encircle her. Black Antelope pulled her close, his touch gentle and reassuring. "Then Black Antelope will do as you say," he answered, "for he wishes to live a long life and to die at the hands of a warrior enemy, not at the hands of his tiny, young wife."

She sniffed and looked up at him, only to see a grin on his face, a most handsome grin. She could not help but laugh then at what she had said, and Black Antelope laughed with her. The laughter turned to smiles, and as their eyes held he could not resist bending down and touching her cheek to his own. Little Flower knew then she would not make him wait long.

"Go to your village and get your belongings," she told him, reaching up around his neck. He lifted her off the ground, pulling her tight against him. "I will build us a hut. When you return, I will be your wife."

There followed a winter of gentle love, and happiness at last for Little Flower. But it all came too late, and as her stomach swelled with the Frenchman's child, she grew weaker. In the spring she gave birth to a son, a sturdy, dark, handsome boy. When Black Antelope entered the hut after the birth, he was shocked at the sight of his young wife. Her eyes were sunk deep into her face, with death written in the circles beneath them. She lay bleeding heavily, just as her own mother had bled and died when she was born some fourteen summers before.

Black Antelope's heart was heavy with grief as he looked at the woman he loved. Her eyes fluttered open at his presence, and she motioned weakly for him to come closer to hear her speak. Black Antelope knelt beside her, leaning over and gently pushing the dark hair back from her face.

"You have been kind to me," she whispered. "And I have loved you, my husband. The spirits call me now . . . but I do not want to go."

"No," he groaned. "They cannot have you. We will have many more years together, Little Flower. Such a short time I have had you. I want you to stay and bear more sons— my sons."

"It cannot be so. I was not made well . . . for such things. And I was too young for this one." She turned her face to look at her beautiful son. "You must promise me he will be cared for."

Black Antelope looked away. She placed her hand gently on his forearm. "It is not the child's fault . . . for what his father was. He is of my body, my blood. He is Cheyenne. I want him raised to be brave and strong like you, my husband. Promise me you will care for him."

He turned back, unable to hide the tears in his eyes. "This I promise," he choked out. "What—what shall I call him?"

"I heard a hawk's cry . . . and saw it flying while I was in the pain," she answered. "It cried out to find its home. My son's eyes are blue. He should be called Blue Hawk . . . and you must help and protect him. You must guide him, for always his soul will cry out to know where it belongs . . . in our world or the *vehoe's* world."

Black Antelope leaned closer and placed his cheek against hers. "Do not leave me, Little Flower. I cannot live without you."

"You will live, my husband, for you are strong . . . and there are many young women who make eyes at my man. You will some day desire one of them. And she will give you more sons . . . the children I could not give you."

"I desire only you." She felt a wetness on her cheek.

"And this you have shown me in the night," she replied softly, breathing in his sweet scent, wanting to remember and take it with her along *Ekutsihimmiyo*, the Hanging Road of stars that led to the heavens where all was peace and happiness. "Better that I have ... had this time in your arms ... than to live to an old age with that evil white man. You have been good to me, Black Antelope. You kept ... your promise."

Black Antelope looked up to see her eyes closed again. Her body shuddered.

"May *Maheo* curse that man forever," he growled.

She grasped a piece of his hair, as though to hang on to life itself. "One more ... promise," she said weakly. He moved closer still, so that her lips were near his ear.

"Tell me," he whispered, "and it shall be done."

"The blue quill necklace.... Keep it ... for my son ... a gift....May he always honor ... his mother by wearing it ... and remember his Cheyenne blood."

"This I will do, Little Flower."

"My ... husband," she whispered lovingly.

Her hand fell away. He looked up and stared at her a moment before realizing the last bit of life had gone out of her. Black Antelope threw back his head and let out a long cry of grief. His woman, the source of such brief happiness and ecstasy, was dead.

Eight-year-old Blue Hawk raced with the other Sioux children into camp, excited that Black Antelope and the other warriors were returning from a raid on the Chippewa. The painted men held up lances in victory, yipping war whoops, some laughing. The women and old ones gathered around the warriors, calling out and praising the men for the successful raid against their old enemy, who weeks before had raided the Sioux village and killed two warriors and one woman. Behind the warriors a herd of stolen Chippewa horses thundered into camp, their nostrils flared in nervousness.

It seemed to Blue Hawk that the very earth was shaking with the thunder of the returning men and horses. He ran to his aunt, Small Hands, who had nursed him and raised him from his birth. She was Black Antelope's sister; since Little Flower's death, Black Antelope and Blue Hawk had lived among the Sioux in the north. To Blue Hawk, Small Hands was like a mother, much more a mother than the new wife Black Antelope had taken just two moons before. She was called Two Stars, and she joined Blue Hawk and Small Hands now, shouting out to Black Antelope as he rode by.

Blue Hawk watched proudly as the man rode past them leading several stolen Chippewa horses. The man handed the ropes to another warrior before turning his mount and riding back to his family, sliding off the painted animal and pulling a tomahawk from his gear. He walked up to them, and Blue Hawk's heart swelled with joy when Black Antelope spoke to him first, handing him the weapon.

"Taken from the enemy," he said proudly. "Now it belongs to you, my son. Some day you will be a great warrior. Already you are strong and wise beyond your years."

Blue Hawk took the weapon proudly, but his happiness was marred when Black Antelope turned to his new wife, love and desire in his eyes. "There is much to celebrate tonight," he told her. "I killed four of the enemy myself, and led the raid. The Chippewa will not bother us again for a long time to come. Tonight there will be feasting and dancing." His eyes were hungry. "And it has been a long time since Black Antelope held his woman."

Two Stars smiled and dropped her eyes, and Black Antelope walked back toward the group of whooping, howling warriors now dancing around a fire sporting scalps on the ends of their lances. Two Stars followed, staying properly behind to watch. Blue Hawk stared after them, his lips puckered in jealousy. Small Hands patted his head.

"Just because Black Antelope seems to have eyes only for Two Stars does not mean he has any less love for you, Blue Hawk. He came to you first, and has given you a treasured enemy weapon. But tonight he will want to be only with Two Stars. That is the way it is for a man with a new wife. When you are grown you will understand. And you should be glad Black Antelope has found someone to make him happy again. For many winters after your mother died he was not a happy man."

Blue Hawk studied the tomahawk. "She will give him sons. I will no longer be the only one." He pouted.

"Ah, but you will be the oldest, and you are special because you are the son of his first woman. He made a vow to Little Flower to love you and raise you to be a great warrior. It is a lucky child you are to be the son of Black Antelope."

"But I am not truly his son." He looked up into his aunt's kind face. "I am the son of a white man, and always I fear Black Antelope will not love me because of this."

"Blood has nothing to do with love. And the only thing white about you is your eyes. Your heart is Indian. Your skin and hair are Indian. And your courage is Indian. Wear the blue quill necklace proudly, and always remember it is a gift of love from your Cheyenne mother, who gave her life for you. You come from two worlds, Blue Hawk. Perhaps you will be the better man for it. Come, let us join the celebrating. Before long you will be riding with Black Antelope on the raids and hunts. You will take much game, and count many coup."

She started to walk away, but Blue Hawk tugged at her tunic.

"Now what is it?" the woman asked, a patient twinkle in her eye.

"I do not understand . . . about the Chippewa and the Americans. Why do the strange Americans want our land, and why do the Chippewa help them?"

Small Hands put an arm around the boy's shoulders. "The Chippewa have long been our enemies, Blue Hawk. They are jealous of our friendship with the Cheyenne. They are afraid that by being friendly with the Cheyenne and inter-marrying with them, we will join together and have too much strength, perhaps chase the Chippewa away. So the Chippewa, too, try to be friendly to the Cheyenne, and are always trying to stir up trouble and hatred against us. But it does not work. Now the Chippewa see another way to bring us trouble and try to chase us away. Some of our people have aided the Red Coat soldiers in keeping this land from the Americans. So now the Chippewa help the Americans, because they are our enemy. But the Chippewa will soon learn that the Americans cannot be trusted."

"How do you know, Small Hands?"

The woman sniffed as though disgusted. "Stories. We hear many stories about other tribes, tribes who lived in the east where the sun rises. They have died from the white man's sickness and from starvation and murder at the hands of the *wasicum*. These Americans call the Indian friend when they need help or favors. But they turn on the Indian, steal his land, murder his people and plunder his villages. Some day the Chippewa will learn this and will no longer help those Americans. This Black Antelope believes. But until then, the Chippewa remain our enemy, for they are jealous and proud."

Blue Hawk frowned, trying to take it all in. "But won't the Red Coats take our land like the Americans are trying to do?"

A warrior rode by and Small Hands waved him on, calling out her pleasure at their victory. "The redcoats like only to trade for our beaver skins," she answered. "This is not their country and they do not settle here. But the Americans, they want the land, my child. Always remember that. They are not satisfied with just taking treasure from it. They want it all for themselves. We hear many stories of what is happening to the Iroquois, the Delaware, and the Shawnee. Some tribes along the shores of the great waters no longer live at all. They are all gone, killed by the Americans or dead from the white man's sickness."

Blue Hawk folded his arms in a manly fashion, as he had seen Black Antelope often do. "I have never seen a pale-skinned man. Yet I hate them all, even though one was my father."

"I have seen two such men, trappers. But mostly they stay out of here and let your father and the others trap the beaver for them. Three Skies and some of the other braves take the skins to a place where they meet with the Red Coats, on the great river, and trade with them for food, honey, beads and blankets. Perhaps one day you will be one who takes the skins and you will see the white men who wear the red coats and those who trap the beaver and trade with us. Your own father was a trapper."

Blue Hawk held the tomahawk tightly. "I do not want to meet them, especially the bad ones like my father."

"Ah, I am afraid some day you will have to meet them, nephew. And I am afraid I see a dark future for us, in spite of our victory today. I see more and more white men coming, and I fear we will have to flee to the land where the sun sets to get away from them. They say the land there is brown and barren and gives no life, and there are great mountains that rise to meet the sky. I would not want to go to such a strange land. And I would miss these deep woods, the green grass and cool trees."

Blue Hawk thought hard about all she had told him, touching the blue quill necklace that hung loosely around his small neck. Often he removed it to admire the brilliant blue color and the little yellow and red designs on it. He wished again he could have known his real mother, who had given him his dark skin. They said she had been very beautiful. He studied the back of his hand, wondering with a child's curiosity just how "white" his father really had been. Would his own skin turn whiter? He hoped not. He did not ever want to be white.

Over the next year, life was happy for Blue Hawk. Black Antelope took him along on several hunts, and man and boy became closer. Blue Hawk all but worshipped his Sioux stepfather, wanting nothing more than to some day be as great a warrior and gain as much respect as Black Antelope. But the brief interlude of peace was soon broken. The Chippewa had cunningly schemed to wait many months before retaliating for the Sioux raid, wanting to have the element of surprise in their favor. They purposely allowed the Sioux to believe that perhaps there would be no retaliation, and they waited until the Sioux were weary from a long hunting season before attacking.

They came from the south, raiding and burning Cheyenne camps along the way, killing men, stealing women and horses. The Chippewa were made braver from whiskey, given to them by the Americans in payment for attacking Indians who were friendly with the British. Chippewa blood was hot, their thirst for vengeance great. Cheyenne runners from other villages who tried to warn the Sioux were cut down by tracking Chippewa, and no one in Black Antelope's village was aware of the impending disaster.

They came in the deep of the night, a time when attack was least expected, a time when the entire Sioux village slept peacefully, secure in the knowledge that their lodges were full of meat and supplies for the winter. It began with one piercing war cry, followed by a well-planned attack on each hut, most of the thatch rooves hit with flaming arrows. As Sioux men, women and children fled their flaming homes, Chippewa warriors struck them down. It was a bloody, grotesque attack, with no mercy. Most of the Sioux were unaware of what was happening until they saw flames and smelled smoke, then felt the horror of hatchet and knife as they fled their homes.

Blue Hawk felt himself grabbed up in his father's strong arms, but rather than send his family through the entrance-way, Black Antelope chopped a hole through the back side of the hut. "Go," he shouted. "Run to the woods." He shoved his wide-eyed young wife through the hole. "Hurry! Run!"

The woman clung to their newborn son, and amid screams of horror, Black Antelope grabbed Blue Hawk and shoved him through the hole. Black Antelope followed, grabbing Blue Hawk and running fast. He picked up Two Stars in his other arm when he caught up with her, carrying both her and Blue Hawk until they reached the woods. "Find a place to hide," he told them quickly.

There was no time for good-bye, no time for parting words of love. The man was quickly gone, returning to the burning village to do what he could against the Chippewa and save the other Sioux women and children. Blue Hawk watched the man's silhouette against the orange flames, and his heart tightened: somehow he knew it was the last time he would see his beloved stepfather alive.

But there was no time to think about it. Two Stars grabbed him and pulled him by the arm deeper into the forest, while behind him people continued to scream and more huts went up in flames. Two Stars spotted an old, rotted log in the moonlight, and she pushed Blue Hawk down and ordered him to crawl inside.

The boy wiggled in, barely fitting, and Two Stars bent down to put the baby inside after him. Just then a horse came crashing out of the darkness, and the next moment Blue Hawk heard a terrible scream and a thud. The baby began to cry, and then there was another thud. The horse galloped away, and in the distance the fighting continued.

Blue Hawk kept his eyes closed, smelling the damp rot of the log and feeling small insects crawl over his body. Instinct told him to stay where he was until there was no more noise. How he wished he were a man so he could crawl out and help his father fight the hated Chippewa. But he knew it was important to save the women and children in battle, to preserve the seed of the tribe. It was his duty to remain safe, to fight another day when he was man enough to do so.

The boy stayed cramped in the bowels of the log for what seemed hours, sometimes crying, sometimes sleeping, sometimes praying for his father's safety. Only when a ray of sunlight filtered through a crack in the log did he dare venture outside. All sound had ceased. Even the birds were still. Death hung in the silent air.

Blue Hawk squeezed through the end of the log, and the stench of smoldering debris filled his nostrils. He brushed off rotted wood, dirt and biting insects before turning to go to the village. It was then he saw Two Stars, lying dead in the thick weeds. His new baby stepbrother lay beside her. Both their heads were split open.

Blue Hawk's eyes widened, and an odd groan escaped his lips. The realization that he might be totally alone began to engulf him, and he ran toward the village, praying fervently that by some miracle Black Antelope would still be alive. When he came upon the village and saw dead bodies strewn everywhere, he knew with awful certainty that Black Antelope could not have survived.

He walked carefully among the dead bodies, afraid to touch them. His nostrils filled with the stench of death as he surveyed the grotesque poses of those who had died fighting. Without knowing it, he began to weep, his chest heaving with sobs of agony. Around him lay old ones, small babies, women, children; all struck down without mercy, their heads smashed, middles split open, limbs severed. Blue Hawk could not stop the choking sobs as he walked among loved ones and friends. He finally found Small Hands, sprawled on her back, naked and obviously raped, her eyes open and filled with terror even in death. A lance was still embedded in her chest, pinning her body to the ground. Blue Hawk gave one great cry and grasped the lance, jerking hard. He groaned in horror when it would not come out and instead moved Small Hands' body when he pulled at it. Steeling himself, he gave one final, desperate tug and the lance came free.

The boy threw the weapon aside and looked around the rest of the village, his eyes so teared that he could no longer see clearly. He stumbled through the village, searching for the one he dreaded finding most—Black Antelope. He found the man lying over the gray ashes of a campfire, a tomahawk still embedded in his chest. Blue Hawk stared at the man he had called father, teacher, friend. He fell to his knees

beside the body, bursting into loud sobbing, digging his
nails into his cheeks to draw blood. It was a ritual act of
sorrow and a vow of vengeance.

For several minutes the boy sat rocking and crying, but
finally he wiped stubbornly at his tears and stood. He ran
to where his hut had been, and amid its smoking embers
he found the tomahawk Black Antelope had given him as
a gift, its handle charred but still solid. He gripped it tightly
as he walked to the river where the ground was soft. He
began to struggle to dig a grave big enough for Black Antelope, Small Hands, Two Stars and the baby. He dug as
fast and hard as he could, caring not that it took hours of
chopping and scooping the dirt. He knew he could not lift
their bodies onto scaffolds for a proper burial, but he would
not let them lie out in the open for the wolves.

Darkness was settling in when he finished digging. He
threw down the tomahawk and searched through the ruins
hurriedly to find some rope. This he tied around Black
Antelope's ankles and around his own waist, sobbing as he
pulled and tugged the man's body to the gravesite. As hard
as he tried, he was unable to stop his tears and the aching
sorrow.

"Father." He groaned as he pushed and shoved the body
into the grave. But he could not stop to mourn. He hurried
back into the woods, taking a deep breath for courage, for
he was afraid to touch dead bodies. He picked up the baby
and carefully put him inside Two Stars' tunic, then tied the
rope around the young woman's ankles and again began
tugging, dragging her bloating body through the weeds into
the village. At the river he stopped several times to rest,
but he was desperate to get all the bodies into the graves
before the wolves came.

By the time darkness had fallen, the boy got the bodies
to the gravesite. He fought a sick feeling in his stomach as
he rolled them into the grave, where they landed beside
Black Antelope. Blue Hawk was grateful that at least Black

Antelope and Two Stars would lie close together, the baby between them.

He left to quickly gather some smoldering embers together, stirring them and adding some fresh wood to get a fire going. It was too dark to search for Small Hands, for already he heard wolves howling not far away. He could only stay close to the grave and keep a fire going, and pray that Small Hands' body would be left untouched until morning when he could put her in the grave and cover the bodies.

He curled up beside the fire, his whole body sore and aching from all the digging and dragging; his chest and throat burning from so much crying. He soon fell into an exhausted sleep, blessedly oblivious to the sounds of wolves when they came later in the night to rip and tear at the remains of his tribe.

Blue Hawk awoke to a cold nuzzle from an old horse that had been left behind by the Chippewa. The boy jumped up, confused at first. He patted the horse, then hugged it around the neck as the memory of what had happened the day before came back to him. But today the tears would not come. It was as though they had all been wrung out of him.

He wearily picked up the rope and walked back to Small Hands' badly bloating body, glad to see that at least the wolves had not touched her. He grimaced as he tied the rope around her ankles and dragged her to the gravesite, pushing her and struggling not to vomit at the odor of rotting flesh. Then began the difficult task of filling in the grave. For hours he scooped and pushed until the bodies were entirely covered. More hours went by as he carried rocks from the riverbank to cover the fresh dirt, so animals could not dig through it.

When he was finally done, the boy just stood staring at the grave. He knew he had to leave, but did not want to bid farewell to his beloved stepfather and precious Small Hands. He knew he must be a man now, and he must make

decisions. Black Antelope would expect it of him. Blue
Hawk looked around at the surrounding woods. There were
more Sioux villages to the north, but he did not know the
people there nearly as well as his Cheyenne relatives to the
south. He promptly decided that was where he should go,
to live with his mother's people. He knew the Cheyenne
would welcome him.

He looked through the rubble again, finding a usable
parfleche. He filled it with berries from the nearby woods
and some dried meat the Chippewa had not stolen. He fashioned a bridle with the rope he had found and put it around
the head of the old horse. Throwing the parfleche over the
animal's neck, Blue Hawk climbed up.

The boy gazed at the grave for one more long moment,
then turned the old horse and headed south. He carried the
treasured tomahawk, a bow and some arrows, all he had
been able to salvage. He was alone. He must be a man now.
For the rest of his life he must make Black Antelope proud.

Chapter Three

B LUE Hawk made his way through the deep forests,
gradually taking pride in his bravery during the dark
nights and his ability as a hunter. He managed to kill
a rabbit with an arrow, after waiting patiently for a long
time near some underbrush where he had seen the tracks.
When the small creature finally ventured out again, Blue
Hawk took careful aim and killed it. He thought of how

proud Black Antelope would be if he had seen the shot. At nine, Blue Hawk was already good with the bow. But the thought of the many lessons Black Antelope had given him, of the man's strong arms holding his small wrists and helping him pull the bow and aim the arrow brought the terrible ache back to Blue Hawk's chest. He wondered if it would ever go away.

"Thank you, rabbit spirit," he said before skinning and cleaning the animal. It was proper to always thank the spirits of those animals killed to provide nourishment and warmth to man. The animal's sacrifice did not go unappreciated.

The boy made the rabbit meat last three days, cooking all of it at once and then keeping the meat in his parfleche. He filled himself with berries to quell his almost constant hunger. He remembered how his father and aunt had teased him about having a stomach that could never be filled, and their laughter echoed as sweet but painful memories.

The adventure of being alone in the forest and finding his own way to his Cheyenne relatives helped distract him from his loss. He came across roaring waterfalls, lush vegetation and fragile flowers, all of which renewed some of the joy in his child's heart. Though he headed south, he was not sure how to find his relatives and knew he would have to search. In the meantime, he remained cautious, sticking to the deep woods to avoid the Chippewa, who would surely kill him, or worse, take him captive.

"Perhaps being alone in my ninth summer is good," he told the old horse he rode, patting its neck. "Now I will be a man before any other Indian boy my age can call himself one." He sat straighter, puffing out his chest and looking around at moss covered tree trunks and blooming wildflowers. "Yes. I would not want to lose my father as I did, but now I am forced to provide for myself, to hunt, to live from the forest, and to be brave and watch for the enemy. These are things I would do many summers from now if I had not been left alone. What do you think, old horse? Do you think I am a man now?"

The animal snorted and shook its head, and Blue Hawk scowled. "What do you know," the boy grumbled. "You are only an old horse."

After another week of travel the land began to look more familiar, and Blue Hawk knew he was nearing his Cheyenne relatives. His heart quickened with the thought of seeing loved ones and knowing he would again have a home. Yet he also grew sad, for he was most certainly more man than child now, and he would make sure his relatives treated him as such. His grandfather would be proud of the fact that he had found his own way to the village, where he had only visited a few times. He had even slept one night among dead bodies, but the night spirits had not harmed him, nor had the wolves.

He wore one foot of the rabbit he had killed around his neck on a rawhide string. "I got you, didn't I, rabbit? I am good with the bow." Beneath the rabbit's foot was the blue quill necklace, which he never removed. He touched it, his thoughts again turning to the mother he never knew, and how his own life had even begun in death.

The afternoon grew warm and lazy, and Blue Hawk's head began to nod as the horse plodded quietly over fallen pine needles. Suddenly, the sound of laughter broke the still air. It startled Blue Hawk to attention, and instinct told him immediately to be cautious. He reined the old horse to a halt and slid off, realizing he was very close to the Cheyenne village. He was sure it was just over the ridge before him, but until he was certain all was well, he would be careful.

He tied the horse and stealthily crept up to the top of the ridge. His moccasined feet were noiseless against the ground carpeted with pine needles. The woods too were silent, and he heard nothing but the wind whispering through the pine branches, and the laughter. When he peeked at the village below, his eyes widened in horror. He wanted to scream out but was paralyzed with disbelief, for below him lay the village of his Cheyenne relatives, burned out and desecrated, just as his own village had been. Bodies lay strewn about, women, children, old people and young warriors. They had apparently been dead for some time; the stench was revolting and bodies were bloated.

Blue Hawk knew the Chippewa had wiped out the village, perhaps even before attacking his own Sioux village. How he hated them! He gripped his tomahawk in rage, gritting his teeth against the tears that wanted to come. He heard the laughter again, and spotted two men moving among the bodies, stealing anything of value they could find. They stumbled as they walked, acting silly and pushing each other around. Blue Hawk knew that an Indian would never walk among dead bodies in that way unless they were either full of the white man's firewater or crazy.

"Chippewa!" He whispered the word in a sneer. He wondered if, in their drunken state, they would be easy to kill. The nine-year-old boy was suddenly a full-grown man indeed, for he felt a thirst for vengeance that made him brave and determined. He smiled, and in spite of his small body and boyish face, the smile was that of a violent, vengeful man. "It is a good day to die," he muttered, "and I shall see that two Chippewa die with me."

There was no time to think or hesitate. It must be done. He reached behind his back and took out an arrow, placing it in his bow. Raising the bow and remembering all that his Sioux father had taught him, he took aim at one of the Chippewa. The boy let the rawhide bowstring snap and the arrow sang through the air, landing squarely between the shoulders of one of the Chippewa braves. Blue Hawk's heart leaped with the joy of revenge. He was a true warrior! If only Black Antelope could have seen his accomplishment.

The wounded man fell forward with a grunt, jerked and went rigid in death. His companion watched in stunned surprise before jumping up and looking around with cautious, frightened eyes. Blue Hawk used the man's surprise as a weapon, quickly leaping over the ridge and running toward his enemy with his tomahawk raised. Screaming war whoops, he gave an amazingly frightening appearance to the startled Chippewa, who at first just stared at the boy.

Blue Hawk reached the man, preparing to land his tomahawk into the hated Chippewa. Instead, the man gave a crushing blow to the side of Blue Hawk's head, and the ground came up and slammed into the boy. His mind reeled, and he felt himself turned onto his back. The Chippewa grabbed his hair and he saw the flash of a blade, but at the same time he realized the tomahawk was still in his hand. With all the strength he could muster, he swung hard with the weapon at the blurry figure that hovered over him. He felt the fine edge of the tomahawk blade sink deeply into his enemy, and he heard a horrified scream.

The Chippewa let go of Blue Hawk's hair and slumped to the ground beside Blue Hawk, the tomahawk buried so deeply in his back that the fall tore the handle from the boy's hand. Blue Hawk's ears began to ring loudly, and he couldn't see clearly. He put a hand to the side of his face and could feel blood and a great swelling. He groped through half blindness to find the tomahawk again, determined not to lose the precious weapon given him by his father. With what little strength he had left, he rolled to his knees and yanked the weapon out of the Chippewa's back.

Blue Hawk tried to get to his feet, but the light of day turned gray, then black, and he fell forward. He sprawled over the Chippewa's body, the tomahawk still in his hand. In his last thoughts he wondered if any Indian boy of only nine had ever killed two enemy warriors as he had just done. He would have been honored and celebrated if his people could have known. How proud Black Antelope would have been!

But Black Antelope would never know, and the wrenching pain of all he had lost was soothed only by the blessed unconsciousness that finally enveloped him.

When first he came to his senses, Blue Hawk felt himself bound tightly but comfortably, his body bouncing gently as he lay on something that was moving. He opened his eyes to see a bright blue sky, and raising his head slightly, saw that he was on a travois, being hauled in the traditional Indian way.

A horrible pain seered through his head, and he lay back down, wondering what Indians had come along to help him. Perhaps they were Cheyenne, for surely no Chippewa would help. They would have taken his scalp and left him for dead. Still, he recalled that everyone in his grandfather's village had been dead. He vaguely remembered the Chippewa, the terrible blow to his face, and burying his tomahawk in a Chippewa's back. Who could have found him?

Perhaps he was a captive of the Chippewa, being taken to torture or slavery, he thought. Ignoring the pain movement caused, he turned his head enough to see a man riding beside the travois, wearing finely cleaned and sewn buckskins. The boy's eyes widened as he realized his situation was even worse than he had feared. His captors were white men. He had never seen one before, but knew that was what the pale-skinned creature with hair on his face he saw riding beside him had to be.

From all he had heard about the white man who had abused his Cheyenne mother and about the Americans who came to steal land from the Indians, Blue Hawk hated pale-skinned men. He wondered what kind of horrors these men had in mind for him. The one riding beside him was leading the boy's old horse, and Blue Hawk wondered why they would steal such a worthless animal. He decided white men did not know much about horses.

The boy tried again to rise, deciding he must run away quickly if possible. But he was bound too tightly, and the effort to free himself brought so much pain he could not help groaning. The sound caused a second man, whose horse was pulling the travois, to halt his mount.

"I think the boy has come around, Tom," the man riding alongside him said. Blue Hawk did not understand the words, but the one called Tom dismounted and walked around to stare down at the Indian boy.

"Well, now, little warrior, how are you feeling?" The man knelt down and smiled, his eyes sparkling with kindness. If Blue Hawk had known anything about white men, he would have known this one was a jovial Irishman. But he was so filled with hatred for the strangers that he did not even notice at first how red the man's beard and hair were. His mind only raged with tales of his mother, and he spit at the man, unable to think of any other way to express his opinion. At least his act showed that even in his helpless condition he was not afraid and would fight the awful things the white man must have in store for him.

"Wasicus." He hissed the Sioux word for white man through gritted teeth, and the red-haired man's eyes widened in surprise. The other man, still mounted, chuckled as the one called Tom wiped the boy's saliva from his beard.

"I told you it was no use tryin' to help that little wildcat," the mounted man said. "Any kid that can take on two grown Chippewa and come out of it alive has got to be a lot to handle. You can't take somethin' like that home to Cora and Sarah, Tom."

The one called Tom only grinned, reaching out to pat Blue Hawk lightly on the shoulder to assure him he intended to help him, not harm him. "You know my Cora," he answered. "She loves everything. She can't even bring herself to kill flies. She's never got over losing our baby, or the fact that she probably can't have any more. Sarah's a treasure, but still, the baby was a boy and Cora still thinks she's let me down somehow by not giving me a son." He studied the dark handsome young boy he had rescued. Yes, he wanted a son, but that was not to be. He couldn't help wondering if there was some reason God had led him to this wounded Indian boy. "Maybe this little varmint will keep Cora busy enough to help her get over her depression. Sure'n it's worth a try, don't you think, friend?"

"The little bugger will probably kill her first chance he gets and light out. And what about Sarah?"

Tom grinned, standing up and walking to his horse to get out a canteen and a piece of cloth from his gear. "My little girl has more energy than all of us put together, and the curiosity of a cat. I don't worry about that one, friend. I'd worry more about the boy being the brunt of that girl's endless questions and stares. She's a brave and daring child who doesn't know the meaning of fear, that she is."

"So you think you can just pick up a wild Indian boy like some stray puppy and take him home to raise, I suppose?"

Tom shrugged, walking back to Blue Hawk and kneeling down beside him. "We'll see, Bo. I couldn't very well leave him like we found him now, could I?"

"Yes, you could," Bo answered.

Tom scowled at him, then wet the cloth he held and placed it gently against the ugly swelling on the side of Blue Hawk's face. The boy tried to jerk away at first, but was tied too tightly. As the white man insisted on keeping the cloth against the swelling, Blue Hawk realized the coolness eased the pain. Blue Hawk looked up at the man curiously, realizing he only meant to help.

The boy stared in wonder then at the red beard, amazed at its color. When he met the pale-skinned man's eyes, he saw nothing of the evil horror he had imagined whenever he envisioned a white man. This man was middle-aged, with hair that hung to his shoulders from beneath a coonskin cap. His eyes were a soft light brown, and they reminded Blue Hawk of the gentle eyes of a puppy. The man was not ugly and his buckskins were clean and well sewn. Two knives hung from a wide leather belt around his waist.

"So, my little warrior, perhaps it is good you are wounded for now," the man said in a gentle voice. "If not, you would kill me before you realized that I mean you no harm." He held the canteen to the boy's lips and gestured that Blue Hawk should drink some water if he wished. The boy raised his head slightly and took a sip, then drank more, suddenly realizing just how thirsty he was.

"Easy now," the man told him, gently pulling the canteen away. He frowned as he corked it. "I'm wondering what terrible things you have seen, little warrior, to leave you orphaned and cause such a child to kill two grown men."

"Indians ain't kids for long," Bo said. "But it's still hard to believe that one there could have killed both those men."

Blue Hawk looked at the man. Bo's hair was a dark blond, and when he pushed his hat back, Blue Hawk saw that his hair had receded. He sported hair under his nose and the hair on his face was not thick like the red-haired man's. It was bristly.

"You saw the bodies," Tom answered. He sat studying the boy a moment, fingering his beard. "They were recently killed compared to the other bodies there, and their blood was all over the boy and his tomahawk. We know the Chippewa have been at it lately with the Sioux and the Cheyenne. What puzzles me is that the boy's clothes and weapons are Sioux, but it was a Cheyenne camp we found him in. His own people must have been killed. See the marks on his cheeks?"

Bo scowled. "Looks like he got in a fight with a bobcat."

"Those are marks of sorrow, scratched into his cheeks with his own hands, I'd guess. Poor boy. Must have come across those two Chippewa and decided to get his revenge— or maybe they attacked him. Either way, it's a damn brave boy we're looking at, Bo. A real warrior. I admire him, and I feel sorry for him."

"You're too softhearted for this land, Tom Sax, you and Cora both. Why you brought a frail woman like that to these parts, I'll never understand."

Tom turned away, saying nothing. No one but he and Cora knew why they had left Saint Louis. "It's pretty country, Bo, and I'm born to wander these forests and trap beaver. I never could live the conventional way, you know. My Cora just happens to love me enough to put up with it."

Bo dismounted and walked over to stare down at Blue Hawk, who still watched them with distrustful eyes. "What do you think of them blue eyes, Tom? It's a fact he's not all Indian."

Tom squinted and studied Blue Hawk. The boy knew the man was wondering about his eyes, and he wished they were not blue. How he hated having a white man's eyes. If not for the eyes, no one would ever know he had any white blood in him.

"Hard to say." Tom kept fingering his beard. "Most Indians out this far haven't seen much of white men yet, especially not the Indian women. But there's no mistaking some white man was through here a few years back and set his eyes on some pretty little Indian maiden...and this little warrior is the result. Those blue eyes set in that Indian face sure make him a handsome one." He pointed to his own chest then. "Tom," he said to the boy. "Tom Sax. Tom Sax." Then he pointed to Blue Hawk, but the boy said nothing. He pointed to himself again. "Tom Sax." He pointed to Blue Hawk again.

"Blue Hawk," the boy finally mumbled in his own tongue.

"What did he say?" Bo asked.

"I think it means Blue Hawk," Tom replied. He pointed to Blue Hawk again. "Blue Hawk," he said in English. "Blue Hawk." He bent closer. "I'm wondering just what kind of Indian you are, boy. Your clothing and weapons are Sioux, but the name you gave me is Cheyenne and we found you in a Cheyenne camp. That pretty necklace you wear looks Cheyenne. How about it, boy? Are you Sioux—*Santee*? Dakota?"

The boy recognized the words and nodded, hope brimming in his eyes. Maybe this man was going to take him to his people.

"Then you're not Cheyenne," Tom added.

Blue Hawk nodded again. "*Shahiena*," he spoke up, using the Sioux word for Cheyenne. "Dakota."

Tom Sax removed his hat and scratched his head, frowning. "Now which in the hell are you—Sioux or Cheyenne?"

Blue Hawk nodded to both, and Bo laughed. "Reckon somehow he's both, friend, with a little white blood in there someplace. I'd bet it's French."

Blue Hawk's eyes darted to the man at the word French. He knew his white father had been called Frenchy.

"Frenchy! *Wasicus!*" He spit again.

Tom Sax chuckled and shook his head. "Well, there's something about white men he sure doesn't like. I guess I'll have to wait till my Cora teaches him some English before I know." He stood up and walked back to his horse, putting away the cloth and the canteen. "We only know enough Cheyenne and Sioux to barter a little, but maybe between the two of us, Bo, we can learn a little from him as we go along, figure out a way for us to understand each other."

Bo returned to his own horse and both men mounted. "I don't know why you're doin' any of this, Tom Sax. You're crazy, far as I'm concerned."

"I'm only doing what Cora would want me to do, my friend. It's a savage land, that's sure, but it doesn't have to make savages out of us."

"Well, that there boy is a savage, mark my words."

"It's my problem. We'd better get moving. We have at least two weeks of riding ahead of us before we reach Fort Dearborn, and I'm missing my Cora."

"We didn't get enough skins this time out. And the kid is slowin' us down. We could do a little more trappin' on the way back."

"The boy needs help, and I've been away too long as it is. We have enough to sell at the fort to get by on. Once we get the boy settled with Cora and Sarah, we'll head out again."

"I say we should have hunted up another tribe and dumped the boy off."

"What tribe? With the warring among the tribes and taking

sides between the British and the Americans, we can't be sure what to expect if we go any farther north or west. We've already come much too far this time to be sure our own hides are safe. The Chippewa are angry, Bo, and they're sworn enemies of the Sioux and Cheyenne. It looks to me like most of the Sioux and Cheyenne in these parts have been wiped out. So what would I do with the poor kid? Besides, we're low on supplies. It's time we headed back."

Blue Hawk felt the travois start moving again, and his heart ached for Black Antelope and his beloved aunt, Small Hands. He sensed he would never see his homeland again, and a terrible ache swelled in his throat. He bent his neck and saw that he still wore the blue quill necklace and the rabbit's foot. At least the pale-skinned man with the red beard had not stolen them.

He looked up at the sky and could tell by the sun that they were headed east. He had never been anywhere east of the deep woods where he had been raised. Small Hands had told him that many white men lived in the lands where the sun rose. Where was this white man taking him? He felt both frightened and excited. Already he had done more than any Indian boy his age, for he had killed two Chippewa warriors. Now he was headed east with white men. Again he must be very brave, but that would be easy; he was a man now.

Chapter
Four

FOR three more days Blue Hawk slipped in and out of consciousness, unable to even sit up until the third day without excruciating pain. Through it all the white man called Tom fed him, gave him water and carried him from the travois to the woods to relieve himself, holding on to the boy so he wouldn't pass out. The man's concern and gentleness confused Blue Hawk, who had convinced himself since he was old enough to remember that white men were cruel and not to be trusted.

By the fourth day, as he sat near the campfire eating fresh fried trout, he began to realize that just as there were good and bad Indians, there must also be good and bad white men. And he knew that he must learn which men to trust and which ones not to trust. It seemed to be the eyes that usually told the story, and the first time he had looked into Tom Sax's eyes, he had sensed that he was a good man.

A few white men's words began to make sense to Blue Hawk, like "go" and "come," "yes" and "no," "eat," "sleep" and "good morning." Neither Tom nor Bo touched Blue Hawk's belongings, and they took good care of his old horse as they traveled to whatever mysterious place they intended to take him. Blue Hawk had been too sick those first few days to try to run off, and now he was farther east than he had ever been in his life. He had no idea where he was or in which direction to run. These men were being kind to him, and if he ran off alone he might encounter enemy Indians, for his father had often told him there were many other tribes of Indians in the "great and mysterious beyond," some even more ruthless than the Chippewa. And there was always the chance of encountering white men who were not as kind as Tom Sax and the one called Bo.

By the time Blue Hawk was well enough to flee, there was no place for him to go; and his attachment to the one called Tom was growing stronger, making him wonder at times if he wanted to leave at all. In spite of the man's red beard and white skin, Tom Sax reminded Blue Hawk of his Sioux father. Like Black Antelope, Tom was brave and strong, apparently honest and kind, a man Blue Hawk sensed could handle himself well in danger. Tom was a capable man, but one who had the same gentleness in his eyes as Black Antelope had had when addressing Blue Hawk.

On the fifth day of their journey, after making camp late in the day, Sax pulled out a long rodlike object from a boot on his saddle. Blue Hawk had eyed the instrument curiously many times, wondering if it was some kind of white man's weapon. "I guess we're far enough out of the most dangerous Indian country to use our guns again, don't you think, Bo? We're low on meat."

"I reckon," Bo replied. "If you'd fired that thing a few days ago, you'd have attracted every redskin devil for miles and we'd both be hairless."

"Maybe so. Maybe not." Tom looked at Blue Hawk and held up the weapon, grinning at the wonder on the boy's face. "Musket," he told the boy. He held it out and Blue Hawk reached for it hesitantly. Tom let go of it, and the boy nearly dropped the gun, surprised at how heavy it was. Tom laughed jovially and took it back from him. "Want to see how it works?"

The boy just stared as the man poured black powder into the end of the gun, then held out a hard, round ball for Blue Hawk to see before dropping it into the end of the long gun. "It's not always easy to hit your target with these," he told

Blue Hawk, "but we'll see what we can do. This one is a flintlock, a little better than the old matchlocks."

Blue Hawk understood little of what the man was saying, only realizing that Tom Sax wanted to show him something. Sax pounded a rod into the barrel, then motioned for Blue Hawk to follow him deeper into the forest. The boy hung back as they walked, wondering if perhaps the man meant to harm him with the strange weapon. He watched as Sax crouched down by an old log, then Blue Hawk stepped warily closer. Sax motioned for him to crouch down beside him, and no sooner had the boy done so when he realized Sax had spotted a rabbit sitting on its hind legs not far off. Its back was to the men, and since the animal was upwind of them, it apparently did not realize they were nearby.

Sax put a finger to his lips, signaling Blue Hawk to be still. He pointed the strange weapon then, balancing it on the log and aiming it at the rabbit. Moments later the weapon seemed to explode, and Blue Hawk jumped back, then ran farther away, his heart pounding. Sax only laughed, pointing at the rabbit. Blue Hawk looked and saw that the rabbit lay dead. He followed Sax as the man walked up to the animal, and Blue Hawk knelt down to study it closer. It's head had a bloody hole in it. He looked from the rabbit to the weapon Sax had called a musket, then reached out and touched the weapon, jerking his hand back quickly at the warmth of the barrel. He wondered if the musket might turn on him and explode again, making a hole in his hand like the one in the rabbit's head.

Sax chuckled again, blowing smoke away from the end of the barrel. "Come on, let's clean our rabbit and eat it." He winked at Blue Hawk, picking up the rabbit and handing it to Blue Hawk. The boy took the animal and walked back with Sax, staring at the weapon, thinking what a powerful and magical thing it was. He marveled at the exciting new things he was learning from this white man and wondered if Tom Sax was the only white man who could do magic.

* * *

As the journey east continued, Blue Hawk watched when the men stopped and checked iron traps for more beaver. He became familiar with the strange contraptions and though had never seen them before, he had heard about them from Black Antelope. He realized that these two white men must be some of those who caught beaver and sold the skins to other white men. He had heard enough to know the furs must be of considerable value to white people, and he wanted to tell Tom Sax he had heard of these traps, that his own white father had used them. There were many things he wanted to tell Tom Sax about himself, but he could not speak the white man's tongue.

Still, in spite of the language barrier, Tom and Blue Hawk set up a form of communication for day-to-day living, and Blue Hawk became more comfortable and less fearful on each day of his journey eastward, although he had refused to show any fear in front of Tom Sax. He was still somewhat suspicious, for they had not yet reached their final destination, and Blue Hawk had no idea what was in store for him. Perhaps the white men would make a slave out of him.

The boy's apprehension grew as they moved farther and farther from his homeland, leaving behind all that was familiar. Blue Hawk recognized no landmarks now, and after more than three weeks of traveling, a new smell invaded his senses, the smell of water. Blue Hawk sensed something very different. His instincts told him the smell was not from just one of the many small inland lakes that dotted this land. This smell filled the air with a sweet dampness that suggested a very large body of water. That night, when they made camp, he could hear an odd rumbling sound in the distance, and the smell of fresh water permeated the air and teased his curiosity. He did not sleep well that night, for something new and, for the moment, menacing lay waiting not far ahead.

The next morning Tom Sax led the boy to a high bluff from which Blue Hawk stared in awe at a great body of water that stretched far into the horizon and beyond. His eyes widened at the huge, crashing waves. White birds he'd never seen before soared over the water, crying shrilly and occasionally diving down to the water, moving up again with fish in their beaks.

A chill swept through Blue Hawk. "*Maxe-ne hanenestse*," the boy muttered softly, his voice full of worship.

"Yes, it is a great lake," Tom Sax told him, smiling at the boy's enraptured look. "The Chippewa and other Indians around here call it *Michigama*. We call it Lake Michigan." The man pointed out over the waters. "Lake Michigan."

"Michi . . . gan," Blue Hawk repeated. He turned to Tom, frowning. "Chippewa?"

Sax reached over and grasped his arm. "It's all right," he told the boy in Cheyenne, hoping he understood. Then he went on in English. "No harm, as long as you're with me." He pointed south. "Fort Dearborn. That's where we're going. It's on a river that flows into Lake Michigan."

Blue Hawk frowned, looking back to the west. How far were they now from his homeland? His chest hurt, and unwanted tears filled his eyes.

"Ah, yes, son, you'll be missing your own people, I know," Sax told him, hoping the boy understood by the inflection of his voice that he sympathized with the child's fears. "But you've got a friend in me, Blue Hawk, and it's sure you'll be like a son to me yet." He squeezed the boy's arm. "*Na-eha*," he said softly.

Blue Hawk looked at him then, studying the man's kind brown eyes. This man called Tom Sax had called him son in Cheyenne. Did he want him to be his son? Perhaps one day he could consider the man his father, but not yet. He missed Black Antelope and his people too much. But the fact remained that part of his blood was white. He suddenly realized he was not totally foreign to the kind of man he was with now. Part of him was their kind, but he had never before considered himself anything but Indian, nor had he even wanted to consider himself any other way. He still did not, but Tom Sax was a good man. He would trust him and go with him wherever this man called home. He had no other choice now. Great changes had come into his life. He stared out at the great lake again. Surely this was the most wondrous thing the Great Spirit had ever created, and good spirits dwelled in this land.

Blue Hawk rode close to Tom and stared in wonder at all the white people in the strange settlement that was surrounded by a pointed wooden wall. Great log buildings sat inside its walls, and outside Blue Hawk had seen smaller log structures, near which more white people stood. Were they these peoples' homes, like the mud and thatch huts of the Indians? He stared at the pointed wooden wall that surrounded the bigger buildings as they rode inside the structure. He wondered if the wall was to keep out enemies, or some frightfully powerful god that ruled the great lake. Inside the structure he saw strange, boxlike contraptions on round pieces of wood that rolled, a fine instrument for carrying things and much bigger than a travois. Outside the wall he had seen much land with the earth dug into and things growing from it in rows. He recognized some of the plants as corn. So the white man also ate corn. He wondered if they had learned about the food from other Indians.

He gawked at two white women who were visiting together. Never in his life had he seen such women, especially not like the one with the golden hair. Both wore dresses that hung to the ground and were made of brightly colored cloth. The two women looked up at him and pointed, one looking at him in contempt, the other with pity in her eyes. Blue Hawk's head turned as he passed them, and one of them held up her chin and walked away, as though somehow insulted by his stare.

The boy continued staring at the pale-skinned people everywhere. Blue Hawk wondered if this was the place where all the white people gathered. Was this all there was? Some of them stared at him, and he sat proudly on his horse, determined they all understand that, in spite of his blue eyes, he was Indian, and in spite of his young age, he was not afraid. He spotted a few Indians, but they were not Chippewa. They eyed him as warily as he eyed them, for he was an Indian from the far west, one with whom they were not familiar. In a sense he knew that made him special, something from a land far away that some of these people had never seen.

They rode to a large building where piles of beaver skins were stacked just outside the door, protected by an over-hanging roof. Tom and Bo dismounted, and Tom motioned for Blue Hawk to do the same. They walked inside the building, where three old men sat around a potbelly stove, empty because of the warm weather. All three stopped talk-ing and stared at Blue Hawk, as did the four other men inside the building. They were all dressed in buckskins like Tom and Bo, garb similar to Blue Hawk's own Indian dress. Blue Hawk gawked at the array of food and supplies inside the building, wondering if all white men were wealthy. He wanted to touch things, but was afraid to and just stayed close to Tom Sax.

Most of the men greeted Tom warmly, giving Blue Hawk curious glances and wondering at the dark bruise still evident on the side of his face. Their eyes were friendly, except those of one man who looked Blue Hawk over with a note of disgust, then spit out something dark brown. The ugly wad landed on Blue Hawk's moccasin, and the boy's eyes immediately narrowed, for he knew he had been insulted. He clenched his fists, but Tom Sax put a hand on his shoul-der, warning him to stay calm.

"Wipe it off, Wiggins," Sax told the man who had spit. Other men in the store backed away.

"I don't wipe the moccasins of no blue-eyed Indian who comes in here dressed like Sioux. What the hell are you doin' bringin' home the litter from some whorin' squaw? Or are you the one she whored with? He your bastard, Sax?"

Sax stepped closer to the man, and Blue Hawk could see

that the one called Wiggins was more than a little afraid of Tom Sax.

"I ought to kill you for that insult, Wiggins," Sax hissed. "It's a disgrace to my Cora. The only reason I don't have it out with you is that I don't want to get the boy upset." He turned to the others. "This is all new to the boy, and he's scared and alone. Bo and I found him out in the wilds, nearly dead from a bad wound to his head." He put a hand on Blue Hawk's shoulder. "He's a brave one. This boy killed two grown Chippewa warriors, one with an arrow, and the other with a tomahawk."

The men stared more intently at Blue Hawk, whispering among themselves, some in astonishment, others in admiration. Blue Hawk sensed Tom Sax had said something good about him, and he straightened more, holding up his chin proudly.

"I nursed this boy back to health," Sax continued. "I'm taking him to Cora." He turned back to Wiggins. "You got any objections, Wiggins?"

Kyle Wiggins' eyes shifted from the boy to Sax. "Maybe the little bastard killed two grown men, but they were Chippewa—our friends. He's Dakota. Dakota fight on the side of the British."

"What does a child like this know about our arguments with the damn British!" Sax spit out the words in an angry voice. "Where he comes from the Sioux and Chippewa are always at each other. That's all he knows. It's something he grew up with. He doesn't understand anything about our fight with the British. Don't tell me you're afraid of one little boy, Wiggins."

Kyle Wiggins clenched his fists. "He'll make trouble. Mark my words."

"That will be my problem. At the moment you're the troublemaker, Wiggins, and I'd advise you to wipe that spittle off the boy's moccasin, or I'll rub your face in it."

Wiggins' eyes darted about the room. He didn't like backing down in front of the others, but he didn't like the thought of tangling with Tom Sax either. The hotheaded Irishman had a reputation with fists and knives. "Just to keep the peace," he finally grumbled. He took out a worn handkerchief from his pocket and bent down, wiping the tobacco wad from Blue Hawk's moccasin. "You're crazy, Sax," he muttered, "takin' a wild half-breed home to your wife and daughter. God only knows what he'll do to them. They say a desire for women comes early to—"

He didn't finish the statement. Sax's fist landed squarely on Wiggins' nose, jolting the man backward and sending him sprawling into a pile of flour sacks. His body slid down and a sack broke over his head, mixing flour with blood and turning him into a cloud of white. Blue Hawk could not suppress a laugh then, and Sax grinned.

"You know better than to insult the family of an Irishman, Wiggins." Sax put a hand on Blue Hawk's shoulder again and turned to the others. "This is Blue Hawk. He says he's part Sioux—Dakota—and part Cheyenne. That's all I can figure for now, except it's obvious he's also got white blood, so I'm not quite sure what's mixed with what. But I'm taking him home with me and we'll make a civilized boy out of him—me, Cora and Sarah. He'll be a Sax, and I want him to have the same respect he'd have if he was my own blood. Do all of you understand?"

"Sure, Tom," the man behind the counter replied for them all. "Feelings are running kind of high, what with the Indians split up and fighting on different sides, that's all."

"You think I don't know that? It isn't just our war, Hugh. Looks like in the interior country there's a lot of warring going on among the tribes. We found Blue Hawk in a burned-out Cheyenne village where more than a hundred had been slaughtered. I think it's more than the Chippewa helping us and the Dakota helping the British. I think it was a vengeance war between the two tribes. At any rate, Bo and I won't be here long. We'll be heading out again in about six weeks, and I'm counting on you men to be kind to the boy and watch out for him, just like you do my Cora and Sarah."

He looked back at a coughing Wiggins. "All of you but Wiggins."

Wiggins got to his feet, shaking flour from his hair. He glared at Sax a moment, then the boy. "You're a fool, Sax," he growled. He stalked out, and Tom turned to the others.

"He goes near my Cora when I'm not around, I want to know," he told them.

"We keep an eye out," one of the men told him, a pipe clamped between his teeth as he spoke. "I expect you'd best not go too far next time you go out. Seems like things are comin' to a head with the British."

Tom sighed, putting a reassuring hand on Blue Hawk's shoulder again. "Sure 'n it does," he commented. He turned to the storekeeper behind the counter. "I'll take a can of tobacco, Hugh, and I've got some furs outside. Oh, and I'm sorry for the mess I made with Wiggins. I'll help clean it up."

"Don't worry about it, Tom. I expect you're anxious to get home."

"That I am."

Blue Hawk looked up at the man with pride, surprised at the strength of the love and respect he felt for him. Tom Sax had clearly stuck up for him, fought because of him. He was indeed a good man, and not afraid of big men like the ugly one who had spit on Blue Hawk's moccasin.

"Bo and I went a lot farther west this time, so we sold most of our skins at Fort Crawford before we started back," Sax told Hugh. "But we collected a few more on the way here."

"How much did you get for them at Fort Crawford?"

"Three dollars a pound. What I have left isn't much. I hope to do better this winter. Things just didn't go too well this time around, a lot of bad luck. That's why we're going back out. Bo was sick for a while, and I got a bad infection in my leg that slowed us up some. Then we came across the boy. We should have been back a month ago."

"True. Cora has been worried. Mentioned it every time

she came in here for supplies. Why don't you go on home? I'll weight up the skins. You know I won't cheat you. Come back later for payment."

Blue Hawk watched in fascination when the man dipped a feather into something dark and began scratching on something thin and white. He wondered what kind of signs the man was making and what they meant.

"That's fine with me, Hugh."

"And like I say, forget about the mess. It was worth it, seeing Kyle Wiggins get what was coming to him."

Tom grinned. "Well, it's sure I'll be spending most of my earnings right here on more supplies, so you won't be out much now, will you, Hugh? You merchants make out better than the rest of us."

Hugh laughed. "Could be."

Tom chuckled as he led Blue Hawk out the door.

"I'll be headin' for the inn and a good, stiff drink," Bo told Tom on the way out.

"Go on with you then," Tom replied. "I'll talk to you tomorrow and we'll figure up a time to head out again."

Both men unhitched their horses, and Blue Hawk unhitched his old mare. The pack mule with its load of skins was left at the store. Blue Hawk noticed the ugly white man called Wiggins sitting nearby, dabbing at a bleeding nose with the dirty handkerchief and eyeing Blue Hawk with such an evil look it gave the boy chills. Already he knew this Wiggins was a bad white man, but he was confused as to why the man should hate him so, for Blue Hawk had done nothing to Kyle Wiggins. Blue Hawk suddenly realized that these people were that strange breed called Americans. He felt like he was walking in an enemy camp, and if not for Tom Sax, he would run way. Perhaps he still would.

Tom walked with his horse and motioned for Blue Hawk to follow. Blue Hawk walked with him through a gate on the other side of the fort and out toward a distant cabin. The structure was small and built of rough-hewn logs, chinked together solidly with something that looked like mud. Blue

Hawk realized it must be the house where Tom Sax lived. They saw a woman hanging some clothing outside, and when she noticed them, she shouted Tom's name. Tom dropped the reins of his mount and began running toward her. Blue Hawk hung back, realizing it must be Tom Sax's woman. It reminded him of the times Black Antelope had come back to camp after a raid or a hunt, and Two Stars would run to greet him.

His heart quickened with curiosity when he saw a little girl running behind the woman, shouting "Daddy! Daddy!" He was not sure what the word meant, but for the moment he was totally fascinated with just watching her. She appeared to be even younger than he, and she was the first little white girl he had ever seen.

The boy slowly walked closer, leading both horses, watching as Tom Sax swept both the woman and the little girl into his arms. A new loneliness engulfed Blue Hawk. How he wished he could see Black Antelope coming to greet him again. But he was in a new land now, with a new people, and he wasn't sure how to get out of it, or if he even wanted out. When the little girl looked at him and pointed, Blue Hawk forgot his loneliness for a moment. She was the prettiest child he had ever seen. Her hair was thick and wavy, hanging to her waist in reddish gold splendor.

Suddenly all three of them were staring at him, and Tom Sax was saying something. Blue Hawk heard his name mentioned, and then they all began walking closer to him. As they approached, Blue Hawk saw that the girl's eyes were a startling green. Yet it was more than the vivid color that took him by surprise. Her eyes were large and brilliantly clear, with a penetrating, all-knowing look that was too mature for such a small thing. Her face was perfect, her skin a soft milky white. Her eyes were even bigger than usual as she stared at Blue Hawk in wonder.

"Blue Hawk," Tom said, forcing the boy to look at him. He led the woman forward, and the boy realized she greatly resembled the little girl, except that the woman's skin was peppered with little brown spots. Her hair was redder than the girl's, but her eyes were the same pretty green, and Blue Hawk felt amazed at how colorful these white people were. "This is my wife, Blue Hawk . . . uh, *na-htseeme*, wife. Cora."

So, this was the Cora Blue Hawk had heard Tom Sax mention so many times. Then the little girl must be Sarah. The woman smiled with genuine affection, putting a hand gently on the side of Blue Hawk's face that was still bruised.

"Oh, Tom, the poor boy," she said softly.

Blue Hawk immediately sensed her genuine concern, and he liked her right away, sensing she was a good woman, like Small Hands. Surely Tom Sax would want only a good woman at his side, for he was a good man. But she looked so frail, as though she would easily break. She had none of the look of strength to her that Indian women had, and Blue Hawk could not even imagine her carrying wood. But surely she did, for that was woman's work.

Tom moved to the little girl. "This is Sarah. Sarah," he repeated, patting the girl's head. "She's our little girl, and if you'll stay on with us, she'll be your sister." He struggled to try to explain in Cheyenne, but Blue Hawk only frowned. Tom sighed and pointed to the cabin. "House. Our home. Come." He waved Blue Hawk forward, but the boy hung back until the little girl boldly grabbed his hand and tugged.

"Come on, Blue Hawk. Don't be afraid," she said in a tiny voice.

The boy let her pull him along, afraid that if he did not follow or offended her in some way, Tom Sax would be angry with him. He still was not sure what these people expected of him: he knew only that Tom apparently wanted him to stay with them for the present. He hoped perhaps Tom Sax would go out to the deep forest again and would take him along, away from this place where there were so many white people.

How he longed for those deep woods, for his beloved

homeland, for Black Antelope. But that was all far away now, and the terrible events he had encountered seemed years rather than only weeks away. He felt strangely removed from himself as the pretty little white girl led him up some wooden steps. They walked through a doorway into a cozy, neat cabin, where the rich smell of something cooking met his nostrils and awakened a keen hunger in his belly. It made him think of sitting around a small fire in a mud hut, watching his aunt cook fresh meat. A thickness came to his throat then, and tears welled uncontrollably in his eyes. The pretty little white girl grabbed his hand again and squeezed it, somehow detecting his loneliness.

"It's all right, Blue Hawk," she told him quietly. "You'll see. You'll like it here. I'll show you everything you need to know. You don't have to be afraid."

He frowned, studying the girl's amazing green eyes. He understood nothing of what she had said, but he sensed it was kind and that he had a trusted friend in the little girl called Sarah. He would not run away yet. He would wait and see what it was like in this place called Fort Dearborn, near the great lake called Lake Michigan. Perhaps he was destined to stay with these people of his other blood, his white blood. Perhaps it was what *Maheo* wished, and for the moment, as a feeling of friendship flooded through him at the touch of Sarah's hand, he didn't mind the thought of staying.

Chapter Five

FROM that day forward, Blue Hawk's life was filled with the struggle to learn. Simply eating at a table was something new, for on his return trip with Tom Sax, they had always eaten around a campfire, much as Indians did. Blue Hawk had no reason to believe Tom Sax would eat any differently at the little log house at Fort Dearborn. He frowned that first night when Tom and Sarah sat down on hard objects at a big, wooden board with legs where food was laid out. Cora took a dish of food and handed it to Blue Hawk, who stood nearby, motioning that he should take it to the wooden board. Confused but hungry, the boy immediately squatted to the floor with the plate and began eating the food with his fingers.

Sarah squealed with laughter, saying something in words he did not understand and pointing at him. Tom Sax said something back to her and she sobered slightly, but Blue Hawk already realized he'd done something wrong, and shame made its red appearance on his face.

Tom Sax only smiled and bent down, taking the plate from him. "Table," he said, pointing to the wooden board. "Table." Then he pointed to the hard objects on which they all sat. "Chair." He sat down in his and held out his hands. "See? When in a house, we sit at a table." He pointed again. "We sit on chairs." He pointed to the hard object again, then indicated that Blue Hawk should sit on the other chair.

The boy stood up and slowly walked to the chair, scowling at the little white girl who had laughed at him. He plunked himself onto the chair and again began eating with his fingers.

"Oh, no, Blue Hawk," the little girl exclaimed with another laugh. She grasped his wrist and held up her own fork. "See? Fork. We eat with a fork." She jabbed the instrument into a piece of turkey, then put the meat in her mouth, smiling warmly at him. Blue Hawk looked at his own fork and picked it up, studying it intently before poking it almost violently into his meat. Sarah covered her mouth to smother more laughter and watched as Blue Hawk slowly put the meat into his mouth. Then he poked another piece, seemingly fascinated by this new way of eating. He put still another piece into his mouth.

"Blue Hawk, look," the little girl spoke up again. The boy met her startling, green eyes, seeing the gentle humor in them. He could not help but grin back at her. She held up another instrument. "Spoon," she told him. She scooped up some of the corn which, for some reason Blue Hawk could not fathom, the woman named Cora had cut from the cob.

Blue Hawk frowned again. Why did they use a fork for meat and a spoon for corn? These white people used too many instruments for eating, he decided. What was wrong with fingers in the first place? Still, he did not want to offend Tom Sax, nor did he want the little white girl to laugh at him again. He picked up his own spoon and dipped it into the corn.

Tom Sax looked at his wife. "I don't think you'll have to work with him too awfully hard, love. Sarah will do it for us."

"I imagine it's easier for him to take lessons from another child than from grownups."

"I can show him lots of things, Daddy," the girl said excitedly.

Tom grinned. "I'm sure you can, pet." He looked back

at Cora, hunger for his woman in his eyes. "I hope we can get the boy settled down early."

Cora Sax reddened, her eyes shining with love. "Yes. So do I."

Blue Hawk became almost enraptured in learning how to eat this new way. The food the white woman cooked was wonderful, potatoes and gravy, turkey and corn, followed by a wonderful treat made of thickened fruit cooked between two crusts of something flaky and sweet. "Pie," Sarah Sax called it. Whatever it was, it was the best thing Blue Hawk had ever tasted.

When he finished he stood up and pointed to the wooden board with legs. "Table," he announced proudly.

Tom Sax grinned, and Sarah clapped her hands. Blue Hawk pointed to the object on which he had sat. "Chair."

There was more applause, and Blue Hawk smiled, happy to show the little white girl and Tom Sax how fast he could learn. He held up the spoon and fork, naming them, then pointed to the little girl. "Sarah," he said. He pointed to the woman. "Cora."

"Oh, Tom, he's very bright, isn't he?" Cora Sax smiled kindly at the boy.

"Of course he is. He'll be your project, love, when I head out again—something to keep you busy and help keep you from worrying and being lonely. You and Sarah can teach the boy things, maybe even show him how to make letters and read." He sobered and took her hand. "I'd like to keep him with us, Cora."

Cora's eyes warmed at the pleading she saw in Tom's eyes, and she knew this boy could fill a great void in both their hearts. "You know whatever you want is fine with me, Tom. But we should give him a Christian name so he'll be better accepted by the others."

Tom shrugged. "We were going to name our son Caleb. Why not give the name to the boy?"

"Are you sure?"

"Sure 'n I am. Caleb. Caleb Sax. It's a fine name."

Her eyes teared. "Then that's what we'll call him." She looked at Sarah. "We're going to name him Caleb, Sarah. Maybe you can help us teach him his new name."

"Oh, yes, Mommy!" The girl got up from her chair and grabbed the boy's hand again. Blue Hawk was so fascinated by her that he continued to let her lead him around. She pointed to herself. "Sarah Sax," she told him. Then she pointed to Blue Hawk. "Caleb," she said. "Caleb Sax." Again she pointed to herself and said her name, then to Blue Hawk again. "Caleb Sax." She went around the room then, pointing. "Tom Sax. Cora Sax. Sarah Sax. Caleb Sax."

Blue Hawk frowned, realizing that for some reason they wanted him to have a name like theirs. Caleb Sax. Whatever the strange reason for wanting to give him such a name, he would go along with it until he decided whether to stay or go.

Caleb's sense of honor left him with little choice but to quietly accept the new ways Tom, Cora and Sarah taught him. Days turned into weeks, and his thoughts of running away began to fade as his affection grew for these people.

It seemed everything about the white man's world was hard or harsh or stiff, including the thick cotton pants he wore that were too hot and the long-sleeved shirt that had to be buttoned to the neck. He did not like the clothing at all, but even Tom dressed in this manner when he was at the fort. The only thing he fought wildly was when Cora Sax wanted to cut his hair. No Indian man wore his hair short without great shame, and though he was half white, he would not recognize that side of himself through short hair. Tom told Cora to leave his hair as it was, knowing Caleb had already been faced with many changes and had enough adjusting to do.

"But he'll never be accepted as a Christian, civilized boy with that hair, Tom," she argued.

"Those who won't accept him aren't worth worrying about, love. The boy has a spirit of his own, and certain things that are special to him. I'll not take those things away from him."

Cora agreed to leave his hair long, but she insisted that Caleb sit for daily lessons in English. She began to teach Caleb to read using a little book she had ordered from the east and had used to teach Sarah. It contained pictures of objects with the names spelled out below each one, and Caleb's ability to learn soon impressed them all.

Caleb himself was determined to cooperate. He was, after all, half white, and he realized knowing that side of himself might be important. Small Hands would probably tell him so. His days were filled with learning new things. But at night, while he slept on the floor in front of the hearth—he had refused a bed in the loft—his heart and dreams were still full of Black Antelope and all those he had loved and lost. He still dreamed of the deep forest and home.

One of the most difficult new lessons was bringing in wood for Cora. This he considered woman's work, and he felt humiliated when he carried it in. At first he had refused completely, but Tom had explained that by white man's custom, all the hard work was done by the men. He had proceeded to carry some wood in himself to show the boy. Caleb supposed that if a rugged man like Tom Sax could lower himself to carry wood, he also could do so, but only because it was for Cora, who was too thin and weak to bring in the wood herself; and for Sarah, who was too little.

He liked Sarah, who eagerly taught him words and writing, and who quickly came to be a good friend. She was sweet and patient, and she had a wonderful laugh that made him feel good inside. It was not long before he and Sarah developed a form of communication that made it possible for Sarah to understand him more easily than the adults.

They were soon becoming family to him, but still, deep in the night, Caleb felt restless, and sometimes he wanted to cry. He missed the smell of the earth and the plants and trees and the feel of the soft earth beneath him when he slept. He missed the aroma of sweet smoke inside a hut,

SAVAGE HORIZONS   (65)

the glory of riding a horse and carrying his own weapons
to the hunt, the winter nights spent huddled in a hut listening
to Black Antelope speak of glorious battles or tell frightening
ghost stories.

Most of all he missed the simple comfort of being around
his own people, missed the soft buckskin clothing, the young
Indian children he used to play with. The few white children
who lived in and around the fort were afraid of him and
would not play with him. Some of them laughed at him and
pointed. But he refused to be ashamed of his Indian blood,
and he still wore the blue quill necklace under his cotton
shirt. It was one item that linked him to his past, as did the
precious tomahawk Black Antelope had given him only a
little over a year before. Those were two things he would
never give up, and would kill to keep if it came to that.

Sometimes the restlessness of his spirit would overwhelm
him, and he would rise in the middle of the night and walk
to a window to look out, feeling like a caged animal. Sometimes it seemed he would suffocate within the four walls of
the cabin, and a wildness would well up inside him that
was difficult to control.

There were many Indians around the fort, mostly Fox,
Sauk and Shawnee. Seeing them made Caleb miss his old
way of life. And whenever he spotted a Chippewa, it was
hard to keep from attacking, but Tom Sax had warned him
that he must not do such things or it could mean trouble,
not just for himself but for Tom as well. The day came,
however, when the boy's Indian ways and proud spirit could
not be quelled, in spite of all of Tom's warnings.

Caleb accompanied Cora and Sarah to the supply store,
while Tom stayed home to chop wood to store up for winter.
Caleb's heart tightened when he saw Kyle Wiggins sitting
on the steps of the store. Wiggins had been gone for quite
some time, and Caleb had hoped he was gone for good. He
sensed that if Tom Sax knew the man had returned, he would
have accompanied his wife and daughter to the store.

Wiggins put a half empty bottle of whiskey to his lips

and watched with threatening eyes as they all walked into
the supply store. Cora refused to even look at the man, and
Sarah stuck out her tongue at him, making Caleb grin. They
both giggled and followed Cora inside, where three old men
sat around the stove. Caleb sometimes wondered if these
regulars ever left their chairs. He stared again in fascination
at all the marvelous items in the store, a place he was sure
he would never get tired of visiting. Cora began to place
her order, and as Hugh cut off a piece of dried meat for
her, Caleb sensed that Wiggins had followed them inside.
He turned, meeting the man's eyes squarely, determined to
show he was not afraid. Wiggins looked him over with an
insulting gaze, smirking at his white man's clothing. The
man plunked a few skins down on the counter, and Caleb
turned up his nose at the smell of the man's soiled buckskins.

"I've got more outside, Hugh," Wiggins said loudly. His
eyes moved to Cora Sax. "Lord knows I'm better at trapping
beaver than Tom Sax."

Cora reddened but said nothing, realizing Wiggins was
drunk and looking for trouble. She walked to another counter
to pick out some cloth.

Wiggins turned back to Caleb. "Bought quite a few of
these here skins from a bunch of Dakota northwest of here
that was hurtin' bad for supplies. The dumb bastards gave
me a whole slew of furs for a few pots and pans and some
flour." Caleb glared at him, not understanding every word,
but sensing he was being insulted. "Injuns ain't too smart
these days," the man continued, his snide grin revealing
yellow teeth. "They're out there fightin' and starvin' each
other out. Makes things easy for us trappers, though, saves
us work." He chuckled and threw a piece of chewing tobacco
in his mouth. "Where's your pa, boy? Ain't that what you
call him now?" He laughed heartily. "Imagine that, ole Tom
Sax takin' in a Injun breed and callin' him son. What do
they call you now, boy? Injun? Breed? Bastard?"

"That will be enough," Cora Sax said angrily, her face
red. "The boy's name is Caleb. He was homeless, and we

have taken him in. You will stop insulting him, unless you want to answer to my husband."

The man looked her over as though she were a delicious piece of pie, and Caleb watched cautiously, hating Kyle Wiggins with every bone in his body. Cora stepped back, pulling Sarah with her. Sarah stuck her tongue out again.

"Go away, Kyle Wiggins," the girl exclaimed, her green eyes blazing. "My daddy will punch you!"

Wiggins chuckled. "That so?" He leaned closer. "You better watch what you say, you pretty little thing, or some day you'll be sorry." He sneered at Cora Sax. "Appears to me you and your husband are raisin' a right spoiled brat here, woman." His eyes shifted to Caleb. "A spoiled brat and a wild breed. Some combination."

"Leave them alone, Kyle," Hugh said from behind the counter.

"Yeah, Wiggins, lay off," one of the men around the stove put in.

"I don't take orders from cowards and old men," the man growled. He turned to Cora. "And I ain't afraid of your man, neither. I can take down Tom Sax anytime I want." He leaned forward and tugged at a piece of lace at the neck of Cora's dress. Caleb was immediately enraged.

"Do not touch her," he said loudly, his fists clenching.

Wiggins' eyebrows arched and he turned to look at the boy. "What was that, boy?"

"You no touch her," Caleb repeated.

Wiggins chuckled. "Well, you've learned some English. You're a pretty sassy thing for bein' just a bastard half-breed in white man's territory, ain't you, boy?"

Cora screamed as Caleb lunged at the man.

Wiggins grabbed the front of Caleb's shirt and let the boy flail away at him while he just laughed. Then he flung Caleb to the floor, ripping his shirt and tearing off the rabbit's foot. The blue quill necklace was revealed by the torn shirt. Wiggins threw down the rabbit's foot and stepped on it, grinding it into the dirt floor.

"That will teach you to smart off to me, breed."

"You're a mean, ugly man," Sarah shouted, tears in her eyes.

"Be still, Sarah," Cora spoke up, pulling the girl away.

Caleb felt hot with shame at being thrown down by Wiggins. After all, he had killed two grown Chippewa men, hadn't he? He could not look so small and weak in front of Sarah. He started for Wiggins again, but Cora grabbed his arm.

"No, Caleb," she said sternly. "He'll hurt you. You must learn to control your temper, son."

The boy hesitated, glaring at Wiggins, who grinned. "That's teachin' him, Mrs. Sax," he said with a mocking bow. "The little wild animal needs some manners, that's a fact. Tell me, ma'am, what all are you teachin' this boy? Perhaps there are some things he's not quite old enough for yet, hmmm?"

Cora Sax reddened deeply, and tears welled in her eyes. "You're a filthy animal, Kyle Wiggins," she replied in a choked voice.

Caleb didn't understand the words completely, but he knew that Cora had been insulted and looked ready to cry. He glanced at the other men in the store and thought all of them cowards, for none of them stood up to defend Cora. In his rage he kicked Kyle Wiggins hard in the shin bone, glad for the first time to be wearing the uncomfortable, sturdy white man's shoes. Wiggins grunted in surprise and pain. Cora backed away, pulling Caleb with her. The boy backed up reluctantly, holding his chin high, ready for whatever Kyle Wiggins wanted to do. He would fight him, grown man or not.

Wiggins glowered at Caleb, coming closer. "You halfbreed brat!" He reached for the boy, but Caleb jerked away. The blue quill necklace came off in Wiggins' hand. Caleb grabbed for it, but Wiggins jerked back his arm, grinning.

"You want your necklace, boy? Come and get it."

"Give it back," Sarah shouted, wanting to cry.

Caleb glared at the man, hesitant.

"Give the child his necklace," Cora demanded.

"No, ma'am. If he wants it, he has to take it himself." He laughed. "Come on, boy. Come and get your necklace. It's special, huh? Did your whorin' Injun ma give it to you maybe?"

In blind fury Caleb turned and grabbed the huge butcher knife Hugh had left lying on the counter. Cora gasped and backed away, and Sarah stared wide-eyed as Caleb waved the knife at Wiggins.

"Give me necklace," the boy growled, looking amazingly menacing for his age. "You no touch woman. I kill you!"

Wiggins stood stock still, a gut feeling telling him the boy knew how to use the knife. "I ought to beat the hell out of you," he snarled.

Caleb held out his arms as though to tempt the man to try. Wiggins swallowed as the boy waved the knife again. "Give necklace."

Wiggins hesitated a moment longer, then threw the necklace to the dirt floor. "I ain't fightin' no damned kid. I got better things to do."

One of the three men at the stove chuckled then. "You lettin' a kid back you down, Wiggins?"

"Shut up!"

Another man snickered. "I think he's remembering the kid there killed two grown Chippewa warriors with his own hands. He's not one to mess with, right Wiggins?"

Wiggins whirled. "I said shut up! I could rip the little bastard's guts out. But grown men don't go around fightin' kids."

"They don't?" The first man laughed harder. "Seems to me that's what you was just doin', Wiggins, and the kid won." They all laughed then and Wiggins stormed out of the store.

Sarah bent down and picked up Caleb's necklace and rabbit's foot, brushing dirt from the rabbit's foot. As she handed the items to Caleb, tears welled up in her eyes.

Caleb laid the knife back on the counter, forcing back his own urge to cry, refusing to do so in front of a little girl. He suddenly did not like this white man's world at all. He wanted to be home, in the deep woods, among his own kind.

"I'm sorry, Caleb," Sarah told him.

The boy looked at Cora, seeing a mixture of sympathy and consternation in her eyes. He dodged past both her and Sarah, running out of the store, running for the Sax cabin. He ran as hard and fast as his young legs would take him, wondering if all the white men would be after him now for holding a knife against Kyle Wiggins. Maybe they would shoot him or hang him.

By the time he reached the cabin his lungs ached and his eyes were blurry with tears. He barged through the door, looking for Tom, but the cabin was empty. He ran outside, looking around the fields and over at the log pile, but the man was nowhere to be seen. He headed for the small log building where Tom kept the horses, his heart pounding with anger and loneliness. He wanted the comfort and security only Tom Sax could give him now, and he found the man inside, brushing down a horse. Tom turned to stare in surprise at Caleb, who stood there panting, tears running down his face, the necklace and rabbit's foot he had taken from Sarah still in his hand.

"White man no take necklace," the boy declared angrily.

Tom frowned, putting down the brush. "What white man?"

"Ugly one. Wiggins." The boy sniffed. "And he no touch Cora!"

Tom's eyes narrowed angrily. "Nobody is going to take your necklace, Caleb. Tell me what happened."

The boy ran to him, burying his face against the man's chest, spilling out the story in broken English and Cheyenne, declaring he wanted to go back to the wilderness to live. Tom Sax gave the boy a reassuring hug and led him over to a stack of hay.

"You sit right there, Caleb, understand? Don't leave this

spot. I'm going to make sure Cora and Sarah are all right and help them bring back their things, and I'll be having a word with Kyle Wiggins. Promise me you won't leave this place."

The boy nodded, wiping angrily at unwanted tears, still holding the necklace tightly. Tom Sax left, and Caleb waited obediently, hoping there would be no trouble for Tom Sax because of what he had done. It seemed an eternity before Sax finally returned, carrying supplies into the house before coming back to the shed to find Caleb wiping off his necklace with his shirt. He looked at Tom anxiously.

"I make trouble?"

Tom smiled patiently and sat down beside the boy. "Not much. Let's just say I don't think Wiggins will give you any more cause to get into trouble in the first place." The man rubbed his hands, and Caleb saw that his knuckles were red, a couple of them bleeding.

"You fight?"

Tom opened and closed his fingers. "Yes." He looked at Caleb. "Wiggins won't give you or my women any more trouble. He knows what I'll do to him if he does." He sighed and put an arm around the boy. "Son, I have a feeling your mixed blood is going to keep bringing you trouble like this. You've got to learn how to control your temper, learn when to get angry and when to let something go."

"Wiggins bad man. I no like. I want go home."

Tom squeezed his shoulders. "You'll like it here all right in time. I can't bring myself to take you back, Caleb. You've made so much progress, and you're such a handsome, intelligent boy. I've grown attached to you, too. Besides, you might as well learn to get along with whites. You're half white anyway, and the day is coming when all Indians will have to learn to get along with them, mark my word. You'll just have a head start. You're a bright boy, and I'd be shucking my duties to God and conscience if I took you back now." He turned the boy, looking into his sky blue eyes. "And I'd miss you, Caleb, that's a fact. I could never take you back and just forget you. Cora and Sarah would miss you, too. You've been good for my Sarah. It's a hard, lonely life for a little girl in this place. There are other children, but they're all older. You're older, too, but you're here all the time, and it's nice for her. She likes teaching you things. Don't you like learning letters and numbers? Don't you like Cora and Sarah and me?"

The boy wiped at a few straggling tears. "I like. You good. Others bad."

"Not all the others, Caleb. There are other good ones." The man sat back and took a pipe from a shirt pocket, then reached into a tobacco pouch he wore on his belt, taking some out to stuff the pipe. "You know, Caleb, my Cora lost a baby not long ago, a boy. I wanted that boy bad—for more reason than you would understand. Cora feels pretty bad about it, but it's not her fault. At any rate, when I found you I thought to myself, 'Tom, a boy is a boy. You lost yours, so what's wrong with this one? Why not take him and make him your son? He needs a father, and you need a son.'"

He stopped to light the pipe, then puffed it for a moment. "Ah, but losing the baby wasn't the only thing that was hard on my Cora. We left Saint Louis because of a bad family misunderstanding with a brother I have there. His name is Terrence, and I guess Terrence and I are as different as two men can be. At any rate, it's been hard on Cora, living up here in less civilized places. And it worries me, raising Sarah here, too. My brother has said we should send her to Saint Louis, where she can have a better life, better schooling." A strange coldness flashed through his eyes for just a moment. "But she's our little girl, and we can't bring ourselves to send her away."

He turned to look at Caleb again. "I guess what I'm trying to say is, since you came along, life has been better for my Cora and for Sarah, and I want you to stay, Caleb. I'm very fond of you. I want you to stay and learn and be a part of our family. I know you're feeling out of place and a little lost. But that will get better as time goes by and you master our language better, learn to read and write, get used to calling us your family."

The boy sighed, puckering his lips in thought. "I stay. But I go with you on next hunt."

Tom's eyes clouded and he puffed the pipe quietly another moment. "Caleb, you can't go with me, at least not this time."

The boy's heart quickened. Surely Tom Sax wouldn't go off and leave him behind. "I go with you!"

Tom faced him, putting a hand on his shoulder. "Caleb, you can't go with me. We've heard there's a new preacher coming to Fort Dearborn who is also a school teacher. Cora feels . . . well, we think you should have some of his professional schooling, some Christian teaching."

"Christian?"

"Yes. Our religion. The preacher could teach you about God, and he can also do a better job of teaching you English and numbers and all those things than Cora can."

The boy scowled. "My god *Wakan Tanka.* Grandfather called him *Maheo.* No Christian. Gods same for all."

Tom rubbed at his eyes. "I know how you feel, Caleb. But just give it a chance. Listen and learn, then decide, about all of it—how you want to live, how you want to worship. Cora and I want the best for you, and I promised Cora that this time when I went out I'd leave you behind, just for this one winter, to be schooled by the preacher."

The boy's eyes teared. "No! I go on hunt. Camp under sky. Be close to earth again."

"Not this time, Caleb."

"You promise I stay with you."

"Not in the way you mean it. I want to keep you, yes. Right here at Fort Dearborn, as my son. But I still have to go out on the hunts to make a living, Caleb. When you're older you can go with me again."

The boy looked away, his heart pounding. He didn't want Tom Sax to leave him among these white people. Tom reached over and rubbed his back. "Caleb, it's just for the winter. Cora's looking forward to showing me how much you've learned when I get back. Please do it for my Cora. She's wanting you to get some Christian teaching, and she and Sarah would have some company over the winter."

The boy's shoulders shook. "I not want be without you."

The man's heart ached for him. "I don't want to be without you, either. But things like this are part of growing up, Caleb. Sometimes it seems all there is to life is saying good-bye. But it's just for this one winter, I promise. If you do well, learn your reading and writing and numbers, and make no trouble, I promise on the Bible that I will take you with me on the spring hunt, and you can be outside again and live the way you like to live."

"You keep promise?"

"I'll keep it. As God is my witness."

The boy breathed deeply, wiping at his eyes. He stood up then, facing Tom, shoulders straight and chin held high. "I stay one winter."

Tom rose then himself, his eyes watery. He reached out and put a hand to the side of Caleb's face. "You're quite a young man, Caleb, and I'm proud of you. You've learned so many things so quickly, and you're proud and brave. I'm not telling you to forget your old ways, Caleb, or forget that you're as much Indian as white. But it's best for you if you learn both ways. Maybe that's why your *Wakan Tanka* led you to me. Come on. Let's go back to the house."

Caleb walked along beside the man, his heart heavy. "Wiggins no like you?"

"Wiggins likes nobody," Tom answered. "He's just a bad man, a no-good drunk. He stole some skins from a partner of mine once, and I accused him of it but could never prove it. He's been itching to make me look bad ever since, but he'll not be doing it by insulting my Cora or Sarah. If he does it again, I'll shoot the man. You needn't worry anymore about Wiggins."

Caleb felt better having talked with Tom Sax. He tied the

blue quill necklace around his neck, glad Wiggins hadn't stolen or broken it.

As he finished tying the necklace, Sarah came racing into the shed. "Caleb, you were so brave, holding a knife on that terrible man. I was so scared for you! Is the necklace all right?"

She ran up and stopped in front of him, fingering the necklace with her tiny hand, her soft fingers touching the skin of his neck.

"No break," Caleb told her.

She looked at him with her intriguing green eyes. "Why did you get so mad, Caleb?"

The boy frowned. "He bad," he answered, not knowing what else to say.

She smiled and ran off then. "Come on, let's go fish at the river."

He watched her, his heart feeling strangely warm. Tom Sax had made him feel better, but he realized now the man wasn't the only reason he wanted to stay. Sarah was so sweet, and she didn't just make him feel safe like Tom did. Sarah made him feel proud . . . and warm. Yes, he would stay for the winter. Sarah was his little sister now, and Cora his mother. He must protect them both.

Chapter
Six

THE weeks passed too quickly, and the glorious autumn beauty of the land was lost to Caleb, who grew sadder as the time for Tom Sax's departure drew near. He did not want to make any more trouble, so he did not tell the man how he feared the dark, condemning eyes of the new preacher who had finally arrived.

"I'll make a good Christian of the boy," the man had said with a pious air the first time he met Caleb. Preacher Stoner was a tall, lanky man, who Caleb guessed was stronger than his lean build suggested. He had a sharp nose and piercing dark eyes that were stern and unforgiving, and he wore dark woolen clothes, as did his daughter, Emily. The girl's mother had died when Emily was very young, or so the preacher told everyone, and Caleb sensed that Emily Stoner was just as lost and lonely as he. What little they had seen of her, the girl had not once smiled, and she always looked over-dressed for the weather. Though she was only slightly older than Caleb, her white-blond hair was worn in a tight bun. Caleb was certain she would be prettier if her hair were worn long and loose, like Sarah was allowed to wear her hair. But soon it was obvious it didn't matter how Emily Stoner wore her hair, for her father seldom allowed her to leave his side, and she was never allowed to play with the other children.

In late October Tom Sax was ready to leave, and Caleb

wondered if the people he loved would always be dying or walking out of his life. When Sax rode off with Bo Sanders, Caleb watched until the horses could no longer be seen, then stood staring at the woods into which they had disappeared, aching to be with the men in the deep and friendly forest.

"You wanted to go, didn't you, Caleb?" little Sarah asked, walking up behind him.

He nodded. "Yes. It is home, the forest."

"Better than here, where it's safe?"

He met her green eyes. "For me, safer there. No like here."

She looked sad then. "I wish you did. I've been a good friend, haven't I?"

He smiled at her. "Yes." Then he looked back in the direction Tom had ridden. "But I like hunt."

"Well, you aren't big enough to go yet."

He turned scowling eyes to her; almost laughing at the ridiculous remark. "I hunt with bow. I kill two Chippewa warriors. I plenty big enough."

Her eyes moved over him. Although he was only three years older than she, he seemed at least twice her age, and in her eyes he was much taller than he really was, for she greatly admired the Indian boy who had come to live with them. "I didn't mean to make you mad, Caleb. I only meant you have to go to school first."

"Why?"

She blinked. "We all have to go to school when we're little."

"Indian children no go school. They be fine men and women. I will go to this school one winter, no more. Then go on hunt with Tom Sax." The words were spoken as a solemn vow before he turned and stalked away.

The only sound was the ticking of the grandfather clock, and the ominous pacing of Preacher Stoner's boots around the table in his parlor. The man had had the stiff, white-

washed wooden house built quickly, refusing to remain in
the small cabin which awaited him when he first arrived at
Fort Dearborn.

"A proper Christian home with hardwood floors and glass
windows is all I shall accept for my daughter," the man had
announced soon after arriving at Fort Dearborn. He told the
small community of settlers that lessons could not begin for
the few children at the fort until such time as the preacher
was truly settled and a proper chapel was built which could
also be used as a schoolroom. All did his bidding, for they
thought him a man of sacrifice and dedication for leaving
civilization to come and preach in the wilds. No one questioned why he had come to such a remote area.

The chapel was built first, and there Caleb was compelled
to sit wearily through long, boring prayer services. He was
not allowed to sit in the middle or at the front of the chapel,
but was asked to sit in the back, where his dark presence
would not disturb the white congregation. Cora Sax did not
fully agree with the decision, but the preacher, she thought,
should know what was best. She was more disturbed, however, when the preacher told her Caleb would not be allowed
in the regular classes with the other children.

"The boy would be a disruption," he had told Cora. "Caleb
Sax is a special child—peculiar in that his skin is so dark
and he insists on wearing his hair sinfully long. And his
blue eyes in that dark face would make children stare at
him. There is also, of course, that certain element of wildness in the boy that could cause confrontations and corrupt
the other children. Caleb will take special teaching, and
would best be taught privately. As soon as my home is
finished, you will bring the child there in the afternoons,
after regular classes."

Again Cora had reluctantly bowed to the stern preacher's
demands, only because she thought it would be good for
Caleb to have the formal learning. Now Caleb sat in the
finished house. His lessons had not begun until almost Jan-

uary, for that was how long it took to finish the preacher's home.

Caleb sat stiffly in the hard chair at the parlor table, dressed in a warm, woolen suit that itched badly and made it difficult to keep from wriggling and almost impossible to pay attention. The preacher's first instructions had been to sit completely still and not to speak. So he sat, awaiting his first lesson, apprehensive around the stern and frightening preacher, but determined to do his best to please Tom and Cora Sax so that he could go on the next hunt. Preacher Stoner paced around and around the big table, then finally stopped at the other end to stand and stare at Caleb. The preacher's daughter, Emily, was nowhere in sight, but Caleb sensed she was nearby, listening and watching.

"I will be blunt with you, Caleb Sax." The preacher's voice boomed at Caleb, startling the boy. "I do not like the fact that you are a bastard and a half-breed."

Caleb blinked, unsure what the words meant, but sure they were an insult. "I not—bastard," he began.

"Silence!" The man's face reddened. "I told you not to speak."

Caleb closed his mouth and swallowed.

"You will be difficult to teach, and it will be especially difficult to make a good Christian of you, Caleb Sax. I am not certain I can ever make you good enough in God's eyes, considering the fact that you are not only part Indian and a bastard, but that you have also murdered two men. I will do my best. But know that you are forbidden to say anything in your Indian language. You will speak only English, and you will learn to speak it well. Perhaps your white blood will give you enough intelligence to grasp some of what I will teach you. But before we begin, you need the devil beaten out of you, to clear the evil Indian spirits from your soul and to show you obedience. You have killed, Caleb Sax, and there is a wildness in you that must be controlled. Remove your suitcoat and your shirt, boy."

Caleb sat rigid, unsure what to do.

"Stand up and remove your shirt," the man roared at him.

Caleb stood up quickly then, knocking over his chair in his haste. He removed his jacket and shirt, then stared straight ahead. But out of the corner of his eye he could see the preacher removing his wide leather belt. His heart pounded with fear, yet he was determined to sit through at least this one lesson, as he had promised to do. Would Tom Sax be angry with him if he ran away his first day?

"May the evil come out of you," the preacher cried a moment before the wide belt snapped across Caleb's back. The blow was so hard it made Caleb stumble forward over the table. The belt came down again and again, until Caleb thought he would pass out from the pain. But he made not one sound, nor did he cry, stubbornly refusing to satisfy the preacher with any sign that he was hurt. He was Indian, and a man. He would bear this, just like young warriors withstood their test of manhood. Yet he already hated this man, much more than even Kyle Wiggins. Wiggins was at least open about what he was, but this man put on a pious air, then beat children behind closed doors.

When the man finally finished, Caleb's head swam and he could barely move his arms to put his shirt back on. He gritted his teeth against a groan as he put the coat on also, and the preacher pushed him roughly back into his chair and began the lessons, while Caleb struggled to pay attention. But the pain seared through him, and the welts on his stiffening back burned and were suffocated by the woolen jacket.

Somehow he managed to get through the next two hours of spelling and mathematics, making some mistakes because of the pain. But overall Caleb did well enough to earn a remark of surprised praise from the preacher, who stressed that if God ever forgave the heathen evil inside him, it would be only because Caleb had some white blood in his veins.

"I will send a letter home with you, Caleb, to tell your mother how well you did. But I warn you," he leaned closer, "do not ever tell Mrs. Sax about your whipping. If you tell her, God's revenge will be great upon you." His face reddened with an almost wild piousness. "Do you understand, Caleb Sax?"

The boy swallowed. "I understand."

"If you tell, God will cast you into a living hell, and I will have to beat you again. You must be good, Caleb, and accept the punishment that is necessary in order to get the evil out of your blood." The man stood up then. "Now, go home and do the lessons I gave you. Bring them back with you tomorrow."

"Yes, sir," Caleb said quietly, raging on the inside. He refused to actually look straight at the preacher, for fear the man would see the hatred in his eyes.

"Stand up, Caleb Sax," the man told him.

Caleb rose, turning toward the man but not raising his eyes. The preacher reached out and pulled at the quill necklace. "This is a heathen token," he said almost angrily. "I have heard how this necklace made you threaten a man's life. That shows how evil it is. Do not wear this necklace in my house again. If you do, I shall destroy it."

Caleb looked up at him then, and their gazes locked challengingly. Caleb wondered if at that moment the man was actually afraid of him, for he immediately let go of the necklace.

"My necklace," Caleb said in a near hiss. "Do not touch."

The preacher grasped the boy's long hair then, pulling on it painfully. "Then do not wear it here again."

Caleb jerked away. "I no wear," he answered. He turned and ran out through the door, slamming it behind him. How could he bring himself to ever go back to the preacher's house? he wondered despairingly. Yet what would Cora and Tom Sax think if he broke his promise to them? Would Tom refuse to take him on the next hunt? That was one possibility Caleb couldn't face.

Caleb ran several yards from the house, then turned and looked back, fearful that the preacher would come after him for some reason. It was then he saw Emily Stoner, staring down at him from an upstairs window. How much had she witnessed? He was ashamed to think she might have seen the beating with the belt, heard the bad words the preacher had said about him. He stared for a moment, wondering why the preacher seldom let her out of the house and would not let her attend school with the other children. She was an outcast, like himself, yet she was the man's own daughter. Caleb turned and ran home.

Inside the house Emily watched him go, curious about the Indian boy and wishing she could talk to him and find out where he had come from. And she felt sorry for him, wincing herself at every blow of her father's belt across the boy's back. She'd felt that belt, knew its sting.

"Get away from that window!" her father yelled behind her, and the girl jumped and whirled to look at him. He stepped closer and slapped her across the face. "Slut! How dare you watch that Indian boy?"

She kept her face turned away then, putting a hand to her numb cheek. "I—I was just watching a bird."

"Don't add lies to your sins, Emily. If I don't watch you closely, you'll turn out just like your mother. You just pray to God that you won't walk the evil path your mother walked. Don't let me catch you staring at a boy again."

The man turned and left the room, and Emily flung herself on her bed, weeping bitterly. She was confused and lonely, trapped in her life which was nothing more than schooling and prayers and chores. What was so terrible about being with others, talking to other children? And what did her father mean about turning out like her mother?

She remembered little about her mother, for she'd been very young when she had died. Emily had had nightmares about her poor mother burning in hell, for that was where her father claimed she had gone for her sinful ways. Emily had never been told what her mother had done wrong. Her only memory of the woman was from an early age, but it was vivid and had always haunted Emily. She remembered it had been night, and her mother was running with her. A strange man ran beside them, and then there were shots and screams, and her father was picking her up and carrying her away. She had never seen her mother again, and soon after they had left the place where they had lived. She didn't even know where that had been, and they had moved several times since. Emily was never allowed to make friends anywhere they had lived. Her father had simply told her that her mother had died, and whenever she asked about the woman, her father simply told her to never mention "that sinful woman" and threatened to beat her if she did so again. Emily had learned to stop asking.

Caleb ran to the horse shed, not wanting to face Cora Sax and her questions until all the anger and humiliation were out of him. The tears came in bitter, wrenching sobs that tore at his young soul. He was not evil. He was not! And he would wear his necklace forever, whether the preacher liked it or not.

He dropped his books and tore off his suitcoat and shirt, unable to bear the cloth against his welts any longer. He threw himself face down into some straw, crying bitterly in loneliness and terror. If only he could have gone with Tom Sax! What should he do now? Should he run away? But where? And was the preacher right when he said he would be punished by the white man's God if he told Cora Sax about the beating?

It was then he heard the voice behind him. "Caleb! What happened to you?"

He whirled, quickly wiping at his eyes, disgraced even more that Sarah had found him crying. "Nothing," he said quickly.

The girl stared for a moment at his bare chest. She'd never seen a shirtless boy before, and his skin was fascinatingly dark. Her heart felt as though it would burst with pity, for she sensed that for an Indian boy to cry, something very bad must have happened.

Sarah walked closer, and Caleb grabbed for his shirt and started to put it on.

"Caleb, let me see your back again. It has big white marks on it. Where did they come from?"

He slipped on one shirtsleeve, then winced as he put his other arm in the second sleeve. "I fall," he told her.

Sarah's eyes teared, for the preacher scared her when she sat in school and church and listened to him roar about sins and the devil.

"Did that preacher man hit you?" she asked, her eyes wide with fear.

Caleb refused to meet her eyes and began to button his shirt. "I cannot say. He tells me—" Caleb stopped. He was not supposed to tell. Then he heard Sarah whimper and he looked at her. "Why you cry?"

"He beat you, I know it. Will he . . . beat me?"

Caleb scowled, wincing again with pain. "No. You white. I Indian. He say I bad."

Sarah sniffed. "But you aren't bad, Caleb!" The look of his back brought terror to her heart. She moved closer, kneeling down near him. "You should tell mother, Caleb. Don't let that man hurt you again."

"No. Cannot tell."

The girl began to cry harder. "But I don't want the preacher to hurt you again. I can't stand for you to be hurt, Caleb." Tears ran down her chubby, rosy cheeks, and for some reason it bothered him terribly to see her cry.

"No hurt. You not cry. It be secret."

Sarah shook her head. "He's a bad man, Caleb. I'm telling mother!" She turned and ran.

"No! Wait!" He wanted to run after her, but felt suddenly dizzy and weak. He sank back down into the hay, rolling over on his side. What would Cora Sax say? What kind of punishment would come to him? He had not meant for Sarah to find him crying. He felt like a fool now. Perhaps he had not been brave enough.

Several minutes later Cora Sax came running out to the

shed. "Caleb!" She rushed to his side. "What is this about welts on your back? What happened. Caleb?"

His stomach churned and he wondered if he was going to vomit. "No hurt. Keep promise. Go back tomorrow."

"Sit up, Caleb, this instant," the woman told him.

The boy obeyed, glancing at Sarah, who just stared as Cora lifted his shirt to see the welts on his back. "Dear God," the woman muttered. "Come to the house and I'll put something on these welts right away."

The boy only scooted back, looking up at her with teary eyes. "I no tell. Sarah tell. Your God no punish?"

The woman frowned, kneeling back down beside him. He stared into her thin face and kind, green eyes. "Punish?"

"Preacher say ... I tell, God punish."

For the first time since he'd known her, Caleb saw true anger in Cora Sax's eyes. "How dare he tell you that!" She reached out and touched his hair. "Our God does not punish innocent little boys, Caleb. He is a good God, a kind God. It is Preacher Stoner who should be punished, for hurting you and telling you those lies about our God."

The boy swallowed back more tears. "Is true? No punish?"

"Of course not. And you'll not go back there, Caleb."

The boy stared at her in joy and disbelief. "I stay here? You teach?"

The woman smiled softly. "I'll teach. I thought it would be good for you to have the preacher's learning, Caleb. But what he has done is unforgivable, and certainly no way to teach a child."

"Caleb not evil?"

The woman grasped his hand. "You're not evil, Caleb."

The boy's lips puckered. "Tom Sax be angry. No take on hunt."

"Oh, yes he will," she answered. "I promise, Caleb. Tom will understand. And he'll be very upset with Preacher Stoner. You pay attention and let me teach you, and when Tom gets home we'll just show him how much you can learn without the preacher's help. We'll do it ourselves, you and I and Sarah. I'll not send my Sarah back to that man, either. Tom will have some words for him, preacher or not, you can be sure!"

Caleb looked at Sarah then, and the girl was smiling at him eagerly. She nodded. "See? I told you we should tell mother."

Caleb breathed deeply. Suddenly his heart felt lighter and even his back seemed less painful. He slowly got to his feet, insisting on doing it alone. Cora picked up his jacket and boots, and Sarah took his hand.

"Come on, Caleb. While you were gone I baked you a pie all by myself! It's my first pie. You have to taste it and tell me what you think of it."

Caleb managed a grin. He was not really hungry. He was in too much pain. But he would taste it for Sarah, and even if it wasn't good, he'd tell her it was, for her heart was good, like her mother's.

Tom Sax fumed, storming back and forth in the small main room of the cabin. "He'll not get away with that," the man grumbled, his fists clenched.

"You can't go getting in a fist fight with a preacher, Tom," Cora tried to calm him.

"Oh, can't I?" He shook a fist in front of his chest. "He's a man no different from any other."

"Not to the community."

Caleb and Sarah listened excitedly, their eyes wide, their mouths quiet. Caleb would like nothing better than to see the fiery Tom Sax punch out the cruel Preacher Stoner for the stinging beating the man had given him.

"The man's a fake," Tom answered. Tom had returned the night before, but Cora had saved the news about Caleb's beating for morning.

"Tom, think for a moment," Cora pleaded. "We know it was wrong. But men like Preacher Stoner can make such things look right. Caleb is Indian. If you go out there and call the preacher out and make a scene about this, it will only make things worse for Caleb. Just because the man is a preacher, a lot of people won't believe us. And some who do will just say the man was right to beat Caleb, because he's Indian. If he were one of their children, it would be a different story. But you'll just draw more attention to Caleb. People will brand him as a trouble-maker, and he doesn't need that. To make a scene will just make the preacher look more right than wrong. You can't just physically beat on a man who is so respected in the community, right as you are. You'll just turn more people against Caleb, and that would hurt more than help him."

Tom stopped and looked at Caleb. "I'm sorry, boy. Damned sorry. I had no idea he'd treat you that way. I should have taken you with me on the hunt."

Caleb watched with hope in his eyes. "You will take me next time? I have learned much from Cora. I can read a lot of words, and write and spell. And I know my numbers."

The man's eyes actually teared. "Of course you can go with me. I promised, didn't I?"

Caleb nodded. Tom shifted his eyes to Sarah. "Did that man ever lay a hand on you, girl?"

Sarah shook her head. "Mama kept me from school anyway. She said she doesn't want the preacher teaching me anymore."

Tom nodded, looking at Cora. "That was good."

"Preacher Stoner came over one day and asked why Sarah wasn't in school." She raised her chin. "I looked him straight in the eyes and I told him I thought he knew why. He turned very red and gave Caleb a terrible look. But he's not bothered us again. Please let it rest, Tom. Do it for me. The man could do or say something to turn the community against Caleb. They all hang on every word the man says. I know he's wrong, but I think it would only hurt Caleb to use him to try to prove the kind of man the preacher is. Perhaps people will figure it out for themselves eventually, just by noticing how the man treats his daughter. The poor girl seems a virtual prisoner in their house. She can never play with the other children or even go out of the house."

Tom sighed deeply, rubbing his chin. "That's a sorry thing over there. But I can't do anything about how he treats his own child. It's my children I have to protect. You were wise to take Sarah out of the school. This all must have been very trying for you."

She looked at her lap. "I was wishing you were here, that's for sure. I'm glad you're back, Tom."

Their eyes met again and Caleb admired the love and support he saw between them. He had heard familiar sounds the night before, sounds he sometimes heard Black Antelope and Two Stars make together if he awoke in the middle of the night.

Tom stepped closer to Caleb. "That man gives you any trouble, you tell me, understand?"

Caleb nodded. "I will tell." He put a hand to the blue quill necklace. "You not let him take necklace?"

"Of course not." Tom leaned down, putting his hands on Caleb's shoulders. "And don't you pay any heed to what that man said. There is nothing evil in being Indian, Caleb. You're a fine young man, and you're smart, too. God loves you the same as he loves all of us. Our God doesn't punish children like that man said, and in His eyes you're no different from anybody else. You be proud of your Indian blood, you hear? Don't you ever be ashamed of it—not ever. You promise me that."

Caleb stared back at him with wide, blue eyes. "I promise. That man did not make me feel ashamed—only angry. He has a bad heart."

"Yes. I think he does." Tom raised up and patted the boy's hair. "You're looking fine, Caleb—taller, more filled out, and by golly I think you're getting more handsome. And in a couple of months Bo and I will be heading out again. You will come along this time. You bring some books, and around the campfire at night, you can read to me. I'll help you with the words you don't understand. How does that sound?"

Caleb grinned, his heart dancing with joy. He could go back into the deep woods, live the way he was meant to live. "I go. I be good hunter, you will see."

Tom smiled. "Now that is something I don't doubt." He turned to Cora. "I'll do like you ask, Cora. But that man had better leave Caleb alone from now on. And we'll not be going to his church services. You can read to us from the Bible and we can pray right in our own house. I know you'll miss church-going, love, but we can't go worship under that man."

Cora nodded. "It's all right, Tom. I'd rather not go myself. After seeing what he did to Caleb, I could never sit and listen to him."

The man's eyes softened. "I'm sorry, Cora. There aren't many of the civilized things here you knew in Saint Louis."

Their eyes held. "You know that doesn't matter," Cora answered in a loving voice. "You belong here, and I belong wherever you are."

Tom sighed very deeply, a strange look on his face that moved from sorrow to near anger. "If not for—" He stopped then, turning away. "I've got to go and take my skins to the supply store." He reached out. "Come on, Caleb. You can come along and help me count them. We did good this time."

Caleb jumped up, eagerly following the man outside.

There was no more talk of Preacher Stoner; and no more problems with him. Tom began keeping Caleb with him often, and life became happier and more secure for the boy. Weeks turned into months, and months into years, years that passed living with a loving family. Caleb learned fast, becoming more like a white man in many ways. He felt more and more comfortable in the new world at Fort Dearborn, but he never forgot his life in the deep forest to the west, or the people there he had loved and lost.

Caleb's English improved, and he learned to read and write as well as any white boy his age. Nearly all his schooling came from Cora, whom he began to call mother; Tom Sax was father, and Sarah seemed truly like a sister to him. Still, as both children grew older, he had many disturbing feelings about Sarah that he knew were not brotherly; but he could not fully understand or explain them.

Life for Caleb became a mixture of civilization and the old ways. He continued to prefer the old ways, and the life he led when he went with Tom hunting and trapping. He supposed the wilderness in his blood would never really leave him, and the winter of his fifteenth year found him perfectly happy sitting in the deep woods far from Fort Dearborn, enjoying a campfire with Tom and Bo and chewing on a piece of bear meat. He basked in the pride of having shot the bear himself, and the cooked meat and warm fire helped ease the cold night air that seemed to penetrate even the wolfskin coat Caleb wore. His coonskin hat was pulled down over his ears, and he wiggled his toes inside the fur-lined moccasins he wore as he listened to Tom and Bo discuss what they thought was an impending war between the British and the Americans.

The cause of the fighting brought confused loyalties to young Caleb's heart. The longer he was associated with whites, the more confused he became. He had never felt truly one of them, and living in the woods, hunting and trapping for weeks at a time, only made him long even more for that kind of life forever. He was happiest when he was in the wilderness, and he hoped that troubles with the British and the Indians would not end the hunting trips, as Tom so often hinted could happen.

"The damned British have turned pretty near all the Indians in these parts against us," Bo grumbled. "Even the Chippewa have gone to their side." The man glanced at Caleb, who perked up at the mention of Chippewa, whom he would hate to his dying day.

"I thought the Chippewa fought on the side of the Americans," he said. "That is part of the reason they slaughtered all of my people."

"Well now, the Chippewa and the Sioux have joined up together with the British, Caleb. Would you believe it?"

Caleb licked bear grease from his fingers. "It is very strange. All that dying for nothing."

Tom nodded. "I agree, son." He grinned then. "I just hope you intend to be on my side if there's any fighting to be done against the British and their Indian allies."

Caleb grinned. Although he was not quite sixteen, he had a tall and gangly build that made him seem more like twenty, and he had an air of threatening darkness about him that made others want to stay out of his way. He was not certain that he was handsome, since handsomeness was a matter of perspective. But others said that he was. He smiled at Tom.

"You know that I would always defend you, Father," he answered. "I owe you my life. But I can understand why so many Indians are on the side of the British. The Americans want their land. The British want only the furs. I cannot say that I blame my people for fighting the American settlers."

Tom puffed a pipe and studied the young man. "That's how you still think of them, even after all these years with us? 'Your people.'"

Caleb stared at the flames of the fire. "I cannot help the blood that flows in my veins."

"Half of it is white, Caleb. And some day that part will come through. You might be settling yourself one day on a ranch or a farm."

Caleb shrugged. "I do not think so." He looked at Tom and frowned. "I have never felt white, Father, even after all this time with you. I have tried, but the feeling will not come."

Tom smiled sympathetically. "A man has to be what he has to be, that's a fact. As far as the Indians fighting against us, I can't completely blame them myself. Why not let the

British use their waterways, if all they use them for is to come for more furs and then leave again? It's natural to support the side that poses the least threat to a man's welfare. But I'm white, Caleb. I've settled at Fort Dearborn, left Saint Louis a long time ago. Cora and I are happy here, and we feel the little piece of land we live on is ours now. If the Indians or the British come to take it, I'll have to fight them."

Caleb poured more coffee for himself. "If I lived with the Indians, I would fight with the British. But while I live with you, I will fight with you."

Tom sighed. "Makes things kind of hard for you, doesn't it?"

Caleb nodded, sipping the coffee.

"Well, Caleb, this is a growing country. Whether the Indians and the British like it or not, American settlers will keep coming, looking for more land to farm, looking for some kind of freedom that always seems to be just a little out of reach. There will be some fighting for sure. But in the end the Americans will win, Caleb, because I think that's the way it's destined to be. They've fled oppression and tyranny and starvation in Europe to come here and be free, to reap the wealth of this land."

"And they in turn will bring oppression and tyranny and starvation to the Indian," Caleb answered quietly, staring at the orange flames of the fire.

"Perhaps. I hope not. I wouldn't do such a thing."

Caleb poked at the fire with a stick, stirring the coals. "The trouble is, most white men are not like you, Father. Sometimes my heart feels torn in half, for there are other white men I hate."

Tom puffed his pipe. "You'll always have some difficult choices, Caleb, more than most men because you're from two worlds. Between the British whiskey and the white man's diseases, as well as the flow of more people into this land, I don't see anything good ahead for the Indian. It's this world you'd best choose, son, in spite of all the pain that comes with it. I know it's been rough for you."

Caleb shrugged. "This is the only time I am happy, here in the wilderness with you, or even alone. It is the only time I find peace. I belong only to myself. I no longer belong with my people, nor with the whites. Because of my blue eyes and dark skin, I can never truly belong anywhere."

Tom puffed the pipe again. "I can't help you there, son. I wish I could."

"I know." Caleb took out his own pipe and filled it, then lit it. It was one of the privileges Tom had granted him for being such a great help and a good hunter on the trips. The boy looked over at the bearskin stretched between two trees, and again he felt the warm pride as he puffed on the pipe, trying to remember when he last felt like a child. He could not remember, but he knew he had not been a child since the day he saw his Sioux father lying dead. He watched the flames of the fire. Fire was a friend to the Indian, and he still believed the flames were dancing, friendly spirits. Surely Black Antelope was there in the fire, watching over him, keeping him warm. The man was dead in body, but not in spirit.

"There's some Indians that ain't on nobody's side," Bo spoke up, scratching his balding head. "Rumor says there's a Shawnee by the name of Tecumseh that's built his own town over in Indian Territory. Calls himself a prophet and calls the place Prophet's Town. Seems there's a lot of Indians, especially Creek and Cherokee from the south, that's listenin' to his preachin' about a separate Indian nation of their own, apart from the British or the Americans. They don't trust either side and figure they have to protect themselves against both. The man's got a lot of power over the other tribes, they say."

Tom nodded. "I've heard the same. It all adds up to nothing but trouble, that's for sure. We'd be best to keep our trapping within a few days of the fort from here on. Fact is, this might be my last hunt this far out for a long time to come. I don't like Cora and Sarah being back there alone with so much trouble brewing. I've got plenty of friends watching out for them, but I'd still rather be there myself. My brother down in Saint Louis is always writing letters saying we should send Sarah down there where it's safer, but Cora won't go back, and she won't consider being separated from our daughter, nor do I like the idea."

"Why will Cora not go there?" Caleb asked.

Tom puffed the pipe quietly a moment. "Long story, son, and one that will never be told."

Caleb frowned with curiosity but knew better than to pursue the subject. "I am glad she will not go," he told the man. "I would miss her very much. And I would miss Sarah's smile and friendship."

Tom grinned. "She's a beauty, that one. I love her to pieces. But like I say, things are getting dangerous. Enemy Indians or the British could try to take Fort Dearborn. It's a strategic point of trade."

Caleb frowned. "Do you think that could happen?"

"Sure 'n it could, son. I know how you like to go on the hunts, but you understand we can't leave the women alone until we know what's going to happen."

Caleb nodded. He felt a need to protect Cora and Sarah as he would his own blood relations. He listened to the rushing water of the Rock River nearby, much of it still unfrozen in spite of the cold. "I would not want them to be harmed."

Tom smiled. "You're a good lad, Caleb. And I hope I'm wrong about Fort Dearborn. If we had to leave, I'm not sure where we'd go." He rose and walked over beside Caleb, putting a hand on his shoulder. "I know how you like it out here, son, the rivers, the animals, the quiet. It will be a sacrifice for you to miss the spring hunt this year, a sacrifice for me also. But I fear we'll have to stay home when the weather warms."

Caleb watched the fire, feeling an odd sensation of being led by outside forces over which he had no control. Many things were changing. How ironic that the Chippewa were fighting alongside the Sioux against the Americans. It seemed nothing in life stayed the same for long, and he wondered how much longer he would have Tom and Cora Sax—and Sarah—the only people he had now who cared about him.

Chapter Seven

THEY returned in April, the Grass Moon to Caleb, and the month of his sixteenth birthday. But this time there was no joy in their return. The spring of 1810 brought something worse than an attack by Indians or the British. It brought pneumonia to Cora Sax. Her delicate constitution could not bear the punishment of frontier life, and while the land awoke to the budding of new life, Cora died. She was buried beneath a wild cherry tree that was in full bloom.

There was no consoling Tom Sax, and for days that turned into weeks, he was withdrawn and unapproachable. Sarah and Caleb grew closer, for the center of their love and nourishment was gone, and they had only each other. Caleb had no idea how to console Tom Sax, who often went off alone; nor did he know what to do for poor Sarah but to simply be there for her. His own pain was great, and in a moment of prayer for guidance he cut his hand and let blood in his sorrow over losing the woman who had been like a mother to him. Again he had lost someone he loved. From deep within the recesses of his Indian upbringing, it seemed proper to let blood.

When he returned home Sarah carried on in a near panic over the bleeding cut, washing it for him and bandaging it.

"Why did you do it, Caleb? I don't understand."

He watched her wrap his hand, noticing her soft white hands, and for a moment his eyes caught the full roundness of her blossoming breasts. Her thirteen-year-old body was blooming into a young woman's. Caleb thought how some Indian girls married at twelve, most by fourteen or fifteen. He shook away the odd thought. This was Sarah, and although she was not a blood relation, he knew he should not think of her this way.

"It is fitting," he told her.

Her wide eyes met his, and there was now a provocativeness to the green pools of beauty that disturbed him. What was this thing that was awakening in him? Were the feelings he was experiencing part of the reasons why a man married? It made him think of Emily Stoner, who had been at Cora's funeral, no longer a girl but a young woman, standing taller than all the other women there, quiet, hidden as always under too many clothes. She had looked at him, a long, penetrating stare that made him feel uncomfortable but also brought the strange urgency he was feeling now as he looked at Sarah. Somehow with Sarah it seemed wrong, for not only was she more like a sister, but she also looked at him with total innocence, and Caleb knew she didn't feel the same strange, wonderful sensations washing over him. But Emily—her look had been different, almost inviting.

"I will never understand Indian ways," Sarah told him as she finished tying the bandage. "If this gets infected, you could lose your hand, maybe your arm."

"I will be all right," he answered.

Her eyes suddenly teared and she picked up an envelope. "A man brought this letter up on a boat today. It's from my Uncle Terrence in Saint Louis." She blinked and one tear slipped down her cheek. "I just know what it says, Caleb. Father wrote him about Mama's death, and now my Uncle Terrence will want me to go to Saint Louis. Caleb, I'm afraid Father will send me this time. He's so different, so sad. And I know he thinks I should leave Fort Dearborn." Her lips puckered. "I don't want to go, Caleb. Every night I cry and cry, missing Mama. If I had to leave you and Father, too, I don't know what I'd do."

Caleb took one of her hands in his good hand. "I would miss you very much, Sarah. But in many ways Father is right. This is a bad place now, with talk of war all the time. Many other children have already gone away with their families. I would not want you to be hurt. And Father is full of sorrow and worry. If he sends you to his brother, you should not argue with him about it. He is already in great sorrow and needs no more worries."

The girl swallowed. "You think he'll send me, don't you?"

He squeezed her hand, his blue eyes holding her own as he spoke. "You must be strong now, like an Indian," he told her. "Wherever you go, our spirits will be with you, mine and Father's. Even Mother is with you. Everywhere you are surrounded by Mother Earth and the animal spirits, as well as our own."

She sniffed, and her chest rose in a sob. "But I don't want to go. Why can't you and Father come with me?"

Caleb frowned. "I do not know why, but there is bad blood between Father and Terrence Sax. Father will not talk about it. And now, in his great sorrow, it would be bad to ask him. I know he would never go to Saint Louis. And if he stays here, we cannot leave him here alone. I should stay with him." He sighed. "Besides, I would never go to a place where there are even more white people. If I ever leave this place, I will go back to my people in the west. I am big enough now to find my own way."

"But . . . wouldn't you come to Saint Louis to see me? I can't leave here, Caleb, if it means I'd never see you and Father again. Promise me you'd come to see me, Caleb. Promise!" She squeezed his hand tightly, more tears running down her cheeks. Always it tore at his heart to see her cry.

"I promise," he told her. "But I could not stay."

She wiped at her tears with a shaking hand "Then maybe ... maybe some day when the danger is past, you could come and get me, you and Father. You could bring me back here or take me with you wherever you go."

He studied her pleading green eyes. "Perhaps," he told her. "But maybe by then you will be a grand and beautiful lady who likes all the comforts of the city. Father says Terrence Sax is a wealthy man."

Sarah cried harder. "I don't care!" She had been kneeling on the floor in front of his chair as they talked, and now she flung her arms around his neck, squeezing tightly so he was compelled to lean forward to embrace her. "I don't care how rich he is," she wailed. "I don't want to go away. I don't want to be alone. I don't know my aunt and uncle, Caleb. Why did Mama have to die? Why is God so mean?"

He breathed deeply of the scent of her thick, red-gold hair. "We cannot fight what destiny brings to us, Sarah. The Indian knows he must merely accept that which comes to him, and by accepting, we are stronger. Death and life are not so far apart. I feel my Indian father, Black Antelope, has always been with me, and Mother will always be with us. Her spirit lingers, Sarah, and you must do what she would have you do. She would not want you to stay here, where it is dangerous. She would want you to go to your uncle. Accept it now, Sarah, so that you can bring a little joy to our father's heart by going willingly."

She hugged him a moment longer, and he felt suddenly manly, protective, wise. She pulled back, her face close to his ... too close. "You would be proud of me if I went willingly, wouldn't you?"

Their eyes held for a moment, a spark of something much more than sibling love lighting up in their eyes for a brief moment, a feeling neither of them even recognized. He leaned forward and kissed her cheek, somehow thinking it would make her feel better, unable to control the urge to do so and tempted to kiss her on the lips. He chided himself inwardly for the strange desire.

"I would be proud," he told her.

She stood up then, taking a handkerchief from her pocket and blowing her nose. "I'll go then, Caleb. For you. But only if you promise to come and see me."

"I said that I would."

She took a deep breath and wiped her eyes. "I'll make us some tea. I hope Father gets home soon. Do you think he'll be drunk again?"

Caleb watched her a moment, then stood up and walked away from her, confused by the new emotions she had created in him. "He has not been sober since Mother died. I think he blames himself, and that is the worst part. He was not here when she got sick. And he thinks it is his fault for bringing her here. She was so frail. She was not made for this place."

He stared out the window at Cora Sax's grave, wondering what it was like to love a woman and lose her. He remembered how terribly unhappy he had been told Black Antelope was when Little Flower died in childbirth. Now Tom Sax seemed to care nothing for life. What was it that made a man love a woman so much that he did not want to live without her?

Fort Dearborn began filling with volunteer American soldiers, and talk of war with the British was rampant. Tom Sax reluctantly made arrangements with several volunteers to take Sarah south as quickly as possible. The women and children of several other families would be leaving also. Some of the settlers urged Preacher Stoner to send his daughter, but the man refused to even let her out of the house alone, let alone be separated from him by so many miles.

Tom prepared a map of Saint Louis showing Terrence Sax's home, and he wrote a letter for his brother. Sarah and Caleb never saw the contents of the sealed document.

"Treat her well, or you will regret the day you were born," it read. "She's a wonderful child, and my little girl deserves the best. I admit you can give her that, and although I hold no brotherly love for you, I am grateful that you will take the child, and trust that you will give her everything she so rightfully deserves.

Above all things, give her love. She has much to give in return, just like Córa did. But Cora is gone now, and I cannot raise such a beautiful girl alone. Sarah needs a woman's touch and all the fine things Saint Louis can give her. I know that your wife can have no children, and you have asked that I send her to you now that Cora is gone. I agree, only because I love my Sarah so much and want the best for her, not because I care to satisfy your own whims.

Take good care of her, and never tell her the reason for the bad feelings between us, brother, or it will be bad for you. I enclose some money which I ask that you set aside for Sarah in your bank in Saint Louis. In spite of our hatred for one another, I know I can trust you with the money, that you will see that Sarah gets it at the proper time.

I don't know when or if I will come for her. Perhaps it is best, once she gets settled, that I do not come at all. We will see.

Thank you for your offer and give my best to your wife.

Tom."

The parting was sad indeed, and a few people stared when Sarah hugged Caleb tightly. They whispered about the Indian boy who lived with Tom Sax and had been accepted as a son, and how they would never let a half-breed hug their daughter that way. But Sarah and Caleb were oblivious to their whispers. Caleb suddenly did not want to let her go. The feeling of protectiveness and manliness returned as he held her, and the thought of not seeing Sarah for months tore at his heart and brought back the loneliness he had felt after his village had been attacked.

"I'll pray for you, Caleb," she told him.

"And I will pray for you." She seemed so small. He towered over her now, for he was a full six feet tall, taller, even, than Tom Sax.

Caleb reluctantly let go of her then, and Sarah turned to hug Tom, who was much thinner, his face drawn and tired.

He looked at her strangely, as though to tell her something very important. But then he just hugged her, not caring that he was crying in front of others. "God bless you, sweet Sarah," he said quietly. "I am so sorry that you must go alone, but these people will take good care of you." He kissed her hair. "I love you, Sarah darling. One of these men is to bring back a message letting me know you arrived safely. I'll be praying for you, girl. Make your mother proud now."

"I will, Father."

She pulled back and he kissed her cheek. "You've surely made this old man proud, Sarah. It's a brave thing you're doing, and a wise one."

"We've got to get going, Sax," one of the men said.

Tom nodded, then lifted Sarah onto the flatboat that would carry them south to the Mississippi River, where they would get on one of the steamboats that had been so much talked about lately. The steamboat would carry Sarah and the others downstream to Saint Louis.

Caleb's chest ached. How many ways were there to say good-bye? It must simply be done. He watched with the old, haunting realization that life was a succession of losses and good-byes. Now still another loved one was leaving him. Sarah had been his best friend during the hard years of being an Indian boy among whites, a stranger in a new land. He remembered how she had giggled that first day when he sat down on the floor to eat. Seven years had gone by since then, swiftly, too swiftly. He waved and watched until the flatboat was out of sight, then turned to Tom Sax, walking up to the man and putting an arm around his waist.

"Come on, Father."

"Let's go to the tavern. I need a drink."

Caleb sighed and helped the man walk, amazed at how so much strength seemed to have gone out of Tom Sax.

"You've got to start eating and quit drinking so much," Caleb told him. "Mother would be angry if she saw you this way, and the day will come when Sarah needs you again."

The man nodded. "I know, son. I'll get back on my feet soon. It's just so hard . . . How can a man explain what a woman has meant to him? She sacrificed so much to come here so I could live my life as I damn well pleased. She put up with so many months of loneliness while I was out tramping the forest. She knew I needed that kind of life, that it was in my blood. Now I wish I had done more for her." They walked arm in arm. "The best thing I can do now is what I've just done, give Sarah the kind of life I could never give Cora. Saint Louis will be good for her, and she'll be the prettiest girl in that whole city, won't she?"

Caleb smiled sadly. He missed her already. "She will, Father. But not just in Saint Louis. She's the prettiest girl anywhere."

Sax nodded, his chest aching. "I'll stop the drinking, but not today, son. Not today."

Caleb understood and walked with the man to the tavern. When they entered, the small saloon was crowded with excited men, their attention turned to one man. Caleb stiffened when he saw Kyle Wiggins. The man had been gone for months, and many thought him either dead or just gone forever from Fort Dearborn. But there he was, standing on a chair, holding a bottle of whiskey.

"I tell you, we gotta be careful how far we let the Injuns go! The damn Shawnee are takin' over practically the whole territory of Indiana. They got a leader called Tecumseh who's roundin' up the Creek, the Cherokee, Choctaw, you name it. They're bandin' together and claimin' half the land from the Gulf of Mexico all the way up to Michigan."

He slugged some of the whiskey and several men joined in his concern and drank with him. Others only watched, waiting for more news, unsure exactly where Wiggins had been.

Wiggins finally noticed Tom and Caleb. He slowly lowered the whiskey bottle, realizing Caleb Sax had grown considerably and was big enough, perhaps, to fight a grown man. He had not forgotten that as a boy Caleb had backed him down in front of others, nor had he forgotten his feud with Tom Sax. The room quieted as the others noticed Wiggins glaring at the two Sax men.

"Well, if it ain't Tom Sax and his scum-breed son," Wiggins sneered. "You're lookin' poorly, Sax."

"Lay off, Wiggins," one of the men in the crowd told him. "The man's wife died."

Wiggins looked unaffected. "That so?" He drank more whiskey and moved his gaze to the crowd. "I'm tellin' you men that war is comin', and soon. We use some Injuns to help us, and the British use others. But there ain't none can be trusted. You'd best be careful even trustin' the Miami around here. They'll turn on you, one day, that's sure." His eyes shifted to Caleb. "The best way to avoid problems is to get rid of every Injun we can." He looked back at the other men. "Like it's rumored the governor of Indiana Territory is aimin' to do. Folks there is thinkin' on attackin' the city the Shawnee have built in Indiana. They call it Prophet's Town, and they look to that there Tecumseh as their prophet—think he's gonna lead them to power. I'm warnin' everybody. This thing could spread if it ain't stopped early on."

Tom and Caleb moved to a table to sit down, too involved at the moment in what Wiggins had to say to order whiskey. Caleb leaned back in his chair, his long legs sprawling away from it as he watched Wiggins, his hatred of the man stronger than ever. Caleb was a man now, his skills honed from his own determination and years of living and hunting in the wilderness with Tom Sax. He often practiced throwing a knife, and Tom sometimes sparred with the boy, teaching him how to fight with his fists, always eager to brag about how the Irish were the best fistfighters ever born.

"How do you know all this?" somebody shouted.

Wiggins took another drink, the whiskey making him feel more important, braver. "I was over in Indiana Territory, trappin' along the Tippecanoe River. That's where I heard about Harrison plannin' this big attack on Prophet's Town." His eyes moved to Caleb again. "I'm thinkin' on goin' back there to help. I can't think of nothin' more pleasurable than wipin' out a bunch of Injuns that think they own more land than they got a right to. The best thing we can do is burn every damned house and out building they own—burn their crops and supplies, too—kill every last one of them savages."

Murmurs filled the room, and men nodded their agreement.

"I'm sure a brave man like yourself will find it easy to kill the women and little children, won't you, Wiggins," a voice spoke up loudly.

Everyone turned. The words had come from Tom Sax, and the room quieted. Wiggins stared at him a moment, then climbed down off his chair and set his whiskey bottle aside. He slowly walked over to Tom while people parted and backed away, letting him through. Wiggins took a stance in front of Sax, and Caleb shifted in his chair, sitting straighter and watching Wiggins carefully. His protective feelings for Tom Sax had never been keener, for he realized how much the man was suffering after Sarah's departure.

"You callin' me a coward, Sax?" Wiggins asked.

Tom Sax didn't care anymore what happened to him. He had beat Wiggins before and he could do it again. Maybe he would kill him this time. The man deserved to die, and he couldn't think of a better time to start a fight with him.

"Everybody knows what you are, Wiggins. I know for a

fact you've raped Indian women; and you're only brave when you've got men standing behind you. Besides that you're a damn thief and everybody knows it. You got no right mouthing off against men who are probably better than you. I'd trust those Indians a lot farther than I'd trust you."

Wiggins' dark eyes narrowed and his fists clenched. "Stand up and call me a coward, you Injun lovin' bastard," he snarled.

"Leave him alone," Caleb spoke up. "He is not well enough to fight."

Wiggins' gaze shifted to Caleb. "Well, then, how about you, boy? You look all growed up now, big enough to take on a man. You're one Injun I wouldn't mind killin' for free."

Tom was out of his chair in an instant, pummeling into Wiggins. Tables, chairs and drinks went flying, and the crowd of men backed away as Tom, in his grief and defense of Caleb, reacted to Wiggins' challenge. But he was considerably weaker than normal. Caleb jumped up, his heart pounding as Tom and Wiggins went crashing to the floor. Tom managed to land a couple of hard blows to Wiggins' face with the old Irish steam, but then Wiggins threw him off. Both men got to their feet, and Wiggins landed a crashing blow to Tom's jaw, sending the man flying across a table. It was then Wiggins pulled a knife.

Caleb realized instantly that the blow to Tom had been hard enough to make him dizzy and confused. Tom was struggling just to rise. In a flash Caleb's own hunting knife was drawn, and he climbed over a table and chair, stepping in front of Wiggins as the man approached Tom.

"Get away from him," Caleb hissed, waving the knife. He faced the man squarely, standing as tall as Wiggins.

Wiggins backed up, then grinned. "Well, well. So you're wavin' a knife at me again, are you, boy?" Wiggins hunched over. "Well, this time nobody can blame me for pickin' on a kid, can they?"

"Caleb! God, no," Tom groaned, struggling to his feet. Two men helped him up, then held on to him.

"Leave it be, Tom," one of them warned. "Let the boy concentrate. You're in no shape to be gettin' in on it."

Tom watched in quiet desperation, not even able to stand without the help of those who held on to him. Would he see the last precious thing left to him be killed before his eyes?

There was no look of fear in Caleb Sax's eyes. The boy was quick and sure, darting quickly out of Wiggins' way at the last moment every time the man lunged or slashed with his knife. Again and again each man slashed out, then jumped back, knocking over tables and drinks. Darting in and out, Wiggins began to sweat and pant while Caleb appeared cool and collected, determined and confident. His long black hair flew out with every quick movement, and his finely tuned body was tense and ready, his blue eyes alert to Wiggins' every move.

Wiggins began slashing relentlessly, apparently deciding he could frighten the boy by his sudden onslaught of seemingly fearless jabs, but Caleb's instincts told the boy that the man was slashing crazily, out of fear. Caleb backed up and fell over a table, but quickly rolled to his feet. It wasn't quick enough. He felt a slight draft as Wiggins' huge blade cut a long slash from Caleb's left cheekbone down and back behind the boy's left ear.

Tom cried out, and it took three men to hold him back. "It's his fight now, Tom. You've got to let it be."

Caleb was crouched and ready again in an instant, ignoring the hot sting and the blood that began flowing freely down over his neck. He backed up more, urging Wiggins out of the tavern and into the street, where he would be able to move more freely. The crowd quickly followed them out, and Tom went with them, his heart pounding from fear.

Outside the two men circled one another, glaring, waiting for the right moment to slash again. Wiggins was panting harder now, and Caleb knew that if he held out long enough, the man would tire sooner than he would. And Wiggins had been drinking, making him slower than Caleb. Caleb was glad he had taken Black Antelope's advice long ago to stay away from whiskey, for the fiery water took away a warrior's ability to think, and took away his strength and speed.

Wiggins began a new onslaught of relentless slashes, making Caleb back up again. But Caleb watched and gauged the thrusts, until with a speed that impressed the onlookers, he suddenly grabbed Wiggins' wrist, stopping the thrust with a strength that amazed Wiggins. Caleb quickly pushed, slamming him to the ground so he lost his breath. Wiggins lay limp for a moment while Caleb held his big knife against the man's Adam's apple. He squeezed Wiggins' wrist until the man released his own knife.

"I didn't want this fight, Wiggins," Caleb said. "But you were going to kill Tom Sax." He nicked Wiggins' skin. "If we were among Indians, you would be a dead man."

He got up then, panting and glaring down at Wiggins. He would like nothing better than to kill the piece of filth before him, but he knew that would be too dangerous in this place. He looked down at Wiggins, victory in his eyes and his Indian pride showing. He had beaten Kyle Wiggins again.

Caleb turned, walking toward Tom. "Let's go home," he said, still panting. But Tom's eyes widened as he looked past Caleb.

"Hey!" someone shouted.

"Look out!" Tom yelled.

Caleb whirled to see that Wiggins had found his breath and had yanked a pistol from the belt of a nearby man. The gun was already raised. Caleb quickly tossed the knife in his hand. It made a whirring sound as it zipped through the air, finding its mark a split second before Wiggins could fire the pistol. There was a thud, then Wiggins grunted.

He stumbled backward, dropping the pistol and staring at Caleb as though he saw something horrible and frightening. The man clutched the knife in his chest and pulled on it frantically, but he knew it would make no difference. The look of horror on his face told others he knew he was dying. He looked down at the blood spurting from the wound and his face turned sickly white. Then his knees buckled and he went down, the life gone out of him. He fell forward, ramming the knife even deeper with the fall, then rolled to his side and lay lifeless.

Caleb stared at his enemy, wanting to shout with exultation at his conquest. How proud Black Antelope would have been to see him kill such an experienced man at such a young age. His joy was great, and his pride swelled. He was glad Wiggins had pulled the gun; it gave him an excuse to do what he wanted to do in the first place. Wiggins was an evil white man and deserved to die. Caleb had no doubt the man had committed atrocious crimes, and the world would be better off without him. But when the boy moved his eyes to look at the others in the crowd, he knew that what he had just done would not set well with them. He held his chin up and looked at them defiantly before going over to Wiggins and yanking his knife from the man's chest.

Several volunteer soldiers who had overtaken the fort rushed into the crowd, the sergeant demanding to know what had happened.

"The breed there just killed Wiggins," someone shouted from the crowd.

"It was self-defense," someone else added.

The soldier looked at Caleb, who stood panting, blood still pouring from the cut on his face. The soldier pulled a gun. "Hand over the knife, boy."

Caleb looked at Tom.

"Hold up there," Tom stormed, stepping closer. "The boy only got in this to protect me. Wiggins started the whole thing and was fixing to kill me. Caleb is my adopted son. He only did what he had to do, and he's just a sixteen-year-old boy! Wiggins could have backed out of the fight, but he wouldn't. Caleb let him go once—had him down and let him go! Then Wiggins tried to shoot him. The boy had no choice!"

The soldier's eyes scanned Caleb's bloody, dirty face and clothes. "He looks older than sixteen," he commented. "And he's killed like a man. He'll be responsible like a man." He waved the pistol. "Now hand over that knife."

"Wait a minute," one of the others spoke up. The man looked around at the others. "All of you know Tom here, know the quality of the man. And you know just as well the kind of man Kyle Wiggins was. Now Tom and Caleb are like father and son. The boy only reacted in defense of Tom, and only killed Wiggins in self-defense. Wiggins could have called a halt but he didn't. We can't stand here and let the boy hang for doing what any of us would have done. We're all Tom's friends."

The man stepped between Caleb and the sergeant, and then another settler from the fort stepped forward, joining the man who had spoken in Caleb's defense. Then another and another stepped closer, surrounding the soldier.

"You'd be wasting a good man if you hang the lad," one of them spoke up. "It was a fair fight, sergeant. Wiggins started it. He's been after Tom and the boy for years, and he had it in mind to kill the both of them if he could. Caleb Sax just happened to be the better man, that's all. We don't want the boy to hang. These are bad times, and we need manpower to defend the fort. Caleb will fight with us if need be."

The soldier studied Caleb haughtily, and Caleb stood proud and silent, his broad chest heaving with tired breaths, his eyes void of any regret for killing Wiggins.

"All right, Caleb Sax," the soldier growled. "I'll let it go. But you'd best remember that things are getting damned hot with the British and the Indians out here. This fort has been shored up for an attack, and anyone with dark skin and long black hair who dresses in buckskins had better be wary. You decide where your loyalties lie, boy, and decide quickly. If I catch you starting any more fights or suspect that you're siding with your red brothers, I'll hang you from the nearest tree. Understood?"

Caleb glared back and half grinned. "My father, Tom Sax, is white. My eyes are blue. I owe much to Tom Sax. My loyalties lie here. I am a man without a people, but for now I am Tom Sax's son. If fighting to defend him means fighting against the British and the Indians, then I will do so." He shoved his knife into its sheath. "I will keep the knife. It is a gift from my white father."

The sergeant backed away. "I'll be watching you, Indian!"

"If you wish to look upon me as Indian, then call me by my Indian name," Caleb sneered. "It is Blue Hawk."

The soldier shoved his gun back in its case. "To me it's just Indian," the man replied. "And you'd best keep yourself out of trouble. We may have some friendly Miami around here, but you're no Miami, I can see that. I don't trust you." The man whirled and walked off.

"Tom," one of the men from the crowd said, "you'd best realize how touchy things are right now. You're a good man, and we agree Caleb's been a decent boy. But there's a wildness in him that all of us can see, a streak of Indian that can't be tamed. Any kid who can wield a knife like that at sixteen is headed for trouble. You keep him in line, or we'll have to forget our feelings for you and deal with him like any other Indian."

"You'll go through me first," Tom grumbled. He grabbed Caleb's arm and headed for their cabin to take care of the cut on the boy's face. Caleb just grinned, caring not at all about the bleeding wound, but basking in his victory.

Chapter Eight

CALEB swung the ax hard, and it rang in the crisp morning air. It was a cool morning for July, a beautiful time that would have been prettier if he knew he could go inside the cabin to a breakfast made by Cora and Sarah. He missed them terribly, and now with Tom gone with Bo for a few days to hunt for badly needed meat, he was alone.

Despite all that had happened, life had to go on. If they were to make it through another winter at the fort, they would need a new supply of dried meat. Other settlers who had remained planted and would harvest their fields of vegetables, and the corn was already getting high. As always, plenty of wood was needed to get through a cold winter of heating and cooking, and Caleb decided to take advantage of the cool morning to split some of the big logs they had already cut and hauled to the cabin.

To Caleb's relief, the message had come that Sarah had arrived safely in Saint Louis, and she had sent her own letter telling of all the new sights, the fine school she would attend and the beautiful home Uncle Terrence owned. Caleb was glad there were enough diversions in Saint Louis to keep Sarah's mind occupied and help her get over her sorrow and fear. Tom seemed more like himself after getting the letter, although he made a grumbling remark about how his brother was good at impressing people with the "wonders of his wealth."

"I'm sure Sarah will want for nothing," he had commented.

"She is not the kind of girl who would care about those things," Caleb had answered.

Tom had smiled and nodded. "True."

Tom was eating better and drinking less, and Caleb was glad Bo had convinced him to go hunting for a few days. Caleb was sure that getting back to the wilds would be good for the man, and he had agreed to stay behind and get some chores done that had been badly neglected after Cora's death, for neither of them had cared.

Caleb raised the ax again, feeling suddenly that he was being watched. He hesitated, the ax in mid-air, his blood tingling. His dark eyes took in the surroundings and saw a woman standing at the fence several yards away. Even from the distance, Caleb recognized Emily Stoner. She wore her customary black dress with long sleeves and a high neck, even in the summer, and a bonnet covered most of her hair and shaded her face.

Caleb whacked the ax into a piece of wood so it stuck fast. At first he just stood watching her, unsure why she was there, wondering where her father was. He began slowly walking toward her then, his dark skin sweaty and glistening in the morning sun. He wore only his buckskin leggings, thinking nothing of his bare chest, unaware that to Emily Stoner he was nearly naked, a fascinating male creature that ate at the curiosity she was forced to keep buried.

To Emily, Caleb Sax was the summation of everything her father would never let her have. Somehow she was sure that if she could talk to Caleb, see him, know him, she would achieve the ultimate rebellion against her father, who always forbade her to speak to or even look at men. But at nineteen she had reached an age where daring and strange desires overwhelmed her fear of going against her father's wishes.

She had sneaked behind her father's back and had easily found a few men at the fort who did not mind secretly satisfying her curiosity. It was not easy fooling her father, but the excitement of it thrilled her. She hated him desperately for all the beatings, the solitude, the loneliness she had experienced, the denial of a normal life that left her almost crazed. She wanted nothing more than to defy her father to the fullest extent possible, and Caleb represented that ultimate denial, the dark Indian boy her father had declared evil and full of sin.

Caleb was innocent of women. She sensed it, and it only made her hunger for him. And he was innocent also of her own indiscretions. Surely he thought her pure and good. She watched the graceful gait of his walk as he approached, felt stirred by his powerful muscles, flat stomach, and his handsome face, even with the scar on his cheek. Now that he had actually killed a grown man in a knife fight, her curiosity knew no bounds. The thought of Caleb's wildness, his skill and bravery, only made him more fascinating.

Caleb stood close then, studying her pale blue eyes beneath the wide brim of the bonnet. "Why do you watch me?" he asked.

She swallowed, twisting a handkerchief in her fingers. "I . . ." She looked around, as though afraid to be seen. "Can we go inside your cabin?"

Caleb frowned. "If someone sees you go into my cabin, it would be trouble for you. I am alone here, and I am Indian. The others do not all trust me."

Her eyes suddenly teared. "Please? I just want to talk to you, just for a little while."

Caleb carefully studied the surrounding woods. "Where is your father?"

"He's very sick. He gave me permission to go and get some supplies. I never get to go out alone and I . . . I just want to meet someone, talk to someone. I can't stay long."

Caleb went against his better instincts, for he had always felt sorry for her, remembering her lonely face in the window so long ago. "Come," he told her. He turned and walked back to the cabin, and Emily hurried behind him, quickly darting inside, where she removed her bonnet and whirled around, laughing a strange, almost insane laugh.

Caleb watched in surprise. He had never pictured this girl smiling, let alone whirling and laughing. She was too pale, he thought, too thin and unusually tall, but pretty in her own way. Pleasant disturbances moved through him at the thought that the mysterious Emily Stoner was in his cabin and they were alone. He'd never been alone with a girl before, not a strange one like Emily.

She stopped whirling and faced him. "You don't know how good it feels to be free, even for one day," she said excitedly. "Here I am, alone in a cabin with an Indian man, one who has killed a skilled trapper, someone who's forbidden in my father's eyes." Her eyes moved over him in a way that made Caleb feel warm and alive. "Thank you, Caleb, for letting me come inside."

She stepped closer and he stepped back. "It is not good that you are here."

"I don't care. Oh, Caleb, ever since that day my father beat you I've thought about you, wanted to tell you how sorry I am for what he did, wondered about you. But Father so seldom lets me leave the house that I never had the chance to talk to you. Even when I did go out it was always with Father." She breathed deeply and whirled around again. "Oh, how I'd love to run away!" She walked closer again. "Take me away, Caleb."

He wanted to move back again, but something held him fast. "I cannot. They would hunt for us. Besides, it is too dangerous now. Why did you choose me?"

She reached out hesitantly, then touched her fingers to the muscles of his chest, lightly tracing them over his skin. "You're so beautiful, Caleb." His blood suddenly felt like it was on fire. "You're the most beautiful man at Fort Dearborn." The use of the word man made his blood burn even hotter, and she touched one of his nipples, a wild look in her eyes. "I . . . don't know anything about men," she lied. "I've never seen a man's bare chest before." She moved a hand to her own small breasts. "Why do you suppose I have these, and you don't?"

She looked up at him and he wondered if she could hear his heart pounding. He knew she was older than he, but it seemed she genuinely did not know about the differences between men and women. He had known since he was a small boy sharing a lodge with Black Antelope and Two Stars. But until now he had not realized how pleasant those differences could be. Caleb swallowed, feeling light-headed and unable to reason clearly, not stopping to wonder how one supposedly so sheltered, so innocent of male and female anatomy could be so bold.

"A woman has breasts to feed her babies," he answered.

She frowned. "How does she get the babies?"

He just stared at her. "You don't know?"

Her eyes widened like a curious little girl. Her hand moved down. "Are you different here?" She touched him between the legs and he jumped back.

"Go away!"

She put a hand to her mouth. "Why?"

"Go away. You should not touch me that way. It is bad ... cruel."

Her eyes teared. "Cruel? Why?"

"Get out! You should not have come here!"

Her eyes teared and she turned and ran out. Caleb wondered if the fire would ever leave his skin, or the ache she had brought to his limbs would subside. He had never mated, never even thought much about it until now. Suddenly all such feelings and needs had been rudely and painfully awakened. He stumbled to the doorway to see Emily Stoner disappearing into the woods, and he felt bad that he had made the strange girl cry.

The night was a restless one for Caleb, his young man's passions awakened to new heights. He lay awake, fantasizing about Emily Stoner, wondering at her strangely twisted mind, hating her father. He would never forget the beating with the wide leather belt, and he wondered what the girl had been through. It made him feel sorry for her, made him want to protect her, and more than anything, he wanted to know about women, what it was like to lie naked next to one.

But to be with someone like Emily would surely be forbidden and wrong. The few times he had considered some day taking a wife, he had always pictured an Indian woman. Yet half of him was white. Why should a white woman be forbidden to him? Caleb instinctively knew it would never be allowed. He told himself to forget about Emily's strange visit, forget about the pleasant urgings she had stirred in him, forget Emily herself.

Yet he could not. The next day he watched for her, but she did not come. He was almost relieved. Darkness fell, and he went inside, stripping to his loincloth and washing, then cutting a piece of venison for his supper. He had worked hard that day, and he ate well before blowing out the lantern and lying down on his bed of robes on the floor. He had never learned to sleep in a bed. It was warm, and he considered sleeping outside but was too weary to bother getting up again. He lay in the dark cabin, and again his thoughts turned unwillingly to Emily Stoner, sometimes to Sarah. For some reason the two of them sometimes swam together in his mind, but he didn't understand why.

He heard a light tap at the door, and his heart quickened. If it was Tom, the man would simply come inside. Caleb sat up. "Who is it?"

"It's me . . . Emily."

Caleb slowly rose, considering telling her to go away.

"Caleb, don't be mad. You didn't really want me to go away before. I just know it. Please let me come in."

The boy knew Tom would tell him to send her away. But natural instincts prevented him from doing so. He lit a lamp and opened the door. She darted inside without a word, then took off her bonnet.

"I don't think anyone saw me," she said, loosening her

hair and removing a cape. She whirled, her white-blond hair brushing over her shoulders enticingly. She stopped and looked at him, her blood burning at the sight of his near nakedness, her curiosity at what lay under the cloth tied around his groin overwhelming. She met his eyes, and she knew instinctively that she had some kind of power over this boy, that even though he was strong, he was weak when she was near.

"Father is sleeping very hard," she told him. "He's still sick, and he's taken some kind of drug to make him sleep. He doesn't even know I'm gone." She laughed then, stepping closer. She took his hand, and he let her move it up and place it against her breast. She inhaled deeply. "I knew it," she whispered. "I knew it would feel wonderful for you to touch me."

He suddenly pulled his hand away and stepped back. "Why do you do this?"

She held his eyes with her strangely wild ones. "Because I want to know. I want to know all the things Father has forbidden me. I want to know about boys. Do you have a special girl, Caleb? A girl you would want for a wife, want to have babies with?"

He felt the fire creeping through his blood again and did not answer.

She smiled. "I could be your girl, couldn't I?"

He frowned. "It is wrong."

A look of wild defiance came into her eyes then, an almost evil cunningness that surprised him. "That is why I'm here," she almost hissed. "Because it *is* wrong! My father says I'm bad, that I should never look at boys or touch them. He beats me. I hate him! Show me what bad is, Caleb. I'll fool him. I'll be what he says I am, and while he sleeps I'll look at a boy, touch a boy." She looked down at his loincloth. "What's there, Caleb? Why did you jump away when I touched you and say that I was cruel?"

He swallowed. "Please. Go away."

She unbuttoned her dress, and he stared in disbelief. "Why are you afraid, Caleb?"

He stiffened. "I am afraid of nothing."

She pulled her dress over her shoulders and down to her waist. "See? I am different from you."

His mouth went dry and he could not move.

"Show me, Caleb. I want to know what is different, what is bad, what mating is." She closed her eyes, breathing deeply with the exhilarating joy of being free, truly free, of doing something she knew instinctively was against everything her cruel father preached.

Caleb could not help allowing his eyes to drop to her young, firm breasts and pink nipples. She moved closer, and her offer was more than he could refuse. His curiosity and young passions were awakened to an agonizing level he couldn't resist.

"I saw a man and woman touch lips once. Touch my lips, Caleb." Emily lifted her face to his.

His eyes glazed with desire, and his lips quivered with the want to taste her so. He bent down, meeting her mouth. It was all the prompting he needed. He pulled her close, kissing her wildly and moving his chest back and forth over her breasts, groaning at the feel of them against his skin. She whimpered, returning his kiss, lost in him, swimming in the forbidden pleasure of being with the mysterious Indian boy.

Caleb felt as if he couldn't get enough. Instinct guided his actions as he lowered her to his robes on the floor and covered her with his body. He did not stop to wonder what his feelings for her truly were. They seemed to have nothing to do with love, only with learning, knowing, awakening, enjoying. She felt wonderful against him, beneath him.

She laughed lightly as he undressed her, then gasped when he removed his loincloth, staring at his manhood. She seemed utterly fascinated by it. When her fingers gently felt him, she pretended to be utterly amazed when it swelled even more. He studied her as she studied him. Her skin was so

white, the hairs that covered her secret places as blond as
the hair on her head. He knew that within it lay that part
of woman with which man mated. He had seen animals
mate, had seen Black Antelope and Two Stars moving under
their blankets.

He moved on top of her, bending down and sucking
curiously at her breasts. The action made her moan with
pleasure, so he did it again. She grasped his head, arching
up to him, whimpering his name, laughing and crying at
the same time. He kissed her all over, her neck, her mouth,
her breasts, her abdomen, fumbling then with himself until
he found his mark, the moist warmth he knew instinctively
lay waiting in her depths. She cried out when he entered
her, and he wondered if he was hurting her, but he could
not stop. In moments a wonderful relief engulfed him as
his life poured into her, and then he felt suddenly weak.

He went limp beside her, then smiled, pulling her against
him.

She looked into his eyes. "Why is it supposed to be bad,
Caleb?" Her act of innocence was decidedly perfect.

"I don't know, except that we should be married, I think.
When an Indian man and woman do this, it is understood
they are married. Are we married now?"

She frowned. "Not by white man's ways. It would have
to be a church wedding, and my father would never allow
it." She sat up slightly. "But it doesn't matter. We'll keep
meeting this way, in secret. I like it better this way. My
father would be furious."

Caleb reached up and stroked her long, blond hair. "You
are a strange girl, Emily Stoner. We should be married so
that it is right."

She smiled. "I don't think I want to be married. It's more
fun this way."

He sighed, not sure what to think of her. "We cannot
meet here again. My father will be back any time."

"Then come to the barn behind our house at night. Give
a call—like a bird or something—and I'll know you're

there. I'll come out to you." She said it as though it were all very simple. She lay down beside him. "Do it to me again, Caleb."

He was too full of the glory of what he had just learned to object or wonder at her strange behavior. It felt wonderful being inside of her, touching her bare skin. If she was willing to let him and didn't care that they weren't married, he would take advantage of the moment, for it was important to learn about women. He was soon lost again in her silken mystery.

Caleb could not resist the meetings. Tom Sax did not return for three more days, and each of those nights Caleb felt drawn to the Stoner home, where he softly whistled a lilting birdcall that told Emily to come to the barn. Each night they continued to explore and discover all the wonders of physical love. There was no more talk of marriage, and Emily didn't seem to care. Defiance against her father was apparently more important to her than anything, and there was a wickedness to her ways that only made her strangely inviting.

Tom noticed an odd restlessness to Caleb after he returned, but Caleb seemed unwilling to talk about it. There were moments when Tom was sure Caleb was about to speak, but the boy seemed afraid. Tom tried to gently prompt him, assuring Caleb he could tell him anything, but Caleb insisted there was nothing to tell. Every night he would disappear, telling Tom he preferred sleeping in the forest in the summers, that winter would be upon them soon enough and he would have to sleep inside.

Caleb's soul was torn. It didn't seem right to mate with a girl who was not his wife, and yet he could not resist going back night after night. His newfound ecstasy was too tempting, but he also felt guilty about it. He often thought of Sarah, and how he would hate it if some young man tried to do such things with her. Sarah was so different from Emily. Sarah would never do these things with anyone but a husband, and Caleb hoped she would find a good, kind man who would not frighten or hurt her.

Somehow, though Emily had been so willing, he knew that her behavior was not natural, that a truly good young woman would never do what Emily was doing, and would perhaps even be afraid of that first awakening to a man. He remembered from his life among the Sioux that a young woman who did what Emily was doing risked being beaten or scarred, perhaps even have her nose cut off. The man who offended her risked being killed. There was a good side to mating and a bad side. Emily seemed to want only the bad. But Caleb was young, and the pleasures of a woman's body were wonderful indeed. He could not bring himself to reason out what was happening, for he was too full of his joyous awakening to manhood.

Caleb let Emily into the barn, closing the door behind her and sweeping her into his arms.

"Oh, Caleb, I'm so afraid every night that you won't come again," she whispered. Their lips met, and all the manly, protective, powerful feelings returned, as they always did. He carried her to the hay and laid her down, able to see her only dimly by the light of a full moon that shone through a gap in the wall.

They spoke little. All their youthful passions were quickly reawakened, and he moved a hand under her flannel gown, knowing she wore nothing beneath it, touching her in all the ways she had told him made her feel excited. He pushed the gown up to her waist and moved a knee between her legs, but then there was the sound of scuffling feet outside.

"Emily!"

Emily gasped and stiffened. Caleb jerked away, and immediately Emily began screaming wildly, ripping at her gown. She lashed out and scratched Caleb's cheek with her fingernails, and the boy jumped up, confused. The barn door burst open, and Preacher Stoner stepped inside, a lantern in one hand and a musket in the other.

"Father," Emily screamed. "He attacked me. That horrible Indian boy attacked me! He touched me in bad places and tried to rip off my gown!" She ran to her father, weeping as though terrified as she clung to him.

Caleb stared dumbfounded, unable to move. What was happening? Why had Emily accused him of attacking her?

"Heathen!" Stoner swung around and hung the lantern on a nail, then raised the musket. "You half-breed scum. I knew you were bad. I should beat you to death!"

Caleb found his feet then. There was no time to ask questions, to wonder why Emily had accused him of attacking her. There was only time to get away with his life. He ducked behind a horse stall as the musket was fired. Stoner pulled a pistol from his belt then, and Caleb darted for the opening in the wall where the board was missing. He squeezed through it just as a shot landed in a board next to him. He ran as hard and fast as his legs would carry him, heading for the shelter of the nearby forest.

In the background he could hear Stoner screaming after him and yelling for help. Two more shots were fired and Caleb kept running until his calves screamed with pain and his heart pounded so hard he thought it might burst. His mind raced with confusion and disgust as he moved deeper into the forest, where he felt welcome and safe. Why? Why had he allowed that crazy white girl to get him into this? If she continued to scream rape, he could never go back. They would believe her. He would be hung before he could speak a word in his own defense.

For three days Caleb lay in a small hollow beneath a log, cautiously coming out for only moments at a time to relieve himself, grab some berries and drink some water at the nearby stream. He hid his tracks each time, retreating to the hollow again and pulling brush around it. Four different times he heard men ride past, voices cursing him for his cleverness in hiding, others swearing they'd hang him on the spot if they found him. The last time they were near, someone mentioned they might as well give up the search.

"He's half Indian," the voice grumbled. "The redskin is probably miles from here by now, headed for his own people where he'll be safe. We'll never find that slick little devil."

"Little?" someone replied questioningly. "He's built like a man, and he was apparently man enough to rape Emily Stoner and destroy that poor girl's honor. I wish to hell we could get our hands on that buck and give him what he deserves!"

The horses moved away then, and for the rest of the cool, quiet night, Caleb stayed in the hollow. All the next day there was only the sound of the animals and the wind. Caleb wondered if everyone back at the fort had finally decided he could not be found. With the danger of venturing away from the fort because of the threat of war, the search may have already ended.

On the fourth night he came out of hiding, taking off his buckskins and washing in the stream. How he hated Emily Stoner! She had branded him. How could he go back to the place he called home, to Tom Sax? Because of Emily Stoner's strange desires he was permanently banished from Fort Dearborn and the great lake. After all the times he had dreamed of going back to the wilderness, he realized now that he didn't really want to go, not yet. But now he had no choice.

Caleb dressed and made his way through the dark woods toward the Sax cabin. Everything was quiet, and when he neared the cabin, his eyes teared. What did Tom think? How could Caleb leave him?

He watched the surrounding area for several minutes, deciding it was safe to head for the cabin. He darted toward it. The night was black, the moon hidden by clouds. He made his way quickly to the wooden door that led to the root cellar beneath the building. With a sigh of relief he found the door unlatched. He quickly opened it and climbed down the stone steps, closing the door behind him. In the clammy, pitch black cellar he felt his way along the ceiling to the trap door that opened into the kitchen. He listened, hearing only the soft squeak of Cora's rocker that Tom had gotten into the habit of using lately.

Caleb tapped on the door that lay beneath a braided rug above, and the rocker stopped squeaking. He heard footsteps, and then a voice close to the door. "Caleb?"

"Yes," the boy answered in a rough whisper.

The door opened. The cabin above was dark. A hand reached down and grabbed Caleb, and he felt a strength flow through him at the touch. Tom helped him up and immediately hugged him tightly.

"Thank God," he muttered. He led Caleb to a chair, and they could see each other from the glow of embers in the hearth. They sat across the table from each other.

"What in God's name happened?" Tom asked.

Caleb sighed, putting his head down on the table. "I don't even know, Father. Emily Stoner came to me, wanted me to . . . do things to her." His eyes teared, and he was glad it was dark. "I knew it was wrong, but she begged me. She came to the cabin when you were gone hunting, snuck away from her father while he was sick." He raised his head. "I could not stop myself. I wanted to, but she . . . she almost insisted. She took off her clothes." He put his head in his hands. "I just want to get away. I feel far away from *Maheo*. I feel bad." He looked at his father. "But I did not attack her like she said. She met me willingly in the barn, and her father found us. That was when she started screaming, and scratched me and said I attacked her."

Tom Sax sighed deeply. "The little bitch. I've suspected for a long time she was a bad one. I can hardly blame her for being a little strange, considering how she's been raised, but she did you a great wrong, Caleb. I suppose she accused you of attacking her because she was afraid of her father's wrath. Whatever the reason, you can't show your face here now. They'd hang you, son." He reached across the table and grasped Caleb's arm. "God knows what she offered would be hard for any boy your age to ignore. But you should have told me, Caleb boy, you should have told me. I knew something was wrong."

Caleb swallowed. "I did not know how to tell you. I did not want you to be angry with me." He rubbed his neck. "I'm sorry, Father, to add to your troubles. I will go away. Can you get some supplies for me? I will need a horse. I will pay you."

"Don't be ridiculous. You needn't pay for what's yours. I told you that gray gelding was yours to keep. But where will you go?"

The thought of leaving Tom Sax created a terrible ache in Caleb's heart. "West. To the wilderness where it would be harder to find me. I do not want to go where there are many white people. I have never been happy among them, and now I know I cannot live among them without trouble. They are too ready to believe I am bad."

"The country to the west is very dangerous now, Caleb. You'd have to be very careful."

"I can do it. I know the ways of my people. I will try to find the Cheyenne."

Tom squeezed his arm. "I'm so sorry, Caleb. I'd go with you, but they'd know if I suddenly left. They'd be more likely to resume a search. Tempers are high, Caleb."

"Are you in danger?"

"No. They know better than to mess with Tom Sax."

"Meet me, Father. Meet me next spring—at the place where the Fox River meets the Mississippi, where sometimes the trappers and Indians used to meet. Come in the Moon of the Greening Grass, in May."

Tom nodded. "I'll do that, son. I'll meet you."

Caleb fought an urge to cry. "Do not tell Sarah why I had to leave."

"I understand," Tom replied. "I won't tell her. I'll just tell her you felt a need to go back west and find your people. She'll understand that."

"And tell her—tell her I will see her again, like I promised. I don't know how, but I will. Tell her I will remember her always."

Tom stood and walked around the table. "I love you, Caleb," he whispered, his voice breaking. Caleb stood up and they embraced.

"I'm so sorry to hurt you, to leave you alone." Caleb groaned.

"You did nothing wrong, Caleb. You fell into a trap, and you're just the victim of all the hatred and prejudice of the times." He patted the boy's shoulder. "Go back into the cellar. I'll knock on the outside doors when everything is ready."

The boy climbed back down the steps and waited in the darkness. Tom closed the door in the floor and put the braided rug back over it. Several minutes later there was a tap on the outer doors. Caleb opened one carefully and climbed out. Tom waited in a shadow of the cabin, holding the bridle of the gray gelding. "He's all packed and ready to go, son. There's food in the parfleche and a change of clothes, a musket and pistol, your hunting knife and tomahawk, your bearskin and some warmer clothes for winter."

Caleb stepped closer, and they embraced again. "Thank you, Father," he whispered. "I will see you in the spring."

"God go with you, Caleb."

"Forever I shall remember you, and honor you as Father." A lump welled so tightly in his throat that he could say no more. He climbed onto the horse. "May you always ride with the wind at your back, Father, and under the blessings of *Wakan Tanka*."

"And the same to you. Good-bye, Caleb." The man's voice choked again and he patted Caleb's thigh. "Go now. Just go."

Caleb rode into the shadows of the surrounding forest. He did not look back. Again his life was changing, and he could not bear to look back at the little cabin and the man who stood there alone.

Chapter
Nine

LONELINESS took on a new meaning for Caleb Sax. He was deeply troubled by the thought that he might never see Sarah again. Emily's actions and betrayal made him miss Sarah even more, almost desperately. And he had shamed and brought trouble to Tom Sax, adding to the man's own loneliness by having to leave. He would dearly miss the man who had been a father to him for over seven years. He wondered sometimes what really made a man a father. His real father was a bad white man, but two men who were not his father by blood had been as dear to him as any natural father could be.

Now both were gone from his life, and he was back in the wilderness. He had no idea if he could find the Cheyenne, let alone anyone who had known him. The rumors back at Fort Dearborn had been that many Sioux and Cheyenne had pushed further west, leaving the land to the eastern Indians who fled the continuing onslaught of American settlers. All sought to flee the diseases the white men brought, diseases that sometimes wiped out whole tribes.

Caleb kept to the thick forest as much as possible, hiding from Indians and British alike, for in the land immediately west of Fort Dearborn neither could be trusted. Day after day he traveled, every mile farther from Tom Sax making his heart hurt more. He consoled himself by remembering that at least they would meet the next spring. He would see

Tom again. And at least he was back in the wilds, close to Mother Earth, moving closer to the people with whom he had once lived. And in spite of his youth, his many hunting trips with Tom, as well as his memory of living in this land as a child, left him capable of taking care of himself.

Perhaps, he reasoned as he headed west, his misfortune would be his good fortune. Perhaps the spirits intended him to go back to his people, return to his roots. He had never been completely happy at Fort Dearborn, and if not for Tom and Cora and Sarah, he would not have stayed as long as he had. Caleb did not regret living with the Saxes because it had taught him much about himself and the white man's world. Yet deep in his heart he realized it was time to return to the world of his Indian heritage. It would be good to live where a man could be truly free, away from the strange confines and rules of the white man. He felt a need to return and grow closer to the earth spirits, to live off the land with none of the white man's trappings.

The deep woods and caves became his home through the loneliest winter of his life. The gray gelding became his best friend, and Caleb thanked the spirits that the horse did not get sick or hurt, for without him Caleb might not survive. The winter was a hard one, with unusually deep snows and cold weather that tested his skills to their limits.

He grew and matured, realizing he must be his own man. He had survived as a nine-year-old boy. He would survive at sixteen. In the eyes of the Indian he was already a man. There was no room that winter for allowing childish feeings of terror to take over. He had been foolish enough by lying with the strange white girl. He had not been strong in resisting her as he should have been, and the shame of it made him determined to be strong now as he penetrated the wilderness. He would bring no more shame upon himself.

Each day became a challenge to survive, and just finding food and enough firewood was a major victory. Caleb was glad for the thick, wolf skin coat Tom had packed for him, as well as the bearskin from the bear he had killed the winter before. He fashioned snowshoes out of slender branches woven together, and found a cave in a rocky hillside to use as a base camp in the worst of the season.

He thought often about Emily, finally wishing he could stop hating her. Perhaps she had done what she had out of fear, and yet it was a terrible lie that brought him shame and loneliness. He knew now she was bad, bad from the inside out. Perhaps it was because of how she had been raised, so hidden from real life that she didn't know how to live at all. That first day in his cabin she had behaved almost like a wild animal just released from its cage, running free once more.

He tried not to think about her too often, for it brought bad feelings to his heart. He preferred to concentrate on Tom . . . and Sarah. Poor Sarah, alone in Saint Louis, Tom alone at Fort Dearborn, and himself alone in the wilderness. Would the three of them ever be together again?

An early thaw in February gave him the ability to travel again, and he struggled mile after mile into the northwest interior, far from the Americans and the British, into a land occupied by Santee and Dakota Sioux, a region that would one day be called Minnesota. This was new, unfamiliar territory, farther west from where he had been born. Caleb saw many signs of Indians, abandoned camps, snow trampled and pawed away by horses to find grass. He cautiously followed the trail left by the large group of people.

The young man's heart quickened with a mixture of hope and apprehension when finally he spotted smoke over a distant rise. He headed in that direction, hoping whoever was camped on the other side was friendly. He was so deep in the wilderness he knew it had to be Indians. He was hungry for human companionship. He would take his chances.

He made his way quietly on foot through thick pines and over soil soggy from melted snow and spongy with wet pine needles, leading the gray horse by the reins. The aroma of pine and wet earth was strong in his nostrils as he climbed the rise, and then he sensed someone was nearby. He stopped and petted the gray gelding.

"I think we have found human life, boy," he told the horse. "The only question is whether they are friend or enemy."

He waited, his eyes slowly scanning the surrounding underbrush and boulders. He called out in Cheyenne, hoping he still spoke it well enough, and that those in hiding were Cheyenne. He called himself friend. The next moment two warriors moved out, one from behind a bush, the other from behind a large boulder. They were dressed in heavy skins and sported brightly beaded weapon belts that held large hunting knives. Beads decorated their hair, and coup feathers were tied into their hair at their necks. They wore knee-high, fur-lined moccasins, and a quiver of arrows and a bow were slung across each of their backs. One wore a split feather that protruded behind his head, indicating he was a man who had been wounded many times in battle. The other wore a feather notched at the top, which Caleb remembered meant the wearer had counted three coup, had touched or killed three of his enemy. His heart took hope, for they were Cheyenne.

Both looked like accomplished warriors, and Caleb could only pray they would be friendly. They eyed him questioningly.

"*Tsis-tsis-tas*," Caleb said, using the Cheyenne word for the People. He pointed to himself and pulled his blue quill necklace from under his heavy coat. "*Tsis-tsis-tas*."

One of them stepped closer, looking at the necklace curiously, then moving his eyes to the scar on Caleb's face. When he saw Caleb's blue eyes, he pointed and frowned. "*Vehoe*."

Caleb shook his head. "Cheyenne," he told them in their own tongue. "My father was a white trapper, my mother Cheyenne. She gave me the necklace. My mother was from the Cheyenne who once lived to the south and east. Many of them were killed by Chippewa long ago. I was raised by the Sioux, Black Antelope was my Sioux father and was also killed by Chippewa. I seek the Cheyenne and my mother's people. Do you know of them? Deer Man? White Bird? Many Bears? Most were killed. Perhaps some escaped."

The warrior who had stayed behind looked surprised and stepped closer, eyeing the necklace. He looked at the first warrior, and they exchanged a look that told Caleb they knew something. The first man put a fist to his chest. "I am a Cheyenne dog soldier," he said in Cheyenne. "Called Proud Eagle."

Caleb met the man's eyes squarely. "I am called Blue Hawk. I am also a warrior, even though I have blue eyes," he told them, thinking perhaps he needed to impress them to be accepted, to prove his own worth. "My family was killed by the Chippewa when I was only nine summers, and when I was alone, I found two Chippewa warriors and killed them, one with the bow, the other with my tomahawk. I was separated from my people then. Now I am trying to find them."

Proud Eagle watched him closely, as though trying to determine if he should believe Caleb. "You killed two Chippewa warriors when only nine summers?"

Caleb nodded. "I have also killed a bad white man." He took out his knife and held it up. "With this. That is when I got the mark on my face.

Proud Eagle frowned. "You are still young."

"In two moons I will be seventeen summers. I am a man."

A hint of a smile passed over the Cheyenne warrior's face. "That you must yet prove." His eyes fell to the necklace again. "You say your mother gave you the necklace?"

Caleb nodded.

"Who made this necklace?"

"The wife of Many Bears, my Cheyenne uncle. She was called Sweet Seed Woman."

The man turned and looked at the second warrior, then

started walking. "Come," he said curtly, walking ahead of Caleb.

Caleb followed, hoping he was not walking to his death.

Caleb stared in surprise at the dwellings below the rise. He had not seen these before. They were arranged in a great circle, with an opening that faced the east, the rising sun. They were cone shaped, with smoke rising from smoke holes in the centers. They appeared to be made of skins and were painted with many scenes, some of war, some of the sun and animals. When he left the Cheyenne, they had not lived in such dwellings.

It was a large village, and as they entered it, they were greeted by an abundance of barking dogs and a sea of curious women and children. A few young girls stared at Caleb and whispered, but most quickly looked away the moment he met their eyes. One, however, daringly held his eyes for a moment, and even after she looked away Caleb stared at her. She was exceedingly beautiful, but also not quite a woman. It had been months since he had learned about women with Emily Stoner, but the memory of how it felt to be with the opposite sex would never leave him. Surely it was much more wonderful to be with a woman who had a good heart.

He shook away the thought. Emily Stoner had brought him bad luck. He must not think about females again for a long time. Proud Eagle led him to a huge campfire at the center of the village where a few old women were cooking meat over the flames. Proud Eagle turned and told Caleb to wait by the fire.

Proud Eagle and the other warrior left then, and Caleb waited with a pounding heart while several elders and children gathered closer, pointing at his blue eyes and talking among themselves about the intruder with the white man's eyes. He tried to show no fear, for he sensed that was very important. He stood proud and straight while some of the old women touched and admired his horse.

In the distance he again caught a glimpse of the pretty young girl he had seen. Though she was wrapped in a blanket of skins and only her lovely face and hair were visible, he was sure that under the blanket there were even more beautiful things. But he scowled then and looked away, not wanting to risk chastisement for letting his eyes linger too long on a girl who appeared to be a young virgin.

He forced himself not to think of her, and concentrated instead on a group of Cheyenne men who were gathering by one of the dwellings, talking together. They approached then, shooing away the women and children and gathering in a circle around the campfire. One young warrior looked challengingly at Caleb and grasped the bridle of the gray gelding, taking the horse away. Caleb decided it would be best not to try to stop the man. He stood alone, a stranger among his own kind, and Proud Eagle signaled for him to sit between himself and an old man who appeared to be some kind of leader. The old man's face was wrinkled and weathered, and when he made the sign of peace at Caleb, Caleb noticed his fingers were gnarled and knotted with the stiffening disease that often came to old ones. Caleb touched his forehead in respect for the old man, then sat down beside him.

"These are our best warriors and our wise elders," Proud Eagle told him. "Beside you is Three Feathers, an honored shaman. Tell these men why you are here. If they accept you, we will smoke the pipe of peace together, and you are welcome in our village."

Caleb knew better than to leave anything out, for the Indian honored truth. He told them the story of his birth, and the necklace, his mother's death, his life among the Sioux and the massacres by the Chippewa. He told them all about how he killed two Chippewa warriors at the age of nine, which brought nods of admiration. Then he told about his rescue by the white man called Tom Sax, how he had been given a white man's name and knew the white man's ways. He was afraid to tell them about why he had been forced to leave, so he told them he had returned west to find his Cheyenne people, hoping someone of his blood still lived.

"It was hard in the white world," he told them, "even though I have white man's eyes. They hold little love for the Indian, and even less for a man who is only half Indian. I was not happy there. But my white father was a good man, and in the Moon of the Greening Grass I will return to the place where the great waters meet, where my white father is to come and meet with me. He would have come with me, but he has a white daughter who still lives in the East, and he stayed for her sake. I have returned to the land of the people I truly consider my own, where I can be free of white man's rules and strange customs, where I feel safe and happy, closer to the spirits. I have come hoping to find someone of my Cheyenne blood."

There was a momentary silence when he finished, and then Three Feathers spoke up. "It is a hard thing to live in two worlds," he said quietly. "A man's soul is torn and he cannot find peace. If we can help the young warrior who at only nine summers counted coup on the Chippewa, we must do so. He was raised by Sioux, who for a time became our enemy. Now we are friends again, and soon we will all fight against the hated Crow, who constantly attack us and steal our food and our women. Perhaps this young warrior can help us."

"He should prove his manhood at the Sun Dance Ritual," one of the others said, looking at Caleb with an almost jealous look in his dark eyes.

"It will be his choice, Fire Wolf," Three Feathers answered.

Caleb sensed an instant rivalry with the one called Fire Wolf. Why, he could not be sure, but he straightened proudly before he spoke. "I will gladly sacrifice my flesh at the Sun Dance," he told them. "As a small boy I dreamed of doing

so. I have not lost that dream. And I will gladly fight beside
you against these Crow. I do not know about them, but if
they are the enemy of the Cheyenne, then they are also my
enemy."

Three Feathers nodded approvingly, but Fire Wolf frowned
and left the circle. Old Three Feathers picked up a long
peace pipe and lit it with a coal from the fire. The sweet
odor of the pipe's contents filled Caleb's nostrils as blue
smoke spiraled from the bowl of the pipe.

Three Feathers took a puff and pointed the pipe toward
the sky. *"Heammawihio,"* he said in a near whisper, speaking to the God of the Sky. He pointed the pipe at the earth.
"Ahktunowihio." Then he pointed the pipe in all four directions, offering it to the gods of the North, South, East
and West. He puffed the pipe again, then passed it to Proud
Eagle, who puffed it and in turn handed it to Caleb. Caleb
knew this was an honor and signified an acceptance by the
tribe, even though it might be temporary, pending his proving his worth. He took the pipe and put it to his lips, puffing
it in reverence and worship.

After the pipe was passed around to the others, Three
Feathers nodded to Proud Eagle. Proud Eagle rose and left
the circle, and Caleb watched curiously, but Three Feathers
drew his attention back to the Council.

"Soon we ride against the Crow," he told Caleb. "They
have stolen many of our horses and some of our women.
We will get them back, and some of their horses and women
also. You will ride with us?"

Caleb could think of nothing more exciting, and all his
Indian warrior instincts were fully aroused. He smiled eagerly. "I will gladly go."

He gazed at the others in the Council, seeing their approval. A movement beyond the group caught his eye and
he saw the pretty young girl peeking at him from between
two older women. He saw too that Fire Wolf was also
watching her, a scowl on his face. His dark eyes moved to
Caleb, and Caleb knew instantly the man did not like the

young girl looking at the new arrival. Was she Fire Wolf's wife? Surely not. She was too young. Perhaps Fire Wolf hoped to marry her when she was ready. Caleb decided to stay away from the girl. He did not want to offend anyone or make enemies in the village that could become his home.

Proud Eagle returned, leading an elderly woman, and Caleb watched her with an odd sense of familiarity. As they entered the circle of men, the woman moved forward away from Proud Eagle on her own, staring at Caleb as though she were seeing a ghost.

"Stand up," Three Feathers told Caleb.

Caleb obeyed, frowning at the old woman whose eyes moved over him carefully. "Let me see necklace," she told Caleb.

Caleb's heart quickened as he reached under his coat and pulled out the necklace again. The old woman gasped and put her hands to her mouth, her eyes quickly filling with tears as she moved them to meet his blue ones.

"Blue Hawk," she exclaimed. "Is it truly you, my nephew?"

Joy began to creep into Caleb's heart. "Nephew?"

"I am Sweet Seed Woman, Deer Man's wife. I made the necklace you wear and let your mother, Little Flower, keep it because she admired it so. She gave it to you before she died."

Caleb swallowed against a lump rising in his throat. To find Sweet Seed Woman, a blood relation, after all these years filled him with indescribable joy. He hesitantly reached out, touching her graying hair.

Her tears ran freely. "Always I wondered what happened to you. I thought you must have been killed by the Chippewa. They came to our camp and murdered nearly all of us. I was able to escape with my sister. Together we fled, nearly dying from hunger and the elements, until we came upon other Cheyenne. They took us in. We knew the Chippewa had gone north and attacked Black Antelope's camp where you lived. We . . . never heard what happened."

Caleb cleared his throat to keep his voice steady. "I was nine summers. Black Antelope's young wife hid me in a hollow log. When I came out, they were all dead." He studied her eyes, full of both joy and sadness. "My grandfather? My uncles?"

"All dead," she told him. She touched his arms. "But I have found you, my nephew. *Maheo* has been good to me this day. My joy knows no bounds."

"Nor mine," he answered, smiling.

The woman threw her blanket over his shoulders in a sign of welcome to a blood relative, then began a song of joy. Other women joined her, their voices trilling in chanting rhythm. Caleb felt his heart swell. Never since living with Black Antelope had he felt so truly at home. He knew there would be dancing and celebrating that night, all in his honor, and he wondered if the pretty Cheyenne girl he had seen would be there.

Caleb was again Blue Hawk.

He joined the tipi of his aunt, who lived with her sister, her sister's husband, Buffalo Man, and their son. He was surprised at the space inside the conical dwellings, and learned that because of the more nomadic life the Cheyenne had begun to follow, this new kind of structure became the most practical, for it could be raised and taken down quickly, rolled up easily and carried on a travois. The women made them of sewn skins, mostly buffalo hides, and they were responsible for their erection and dismantling. Different tipis were painted with different signs, according to the owners, and Blue Hawk quickly learned to recognize the tipi of a leader as opposed to a dog soldier or a shaman.

The rest of the winter moved quickly. Blue Hawk helped on hunts when the weather permitted, and eagerly joined the gatherings for story telling, listening raptly to tales of spirits and ancestors as well as accomplishments at war with the Crow. Crow scalps hung from many a warrior's belt.

He often caught sight of the pretty girl, whom his aunt told him was Walking Grass.

"You had better be careful, nephew," she warned. "Fire Wolf has his eyes on that one."

"Has he bought her? Is she promised to him?"

"No."

"Then she is not his, and perhaps I have eyes on her, too."

"And Fire Wolf has a temper. Be careful, Blue Hawk."

Blue Hawk just shrugged. He was not afraid of Fire Wolf. In fact, the challenge only made him more interested in Walking Grass, a fitting name for such a lithe, willowy creature. She was the daughter of Two Bears, a feisty old man who would probably demand much from any man who wanted his daughter. Blue Hawk decided it was time to start proving his worth, and was overjoyed when the opportunity to ride with several others on a raid against the Crow finally arose. He barely slept the night before they were to leave.

In the morning, Buffalo Man offered Blue Hawk a sturdy, painted roan mare that had powerful front legs and shoulders, and spirit in her eyes.

"You need a special kind of horse for making war, Blue Hawk," the man told him. "Your gray is good for travel, and a good companion. This horse likes the smell of fighting and will know what to do without you even telling her. Take her. It is my gift for bringing joy to my sister-in-law, for she has had a sad heart for many moons because of the loss of her family so long ago."

Blue Hawk was touched. The gift of a horse was a sign of great honor and acceptance. "Thank you, Buffalo Man. Always I will honor and remember you for this. Your heart is good."

"As is yours. May the wind be at your back, Blue Hawk."

Blue Hawk slid onto the back of the restless animal, feeling its power beneath him, knowing instantly it was a grand horse. All was ready, his lance, knife, tomahawk, bow and arrows, and sling. He even had something that made him even more honored as a warrior: he had a pistol. He smiled at the memory of the jealous look he had seen in Fire Wolf's eyes the day he had shown the others what it could do. It had brought him even more respect among the others, and he would take it into battle.

The camp was alive with activity as the men prepared to leave. Women and old ones lined up to wish the warriors well. Scouts had spotted a Crow camp several miles to the west. They were certain the Crow intended to raid their Cheyenne village and decided to beat them at their own game.

The weather had warmed, but there was still some snow on the ground. Blue Hawk wore his buckskin leggings and shirt, but his wolf skin coat was rolled and tied behind him. He was determined that he would take Crow scalps and count many coup on this raid, to show the others just how good a warrior he was. His face had been carefully painted for war by Sweet Seed Woman, who helped him understand all the warrior ways. The blue quill necklace he wore at his neck made him feel even more Cheyenne, for it reminded him that his mother was one of these people, and he was beginning to feel that the necklace was a talisman. His hair was clean and brushed, one side of it braided, beads and feathers for luck wound into it. Sweet Seed Woman had carried on before he left about how magnificent he looked.

"You are the most handsome warrior in this village," she had told him. "All the young women look at you, Blue Hawk, for your blue eyes fascinate them and make you special. You are strong and beautiful. I am proud that this day you ride out against the Crow. Bring back a Crow scalp for me. Make me proud, Blue Hawk."

The young man had promised he would do just that, and he cared not that all the young girls watched him. There was ony one whose attention and admiration he craved: Walking Grass. He searched for her as he rode proudly through the village, joined by other warriors as he moved. And then he saw her, standing with some other women, admiration in her eyes as she watched him. She suddenly broke away from the group, running up to him and handing him a beautiful war shield, a detailed blue hawk with the sun behind the bird painted on the front.

"For you, Blue Hawk, for good luck," she told him quickly. "Come back."

Their eyes held for a brief moment, and he was so startled by the gift he didn't know what to say. He knew it was a sign that she favored him, and his pride and self-confidence knew no bounds. At close range she was even more beautiful than he had realized. She whirled then and he started to call after her, but a white horse was suddenly beside him, bumping against his leg.

"You would do best to concentrate on the battle to come, white-eyes. To think of a woman when going into battle could shorten your life." The words were hissed threateningly, and Blue Hawk stared into Fire Wolf's dark eyes, his youthful temper surfacing.

"I will think what I want," he answered steadily. "Do not worry about me in battle, my friend. I will take more scalps than you."

Fire Wolf grinned wickedly. "We shall see. But perhaps your death will not come from the Crow. Anyone can be an enemy, Blue Hawk. Do not call me friend again. And stay away from Walking Grass."

Blue Hawk smiled. "She has shown me favor. She does not belong to you, she belongs to the better man."

Fire Wolf just glared at him, then swung the lance he held in his hand and knocked the new war shield from Blue Hawk's hands. It whirled in the air and spun to the ground, and Fire Wolf quickly rode off, his horse trampling the shield. Blue Hawk started after him.

"Blue Hawk!" The words were almost growled, and a lance barred him from the other side. "No."

He turned to see Proud Eagle.

"He deliberately soiled the gift Walking Grass gave to me."

"We are riding into war. If you have something against Fire Wolf, save it for when we return and bring it before the Council. Do not forget that you are not truly one of us—yet. In battle we must work together or we fail."

Blue Hawk's eyes were an angry, icy blue. He dismounted and picked up the war shield, brushing it off and fuming that one slender branch that formed the edge of it was cracked. The shield was, however, still usable, and he slipped the holder on the back of it over his wrist and remounted his war horse.

"After we ride against the Crow," he told Proud Eagle, "I will be one of you. You will see what I can do. And if Fire Wolf ever touches anything of mine again, I will kill him." He rode off then, and Proud Eagle and others followed, sod flying from beneath the hooves of the swift ponies that would carry them into battle.

Chapter Ten

THE surprise attack was planned for early dawn. There was a side of Blue Hawk that wanted the wild excitement, and a side that did not. But living with the Cheyenne the past weeks and his desire to be one of them outweighed any hesitancy his white blood might create. In his youth his Sioux people had warred against enemy tribes, and it had simply been their way of life. But his years at Fort Dearborn with white men had planted a seed of doubt. Tom had said many times that the Indians were only hurting their own cause by warring against each other. But here, in the wilds, as they began charging the village of the hated Crow, that didn't seem to matter. What mattered was revenge for the Cheyenne and proving his worth.

In moments the Crow village was surrounded. Women screamed and families began pouring out of their tipis, the warriors scrambling for weapons and horses. But the Cheyenne were quickly upon them, charging right through tipis, swinging tomahawks and plunging lances. The fight for territory had begun, and for the Cheyenne, the only way to keep their hunting territory was to show the Crow by force that they did not belong, had no right to steal Cheyenne women and horses. The Cheyenne would strike back.

The horse Buffalo Man had given Blue Hawk went into action easily, prancing out of reach of Crow warriors who grabbed for him or tried to wound him with a weapon. Blue Hawk whirled the stone of his sling, hitting a Crow warrior's head and knocking the man to the ground. He pulled his musket from its boot and fired, opening a hole in the Crow warrior's forehead. He quickly dismounted and stole the eagle feathers from the warrior's hair, an act of humiliation. He had touched the enemy and now deserved at least one coup feather along with those he had just stolen.

He quickly stuffed the feathers into his belt and started to remount when a second Crow man screamed and attacked him from behind. Blue Hawk whirled, kicking up his leg and hoping it would do some kind of damage. It caught the man's upraised arm, knocking a tomahawk out of it. Blue Hawk lunged for the tomahawk as it fell while the Crow man went flying backward. But the Crow man was quick, and just as he picked up the tomahawk the Crow warrior was lunging into him again, hitting Blue Hawk so hard the breath went out of him.

Blue Hawk was as big, if not bigger than the Crow man, but he lacked his full potential, for this was all new to him, and he still did not have the full power and size of the man he would eventually become. But when he thought about

Walking Grass he felt renewed. He kept a grip on the tom-ahawk as the huge Crow warrior on top of him tried to wrest it away. They struggled violently, Blue Hawk gasping for breath but refusing to let go of the tomahawk. The thought of being beaten in his first raid brought so much shame that it made him angry, and he suddenly felt a burst of energy that helped him roll the Crow man over.

Horses thundered by them, other warriors fought hand-to-hand nearby, but Blue Hawk concentrated only on the man under him, who grasped Blue Hawk's wrist and held the murderous weapon away. Blue Hawk straightened his left leg, raising his body and bending his right knee, ram-ming it up under the jaw of the Crow, knocking him sense-less. He yanked the tomahawk from the man's hand and slammed it into his skull, then used it to quickly carve a tuft of scalp from the man's head.

He jumped up, shoving the fresh scalp into his belt along-side the eagle feathers, grinning with the sweet taste of victory. But he could not celebrate long, as yet another Crow came at him, his knife poised. Blue Hawk lunged sideways, swinging the tomahawk and catching the Crow hard in the side with it, but not before the Crow managed to knife Blue Hawk just below the ribs and draw blood. The Crow went down and Blue Hawk was on him immediately, cutting off part of the man's scalp. He put a hand to his side where the Crow's knife had managed to slice through his buckskin shirt and pierce his skin. It stung terribly, and blood made a growing stain on his shirt. But the wound seemed almost worth it. It was that much more proof of how close he had come to his enemy.

Blue Hawk quickly looked for his horse, and to his delight the animal stood nearby. Buffalo Man had been right: this horse knew what to do in war. Blue Hawk started for the animal, while all around him the fight continued. He realized the Cheyenne were slowly but surely winning, and the battle could not last much longer. He had not quite reached his mount when he heard a horse thundering up behind him.

Blue Hawk didn't think the Crow men had had time to get to their horses, and when he turned at the last minute, he didn't realize right away what was happening.

A white horse slammed into him sideways, knocking him over. He felt himself growing weaker from the stab wound and he hoped he had enough strength left for this next warrior. He got to his knees, then his feet, somewhat stunned. He grabbed the tomahawk that had been knocked from his hand and whirled to see the warrior coming at him again. It was not a Crow. It was Fire Wolf. The man's eyes were alive with a desire to kill as he bore down on Blue Hawk. He stood his ground until the man was nearly on top of him, then ducked sideways, turning and grabbing Fire Wolf's ankle just as he went by. He hung on, stumbling backward as Fire Wolf kept his horse at a hard run.

Blue Hawk looked up and saw the man's arm raised, his knife ready to plunge into Caleb's neck. He let go of the man's ankle and darted away, Fire Wolf's laughter ringing in his ears. Blue Hawk ran for his mount, leaping onto its back and whirling the animal to face Fire Wolf, who was coming at him again, this time with a lance. He yanked out his own lance and headed straight for Fire Wolf, realizing there would be no more chances to save himself. He had only to think of this man lying with the pretty Walking Grass to have the courage and skill he needed. He wished his musket was loaded and at hand, yet he sensed that to kill Fire Wolf with his lance was more honorable.

He charged toward Fire Wolf, and the moment Fire Wolf was close enough he hung sideways so he could hit the man's lance with his own, and knock it out of Fire Wolf's grasp. Blue Hawk quickly whirled his sure-footed mount and charged Fire Wolf before the man could even stop his horse and turn. He was nearly upon him before Fire Wolf realized it. The man yanked out his tomahawk and again headed toward Blue Hawk, thinking to snap Blue Hawk's lance with the tomahawk. But Blue Hawk did not hold onto the lance as Fire Wolf thought he would. At the last possible moment he threw it hard, then whirled the roan mare immediately to the left so that Fire Wolf could not reach him.

Fire Wolf rode on for several yards with the lance sticking out of his chest before finally falling to the ground. Blue Hawk turned his horse and neared the man, dismounting to yank his lance from the dead man's body. He stared at him for a moment, panting, his side bleeding badly. He hadn't wanted to kill Fire Wolf. The man was a respected warrior. But he had left Blue Hawk no choice.

Blue Hawk felt dizzy and sick, and when he turned to shove his lance back into the loop that held it, he realized the fighting had ended and several Cheyenne warriors had gathered around him.

Proud Eagle was one of them. His dark eyes moved from Blue Hawk to Fire Wolf and back to Blue Hawk. "This is bad medicine, Blue Hawk. You have killed one of our own."

"He tried to kill me," Blue Hawk answered quietly, regret in his eyes. "I had to defend myself."

"I saw Fire Wolf attack him," one of the other warriors said.

Proud Eagle studied Blue Hawk. He liked him, but what he had done was not good, for many had seen Blue Hawk and Fire Wolf fighting before they left camp, fighting over the shield given by Walking Grass. Among the tribe it was understood Walking Grass would go to Fire Wolf, and now this blue-eyed Cheyenne had come along and had already practically claimed her, even though he had not formally expressed an interest and hardly knew the girl.

"This must go before the Council," Proud Eagle told the young man. "All will have their turn at telling what they saw, and you, too, will be allowed to speak. I cannot say what will be done, Blue Hawk. The elders might banish you."

Blue Hawk thought of Walking Grass and his aunt and the fact that he had just this day proven his worth as a warrior. But now his reputation was damaged and his credibility was being questioned because of Fire Wolf.

"I did nothing wrong," he told Proud Eagle. He yanked the scalps and feathers from his belt. "Look. I took two Crow scalps, and I stole these eagle feathers from a third. All are dead." He held up the tomahawk. "This weapon I took from a Crow. I counted many coup this day. I helped the Cheyenne fight the hated Crow. Is banishment my reward because a Cheyenne does not know how to master his envy?"

"I cannot say. What you have done today against the Crow will be considered. But Fire Wolf was a respected warrior, and his family will be angry. Come. We must prepare to return to the village." The man told a couple of other warriors to wrap Fire Wolf's body and tie it to a horse. He would be brought back to the village for proper burial by his own family.

There were no other Cheyenne deaths, but there were wounded, and time was taken to tend the wounds before they started back. Three young Crow women were kept tied and watched, but they refused to look afraid. Blue Hawk knew it would not be long before they resigned themselves to being slaves, and most likely would end up marrying Cheyenne men, the usual fate of women prisoners.

Two Cheyenne women, relatives retrieved from the Crow, had been rescued. One had been badly beaten and abused, and Blue Hawk thought how terrible it would be if Walking Grass were ever taken by Crow. It was possible many braves would force themselves upon her, and the thought of it brought a surprisingly fiery jealousy and hatred to his heart. He vowed he would never let anything bad happen to Walking Grass.

But perhaps there would be nothing he could do about it. Perhaps he would be banished from the tribe, just when he was growing accustomed to the people and their way of life again. The thought of being forced to leave the Cheyenne saddened him. He wondered how he managed to keep doing the wrong thing. He had had to flee Fort Dearborn, but he did not want to leave here. He wanted to stay and make his life with these people. He belonged to this wild land.

The fire burned brightly, and Blue Hawk watched the flames, hoping the spirit of Black Antelope was watching over him now as he faced the Council. Fire Wolf's family were among those present, his mother glaring at Blue Hawk. Her wailing had been great when they first returned, but the honor of Fire Wolf's death was diminished when it was learned he had not died at the hands of the Crow, but at the hands of the blue-eyed Cheyenne.

At a word from Three Feathers, Blue Hawk stood, ready to defend himself, still weak from his own wound but refusing to show it. He had deliberately worn the torn and bloody buckskin shirt he'd had on the day of the battle, to prove he had almost been mortally wounded. On his lance, which he held in his hand, he had tied the two Crow scalps and the eagle feathers, and in the other hand he held the Crow tomahawk.

Witnesses rose to speak of how they had seen Blue Hawk kill Fire Wolf, including the one man who had seen Fire Wolf attack first. Proud Eagle spoke in Blue Hawk's behalf, and then it was his turn to speak. The fire crackled as all eyes turned to him, some friendly, some eager to banish him.

"Speak Blue Hawk," Three Feathers said. "It is fair that you have your say."

Blue Hawk stepped forward, his blue eyes flashing with pride. "I am Cheyenne. My eyes are blue, but I never knew my white father, and I was raised to love my people. I never stopped wearing the blue quill necklace from my Cheyenne mother. When I was old enough, I left the white village where I had been taken and came searching for my people, for the source of my blood." His eyes scanned them all. "I found it here, with my beloved aunt whom I thought dead. I found it here, among my own kind, people I have learned to call friend. I made you a promise when I came that I would fight with you like a true warrior. I have shown no fear, given you no reason to be ashamed of me. In the battle with the Crow, I killed three warriors, took two scalps, eagle feathers and a tomahawk. I would have killed even more if Fire Wolf had not stopped me."

He looked straight at Three Feathers. "I never did anything to make Fire Wolf hate me, yet from my first day here he looked at me with hate and envy in his eyes. He thought that I wanted the woman that he, too, wanted. I never said that I did, and I did not do anything shameful or lead Fire Wolf to believe I was stealing something from him. The woman belonged to no one, not even Fire Wolf. You know of whom I speak."

In the shadows Walking Grass listened, her heart pounding. How she adored the handsome young man with the blue eyes who had come to her village. How she feared for him now. She never thought giving him the shield would bring him so much trouble. She was glad Fire Wolf was dead, for she did not want to be his wife. But his death might mean banishment for the handsome half-breed, and she did not want him to go away.

Three Feathers nodded. "I know. Go on, Blue Hawk."

"The day we rode out of this village, the woman gave me a war shield she had made herself, a gift of good luck and a sign I am favored. I did nothing to lead her to this. It was her choice. Fire Wolf was jealous, and he knocked the shield from my hand and rode his horse over it. That was a disgrace to the spirits in the shield. But because he was a great warrior he was allowed to ride with us into battle. He must have decided that it would be easy to kill me and blame it on the Crow, so he waited until I was wounded to try to kill me. What I did was in self-defense. I did not want to kill Fire Wolf, but if I had not he would have killed me. I tell you now, I am your friend. I would die for the Cheyenne. I proved that in battle. My wound proves it. My scalps and feathers prove it."

He sat beside Proud Eagle, his heart pounding with apprehension. Leaving would be bad enough, but if he was banished he would be leaving in shame. Three Feathers looked at Fire Wolf's father. "What do you say, Black Eagle?"

The man studied Blue Hawk, then held up a skewer. "The white belly says he is brave and a good warrior. Perhaps he has shown this by the fight with the Crow, the scalps and feathers. But until he makes the sacrifice of the Sun Dance, he cannot say he is one of us, or that he is truly brave. It is one thing to count coup in the excitement of war. It is easy to be brave then." He waved the skewer. "Let us see how brave the white belly is when these sticks are put through his skin and he is raised to hang until the skin tears away. I say he must prove himself at the Sun Dance. I say he can stay until then. If he refuses to participate, he is banished. If he cries out, he is banished."

Three Feathers looked at Blue Hawk. "Do you agree to this, Blue Hawk?"

Blue Hawk stared boldly at Black Eagle. "I agree," he said. "I am not afraid of the Sun Dance. You will know then I am Cheyenne." He turned to Three Feathers. "I made a promise to the white man who raised me to meet him in the Moon of the Greening Grass. I must keep this promise. I will leave to meet him, but I will return in time for the summer celebration."

Black Eagle grinned. "Already the white belly is thinking of a way to leave without looking like a coward."

Blue Hawk jumped to his feet, slamming his lance into the ground. "I am no coward. I will leave soon, but I will return."

"So be it," Three Feathers said with finality. "Soon we leave for the north, following the river on which we are camped to the country where the Sioux gather. Blue Hawk will keep his promise to the white man with the good heart. Then he will come and meet us in the northern camp at the time of the Moon When the Chokecherries Ripen. If he does not come back in time for the Sun Dance, he is forever

banished and can never show his face among us." He looked
up at Blue Hawk. "Do you agree to this?"

"I agree."

"And until then," Three Feathers continued, "you are not
to pursue your feelings for the girl. Until you have proven
your manhood, you are not worthy of looking upon any
Cheyenne maiden."

Blue Hawk looked at Three Feathers, wanting to defend
himself more, but then thought better of it. He was being
given a chance to stay, and he would take it. He walked off
toward his tipi, but once he was away from the firelight,
someone whispered his name. He stopped, looking around,
but saw no one. Suddenly Walking Grass was beside him,
and old, pleasant urgings stirred within him.

"I do not think you are a coward," she whispered. "I
would never think it. And I know you will come back, Blue
Hawk."

He turned away, wanting her but afraid of trouble. He
felt better knowing that Walking Grass did not think less of
him.

"I cannot be seen talking to you, or it will be my death."

"I know. I will leave quickly. I only want to . . . to thank
you for killing Fire Wolf. I did not want to go to him." She
quickly embraced him, a bold act for a Cheyenne maiden,
then she was gone.

Blue Hawk stood there a moment, for some reason thinking about Sarah. The Cheyenne girl reminded him of Sarah,
her innocence, her youth, her sweet heart. Sarah was out
of his life now, and he might never see her again. But
perhaps he could recapture some of the joy he had known
with Sarah with this beautiful Indian maiden who was so
like her. To have Walking Grass would be to have some of
that happiness again. His mind and body were full of the
challenge of the Sun Dance, which brought forth pride in
the youth and made him a man. By mastering the Sun Dance
he would win Walking Grass, and that was all important
now. He hardly knew her, yet he wanted her. He had been

so lonely. Perhaps marrying and having babies would take it away. To suffer the Sun Dance and marry a Cheyenne girl would mean he was truly there to stay. Surely this was the best place for him. He liked the freedom, the hunting, the warring, the warm glow of a tipi fire, the feeling of being close to the spirits. It was where he belonged.

He would go and meet Tom, but he would definitely be back. Perhaps Tom would want to return with him, to witness the Sun Dance. It would make Blue Hawk proud to make the sacrifice in front of Tom Sax and show Walking Grass to the man, show Tom how pretty she was. Yes, he would ask Tom to come back with him, away from Fort Dearborn where it was so dangerous. It gladdened his heart to think of seeing Tom again. The winter had passed more quickly than he had realized. He was nearly seventeen now, a full-grown man who had made war against the Chippewa and the Crow. Black Antelope would be proud.

When he went to his tipi, his aunt was waiting.

"Well?" she asked.

"I can stay. I will leave soon to meet with Tom Sax, but I am to return by the Moon When the Chokecherries Ripen to participate in the Sun Dance. If I do not return, I am forever banished."

"And if you do not return, you can never hope to have Walking Grass." Sweet Seed Woman grinned slyly. "You will return—for more than proving your manhood, my nephew."

Blue Hawk grinned and set his lance aside. "Do not look at me that way, old woman. I want something to eat."

Sweet Seed Woman laughed lightly, taking a piece of rabbit from a skewer and putting it on a plate made of bone. She handed it to him. "Eat up, nephew. It is a long journey to the place where you will meet this Tom Sax. You had better leave soon, so you can be sure to be back in time."

Blue Hawk arrived at the meeting place in late May. At one time many trappers and Indians had met there to exchange furs for supplies. But the war between the British and Americans had nearly put an end to the trading because no man, Indian or white, could be trusted. But dangerous or not, Blue Hawk knew Tom would come. He only hoped it would be soon enough for him to get back to the Cheyenne to prove to them his honesty and bravery.

His heart beat with the anticipation of seeing Tom Sax again. He had missed the man. There was so much to talk about, so many things there had not been time to talk about the night he left. He wanted to know if Tom had heard from Sarah, and he was anxious to tell Tom about all his experiences with the Cheyenne, about his victory with the Crow— and about Walking Grass. He needed the man's advice about the girl, and although he preferred to remain with the Cheyenne, he wanted to know what was happening at Fort Dearborn and with Sarah.

He scouted the area carefully, but it seemed the place was abandoned. He was again alone, but at least now he had a place to which he could return. After the Council fire, most of the Cheyenne had remained hospitable, but Fire Wolf's family wanted nothing to do with him, and they had laughed and thrown stones at him when he left, calling him a coward who would not return. It angered Blue Hawk that they tried to make him look bad. He would have gladly challenged Fire Wolf in a legal fight, a test of skills. It had been Fire Wolf's choice to try to kill him.

Blue Hawk rode to the edge of the Mississippi, its waters high over the banks from the spring melt. It was a pretty area, peaceful and welcoming. It seemed to him that land hardly touched by the white man was always this way. The white man always sought to control the land rather than exist in it, and Blue Hawk hoped this river was the very last boundary of American expansion.

Birds flitted and sang everywhere, and the welcome sun warmed his shoulders. Watching the river, he was deeply reminded that he was a man of two worlds; he was Cheyenne now, yet part of his past was the white man's world. It was strange to be so much a part of both worlds, and he wondered if he would ever truly belong to either one.

He made camp, realizing it could be several days before Tom showed up. Blue Hawk chose a campsite just below a small hill along the river, a low spot that offered protection and seclusion. He spent the next four days meditating about his two worlds, experimenting with his Indian powers of concentration and using them to pray to *Maheo* for help and guidance at the Sun Dance. He had been told he must not cry out, something he knew would be the most difficult task of his life. He must be ready, mentally as well as physically. When Tom still did not arrive, he began running to help strengthen his legs. He swam in the icy water to test his stamina, and he practiced concentrating his mental powers in an effort to learn how to remove his thoughts from all physical feeling. The Sun Dance would be a great test and a great experience, for it was a time for visions.

After six days Blue Hawk grew concerned. Camping in one place for too long could alert enemy Indians, whose keen senses would easily pick up the scent of accumulating horse dung and the smoke of his fires. He considered moving his camp, but he couldn't go too far or Tom might not find him. It was that same morning that he heard the familiar call he and Tom and Bo had devised while hunting and trapping, a trilling birdcall to be used in times when calling out could be dangerous. He rose from his campfire, eager and happy. He called back and ran to the top of the small hill where he saw a rider approaching. The man waved and came closer, and Blue Hawk's heart fell when he saw that it was Bo Sanders. His smile faded.

"Is it you, Caleb?" Bo laughed, riding closer and dismounting. He walked up to the young man and they shook hands heartily. "Ah, you've grown, boy. And if I didn't know you I'd think twice about showing myself to you at all. You're all Indian, I see."

Blue Hawk grinned. "It is good to see you, Bo." He looked past the man with hope in his eyes. Bo's smile faded.

"He couldn't come, Caleb. It just about broke his heart, but he couldn't make it. I promised I'd come in his place so you'd not worry and wonder."

A quick wave of fear pierced Blue Hawk's heart. "What is wrong?"

Bo took off his hat and scratched his head. "A week before we were set to leave Tom got his foot caught in one of his own traps. Injured him pretty bad, Caleb, and he's still laid up. We were mighty worried about infection, but it looks like there won't be any." The man sighed and scratched at a several-day-old beard.

Blue Hawk looked deeply into Bo's eyes. "He'll be all right?"

Bo nodded. "Sure. He'll be fine, 'cept for his disappointment in not being able to meet you."

Blue Hawk turned around so that Bo would not see the tears in his eyes. "Come down and have some breakfast, Bo."

The man followed, marveling at how the winter had turned Blue Hawk from boy to man.

"I have to leave camp soon," Blue Hawk said. "I have been here too long already. Unwanted company could show up any time." He turned and faced Bo when they reached the campfire. "I am glad that you at least came. It was dangerous for you. You are a good friend."

Bo reached out and squeezed the young man's shoulder. "Tom's been my best friend for years. A man doesn't hunt and trap with another man as long as I've been with Tom without lovin' him and those he loves." His eyes filled with sorrow. "He's a lonely man, Caleb. He's took to drinkin' again. That's how he had the accident, tryin' to set a trap when he'd had too much whiskey."

Blue Hawk turned to pour some strong tea into a tin cup. He wondered if he had ever been more disappointed in his life, and he felt guilty for Tom's renewed drinking. He rose and the handed to tea to Bo.

"Am I still wanted? Is Emily Stoner still there?"

Bo nodded. "If you're thinkin' of goin' back to see Tom, you'd best think twice, son. Lord knows what happened wasn't all your fault. That girl is bad. Some have a suspicion now that you weren't the only one she got into her bed. I have a feelin' you were just the first one she was caught with. That's why she put up the fuss. There's plenty of other lonely men at that fort who'd willingly get under that one's dress if she offered, and I think she's offered plenty behind her pa's back."

"Damn! I was such a fool. I actually felt sorry for her." His blue eyes turned to ice. "I would like to put my hands around her throat and squeeze until there is no life left in her."

"Well that would surely get you a hangin'."

Blue Hawk stared out at the meandering waters of the Mississippi. "I would risk going back if I could. But there is something I must do." He turned to face Bo. "I am living with the Cheyenne. I have even found a blood relative, my aunt."

Bo nodded. "That should make you right happy, son."

"It does. But I made one enemy. When we warred against the Crow, he came for me, thinking he could kill me and blame it on the Crow. I fought back and killed him instead, and this brought me trouble." He poured himself some tea, then looked at Bo. "I have to go back. Please explain to Tom. I have to go back for the Sun Dance Ritual to prove my worth. If I do not go back, I will be forever banished from them. I have no choice, Bo. My aunt is there, and I have made friends with many of them. I do not want to have to seek a home with a different tribe." He sighed deeply. "And there is a girl. A pretty Cheyenne girl called Walking Grass. I promised her I would return."

Bo chuckled. "That man you killed, it wouldn't have been over the girl, would it?"

Blue Hawk smiled in return. "Maybe."

Bo finished his tea. "Well, son, Tom will understand. He's always had patience with the Indian side of you. You're probably right where you've always belonged. You can always meet again next year, Lord willin'. Things are gettin' messy with the British, boy. But you know you don't have to be face-to-face with Tom to be with him. Many times you both talked about how spirits can be together, through prayer and concentration. You used to talk about how you sometimes saw your Sioux father's face in the flames of your campfire. It can be the same with you and Tom. Tom knows how you feel about him, and he knows that if not for your promise to the Cheyenne and your need to prove your word, you'd risk your life to go see him. You simply can't do it, just like Tom couldn't come here because of his wound." The man sat down on an old log beside the fire. "Come on, boy. Sit down here and tell me everything that's happened since you've been out here—every little detail. Tom will want to know. He'll be pullin' my tail to tell him all of it when I get back, that's for sure."

Blue Hawk smiled sadly and sat down across from the man. "First tell me if Tom has heard from Sarah."

Bo frowned. "Yes. A couple of times. She sounds reasonably happy, gettin' a fine education and livin' right well. But you know the girl's heart. She misses you and Tom too much to be really happy. There's nothin' she'd want more than to see the both of you."

Blue Hawk nodded, setting his cup aside. "Yes. But I fear I will never see her again. This land and the Cheyenne are my home now."

Bo studied him closely. "You're pretty young to be thinkin' this is all there will ever be for you, Caleb. The country is growin' fast, and the whites will move right into Cheyenne country, mark my word. Half of you is white, Caleb. All kinds of things will happen to you before you're an old man. For all you know, you'll settle some day in the white man's world."

Blue Hawk shook his head. "I do not think so."

Bo took out a pipe. "Well, when I was your age I thought

I had my life all figured out, too. But none of it went the way I thought it would. Life has a way of doin' that."

Blue Hawk swallowed a lump in his throat, feeling like a little boy at the moment. "Yes. It does." How he had looked forward to seeing Tom. Why did life have to present people with such difficult choices? He should go and see Tom in spite of the danger. But if he didn't keep his promise to the Cheyenne, he would be forever shamed. This life, this land, were the most important thing to him right now. He had to prove his right to stay.

Chapter Eleven

EVERY summer, when the Cheyenne gathered for the buffalo hunt, several rituals took place while all the tribes were together, including courting dances and ceremonies to renew the warriors' medicine. But the most important ritual was the Sun Dance, during which warriors and sometimes even women strove to be as close to the spirits as possible. They fasted, prayed, and sacrificed flesh in hopes of receiving visions that would guide them through life. Through the ceremony the Cheyenne also celebrated the rebirth of the earth and the return of the season of growth. The Sun Dance Ritual was considered so important that all Cheyenne attended, believing misfortune would befall anyone who failed to be present.

Blue Hawk was determined to go through with his vow to participate in the twelve-day ritual; somehow it seemed

that the sacrifice would not only prove to the Cheyenne and
Walking Grass that he was brave and honest, but he felt it
would also vindicate his mistake of lying with Emily Stoner.
He vowed he would never be that foolish again. From then
on he would not only be strong and brave, but wise as well.

The days of fasting began soon after Blue Hawk returned,
continuing until he and the other participants were weak
from hunger and thirst. Sweet Seed Woman painted Blue
Hawk's nearly naked body with horses and flowers; custom
dictated that Sun Dance participants be brightly painted by
loved ones before undergoing their ordeal.

Several days into the ceremony, Sweet Seed Woman and
Walking Grass watched proudly as Blue Hawk was led to
the Sun Dance Pole in the central gathering place. The area
was crowded with celebrating Cheyenne, their voices mixing with beating drums and jingling bells to create a festive
atmosphere. But Blue Hawk and the others participating
were hardly aware of anything around them, for they were
nearly in a trance from hunger.

Blue Hawk felt himself being led to the pole, and he drew
on his deepest reserves, thinking only of Black Antelope
and his grandfather and uncles, whose spirits must surely
be with him. He also thought of Tom, how proud the man
would be if only he were here. He knew Walking Grass
was watching, and his aunt, and he threw back his head
and waited, anticipating the glory the celebration would
bring him.

He winced but did not cry out when the skewers were
shoved through slits cut into the skin of his breasts, and
again through cuts on his upper back. Rawhide strips were
attached to the skewers and the pole, and then his body was
raised slightly off the ground. Skewers were inserted into
the calves of his legs and buffalo skulls were hung on them
as weights so that his skin was pulled painfully. Blue Hawk
closed his eyes, calling on that power within him that removed him from physical pain.

Someone began spinning him, and he opened his eyes,

aware of the bright sun and blue sky. He stared at a cloud above him, blowing hard on the bone whistle that had been put in his mouth to use when he felt like crying out. The whistle was sacred, something he would keep forever in his special medicine bag, along with his rabbit's foot and eagle feathers. The medicine bag would be his protector, his power, as was the blue quill necklace which he never removed.

Many faces passed before his eyes, Black Antelope, his grandfather and uncles, Small Hands and Two Stars, Cora Sax—all beloved people gone from his life. But some still lived. Tom and Sarah still lived. Sarah. Why did her face suddenly come to clear to him? It was as though she were right there, calling out to him, crying. He tried to answer, but in reality he only blew the whistle again.

Then he saw a blue hawk, flying and soaring above the land. The hawk turned white and separated into two birds, the other one red.

"Forever you must live in two worlds, my son," a woman's voice said. "You must learn to live in both, but always your heart will belong to me, to the Cheyenne."

He knew in his soul it was his mother speaking to him. He strained to see her face, but it would not come to him. The two birds melded together and the blue hawk flew away. After that there was only blackness.

When he awoke, Blue Hawk saw only blurred images. He could smell the sweet smoke of a hickory fire cooking venison, but when he tried to focus his eyes and rise, pain seered through his body.

"Do not move," said a gentle voice. "You must lie still, Blue Hawk. I will care for you until you are better."

He recognized his aunt's voice. He felt something wet at his lips then, and water was squeezed into his mouth.

"Drink just a little, my warrior. Soon you will eat, and in a few days you will be strong. You did well, nephew. You did not cry out. You are a true Cheyenne brave now, and can sit with the Council and ride into battle. You have proven your word and your bravery, and Sweet Seed Woman is proud of you."

Blue Hawk let the water trickle into his dry throat. "Walking . . . Grass?"

Sweet Seed Woman smiled. "She saw. She too is proud. The spirits of your ancestors are also proud. You are truly one of us now, Blue Hawk."

"My . . . mother. She spoke to me—"

The woman put her fingers to his lips. "You must not tell me of your vision, nephew. That is only for the shaman to hear if you choose to tell."

The words sounded far away. For several days thereafter there was nothing but sleeping and eating, with special herbs and oils put on his wounds to help them heal. And he would heal. He had lived through the Sun Dance Ritual and had done so with honor.

When he was strong again, Blue Hawk sat with the others and watched as the women danced in a circle around a fire. It was a night to relax and have a good time. The summer hunt had been good, and tipis were full of dried meat and piles of turnips and berries. There were many new skins for clothing, blankets and tipis; bones for utensils of endless uses. Many pounds of pemmican had been prepared to help get them through the winter and for warriors to take on hunts and raids. The pemmican was a combination of dried buffalo and venison mixed with melted fat and berries. When properly prepared, it lasted several months, providing nourishment in times when food became scarce and the hunts were not good.

But this summer the hunts had been excellent, and now they celebrated. Blue Hawk sat next to Proud Eagle, each of them smoking homemade pipes and watching the women. Some were married, others were maidens who in these dances were allowed to flaunt themselves and give signals to their own favorite male, displaying their particular preferences. Blue Hawk watched with a quickening heart as Walking Grass whirled by him, smiling, swaying her hips seductively, opening her blanket and then closing it again and continuing the skipping step of the dance, staying within the circle of women.

"You still have eyes for the one who nearly got you banished?" Proud Eagle asked with a grin.

"I do."

Proud Eagle reached into the waist of his leggings, handing Blue Hawk something carved from bone. "Here. I made this for you."

Blue Hawk took the carving, studying it and frowning. "What is it?"

Proud Eagle laughed. "It is your own flute. Do you not know that to court a Cheyenne maiden you must play a special tune, just for her? Is it not time you began presenting her parents with gifts, for them and for Walking Grass?"

Blue Hawk turned the instrument in his hands. "I do not know how to play."

"You do not have to. Practice with it until you have decided on your own special song. Then go near her tipi and play it every night. She will know."

The young woman danced around again. She was fifteen summers, old enough to court. And she was not only pretty, but also daring and proud. Blue Hawk had been told that once, when Crows attacked, she saved her grandmother by knifing a Crow warrior all by herself, then half carrying her frail grandmother to safety. Blue Hawk could not imagine the girl doing such a thing, for she was herself just a small thing, with hips that were narrow but perfectly rounded in the back, a tiny waist and slender legs. Many times Blue Hawk had tried to envision how she would look naked, how it would feel to be with her that way. She was so different from Emily Stoner, and he knew instinctively that Walking Grass would never be bad like that, never bring him shame. He had known her only five months, yet he knew he loved her. She was sweet and delicate, yet brave, and of strong character.

Again she disappeared, but some of the women began

leaving the circle to throw their blankets over their husbands, some single women choosing their favorite warrior to sit with them under the blanket as custom allowed. With the single maidens, the man was never to touch her rudely. The blanket was only a symbol, and for several minutes they would sit beneath it and talk, learn whether or not they would like to talk again, and if there was an interest in more than talk.

Men and women laughed and cheered. It was fun making bets on who the young maidens would choose, fun teasing those under the blankets. Again Walking Grass came around. She opened her blanket in front of Blue Hawk, swaying seductively in a bleached doeskin dress, her hair hanging loose. He felt lost, as if he were at her mercy, and was suddenly very nervous when she left the circle and moved toward him. She threw her blanket over them, and Blue Hawk could hear Proud Eagle and others cheering and laughing.

Sitting under the blanket with the beauty he had looked at from afar for months was tempting indeed. But Blue Hawk knew better than to touch her wrongly. He breathed in her sweet scent, and she in turn thought how clean and masculine Blue Hawk smelled. Her heart swelled with love for him, for he was the most beautiful young man in their village, she was sure. But she dared not speak too boldly.

"I watched you at the Sun Dance. I was proud," she said.

"I told you I would come back," he replied, allowing his arm to touch hers and feeling on fire when he did so.

"Why did you come back, Blue Hawk?"

"To fulfill my vow and retain my honor."

"Why else?" she teased.

Blue Hawk swallowed. "Maybe . . . for you."

"Maybe?"

"Maybe."

"Will you play the flute for me some night, Blue Hawk? I would like it if you did."

"Then I will do it."

"Sing the tune you will play."

"I—" Blue Hawk had never felt so ridiculously nervous in his life. "I cannot. I have to learn first. But you will know."

"I want to talk more, Blue Hawk. If you wish, you may come to our tipi, and we can talk in the presence of my family, but I will not be allowed to look straight into your eyes."

"I understand. I will come. I would like to talk, too."

"Will you tell me about the white man's world?"

"If you wish."

He felt her leaning closer. "You may touch my cheek, Blue Hawk, if you wish."

He longed to put his mouth on hers. His curiosity about how she would react was almost painful, for she knew nothing of kissing the white man's way. He longed to teach her about loving and hear her cry out his name in ecstasy. The thought of a wife and perhaps a son of his own seemed suddenly wonderful. He leaned forward, touching her cheek, and he could not help allowing his lips to brush her ear.

"You are a most beautiful creature, Walking Grass," he whispered.

She wondered if she would faint from his touch. She reached up and touched her slender fingers to his lips. "I think the same of you," she answered.

Suddenly both blanket and girl were gone, and Blue Hawk blinked at the abrupt return to reality. He watched in surprise as Walking Grass ran off into the shadows. He started after her, but Proud Eagle grabbed his arm.

"No. It must be the right way. Do not go after her tonight or you will offend her pride and her family."

Blue Hawk slowly sat down and Proud Eagle grinned. "You look like a stud horse who has smelled the mare in heat, my friend. But someone else owns the mare. You cannot break loose from your rope and go into her pasture."

Blue Hawk shook back his hair and stared into the shadows. "One day she and I will share the same pasture," he said in a determined voice.

Proud Eagle chuckled. "First she has to be ready for you. An unwilling mare kicks hard and bites."

Blue Hawk put his pipe in his mouth and puffed it a moment. "She will not kick and bite," he answered then. "She will whinny and nuzzle."

They both laughed then, and Blue Hawk wondered which would prove more painful—the Sun Dance Ritual or waiting for the woman he wanted.

After that the courting began in earnest. Blue Hawk was determined not to waste any time. He wanted Walking Grass, and was determined to have her soon. Every night he played his flute outside her tipi. By day he asked her parents' permission to sit with her inside their tipi and talk. There were many such talks, as each discovered the beauty of the other. Blue Hawk wore the tail of a white-tailed deer around his neck, and more such tails on his weapons belt, for the talismans were considered good luck in love. He presented the girl's father, Two Bears, with gifts of fresh meat and fine skins, as well as his Crow tomahawk. He also offered some of the white man's tobacco, which Bo Sanders had given him when they met.

Finally Two Bears agreed to the marriage, and Walking Grass began preparing skins for a tipi of their own. Until it was ready, she could not be Blue Hawk's wife. Walking Grass took painstaking care to sew the finest tipi of the village, carefully painting it with blue hawks and battle scenes showing her blue-eyed warrior felling Crow men. Blue Hawk had four horses of his own now, and was considered wealthy by Cheyenne standards. Walking Grass painted pictures of each one on the tipi; the gray gelding, the roan mare Buffalo Man had given him, and two spotted horses stolen from the Crow in a recent raid. She smiled when painting the spotted horses, her heart bursting with pride at her future husband's accomplishments in war. He had brought home not only the two spotted horses, but two others, a gray and a black, for Two Bears. The man was pleased, and Blue Hawk's standing as an honorable warrior had been more than met.

The morning of the wedding dawned with the sound of thundering horses and loud war whoops. Blue Hawk bolted upright, grabbing his weapons belt and quickly tying it around his bare stomach. He wore only a loincloth, but he knew there would be no time to put on clothes. In the next instant a fiery arrow landed in the side of his tipi.

"Crow," Blue Hawk yelled. "Get out!" He pushed Sweet Seed Woman and her sister, both of whom wore nothing but blankets wrapped around them, while Buffalo Man grabbed his lance. "Hurry," Blue Hawk yelled. *"Hopo! Hopo!"*

They were hardly out before the tipi began to crumble. The women headed for the riverbank, where trenches had been dug for just such an emergency. They would hide in the trenches, where it would be more difficult for a Crow warrior to reach down and grab them.

Blue Hawk whirled, shooting one warrior with his pistol, giving his aunt and her sister time to get away. Buffalo Man went after another warrior with his lance, and Blue Hawk searched desperately for Walking Grass. He ran toward her father's tipi, where he saw the girl's mother coming out, helping Walking Grass' old grandmother toward the trenches. But the old woman could not walk fast enough. Two Bears stayed beside them, waving his lance and tomahawk, determined to protect them until they were safe. Walking Grass ran out then, a blanket wrapped around herself. Her wide, frightened eyes met Blue Hawk's.

"Go with them," he shouted. "I will help your father protect you."

She hurried up beside her grandmother, and Blue Hawk turned and lanced a warrior that rode down on them. He yanked it out immediately, and the man rode on farther before finally falling from his horse. Blue Hawk stood near

Walking Grass, who moved slowly with her mother and grandmother. In a moment two warriors came at them, and while Blue Hawk was busy readying himself for one, the other managed to hit Two Bears' head with a stone from his sling, knocking him down. Walking Grass screamed and ran to her father, and another warrior came along and swooped her up onto his horse. Blue Hawk pulled the first warrior from his horse, and in an instant his tomahawk was buried in the Crow man's head.

He jerked out the tomahawk and turned to see Walking Grass' mother and grandmother still running, but Walking Grass was gone. His eyes widened in horror at the sight of Two Bears on the ground. He heard Walking Grass scream his name, and turned to see her struggling with a Crow man on a horse, pulling viciously at the man's hair and biting his nose. Her blanket had fallen away and she was completely naked, but oblivious to her nudity. Blue Hawk ran over to them, trying to get close to the Crow's horse as it turned in confusion while Walking Grass fought with its master.

Blue Hawk finally reached up and pulled her down, then jumped onto the warrior's horse, knocking the dizzy, bleeding warrior from his mount. They both landed hard, and Blue Hawk whipped out his knife and shoved it into the man's heart. An instant later another Crow warrior landed with a thud beside him. Blue Hawk whirled on his knees to see Walking Grass standing near him, holding a tomahawk in her hand. She had apparently grabbed it from the man's mount and used it on the second warrior, who had obviously come up behind Blue Hawk to kill him.

The fighting had moved farther from camp by then as the Cheyenne gained control. Blue Hawk stared at Walking Grass, his eyes moving over her incredibly beautiful body. He met her eyes then, and their gazes held in a moment of lightning desire. She knew by the way he looked at her that he was pleased with what he saw, and the thought of being his wife filled her with a passion beyond anything she had ever experienced.

Blue Hawk rose and put his knife into its sheath. He grabbed a blanket from the Crow warrior's horse and walked up to her, opening the blanket and putting it around her. She kept her eyes on his blue ones, then let him pull her into his arms.

"You saved my life." He held her close.

"You saved mine," she replied.

"The Crow would not have killed you. But he would have done something to you that would have been harder for me to face than your death," he said.

She raised her face and met his eyes again, eyes that made her feel weak. "And for me, death would have been better than to belong to any man but you."

He picked her up in his strong arms and walked toward the river with her. "Look, Walking Grass. The tipi you were making for us still stands. Everything else around it is burned."

She looked at the lovely dwelling, the morning sun lighting up the brilliant blue hawks painted on it. She looked at him and smiled. "It is a good sign. It means it is good that we will marry."

The soft night breeze and fresh scent of pine washed over Blue Hawk as he held back the flap of the wedding tipi. The ceremony had been put off until Two Bears recovered from his head wound. Not much damage had been done other than several tipis being burned, and there had been a celebration over the fact that the Cheyenne were better warriors than the Crow. Blue Hawk's impatience to make Walking Grass his wife was finally satisfied, and now she stepped inside their tipi bashfully. Blue Hawk followed, his heart full of pride in his new wife, her courage, the lovely dwelling she had made for them, her beauty.

The young woman stood trembling, not really afraid of Blue Hawk, but of not pleasing him, for she wasn't sure what she should do. In her bleached doeskin dress she looked soft and velvety, her dark skin a lovely contrast to the dress, which was decorated with fringes and quills and beads, representing many hours of labor by her mother. The dress was matched in beauty only by its wearer.

Blue Hawk removed the white vest he wore and quickly made a fire, while outside drums beat and bells jingled in rhythmic dancing. The celebrating over the Crow defeat continued even now, but Blue Hawk and Walking Grass had their own celebrating to do.

The fire began to crackle, warming the tipi against the cold September night. Blue Hawk turned and removed the fine buckskin shirt and leggings he had worn for his wedding. Walking Grass watched curiously, alive with desire but also nervous and afraid. She studied the hard ripple of his muscles as he discarded all his clothing but his loin cloth. He straightened and stood in all his manly glory, the most handsome man ever created as far as Walking Grass was concerned. He walked up to her and stroked her cheek with the back of his hand.

"Why do you tremble so?" he asked, touching her lips with his fingers. "We have talked many times. We are friends. I would never hurt you, Walking Grass."

She swallowed. Oh, how she loved him! But still she was afraid. "I . . . I do not know what to do."

He smiled. "I will show you. But it is your right to refuse me."

She met his eyes. "I do not refuse," she whispered.

His eyes shone with desire as he untied the laces of her tunic and let it drop to her waist, revealing full, satiny breasts. Gently he caressed them, his body on fire for her. Her nipples grew taught with her own desire, and her eyes did not leave his. His hand moved to her chin and he brought his mouth down to meet hers, gently biting at her lips, using his tongue and light kisses to draw out her natural desires. He knew she was not really afraid of him, but only of what it would be like to be taken for the first time. Walking Grass seemed like a frightened little deer, so innocent. He knew he had to be very careful.

Her breath came in little gasps as he pulled her close, encircling her in his arms and rubbing her breasts against his bare chest while he kissed her the white man's way, searching her mouth, his hands running gently over her bare back.

Blue Hawk trembled with the great joy of finally holding her, finally having her for himself, and with the knowledge that she did not choose to wait. She would shed the chastity rope this very first night, for he knew she wanted very much to please him. She would be a good wife, the best a man could want.

"You are so beautiful, Walking Grass," he whispered, untying the rawhide belt at her waist. He pulled it away and let the dress fall to her feet, his breath catching at the sight of her. Seeing her this way was much more pleasing than when he had seen her naked the day of the Crow battle; this time she was his wife. He looked her over, her full, delicious breasts, slender waist and flat belly, the small patch of hair covering what he desired most, her slim thighs and firm bottom. He turned and retrieved his knife from his weapons belt, then turned to her and held it to the chastity rope, quickly cutting it.

After putting his knife away Blue Hawk picked her up and lay her on the bed of robes she had prepared for them. When he straightened and removed his loincloth, he saw her swallow with wonder and apprehension. He knelt down beside her, reaching over to a bowl of scented oil and dipping his hands into it.

"Soon it will be over," he told her, rubbing the oil onto his hands and then placing them on her shoulders, gently rubbing, massaging in circular motions down and over her breasts, her stomach, his fingers coming daringly close to her secret place.

She wanted to curl up in bashfulness, yet his gentle touch

made her lie still, glad that she saw great satisfaction in his eyes at the sight of her nakedness.

"There will be some pain," he told her. "I will not lie to you. But that is always the way it is. And then the pain goes away. This I promise. Once, twice, three times I will make love to you before it goes away completely." His hands moved over her thighs and then her calves, all the way to her feet and up again.

"Turn over, my wife," he told her. She obeyed, her trembling lessened by his relaxing massage. Again he oiled his hands, and again he placed them at her shoulders, moving down her back and over her bottom, thighs and calves. "Soon you will want me as eagerly as I want you this moment. Sometimes it will be you who comes after me in the night."

His hands moved up again, and she gasped as he gently moved one hand between her legs. He felt the warm moistness that told him she shared his desire. He bent down and kissed her bottom, and fire swept through her in a raging inferno.

After that everything seemed like a strange dream. He turned her over again, and then he was hovering over her, his mouth gently sucking at her breasts, drawing out her wild desires. His hands were searching, his fingers pushing inside of her and making her cry out in eager, youthful desire until a great explosion ripped through her insides, a glorious wave of heated ecstasy making her cry out his name. In the next moment he was on top of her, his manhood pressing against her belly, his mouth searching her own, whispering beautiful words of love, apologizing that he would hurt her. But it didn't matter.

And then came the surprising pain that made her gasp. He grasped her bottom and pushed, knowing he was hurting her but unable to stop himself. It must be done. And this was not like anything he had experienced with Emily Stoner. This was so much more fulfilling, for he loved this woman, and she loved him. They had fought side by side and saved each other's lives. He had killed the man who would have claimed her, and the thought of Fire Wolf doing this to her brought forth a jealousy that made him push deeper.

He moved gently but rhythmically, allowing his life to spill into her quickly so she did not have to endure the pain for too long.

It was over then. She was his wife in every sense, and never in his life had Blue Hawk been happier. He was in love, and he had claimed the virgin he had wanted since the first day he rode into her village many months before. It seemed this was the seal of his vow to stay in this land forever, with these people. He would never go back to the white man's world.

Chapter Twelve

THE winter of 1811–1812 brought to Blue Hawk what seemed to be his final peace, his final home, his final family. He forgot Bo's words about how young he was, how he would experience many things in life. Walking Grass was all he wanted to experience, and through that late winter her belly grew with his child. His joy knew no bounds. She was more than he could have ever hoped for, and it seemed their passion only grew with time. Now it was Walking Grass who wore the blue quill necklace, a love gift from Blue Hawk. It seemed all his life he had been searching to belong, and now he did, here in the wilds that

bordered the Great Plains, with the Cheyenne, with Walking
Grass.

But he did not forget his promise to Tom Sax, and in the
spring he made a very difficult decision. Walking Grass was
with child and could not make the trip with him, but he
could not allow Tom to go to the meeting place and find
no one there. He had hurt the man enough. Blue Hawk had
received nothing but love and devotion from Tom Sax, and
he couldn't simply walk out on Tom without a word. Tom
would go to meet him, and Blue Hawk must go, too. Walking Grass understood, and she sent him off with her prayers
and a good supply of food.

When neither Tom Sax nor Bo Sanders showed up at the
meeting place, Blue Hawk knew something was wrong. A
feeling of doom settled over him. If not for Walking Grass,
he would have gone to Fort Dearborn to find out what had
happened, but that was impossible. He waited as long as
he could, then headed back to the Cheyenne, his heart heavy.
It hurt to think he had never seen Tom after the night he
fled, leaving the already devastated man even more alone.
When he thought of it, he also thought of Emily Stoner,
and he hated her all the more. Now he would have to wait
another whole winter to find out what had happened to Tom.
Already two years had gone by since he had fled Fort Dearborn. At eighteen he looked and felt much older. Tom Sax
would be ageing. Was he even alive? What would he do if
the man again did not show the next spring? He could not
go all the way back and leave Walking Grass alone for so
long, nor could he take her to that place. He could only
hope and pray that Tom would be there when he came back
again, and pray that in the meantime the man knew Blue
Hawk was with him in spirit.

The feeling of doom would not leave him, not even after
he returned to find Walking Grass well and unharmed; not
even when she gave birth to a fine, healthy son. Although
the boy was born a Cheyenne among Cheyenne, Blue Hawk
chose to call him Tom. He was born in late June of 1812

during the Moon of the Ripening Strawberries. The tribe left the next month to travel north for the Sun Dance. Sixteen-year-old Walking Grass rode proudly beside her husband on the gray gelding, the papoose on her back. For a wife to ride on her own horse was a sign of prominence, the woman of a good warrior who had many horses. Since their belongings were packed on their other two mounts, they did not even need a travois.

Walking Grass had only been delivered for three weeks, but she felt strong and enjoyed the journey. It was a good time, a happy time, but Blue Hawk could not stop thinking about Tom, nor shake the dark feeling that hung over him. It was on a morning just as they were awakening to break camp and keep traveling that the darkness fell.

The Crow came to reclaim some of their own women, to win back their horses and avenge Cheyenne attacks on their villages. It was a neverending saga, and no one knew where it had started. This time there was no opportunity for Caleb to grab even his weapons belt. A horse thundering by and their tipi being sliced with a hunting knife was what woke them.

Blue Hawk grabbed his tomahawk, the same trusty Chippewa weapon Black Antelope had given him.

"Out! Get out," he yelled to Walking Grass, who grabbed up the baby and ran, stark naked, out of the tipi. Blue Hawk followed, wearing only his loin cloth.

This time there were many Crow, and their attack was well planned. They seemed to be everywhere, and Cheyenne men, women and children were running helter-skelter, screaming, heading for a ravine not far away. Men scrambled for weapons and horses, and Blue Hawk saw Proud Eagle go down.

Blue Hawk ducked and leaped, swinging his tomahawk in every direction. Out of the corner of his eye he saw Walking Grass suddenly grabbed by the hair and lifted, still clinging to her son. Sweet Seed Woman ran past, knowing what must be done. She had no hope of helping Walking

Grass, so she grabbed the baby from the young woman's arms and ran with him toward the ravine, while a Crow warrior, his face painted grotesquely in black, hung on to Walking Grass.

Blue Hawk ran toward the Crow warrior who was trying to get Walking Grass onto his mount. He grabbed at Walking Grass but could not get a good hold on her because of the Crow's swinging tomahawk, which Blue Hawk feared would end up hurting his wife. Her slender body was tossed and battered, but she kept screaming and reaching up, trying to scratch at the Crow man. The grinning warrior kept moving his horse in different directions, dodging and teasing Blue Hawk while dragging Walking Grass by the hair. Blue Hawk kept going for him, oblivious to the screams and fighting going on around him while the entire village was savagely attacked, oblivious to the fact that their own beautifully painted tipi was burning to the ground.

He finally managed to land his tomahawk in the horse, digging into the animal's rump to make it fall. Horse and warrior went crashing down, and the animal landed full force on Walking Grass. Blue Hawk's eyes widened in horror, and he dove into the Crow man, slamming his tomahawk into the man's face, then striking again and again like a madman.

The fighting had moved toward the ravine, and some of the Cheyenne men had managed to get to their mounts and were beginning to ride after the Crow, who were fleeing with stolen horses and women. The Cheyenne men would pursue and get their property back.

But Blue Hawk would not go with them. He turned and crawled to Walking Grass, who lay sprawled under the horse, one arm flung out away from it. The animal whinnied and struggled wildly, each time kicking at Walking Grass until finally it rolled off her. She lay still, naked and crushed. A horrible wail was torn from somewhere deep in Blue Hawk's soul, and he began to tremble violently. It could not be. He could not live without Walking Grass. He stared at her young, beautiful face, still in death, then threw back his head and let out a long scream, crying his anguish to the heavens, digging his fingernails into his cheeks in sorrow.

His eyes were suddenly the wild eyes of a crazed man. He stumbled to the charred tipi, blindly sifting through its ruins until he found the knife Tom Sax had given him. It burned his palm when he picked it up, but he felt no pain. He began slashing himself with the knife, growling like an animal. Blood spilled from his chest and arms. How many times he cut himself he didn't know, nor did he care. He threw himself over Walking Grass' body, weeping bitterly, numb with the enormity of his loss.

How long he lay there weeping he could not be sure. The sun was high by the time he finally struggled to get to his knees. Others were searching out loved ones, picking through the ruins to salvage what they could. Several had seen Blue Hawk lying in mourning over his young wife, and none dared go near him. Blue Hawk sat looking down at Walking Grass, and it was only then that he saw the blue quill necklace in her hand. She had apparently grabbed it as she ran from the tipi, realizing it might be burned and the necklace might be lost. She had actually clung to it while the Crow warrior dragged and battered her, he realized. She had known how special the necklace was to Blue Hawk, and she had saved it for him.

The realization of her sweet devotion in those last moments of horror filled him with a grief beyond measure. Revenge was already building in his soul, a thirst that would not be quenched for a long time to come. The Crow would pay. If he had to wage a one-man war, they would pay and pay until his own life was smothered out by them.

He stood up, turning at the sound of his name. Sweet Seed Woman stood nearby with his son in her arms.

"The child lives," she told him.

Blue Hawk just stared at her, covered with his own blood. He threw down the blue quill necklace. "What does it matter." He stumbled off, disappearing into the forest beyond the camp.

It was the beginning of even more fierce wars between the Crow and Cheyenne, wars that continued into the following spring and summer of 1813. No Cheyenne warrior was more vicious or vengeful than the one called Blue Hawk, who had lost not only his young wife, but also his best friend, Proud Eagle. In a very short time he became a legend among the Crow. Many feared him, for he seemed possessed by a demon, and his thirst for vengeance knew no bounds. Little Tom was left with a nursing Cheyenne woman who had lost her own baby while Blue Hawk went on a rampage that was food for many campfire stories among the Cheyenne and Crow alike. He did not even stop for the spring visit to meet Tom Sax, he was so consumed with a blind need for vengeance.

Blue Hawk led many raids himself, and after only a few weeks, his clothes and belt were decorated with many Crow scalps. He kept to himself, a wild look about him that frightened even the Cheyenne. Nothing, no amount of killings, seemed to satisfy the once-gentle man. All the scalps and blood could not take away the pain of losing Walking Grass, his love, his life, the security and family he had finally found. Hatred burned in his soul like a torch. Again he had lost everything, and now it seemed he had even lost contact with the spirits. There was no peace or joy for him, and he could no longer pray.

Soon he began raiding alone, not waiting for the war dance and other rituals the tribe believed must be performed before going into battle.

"To ignore the proper prayers and sacrifices to the spirits will bring you bad luck, Blue Hawk," Three Feathers warned him as Blue Hawk painted his face for yet another raid. "You are counting on yourself alone to win the battles, but it is only when the spirits are with us and when we make the proper prayers and sacrifices that we can win the battle. If you displease the spirits, you will die."

"Then I shall die," Blue Hawk snapped. "There is nothing left to live for. Why do you think I go out alone? It is in the hope that one day a Crow warrior will manage to sink his lance into my heart and end this misery in which I live." His voice was cold. "But I have yet to find a Crow warrior who is better than I." He threw down the colored clay with which he had painted his face and slung his quiver of arrows over his shoulder.

"There is always something to live for. You have a son, Blue Hawk. Already the boy is over a year old, and he hardly knows his father."

Blue Hawk's eyes softened slightly. "I know."

Three Feathers sighed. "It is not such a bad thing to die, Blue Hawk, but it is bad to die with your back turned to the spirits and your heart hard and bitter. Who would bless you and welcome you along the Hanging Road if you deny the existence of *Maheo*? Do not go out, Blue Hawk. You are being ignorant. Many of us have lost loved ones. But we go on, for we are all one with the spirits and the earth and sky. It is not for us to choose when we die, that is the spirits' choice. Stop going out alone, Blue Hawk. I care much for you."

Blue Hawk faced him, fists clenched and shaking. There were tears in the wild, blue eyes. "I cannot stop," he replied in a hoarse, broken voice. "If I stop, I will go crazy with my grief! Sometimes . . . I wish that I could stop and find peace again in my soul. But it will not come." He turned and mounted his roan mare, then looked down at the old man, whom he had learned to love and respect. "I am not ungrateful for all you have done for me, Three Feathers. You gave me a home among the Cheyenne and led me to Sweet Seed Woman. Before the death of Walking Grass, I never knew a happier time than my years with the Cheyenne in this land." His tears flowed more freely then, but he sat rigid, his face hard.

Three Feathers reached up with a brown, wrinkled hand and touched his arm. "I will pray that you find peace, Blue Hawk. Walking Grass is gone, and you are still young. You must try to find another woman to marry, one who will give you more children. For now there is your son, who needs his father."

"Perhaps my son needs me," Blue Hawk replied, "but I do not need him, not now. All I need is Crow blood!" He whirled his horse and rode away.

Three Feathers shook his head. *"E-have-se-va,"* he whispered. "It is bad, Blue Hawk. It is bad."

The hoot of an owl penetrated the dark night, and the two Crow men looked at each other across their campfire. How many times had that sound been heard in the night, followed with a vicious attack by one wild Cheyenne warrior? Their blood chilled, and one of them dove for his tomahawk, but too late. The swift and sure-footed roan mare was upon them, and a club landed on the side of the warrior's head. He never even saw the attacker. But the second man did. It was the same one, the Cheyenne who always painted red and black stripes on his face, a blue quill necklace around his neck. Some had seen him close in the light of day, and said he had a long scar on his left cheek.

The warrior grasped his tomahawk. Anyone who could kill this ghostlike Cheyenne who had a habit of raiding after dark would be famous and honored indeed. He whirled, waiting, but the Cheyenne had disappeared again into the darkness. The two Crow warriors had been out alone, scouting. The second man thought of running, but the thirst to be the one to kill the Cheyenne warrior was too great.

He waited, crouched, his eyes darting about the shadows beyond the campfire, his muscles tensed, his heart pounding. There was no sound but the night wind. He turned slowly, studying every angle, his hand squeezing the tomahawk so tightly his knuckles were white. Suddenly his enemy lunged on foot from the darkness behind him roaring like a bear and slamming into the Crow and knocking him face down. Before the Crow could turn and wield his tomahawk, a knife was in his back.

Blue Hawk turned the man over, slitting his throat and slicing off a piece of scalp. It was done. Two more Crow were dead. He fought the sick feeling he was beginning to get with each new killing. He must not let it stop him. He could not spill enough blood in retribution for Walking Grass, and the Crow would learn that. They would regret the day of Walking Grass' death.

He stood up, shoving the scalp into his belt. He walked back into the darkness, grasping the roan mare by the bridle and leading it away. Why did he have this growing feeling of guilt, so like the emotion he had had after lying with Emily Stoner? Killing Crow men for what had happened to Walking Grass could not be wrong. But perhaps Three Feathers was right. Perhaps his guilt was brought on by angry spirits. But *Maheo* had not protected Walking Grass. He could not pray to *Maheo* again. He would continue to go against Cheyenne custom and raid in the night, when all evil spirits came out to do bad things. He would join them.

For two weeks he remained alone, raiding at will, harassing the Crow, murdering, burning, striking out from the darkness like a demon, until the morning five Crow warriors happened upon his campsite. Blue Hawk lay asleep, exhausted after a night of raiding. The Crow men rode out of a stand of trees, then halted their horses when they saw a small campfire and a lone man just across the narrow river they had come upon. Their leader gave quiet hand signals, for even from a distance they recognized the Cheyenne clothing and the painted roan mare. They waited quietly for a moment, readying their weapons, then charged.

The moment a horse's hoof hit the water, Blue Hawk was awake. He bolted for his musket, already primed, whirling around and firing it toward the oncoming Crow, planting a large iron ball into the face of one of the men. He quickly whipped an arrow from its quiver that lay nearby, steadying it in his bow and letting the arrow sing, right into the chest of a second warrior.

They were across the stream by then, blood in their eyes. Blue Hawk jerked out his hunting knife and threw it, catching a third warrior in the heart. The two remaining Crow brought their mounts to an abrupt halt, staring at Blue Hawk as he stood there, his tomahawk in hand. His arms were out, ready to fight. They looked at each other and grinned, then slid off their horses and began to circle Blue Hawk.

One of the warriors lashed out at him with his tomahawk, but he grabbed it and swung back, wounding the man's arm with his own weapon. The Crow jumped back, looking down at his bleeding arm in surprise. Blue Hawk sensed the other Crow was upon him, and he whirled. The man had an arm raised in midair, ready to bring a tomahawk down on Blue Hawk. But he froze in place when he realized who he was up against.

"Are you a coward?" Blue Hawk sneered. "Like all Crow are cowards?"

The Crow's lips appeared redder than normal because of the heavy black paint on his face. His eyes were encircled in white, and he looked like the epitome of evil. His lips curled in a returning sneer. "Two Eagles is not a coward," he growled.

Blue Hawk grinned. "Then come and take my scalp," he dared. "Think what an honored man you would be."

The Crow took the bait and lunged at Blue Hawk, swinging his tomahawk viciously. This time Blue Hawk did not dart away in time, and the sharp blade sliced into his side. But in the next instant his own tomahawk hit the Crow's shoulder. The man cried out and had no time to retaliate before the tomahawk was yanked out of his shoulder and was buried in his neck.

Blood poured down the front of the Crow and his body collapsed to the ground, his head nearly severed from the trunk. Blue Hawk yanked out his tomahawk again, grasping the man's hair and taking a quick slice of the scalp. He grinned and kicked at the body, then shoved the scalp into his belt. He turned, glaring at the remaining wounded Crow, who stood trembling, looking at Blue Hawk as though he were an evil spirit. The man turned and started running. Blue Hawk laughed wildly, flinging his tomahawk and landing it in the man's back.

It was done. Blue Hawk quickly scalped the other four, ignoring the wound in his side, but moments later a terrible weakness enveloped him and he knew it was from loss of blood. He looked down for the first time at his wound and realized just how grave it was. He remembered Three Feathers warning him about going out alone without the blessings of the spirits. Perhaps the old man had been right and he would die.

He stumbled to the roan mare, clinging to its neck for a moment, suddenly not wanting to die without the proper blessings, suddenly thinking of his little son. He could not die without seeing his son once again, leaving the boy his possessions.

He managed to climb up on the horse, then leaned forward against the trusty animal's neck, kicking its sides with what strength he could muster.

"Take me . . . to the People," he whispered.

"I told him the spirits would be displeased," Three Feathers mourned as he watched the shaman chant over Blue Hawk's body.

Since his arrival two days before, Blue Hawk had lain near death while the Cheyenne medicine man packed the wound with healing plants and forced concoctions of herbs and healing waters down Blue Hawk's throat. Then he had chanted over him with special smoke and prayers.

Blue Hawk's only hope for life was his own strength, his will to live, and the blessings of the spirits, who must surely be angry with him. And so the shaman did not stop to rest, sure that Blue Hawk needed more offerings and prayers than the average man. In his beliefs and dedication, the shaman continued the important healing ritual night and day.

The young man had arrived on the roan mare, falling from his horse at the edge of camp. Five fresh Crow scalps were in his belt, and everyone knew he had warred alone. He was indeed a brave and feared warrior, but all thought him a fool to go without the blessings of *Maheo*.

Three Feathers watched him with quiet tears, for Blue Hawk had become like a son to him, and he had had a heavy heart the last time the young man had ridden away. The old man was glad Blue Hawk had returned still alive. Perhaps it was a sign that the spirits were not totally displeased with him. But Blue Hawk's loss of blood and the infection in his side could prove otherwise, and the young man's soul had been so full of hatred that Three Feathers feared it had weakened his will to live.

After three more days Blue Hawk began to stir, but there was a terrible restlessness to his movements, and his groans were deep, sorrowful shudders. Three Feathers understood the war that raged inside the man, and he prayed for him. By the next day Blue Hawk began to sleep more calmly, and by that night the fever finally left his body. He opened his eyes to the dim light of a small fire. The first thing he saw was the wrinkled face of old Three Feathers.

"The spirits are no longer angry with me," Blue Hawk said in a weak voice. "I feel . . . a peace." The few words were difficult, and he was already tired from speaking them.

Three Feathers smiled at him. "Then the spirits have answered my prayers, Blue Hawk. They have let you live, for they know that deep in your heart your faith is still strong and good, that one day you will find love again. They have helped heal your sorrow for Walking Grass."

Blue Hawk closed his eyes. "I hurt all over."

"The pain will leave you soon enough. It is the pain inside that has taken long to heal."

"Go back," Blue Hawk whispered.

Three Feathers frowned, leaning closer. "What is it, Blue Hawk?"

"I must go back. Faces. I saw . . . faces. All those I have loved and lost. But one face was Tom Sax . . . calling me. I fear he is . . . dead. I must go back, must know."

The old man touched his shoulder. "And what of your son?"

"I will return for him."

Three Feathers sat back and sighed. "So, you will leave us after all, Blue Hawk. The white blood in you calls again." His eyes teared. "You will return, but only for your son. Then you will go again. You will never live among the Cheyenne again. My old eyes see it, my old heart knows. You have answered your Indian calling. Now you must go back to the white man's world. May *Maheo* be with you."

The old man rose and left so that the shaman would not see the tears in his eyes.

Chapter Thirteen

BLUE Hawk spent his months of healing getting to know his little son, a beautiful, solidly built boy with snappy brown eyes, black hair, and a bright smile that always beamed when his father was near. In June of 1814 the boy was already two years old and was the center of Blue Hawk's soul, his purpose for living, finally the answer to his sorrow over Walking Grass. But Blue Hawk felt a calling, and because of the vision of Tom Sax he had

had when lying near death, he knew he must go back to
Fort Dearborn and find out what had happened to the man.

And there was Sarah, too. What had happened to her?
He had promised he would go and see her. Nearly four years
had gone by since that promise. Too many questions were
unanswered, and life with the Cheyenne brought back too
many familiar and painful memories. He would never truly
get over Walking Grass if he did not get away from this
place. But he didn't know what to expect. There could be
a full-scale war going on between the Americans and the
British for all he knew. Out in the wilds a man had little
knowledge of what was happening in the white man's world.

Things had calmed between the Cheyenne and the Crow.
He could not take little Tom with him at such a young age,
and so the boy was left with Sweet Seed Woman, who Blue
Hawk knew would take fine care of him while he went East.
To leave the boy would not be easy, but it seemed life had
become a series of terrible decisions for Blue Hawk. He
had to decide again, and he knew he would never be calm
in his soul until he knew what had happened to Tom Sax.
He left in the next month.

It was early November when Caleb reached Fort Dearborn. He stared in disbelief at the black, burned out fort.
Slowly dismounting, he walked closer, leading the gray
gelding by the reins. Behind it was a spotted Appaloosa he
used for a packhorse, a splendid animal he had stolen from
the Crow and had intended to give to Tom.

But there was no Tom Sax, no fort, no sign of human
life. Fort Dearborn lay in ruins. Caleb's eyes brimmed with
tears. Why did he continue to lose everyone and everything
he loved? What had happened here? He stumbled through
the debris, heading through the fort and toward the cabin
he had shared with Tom and Cora and Sarah.

Sarah. What would she think of this? What had happened
to her? And what had happened to Tom Sax? Had he escaped
this? Caleb neared the cabin, and then turned away, crying

against his horse's neck. How much more was he supposed to bear? The cabin had been burned to the ground.

For several minutes Caleb just wept. Did seeing Tom Sax in his vision mean the man was dead? But he had not seen Sarah. He suddenly missed her desperately and felt frantic to see her. He must go to Saint Louis and try to find her, he decided, in spite of his aversion to going where so many white people lived.

He threw his head back and breathed deeply, leading the horses to Cora Sax's gravesite. The crude stone they had made for it was still there. He knelt down bedside it. "You are lucky, Cora Sax, that you left this life when you did. But I miss you." He closed his eyes and raised his arms, praying to *Maheo* to protect the woman's spirit. It was then someone called out.

"Yo! Who be you?"

Caleb jumped up, drawing his pistol and aiming it in the direction of the voice.

"I'm a friend. Don't shoot!"

Caleb watched warily as a man in buckskins came out from the thick trees, leading a horse and two mules. He was a large, aging man, and Caleb vaguely remembered him from the fort when he lived there. The man came closer, holding up his rifle.

"You from this place, young fella?"

Caleb stayed ready to defend himself. "I am Caleb Sax."

The man's eyes widened, and he looked Caleb over carefully. "I'll be damned! It's the half-breed son of Tom Sax." The man shoved his rifle into its boot and put out his hand, his eyes actually seeming to tear. "I'll be damned! Where have you been, boy?"

Caleb slowly put the pistol back in his belt, then shook the man's hand firmly. "John Brady?"

"Sure am."

"I have been with the Cheyenne. Tom Sax was supposed to meet me last spring, but he never did, nor this spring. I came to see what was wrong."

They broke the handshake, and Brady looked around at the ruins of the fort. "You don't know then."

"Know what? What happened here?" Caleb asked.

The man sighed deeply, meeting Caleb's eyes again. "Son, things got real bad. The British cut off the supply route and the fort had to be abandoned. People were starving. The soldiers ordered everybody to head south to Fort Wayne. Tom, he went along, wanting to get word to Sarah, I think. Me, I headed out on my own, and it's a good thing I did." He frowned with concern. "Most of them never made it, Caleb. That was, oh, maybe a year ago. I've been down to Fort Wayne since then, and that's where I learned what happened. The whole bunch of them was attacked by Potawatomi, son. There was close to four hundred of the redskins, I heard. They murdered nearly every last settler, took a few captives, mostly women, then come back here and burned the fort. Some that were later released went on to Fort Wayne. I seen Hugh there, the storekeeper. You remember him?"

Caleb nodded.

"Hugh, he was thin—pretty near a broken man. He was one of the prisoners let go. He told me he seen both Tom Sax and his friend Bo Sanders go down fightin' under Potawatomi tomahawks and lances. Them redskins chopped some of them men up in a hundred pieces."

Caleb turned away, hanging his head. He breathed deeply to stay in control. How strange it all was. He had murdered many Crow and it had seemed so right. Now Indians had murdered his beloved Tom Sax. How could he bear the guilt of not being by his father's side? What a horrible death he had suffered. But Caleb was sure in his heart Tom Sax had fought bravely and fiercely.

"The Potawatomi," he asked, "they did it for the British?"

"No doubt in my mind the British was behind it."

Caleb threw back his head. "So now the British are my enemy. I once thought they were friends because they seemed to be on the side of the Indian. Perhaps they are, but they murdered Tom Sax and many people I once knew."

Brady rubbed his chin. "I heard tell some army fella by the name of Andrew Jackson is aimin' to take Florida from Spain and head on to New Orleans to fight the British. If you've got an itch to fight the Redcoats, you might want to head south and see what's goin' on."

Caleb stared at Cora's grave. "Perhaps I will. I must go to Saint Louis anyway. I must find Sarah Sax. Even after a year she might not know if Tom were killed with the others or taken captive." He turned and faced Brady. "I guess it does not matter anymore why I left Fort Dearborn."

Brady looked him over. "After a time we learned you wasn't the only one, Caleb. But it don't matter much anymore. That Emily Stoner was took by the Indians, I heard. Her pa was killed. Hugh told me that when he was released, the Stoner girl was still a captive. She'd been took off to some other village. He don't know what happened to her. Only reason he was set free was because he took sick and the Potawatomi didn't figure he was worth nothin'."

Caleb sighed bitterly. "So, it was all for nothing. I was forced to leave because of that girl, and now I will never see Tom Sax again."

"Life takes strange turns, son," Brady said.

Caleb thought about Bo Sanders telling him how many things would happen to him before he was old. He nodded. "I have a son," he told the man. "He is with the Cheyenne and I must go back for him. But first I will try to find Sarah in Saint Louis. Then maybe I will go on down to New Orleans and see if this Jackson is there. If there are British to fight, I would like to be part of it."

Brady put out his hand again. "Then you'd better be leavin' mighty quick. It's a ways." They shook hands again. "You'd make your best time by ridin' hard for Fort Clark and then catchin' a steamboat south on the Illinois River to the Mississippi and Saint Louis. Don't stay long in Saint Louis, or you might miss your chance at some Redcoats.

That Jackson will be needin' volunteers. I hear tell the British could be sendin' a real big army to attack at New Orleans, so keep to the steamboats on down the Mississippi. They'll get you there a lot faster than a horse."

"Thank you," Caleb replied, releasing his hand. "I have never seen one of these steamboats."

The man grinned. "Quite an invention. Real nice way to travel the river. You got money?"

Caleb nodded. "I have money that Tom Sax gave me before I left. I did not need it when I lived among the Cheyenne."

"Well, you'll need it in the white man's world, that's for sure. If you've got enough to get you to New Orleans, I expect Jackson volunteers will get paid for helpin', so you can pick up a little gold there."

Caleb turned and mounted his horse, wincing with the pain of his wound, which still gave him trouble at times. "I will leave right away." He looked down at Brady. "I thank you for your trouble." He looked around. "Is it not dangerous for you here?"

"Not so much. The Americans have took back most of this territory, and neither side is much interested in one ole man who's lookin' to just be left alone. Good luck to you, boy. I'm damn sorry about Tom."

Caleb struggled to keep his composure, not wanting to show weakness in front of John Brady. He simply nodded, then turned his horse and headed south.

Twenty-year-old Caleb halted his horse in front of the white fence that surrounded the two-story frame house with blue trim. It was a lovely home, one that could only belong to a wealthy man. Everything was neat and perfect, and Caleb was suddenly hesitant. What would she be like? She was seventeen now, surely sophisticated and educated. Maybe she didn't care if she ever saw him again. But it was only fitting she should know about Tom Sax.

He dismounted and tied the gray gelding and the Appaloosa. He was wearing his best buckskins, bleached nearly white and softened by Walking Grass' expert hands and sewn perfectly. He felt he owed it to Sarah to be as presentable as possible, but he would not wear the white man's clothing that he hated. The buckskins were brightly decorated with red, yellow and blue beads and quills, with a hand-painted eagle on the back. He wore no weapons other than his large hunting knife attached to a beaded leather belt. The handsome blue quill necklace adorned his neck, peeking out from the open ties of his shirt. His hair was clean and tied into two queues with beaded rawhide, and a round beaded hair ornament adorned one side of his hair.

He started toward the house, going through the little white gate and up onto the veranda, mounting the steps and knocking at the front door. There was no answer and he knocked again. Finally the door opened a crack, and his heart leaped without control when familiar green eyes peered out at him. The door opened wider. Her beauty was startling, stirring.

"Sarah?"

Her eyes widened, and her full lips spread in a joyous smile that revealed her even white teeth. "Caleb!"

She flung her arms around his neck, hugging him tightly. She smelled of sweet lilacs, and her long thick hair brushed the backs of his hands as his arms moved around her.

"Oh, Caleb, Caleb! It's really you," she exclaimed. "I don't believe it. You really came."

He didn't know what to say, he was so struck by her beauty and holding her close.

A woman in an apron and cap came into the hallway. "Miss Sarah, what is it?"

Sarah reluctantly released him and turned, wiping at tears. "Joline, this is Caleb. Caleb Sax. The boy I told you was like a brother to me at Fort Dearborn."

The woman in the apron eyed him up and down. "Boy? Appears more like a man to me, and a wild Indian at that."

Sarah looked at Caleb and reddened deeply, breaking into light laughter. "Yes, he is certainly a man." Her eyes glowed.

"You do look wild in these parts, Caleb, but you look wonderful. Such beautiful beadwork!" She took his hand. "Caleb, this is Joline, one of our maids." She didn't even give him a chance to reply. She pulled him along, much as she had done that first day, leading him to the cabin and assuring him everything would be all right. She still held the same sweet innocence, the same joy and love. "Joline, get us something to drink. It's so cold and damp outside. Perhaps Caleb would like some tea."

She led Caleb over highly polished floors into a lovely room decorated with Oriental rugs, paintings and many plants and pretty vases. A fire crackled in a fireplace, and Sarah urged Caleb to sit down on a loveseat covered with mauve taffeta. He felt out of place in such a lovely home and was still at a loss for words. He had not expected her to be so beautiful, and yet still so much like the Sarah who had left Fort Dearborn. She sat down beside him, taking his hand again and holding it tightly between her own.

"Oh, Caleb, I can't believe you've really come. It's been four years! Where have you been?" Her eyes moved over him, and she felt strange new urgings at the sight of him, the magnificent bleached buckskins, his handsome face and rugged, wild look.

"I have been living among the Cheyenne. There is much to tell you, Sarah." He searched her green eyes, eyes he thought he could drown in. "I have a son . . . he is still with the Cheyenne. I could not bring him because he is still small, and I did not know what I would find at Fort Dearborn. He is over two years old now."

Her eyes widened, and she fought a sudden surge of jealousy. "A son?" Of course. She could not blame him. She had her own life now, and he had his. She smiled warmly. "Oh, Caleb, just look at you—you look like a true Indian. Father wrote and told me you killed that awful Kyle Wiggins, and that people were against you and you had to leave Fort Dearborn." She stopped, her eyes quickly tearing. "Surely you know by now that Father is dead."

So Tom had never told her about Emily Stoner. It was just as well, Caleb decided. His eyes filled with sadness. "I know. That is part of the reason I came. I was not sure that you knew. I did not know until only a few weeks ago. He was to meet me . . ." He swallowed, and her heart ached at the tears in his eyes. "But he never came. So I came here to find you."

She squeezed his hand tighter. "Oh, Caleb, I never saw him again either. When we heard about the massacre and that there were some refugees at Fort Wayne, I begged Uncle Terrence to send someone to find out if Father was among them. The man learned that Father and Bo Sanders had both been killed. My only consolation was to know you weren't with them. I've prayed every night since then that somehow, some day, you'd come. Oh, Caleb, it was so terrible. I've been so lonely here, and then never seeing father . . . I wondered if I would ever see another loved one again. And now you're here. It's so wonderful to see you. Tell me about your son, and his mother."

He pulled his hand away and leaned forward, his elbows on his knees. "His mother is dead. Walking Grass was killed in a raid by enemy Indians. We were only married for eleven months when it happened. Our son was still a baby."

She put a hand on his arm. "Oh, Caleb. I'm so sorry."

He looked at her, seeing the sincerity in her eyes. His sweet hearted Sarah. She had not changed. "We have many things to talk about," he told her. "But I am on my way to New Orleans to join the volunteers who will fight the British. I will come back, Sarah, and this time I promise not to take so long."

"Oh, but you must stay a little while—stay for supper, at least. Uncle Terrence and Aunt Mary will be home soon. They must meet you. I've told them so much about you."

Their eyes held, and he felt warm and wonderful and loved. "I will stay that long. I am to get back on a steamboat by dark."

"Oh, Caleb, must you go at all? It will be dangerous.

We've heard about the British coming to New Orleans. There will be thousands of them. What if something happens to you, too? I don't think I could bear it."

He smiled consolingly. "You hardly know me anymore. Even if I did not go, I would have to go back to the Cheyenne because of my son. But I go to fight the British, at least once, to avenge Tom Sax's memory. It will not be the first time I have killed for vengeance. It is my way of facing grief. It's the only way I know. When Walking Grass was killed, I rode on many raids against the Crow, our enemy. I have killed many men, Sarah. Perhaps I should not even be sitting here talking to one so beautiful and civilized."

"Don't be silly, Caleb. You're my brother."

Their eyes held, saying with only a look that there was more between them than sibling love. She reddened slightly, grateful that Joline came in then with a tea tray and two cups.

The maid set them down on a table in front of Sarah and Caleb. "There you are, ma'am."

"Thank you, Joline."

The woman eyed Caleb warily. "Are you all right?"

Sarah laughed, a delightful, lilting sound. "Of course I'm all right. You can go, Joline."

The woman left reluctantly, and Sarah poured Caleb a cup of tea. He took it, the tiny cup feeling awkward in his large hand.

"It must have been terrible for you, Caleb, losing a new wife and being left with a little baby." She picked up her own cup. "Oh, Caleb, tell me about your son. What is his name?"

Caleb sipped some tea and set the cup back on the table. "I named him Tom, after our Tom. He is a strong boy. I miss him."

"Oh, of course you do. Will you go back for him after New Orleans, Caleb?"

He shrugged and sighed. "I do not know right now. First

I will come back here and see you again. Perhaps after that I will stay with the Cheyenne."

She frowned, suddenly not wanting him to go away again, at least not to stay. "Oh, Caleb, life out there must be so dangerous. You should bring your son back here, where he can go to school and have the care of a doctor if he gets sick."

He smiled patiently. "The Indians have been taking care of themselves for hundreds of years without white man's doctors. I am myself just healed from a wound that would probably have killed a white man."

She set her cup aside, concern in her eyes. "Oh, Caleb, what happened? I thought you looked thin."

"My raids against the Crow. I finally was wounded by one of them with a tomahawk in my side. It was very bad. While I lay healing, I thought about Tom, wondered why he never came to meet me as planned. With Walking Grass dead, everything there was too familiar to me and hurt too much. So I decided to return to Fort Dearborn and find out about Tom."

She studied him a moment, thinking how wild and beautiful he looked. It seemed incredible that he was sitting beside her, this young man who had killed enemy Indians in battle. How strange that her sweet Caleb could be so vicious. She saw nothing vicious about him now, but she knew he was strong and skilled, and knew instinctively that he was the kind of man who would risk his life to defend her.

"I miss Tom Sax," he said quietly. "I wanted to talk to him, ask his advice. I have lost so much these last four years."

She wiped at her own quiet tears. "Yes. We both have lost much. And I thought perhaps I'd never see you again. It's been so lonely, Caleb. I never saw Father again, either, and for so long I've wondered about you, remembering the happy days at Fort Dearborn when I helped Mother teach you things."

He studied her, seeing a sadness in her eyes that was more than just the loss of her father and mother. "What is it like here, Sarah?" he asked. "Are you happy?"

She looked at her lap. "It's all right. I mean, Uncle Terrence has been wonderful. I have a closet full of the latest fashions, a good education and all of that. But it isn't nearly as much fun as Fort Dearborn was for me. I miss the little cabin, the deep woods, the big lake. Those were my happiest years." She met his eyes again. "Uncle Terrence didn't seem terribly upset by father's death. I always suspected there were bad feelings between them. Whenever I bring up the subject of Father, Uncle Terrence refuses to talk about him, and that makes me lonelier. But in every other way he's been very kind to me, and so has Aunt Mary. But—" She stopped, reddening again. "Oh, it's silly, and why should you care? You have your son and your own life now."

He frowned, leaning forward and making her look at him again. "What is silly? Is something wrong?"

She shrugged. "Oh, nothing, really. Uncle Terrence is just after me to accompany a certain young man to the theater and such. He's good friends with the young man's father and the two of them want us to marry, I think. But I don't like him. He drinks, and he's arrogant and spoiled. He comes around all the time and I'm not sure how to get rid of him. Uncle Terrence has been so good to me. I don't want to disappoint him."

A surprising jealousy crept into Caleb's heart. Whoever the young man was, he already did not like him. A feeling of protectiveness began to take hold in his blood. This was Sarah, beautiful, sweet, innocent Sarah. She should never go to some man she did not like. He remembered his first night with Walking Grass, how frightened she had been. What if some scoundrel—He suddenly stood, surprised he had thought of it at all.

"Your uncle cannot force you to marry this young man, can he?" he asked, thinking about Fire Wolf.

"Oh, no. I don't think he'd ever do that. It's just that

Byron—that's his name—comes around so often. It's obvious he's interested, and Uncle Terrence thinks it's wonderful."

He turned and looked at her. "Is there something I can do?"

Their eyes held for a moment, then Sarah turned away with a blush. "No. I suppose not. I just wish—" She reddened again and looked at her cup of tea. "I used to wish you would come and maybe take me away somewhere. We've been like brother and sister, and there is no law that says I must stay with Uncle Terrence. I used to wish you would come back to civilization and maybe . . . I don't know, be a rancher or a farmer or something like that. And you'd send for me and we'd live like we used to."

Her eyes met his again, and a wave of desire swept through him so forcefully that he felt guilty. This was Sarah . . . little Sarah.

"I could perhaps try living the white man's way again. But we are not blood brother and sister. I'm sure your uncle would object. Tom meant for you to be raised by him. That is why he sent you here."

She rose, sighing deeply. "I know. It's just that I've missed that life, Caleb, the cabin, helping plant mother's garden and then harvesting and canning the vegetables, sewing our own clothes. I belonged there. Here I don't belong." She met his eyes again. "Do you know what I mean?"

Their eyes held for a long time. "I know. For me it is worse, for in many ways I belong nowhere, neither in this world or the Indian's. But I am more at home in the wilds. I have given much thought to my son, my life. Somehow I must decide what I, too, will do, how I should raise him. But he should have—" He stopped short, feeling suddenly nervous and awkward. "He must have a mother, and I am not ready to feel that way again about any woman."

Her eyes brightened. "I'm like his aunt, Caleb, aren't I? You could go and get your son, and we could all live together. If you aren't ready for a wife again, there would at least be a woman around. And having a loving aunt is just about as close as you can come to a mother."

She looked at him with eyes full of hope. He was struck by the fact that she was totally serious, but suddenly he could not imagine living with her as a sister and brother should. "I don't think—"

The front door burst open. "We're home," a man's voice boomed. The voice reminded Caleb very much of Tom. "Who owns the horse and gear out front? They look In—"

He stopped at the entrance to the parlor, and his face actually paled at the sight of Caleb standing there, looking very Indian, very wild. "Who the hell are you?"

"Uncle Terrence, this is Caleb," Sarah told him excitedly. "Caleb Sax, the young Indian boy I told you father adopted and brought to live with us at Fort Dearborn."

Caleb stared in near shock, for the man greatly resembled his brother. His hair was a bright red but graying, and he sported a red mustache. He was not as burly as Tom Sax, perhaps because he had not led the rugged life that Tom had. A rather plain and plump woman walked up beside the man and gawked at Caleb.

"Hello," Caleb said to them both. "I came to see Sarah. It has been many years, and I was not sure she knew about Tom's death."

Terrence Sax looked him over suspiciously. "Well she does know. And you don't exactly look like the kind of young man who likes civilized places, so I suppose you'll be leaving soon?"

Caleb was shocked by the man's rudeness, but said nothing for Sarah's sake. Sarah reddened at the remark, and Caleb quickly gathered that, although this household was one of wealth and comfort, it did not hold a great deal of warmth and love, two things Sarah Sax had grown up with, things she needed very much.

"I will be," he answered. "I am heading for New Orleans,

to join the volunteers there who will fight under Jackson against the British."

Terrence Sax's eyebrows arched, and the man looked pleased that Caleb would be going into battle. "That so? Well, that's a noble thing to do." He stepped up and put out his hand. Caleb took it, thinking how clammy and thin it was and how easy it would be to throw the man across the room. Terrence turned and put out his hand to the woman. "This is my wife, Mary." He put up both arms then, indicating that Caleb should look around the room. "And this is the home to which Tom Sax sent his daughter to be raised. Surely you can see that we have provided her with a fine home."

Caleb kept his cool, blue eyes on the man. "Yes. It is very nice."

"Nice?" The man chuckled. "Yes, indeed. I have kept my word to Tom to take good care of Sarah." The man put an arm around her. "She wants for nothing, Caleb. So if you are concerned about her as a brother would be about a sister, you have no worries. Where will you go after New Orleans?"

Caleb decided not to mention that he might return to Saint Louis. "I am not sure. I have a son in the west with the Cheyenne. I must go back to him."

Sax looked relieved. "Well, a son! That's very nice. And you look as though you fit that land, more Indian than white, if you know what I mean. I don't have a lot of use for Indians, mind you, or that wild kind of life Tom led. It killed poor Cora." He moved away from Sarah and walked to a buffet where he poured himself a drink. Caleb glanced at Sarah as the man talked, sensing she was more unhappy than she had even let on. "But since Sarah was always so fond of you, you are welcome in our home as her friend and brother. Will you stay for supper?"

"I will stay. Sarah has already invited me. After that I must catch a steamboat to New Orleans."

"Fine. Fine." The man held up a bottle of whiskey. "Would you like a drink? This is some of the best."

Caleb shook his head. "No. I seldom drink the firewater."

"Firewater?" The man laughed heartily. "Firewater! You certainly are Indian."

Caleb could hardly believe the man was Tom Sax's brother. He looked again at Sarah, who blushed at her uncle's rudeness. Terrence Sax made sure after that that Sarah and Caleb had no time to talk alone. He wanted to know all about the "wilderness" and the "wild Indians." Through supper he kept the conversation going, but it hung dangerously when the man accused Tom Sax again of killing Cora. The man obviously disliked Tom greatly, and Caleb did not like his verbal attacks. Caleb wondered at the strange hatred between the two men, but Tom was gone now and would never be able to tell his side, even if Terrence did tell, which he did not seem willing to do. But Caleb did not like it when a person spoke only bad things about a dead man.

It was a tense meal, and Caleb felt the walls closing in on him. He knew he could never live in such a house, a house full of so many rules and manners. He almost felt as though he could not breathe, and he made an excuse to leave sooner than he had planned, saying he was afraid he would miss the steamship. Sax would not leave Sarah's side as Caleb went to the door, and Caleb felt too awkward by then to try to embrace the girl, although he wanted very much to hold her for just a moment and assure her he would come back and help her in any way he could. It seemed strange that she would need any help at all, for she had a good life. But there were some things more important than wealth and material possessions. Sarah was perfectly cared for, but starving for affection, and apparently somewhat afraid of the young man called Byron.

Caleb turned and left, and Sarah went to her room, but as soon as she got inside she closed the door and hurried to double windows that opened out on to a second story terrace. She parted the lacy curtains and climbed out, her old tomboy nature taking over as she threw her legs over the railing around the terrace and climbed down a rose trellis, running over the lawn before calling out Caleb's name. The young man was already mounted and heading down the street. He turned at her voice, then swung his leg over the gray gelding and slid off, walking up to meet her.

They walked behind a hedge and embraced.

"I just wanted to say good-bye alone, Caleb, and wish you good luck."

He pulled away, grasping her arms. "I will come back. If I can help you some way, I will find it. You must decide, Sarah, if you want to stay in Saint Louis or not. I am a man unsettled. But maybe I can think of something."

"Oh, Caleb, after leaving you and father at Fort Dearborn, I've been so lonely. They're good to me, but I'm not happy. I told Father I was in my letters just so he wouldn't worry. When you came to the door today I was never so happy to see someone in my life. Maybe there is nothing you can do, but at least come back once more. Promise me."

Their eyes held, and again he felt strangely possessive. Was it just brotherly concern? The thought of the man named Byron made him angry. "I will come back," he told her. "This is something I must do, and it will give you time to think. Do not be afraid. I will help you if I can."

Her eyes teared, and she leaned up and kissed his cheek. "Thank you, Caleb. I'm so glad you're all right and I've seen you again. God bless you." She turned and hurried off then, looking back once to wave at him.

He watched until she was gone, then remounted his horse. What a strange visit it had been, so much to say and so little time to say it. They had been apart for years, and yet after moments with her it was as though they had not been apart at all. She was still sweet Sarah, but so grown up, so very beautiful. His mind was filled with her as he headed for the docks.

Chapter
Fourteen

EARLY January of 1815 found Caleb marching through a chilly fog that shrouded the Louisiana cypress trees. The dampness made him shiver. He knew that if he were still in the northwest it would be much colder, yet the humidity of this cold air made it seem colder than it was, and he felt like the fog was penetrating his bones.

His horses waited at a livery, and he walked among hundreds of Tennessee volunteers, his long musket slung over his shoulder. Most of the volunteers paid little heed to the quiet, blue-eyed Indian, and Caleb was glad. He didn't want to make friends with any of them. He wanted only to kill some British soldiers, and joining forces with Major General Andrew Jackson was a sure way to meet the enemy. It seemed to Caleb that most men were his enemy in one way or another. But for the moment the British were the most hated enemy, for it was they who helped instigate the attack by the Potawatomi against those who fled Fort Dearborn.

How glad he was that Sarah had been sent away sooner. What if she had been with Tom that day? She was so beautiful, the Indians would have saved her for a slave, and the thought of it made him angrier. Yet if she were his to care for. . . .

He shook away the thought, again reminding himself it was Sarah, his sweet sister. He could not stop thinking about her, worrying about her unhappiness, wondering how in the world he could help her. Surely there was a way, but he knew that Terrence Sax would never let her simply leave and go to live someplace with her Indian stepbrother. He wished he had more to offer her. Then too there was little Tom to think about. He had to go and get the boy.

He missed his baby son. Caleb wanted to get back before the boy had grown too much. He would be the best father he could be, for this son came from Walking Grass, and she would expect him to give the boy only the best. But it was more than that. It was the simple fact that the boy was his son, his own son. It seemed incredible that he had a child. He felt that only now was he realizing the full wonder of it.

He quelled the terrible hurt and sorrow that always engulfed him when he thought of Walking Grass. He must pay attention to the problems at hand. He marched with volunteers preparing to fight the British, and it struck him how savage people could be on the one hand, and how kind on the other. Sometimes friends were enemies, and enemies were really friends. He could only hope he was doing the right thing. It seemed as though the whole world was a matter of survival of the fittest, strength in numbers, like a pack of wolves devouring a single prey. Now he and Jackson's volunteers would be the wolves, the British the prey.

Jackson had been in New Orleans for nearly a month already, and Caleb was among some of the last volunteers who had come to join the impending battle. He pulled a strip of jerky from a pouch at his waist and bit off a piece, wishing there were some way to gather those he loved around him and protect them forever.

His thoughts were interrupted when someone yelled that they were approaching the city. Looking up, Caleb could see people in the streets waiting to cheer them on.

"Make way, boys," someone shouted. "Here comes Ole Hickory!"

Caleb looked up and watched curiously as he stepped back.

"It's Jackson," someone commented.

The man rode through the middle of the volunteers as they entered the city. He had come to greet them, and he stopped often to thank some of them individually for volunteering their lives in America's defense. He seemed to look at each man as his equal, but Caleb had doubts. He was only fighting with this man so he could fight the British. But he was not so sure he supported Andrew Jackson himself. The man had cleverly turned Cherokee against Creek at the Battle of Horseshoe Bend, slaughtering a large number of Creek and promising the Cherokee protection from exile if they helped him. The man was just as adept at turning Indian against Indian as he was at stirring up the Americans against the British, and although he was a great leader and spokesman, and claimed to be a friend of the Indian, Caleb had trouble believing it. If the man was truly for America that meant he was for American settlement and expansion, which meant that some day the Indians would have to go. Whose side would Jackson be on then?

Still, the man's stature demanded respect. He was a big man who rode a big horse. His appearance was commanding in spite of his gaunt and obviously ill condition. His ability to remain in command and keep the motley crew of volunteers together and in order, in spite of his own pain and illness, was an inspiration to Caleb and the others. Caleb supposed that for a white man, Andrew Jackson was a great man, and it was rumored he would be the leader of the entire nation some day.

Everyone there was eager and ready to fight. The British were coming to New Orleans, and when they did, the Americans would be ready. If Andrew Jackson won this battle, it would be one of his greatest victories. They would be facing hundreds, perhaps thousands of Redcoats, but they were ready for a fight. Caleb fought more for his own vengeance than for the Americans. He only hoped it would end soon.

The volunteers and people in the street cheered Jackson, and the air was thick with excitement. Jackson had a way of recruiting men just by inspiration, and had even accepted the aid of pirates led by Jean Laffite. In all, there were about five thousand men ready for battle, surely more than enough to defeat the British.

Led by Jackson, they continued their march into the city. Friendly faces and waving hands greeted them along the way, New Orleans citizens who, up until the last two months, had occupied an almost defenseless city and had worried the British would take the town with little or no opposition. Now Jackson had arrived, and it was a time to celebrate and bask in a victory they had not yet even realized.

Caleb could not help catching the eyes of a few young girls along the way. Some stared back, fascinated by his Indian dress and long hair, not a few of them struck by his tall, rugged handsomeness. In spite of his sorrow over Walking Grass, certain needs were awakened in him, for it had been over two years since her death, and he had not been with a woman since. He had considered visiting one of the many brothels he had heard dotted New Orleans, but the thought of it made him uncomfortable, for he had never quite gotten over the guilt of his sexual encounters with Emily Stoner. Besides, Indians were probably not even allowed in such a place in this white man's world.

His eyes moved from a pretty young girl back to the troops so he would not lose his place in line. Then he glanced back into the crowd again, and it was then he saw her, just as they neared the edge of town and prepared to march into the surrounding marshlands. She stood on the veranda with several women who were very obviously prostitutes, her white-blond hair hanging nearly to her waist. She stood taller than any of the other women and looked thin and gaunt. She wore a purple taffeta dress that dipped low to reveal nearly every inch of her breasts, but his eyes moved quickly to her face again to be sure. Yes. Though part of a black lace shawl concealed one cheek, the pale blue eyes that looked back at him sullenly were familiar. It was Emily Stoner.

She stared back at him with a mixture of shock, guilt and fear, then turned and ran inside the building. Caleb had a sudden urge to break rank and follow her, not sure what he would do when he reached her other than plant his hands around her throat and squeeze until the life went out of her. How he hated her! Because of Emily Stoner he had never seen Tom Sax again. Yet he could not help but wonder what she had been through since that awful day they were caught. After all, she had lived as a slave to the Potawatomi.

Caleb stared so long at the doorway through which Emily disappeared that he stumbled, and the soldier behind him gave him a shove.

"Keep movin', Indian," he joked. "Don't be gapin' at the ladies. They'll come after the fight."

Several men laughed and whistled, some of them joking about how the white whores liked Indians.

Caleb was oblivious to their remarks, still in shock at seeing Emily Stoner standing amid prostitutes and dressed like one. He would most definitely go back to that place when the fighting was over, he decided. There were things to be settled with that one.

There was little time to think of Emily or even Sarah after that, there was only time to make ready to fight. They would be using a new tactic devised by Jackson, and the volunteers were busy preparing that tactic. As Caleb helped dig one of the trenches, he thought Andrew Jackson was a very clever man. The major general intended to line the men up in trenches, one line behind another, so that men would be firing at all times. The first would fire, then duck into the trenches while the next row fired. It was an ingenious idea, and Jackson's leadership abilities could not be denied.

All through the next day orders were shouted, guns were cleaned, and directions given over and over again so the men knew how Jackson's idea should work. First line fires, then reloads while the second line fires, which reloads while the third line fires. A leader for each line would shout when it was their turn to rise and fire again. The result would be continuous firing, in spite of having to take time to reload.

Excitement filled the men's blood with fire like a beckoning woman. The trenches were dug and ready. The air was still and damp on the morning of January 8, 1815, and soon in the distance they could hear the drums of the British soldiers, which scouts had already told them had landed and were coming in. Caleb's heart beat with anticipation and not a little fear, for it was said there could be up to eight thousand Redcoats coming, many more than they had expected.

Jackson kept scouts moving back and forth in the dense fog, keeping track of just how close the British were, for it was impossible to tell. Visibility was poor, and the thick fog distorted sound. Hearing the steadily beating drums to which the British soldiers marched but not being able to see anything made the morning eerie and unreal.

Caleb and the others remained silent, waiting like bobcats ready to spring upon their prey. The waiting seemed an eternity, the drums teasing them, threatening them. They knew that they were greatly outnumbered, but all had confidence in Jackson's ability and in their plan for continuous fire.

Hands tightened on rifles as the sound of the drums seemed so close that they could surely reach out and touch the British, but whispered orders to continue to hold moved up and down the ranks. Finally the first columns of British suddenly emerged from the fog, and shouts of "Fire!" exploded in the first line. Volunteers popped up from their earthen trenches and fired, then quickly ducked down to reload while the next line stood up and fired, then the next and the next.

Gunfire exploded around Caleb's ears, and he trembled with the terrible and wonderful excitement of the moment. This was certainly noisier than Indian fighting, for the Indians did not yet have firearms. The trenches proved an amazingly successful strategy, more perfectly executed than even Jackson had imagined. The British fell like wooden targets amid the cheers and exultant war whoops of the southern volunteers. There was actually laughter among the men as the firing continued, and Caleb guessed there was not an ounce of fear left among them.

The foolish British continued to march according to the rulebook, approaching the Americans in columns and being mowed down like long grass cut with a scythe. By the time the fighting was over, three hundred British were dead, well over a thousand wounded and at least five hundred more captured, with minimal American casualties.

Caleb guessed he had killed at least ten Redcoats himself, aside from those he had wounded, and he hoped that wherever Tom Sax was, he knew. But the thought of the man brought a sharp pain to his heart, and he did not feel the wonderful joy of vengeance he thought he would feel. Killing the British had not brought back Tom Sax, just as his raids against the Crow had not brought back Walking Grass.

His vengeance soured even more when he saw that many of the wounded and dead soldiers he helped pick up were mere boys, many of whom looked much younger than he. He felt a sudden admiration for them, realizing it had taken great courage for them to continue marching toward the constantly firing volunteers.

Caleb's emotions were in a turmoil. He had fought the British in anger over what had happened to Tom, yet the very Americans with whom he served would surely one day bring great sorrow to the Indian. Where did it stop? Who was really right? And what would happen to the Indian in the end? Already many eastern Indians had been exterminated through greed and disease and exile. Many of them had filtered into western lands, hoping to find a place where the white man would not go.

All around him volunteers joked and laughed, talking about how America belonged to them and that the British could get out and stay out.

"We showed them that once," one man bragged, holding up his musket. "Then the damn fools tried to fight us again. When will they learn?"

"It's God's plan, I tell you," another shouted. "One day we'll own this country from the Atlantic to the Pacific."

There was more laughter, and Caleb hung back. He realized that the cause of his worst anguish was Emily Stoner. Maybe things would have been different if he had not had to flee Fort Dearborn. He decided then that he was through with this army. He would get his pay and go back to find Emily.

An attractive French woman opened the door to the brothel, looking Caleb over with appreciative eyes. "I am afraid we do not service Indians here, *monsieur*."

Caleb removed his floppy leather hat, feeling awkward in his fringed buckskins. "I do not wish such service. I only want to see someone who works here, talk to her."

The woman's eyebrows arched, and she smiled. "Talk? I am not in business for friendly conversations, *monsieur*." She started to close the door, but Caleb put out his hand and stopped her.

"Please. I want to see Emily Stoner. I know she works here. I saw her standing on your steps when we marched through here."

She looked him over carefully again. "You were a volunteer? You helped win that fight?"

"Yes, ma'am."

She shrugged. "Well, you do have blue eyes." She stepped back and let him enter. "Why would you want to 'just talk' with our Emily?"

"I knew her at Fort Dearborn years ago."

The woman frowned. "And you have not seen her since?"
"No."

She folded her arms. "That one, she suffered much at the hands of the Indians, you know." She looked him over as though wondering if he was some savage come to do the girl more harm.

"I heard," he replied. "I assure you, I simply want to talk to her. Could you please tell her I am here? My name is Caleb Sax."

The woman eyed him a moment longer, then nodded slowly. "I will tell her, but if she does not want to see you, you must leave. I have men here who will make you leave if necessary. And if you bed her, you had better pay like everybody else."

Caleb nodded in agreement, hardly able to believe the once-sheltered Emily Stoner lived in a place like this, selling her body to men. The French woman ascended a curving stairway, and Caleb looked around the exotic entranceway. A thick red carpet led down a hallway, and from one room he could hear women and men laughing, a piano playing, glasses clinking. He walked closer to the sounds, unable to help his curiosity.

He moved close enough to the arched open entrance of the room to see inside, where several men sat around tables gambling and drinking. Smoke filled the room, and half dressed women catered to the men. His eyes widened at the sight of them, some pretty, some not so pretty, all looking hard and used, their faces painted, their clothes sparkling and brightly colored. He had heard of such women, but this was the first time he had seen them so close. He thought what a contrast they were to the chaste Indian maidens and women like Sarah Sax. These women fascinated him, but he had no desire or respect for them, and it seemed incredible that Emily was really one of them.

A man and woman sat on a velvet loveseat kissing. The man's hand moved over the woman's generously exposed breasts, then dipped inside the low cut dress to caress her breast fully. The woman giggled. "Wait till we get to the room," she chided, pulling his hand away. "It won't be much longer, honey. Carla is changing the bedding."

Again old needs stirred in him, but he did not want to meet them in this place.

"*Monsieur*," the French woman called from above, "do not look unless you are willing to pay."

Caleb looked up, embarrassed at being caught watching, and the woman laughed. In that moment he hated her, hated all of them. He felt suddenly stifled and out of place, and longed for the freedom of the forest.

"She says you may come up as long as you mean her no harm," the French woman said. "Her customer is leaving now."

Customer. The thought brought a sick feeling to Caleb's stomach. He moved up the stairs, and a well-dressed man passed him, turning and shouting up to the French woman, "Thanks, Marie. She was everything you said she'd be."

Caleb watched the man descend and go out the door, then looked up at Marie, who stood there smiling. "Remember now. If you get a piece of her, you pay."

He wanted to hit the woman, but held himself in check, following her to one of several doors along the hallway. She knocked, and a soft voice told her to come in. Marie opened the door and motioned for Caleb to go inside.

Caleb went in, and his nose twitched at the smell of cheap perfume and the lingering odor of heated bodies and love-making—if it could be called lovemaking. The bed was in disarray, and a woman with long blond hair stood at a washbasin, her back to him. She wore a soft green shift of a very thin material, and he could see the outline of her hips beneath it, the slim dark shadow of the center of her naked bottom.

She turned then, her eyes widening at his handsome, manly stature. A myriad of emotions ran through both of them. Caleb's blue eyes drifted over her slender form. The robe was so thin he could see her nipples and the patch of hair between her thighs. Some of her blond hair fell over one side of her face, nearly covering one eye and cheek, and it was tangled and damp.

"Hello, Caleb," she said in a sultry voice. "I knew you'd come."

He just stared at her.

She swallowed. "You look . . . wonderful. I always knew you'd turn into a marvelously handsome young man." Her eyes moved over his magnificent build, coming to rest again on his beautiful face and blue eyes. She could not quite read his eyes. Were they full of hatred? Pity? Contempt? It seemed to be all those things and more.

"Do you want me to stay, or send up a guard?" Marie asked.

Emily held Caleb's eyes steadily. "No," she finally answered. "You can close the door, Marie."

The woman left, and Caleb stood there wondering why he had come at all. Emily folded her arms, watching him carefully.

"Well? Say your piece, Caleb. Surely you have some reason for coming, probably to tell me how much you hate me for getting you into all that trouble." She sauntered to a nightstand and picked up a thin cigar, lighting it and taking a puff, turning and facing him again, holding the cigar in her hand. "I don't blame you, but I had little choice at the time. I was deathly afraid of my father." She took another puff on the cigar, walking to a window. "Dear God, how I hated him!" She whirled. "You were lucky, you know. All you got was one beating and then you could leave and never come back. I never had that privilege."

His eyes softened a little as she moved to another table, pouring herself a drink. He wasn't sure at the moment whether to hate her or feel sorry for her. If not for her cruel father, she might have turned out differently.

"Do you want a drink, Caleb?"

"No," he finally spoke up. "Whiskey and Indians do not mix. Nor, I suppose, do Indians and white women."

His words were bitter. She sighed, quickly drinking down her own shot and setting the glass back down. "I'm sorry, Caleb," she said, meeting his eyes. "I really am."

He stepped closer, his eyes still unreadable. "Because of your trick, I never saw Tom Sax again," he hissed. "I had to leave him alone and lonely, and then he was killed! Maybe if I had been there—"

"If you had been there you would have died with the rest of them," she interrupted coldly. "Don't be a fool, Caleb! What happened would have happened whether you were there or not. Do you really think your presence would have changed anything? Could you have fought off all those Indians single-handedly? No one escaped that day, Caleb. No one. It was either death right then, death by torture, or enslavement. I should know. That's where I got this."

She flung back her hair, exposing the cheek it had hidden. An ugly, wrinkled scar ran from her cheekbone back to her ear, and from the temple down to her jawbone. Caleb's eyes widened in shock at the terrible disfigurement, and he felt his hatred vanishing.

"Pretty, isn't it?" she commented, turning back and pouring herself another drink. "You being there wouldn't have changed a thing. You'd just be dead now. I'm sure Tom Sax would have wanted it this way, you still alive." She swallowed the whiskey. "They took me for a slave, because of my youth and my light hair, I suppose. Then one of them decided to make me his wife—after several others had sampled me, of course. I had no choice in the matter. The one who 'wed' me was cruel, but I put up with him because I knew I'd be killed if I didn't. Then my 'husband' decided to make sure none of the other men would mess with me, and he proceeded to brand me with a hot coal while I was tied and helpless. He said it was his mark, that I belonged to him, like a man's horse."

The words came out bitterly, and Caleb's angry heart turned to pity. He stepped closer behind her, reaching out and hesitantly touching her hair. "I am sorry, Emily."

She laughed with a note of sarcasm. "Well, then, we both have something to be sorry for, don't we?" She shrugged and stepped away. "You had a right to hate me. I took advantage of your young, budding emotions. You weren't the only one, you know, nor the first. You just thought you were." She turned to face him, her eyes and smile hard. "I suppose by now you're schooled in the ways of women and are no longer the eager boy who came to see me in the barn."

He smiled sadly. "I have been living among the Cheyenne. I took a wife. She was killed, but she left me with a little son. I will go back for him soon."

Some of the brittleness in her eyes vanished and she nodded. "I'm sorry she died, but it's nice that you have son."

He looked around the room. "Why this, Emily? Your father is dead now. you can make a life for yourself."

She threw back her head and laughed. "What kind of life do you think someone like me can have? What decent man would have a woman who was an Indian captive and branded to boot?" She sauntered away from him, still laughing. "I fooled them good, Caleb. You'd have been proud of me— a real warrior. One night while my Indian husband slept, I decided I couldn't take another day in that filth, never knowing what he'd do to me next. So I took his hunting knife and I plunged it right into his heart." She tossed her hair as she whirled to face him again. "It felt wonderful! I'm sure you know the feeling of such victory." She ran a hand through her tangled hair. "And then I ran, just as hard and fast as I could run, through the dark forest with no idea where I was going. For some reason they never bothered coming after me." She walked over and poured herself yet another drink. "At any rate, I was dirty and wore only a tunic. I had nothing. The first place I stumbled on to was a farm, run by an old widowed man." She met his eyes again. "He helped me get farther east. He said he knew a woman who would help me. And she did. But she was a madam. Thus my illustrious career began." She stepped closer. "But it's not so bad, Caleb. I have a feeling I'd have turned out this way in spite of the Indians. I was already doing it back at the fort for free. It was the only way I could show my father just how much I hated him. I hope he's up there on his golden throne looking down and choking on his own vomit!"

He grasped her arms. "Come away from here, Emily. You do not need to do this."

She laughed again, the strange, insane look coming into her eyes that he remembered from the first day she had visited him at the fort. She grasped his wrists. "Caleb, sweet Caleb. Right now you remind me of that boy I knew years ago." Her eyes softened. "I can't leave here, Caleb. My life can never be any different. You just go on back to the Cheyenne and your little boy and forget you ever found me." She reached up around his neck then, breathing deeply of his manly scent. "Unless you first want to refresh your memory on what it was like to make love to me.".

Their eyes held and he was tempted. But he could not quite totally forgive her for what she had done at Fort Dearborn and making him leave Tom Sax. And for some strange reason, Sarah again crept into his mind and heart. Sarah would think it terribly wrong for him to bed this whore: that was all Emily Stoner was now—or ever had been, for that matter. He needed a woman, but he could not bring himself to lie with this one. There were too many bad memories.

He pushed her away, keeping hold of her arms for a moment. "I wish you would leave here and change all this," he told her. "But it is your choice. I cannot make your decisions for you. I must leave now. I am going to Saint Louis to see Sarah Sax again before going to get my son."

She struggled to hide the disappointment in her eyes, for she wanted to be bedded by him again, remembering how much he'd had to offer as a boy and knowing he surely had much more to offer as a man.

"Sure," she answered. She sighed deeply as she followed him to the door. "What will you do after you get your son, Caleb Sax? Stay out in the wilds forever? There are a few better things you could do with your life, too, you know."

Caleb shrugged. "Perhaps." He thought of Sarah again, suddenly anxious to see her. "I am not sure."

Their eyes held and hers teared a little. "Well, I suppose we'll never see each other again."

He touched the scar with the back of his hand. "I suppose. Good-bye, Emily Stoner."

She smiled sadly. "Good-bye, Caleb. Good luck."

He saw a sudden, horrible loneliness in her eyes, and he was compelled to reach out and embrace her. They clung together in a moment of remembered childish fears and disappointments, two young people whose lives had been led by fate to their own particular sorrows and losses.

"I'm glad you came, Caleb."

"I am glad, too. Good-bye." He pulled back, giving her a reassuring smile, then turned and left. She watched him go down the stairs and out the front door, then closed her own door and walked to her bed, covering her face with her hands and bursting into tears. Moments later Marie was at the door.

"I have another customer for you, Emily," the woman yelled from outside. "You ready for him?"

Emily sniffed and stood up, wiping at her eyes. "Sure," she answered in a shaking voice. "Send him in." She quickly tossed her hair around to hide the scar.

Chapter Fifteen

IT was a wonderfully warm day for February, even in Missouri, and Sarah's birthday party was moved to the back lawn. There had been very little precipitation that winter, and that combined with a warm break in the weather left the lawn in fine shape for dancing.

Terrence Sax had spared no expense preparing the party. His niece's eighteenth birthday was an occasion to show off his wealth. All of Sarah's friends were invited, as were many of his own. A small band was hired, and they even brought a piano, the instrument loaded up on a wagon and driven to the Sax residence.

Sarah was almost embarrassed by all the fuss, but Terrence Sax insisted it was the least he could do. After all, turning eighteen was like announcing she had become a woman. But Sarah did not miss the eagerness in his voice when he talked about how soon she would be marrying. She knew who he would like her to marry, and she wanted nothing to do with Byron Clawson. But as Terrence kept telling her, Byron was the "most promising young man in town," with a "great future ahead of him, probably in politics."

Sarah didn't really care. Byron Clawson was not the kind of young man she wanted to marry, Harvard degree or not. He was nearly seven years her senior, and never failed to let her know he'd had many women already, as if the knowl-

edge would impress her. Sarah didn't believe much of what
Byron told her. He was arrogant and always had whiskey
on his breath, and something about him frightened her.

What surprised her was that when she really thought about
the kind of man she'd like to marry, she always thought of
Caleb. She missed him desperately, and found she could
think of little else but seeing him again.

She was not in the mood for a party. She could not help
wondering if Caleb had been wounded or even killed in
New Orleans. How would she ever know? And what if he
was never coming back? What would she do about Byron
Clawson? It seemed like a situation she could not fight, but
when she thought of Caleb she felt better, somehow protected. Caleb would surely think of some way to help her.
But he still hadn't come, and she was growing fearful.

As she cut her birthday cake amid the laughter and talking
of the crowd around her, she barely heard the small band
or noticed the well-dressed people on the beautifully man-
icured lawn. Sarah moved away slightly from Byron, who
had obviously been drinking before he arrived. He had been
more attentive all afternoon than Sarah would have preferred. She felt like she was always running away from him.
There was no use complaining to her uncle, for he had very
happily shaken hands with Byron when the young man
arrived earlier, and he had been eyeing the two of them
eagerly all day.

It wasn't that Byron was ugly, although he was far from
handsome. She could bear his thin frame and beady, gray
eyes and even his long, sharp nose, if only he were not so
cocky, and if only his hands were not so cold when he
touched her. He wore his thick, blond hair in natural waves
combed back from his face and held in place with something
greasy, and she dreaded the thought of ever kissing his thin
lips.

She was glad when a girlfriend pulled her away to open
presents, while others served the cake and Byron Clawson
took another drink from a tray one of the maids was carrying.

Sarah opened gifts of perfume and jewelry and gloves, clothing, and from her Aunt Mary a short fur jacket. Finally came a small box from her Uncle Terrence. She opened it to find an exquisite diamond necklace.

"Oh, Uncle Terrence, it's beautiful," she exclaimed. The man took it from the box and fastened it around her neck. "How can I ever thank you?"

The man leaned closer and spoke quietly into her ear. "You can thank me by being nicer to Byron," he answered. "Everyone can see how you're avoiding him. It isn't very nice of you, Sarah, dear. He's very interested, you know. You're the first young lady he's been this serious about."

She turned to face him, kissing his cheek. "But I don't like him. Can't you tell he's been drinking?"

The man only chuckled, patting her shoulder. "All men drink a little, darling. You just have a lot to learn about men. Come now. Make your old uncle happy and give him a little more attention. Give him a chance, Sarah."

She sighed and looked down, putting her fingers to her necklace. "All right—just for tonight." She looked at him and smiled then. "And thank you for the necklace."

Byron approached them, grinning at her with the leering smile she hated. "How about a short stroll, Sarah, dear?" he asked before looking at Terrence. "You don't mind, do you, sir?"

Terrence met Sarah's pleading eyes, but warned her with his own that she had made a promise. "Of course not," he answered.

Byron thanked the man and took Sarah by the arm, guiding her toward a pathway that led through a thick stand of trees behind the Sax home. She followed unwillingly, not wanting to make a scene at her own birthday party. Others watched and whispered about how lucky Sarah Sax was to be eyed by the wealthy Byron Clawson, the most eligible bachelor around, but Sarah did not feel lucky at all.

Byron led her along the pathway, grinning as he babbled about the warm weather. He led her down a little embankment to a place where a creek flowed and they were out of sight of the crowd. Byron took the opportunity to slip his arm about Sarah's waist, jerking her around and pulling her tightly against himself, startling her with the sudden movement. She tried to pull away, but the movement only seemed to excite him. He laughed as he backed her against the trunk of a large tree.

"Sarah, Sarah," he told her in a husky voice. "Don't you want to be sophisticated like the women back East?"

She turned her face away from his whiskey breath, terrified he would try to kiss her. "I don't know what you mean. Please let me go, Byron."

She gasped when he nuzzled at her neck, gripping her wrists behind her so tightly that she was helpless. The tree bark was rough and painful at her back. "You're eighteen, Sarah, and you've never been with a man, have you? That's all that's wrong, Sarah dear. But I can teach you."

"Please, Byron—"

He quickly moved his mouth to hers, kissing her so forcefully that it hurt her lips. She twisted her face until finally he left her lips, but he kept her backed against the tree while his mouth moved down over her neck, searching for her young breasts, kissing the skin exposed by the green silk dress she wore.

She struggled even harder then, her voice rising. "Byron, stop it," she whimpered. "I'll scream!"

He raised his head, grinning. "You won't scream and make a scene at your own party. Your problem, Sarah, is that you're just afraid. Oh, I don't mean to get under your skirts right here, but the next time I take you out, we could go to a hotel—"

"There won't be a next time," she hissed, struggling furiously. "You're drunk! You're always drunk. And I can't stand you. Now let go of me, Byron Clawson."

He only gripped her tighter, his gray eyes narrowing. "You haughty little bitch. You scream and I'll tell them all you were the one who tried to seduce me, that you flaunted yourself and tempted me and then made a scene. I'll make you look like the worst little whore in Saint Louis." He shook her. "Why don't you admit that you want to go to bed with Byron Clawson and be done with it, little Miss Sax? Are you that concerned about your reputation? Or maybe you really are teasing me on purpose."

He tried to kiss her again, but suddenly a strong arm circled his neck from behind, jerking his head and yanking him backward so hard that he was forced to let go of Sarah. He was dragged farther back, and a knife flashed in front of Byron's eyes before coming to rest against his cheek.

"Do not ever touch her again, or I will kill you," a man's voice hissed. "And you will not die quickly."

The knife moved away and Byron was shoved so hard that he fell to his knees.

Sarah stared in surprise, watching as Caleb Sax re-sheathed his knife and walked toward her, a look of determined possession on his face. He wore his usual Indian garb, his hair pulled into one thick braid at the side. Their eyes held a moment, and his look of possession was matched by her own feelings of belonging.

"Are you all right, Sarah?"

She swallowed and nodded, still shaking, while Byron got to his feet, his face beet red with anger. "Who the hell are you?" he growled at Caleb.

Caleb turned, the warning look in his icy blue eyes putting fear in Byron Clawson's heart. "I am Caleb Sax. Sarah and I were like brother and sister at Fort Dearborn, and I do not like seeing her hurt. She said she does not like you, so leave her alone. If you were a Cheyenne you would die for touching a maiden that way, and if we were not in a civilized place, I would gladly do the killing."

Byron straightened, trying to appear unafraid by holding up his chin haughtily. "Hurt me and you'll hang, Indian! I'm important in this town and so is my father. You can't come here and threaten me and tell me whether I can or can't touch a woman."

Caleb stepped closer, towering over him. "Can't I, white eyes?" In a split second his knee rammed up between the man's legs, making Byron buckle with pain. "You will not say anything about this, Byron Clawson, and you will not touch Sarah again," Caleb warned, kneeling close to be sure the man heard him. "Because if you do, you will always have to walk looking over your shoulder. You will never know when I will come for you, just as today you did not know was I was near. I am in the shadows, in the wind. I have killed many men, so why should I stop with a useless coward like you? I suggest that when you are able to walk you go home. Sarah will make an excuse for you."

Caleb rose then, leaving Byron bent over and groaning. He took Sarah's arm and led the trembling girl farther along the creek to a place where they could climb back up the embankment without being seen by the others. Then he embraced her. "I am sorry. I did not want to be violent in front of you, but he made me angry."

She broke into tears and hugged him tightly. "I'm just glad you came. Oh, Caleb, I was so afraid something had happened to you in New Orleans. I thought you weren't coming back."

"I just arrived to visit you again. When I noticed all the people I was sure I would not be completely welcome, so I held back, watching you, and saw that excuse of a man take you into the trees. I almost didn't follow. I thought perhaps you would rather I didn't, but I was afraid he was the one you told me about, and when I saw him hurting you, I knew he was."

She raised her tear stained face to look at him, and he suddenly wanted nothing more than to kiss her himself, but he held back. This was Sarah. It was not right to have these strange, wonderful feelings for her. It was not right to be so jealous at the sight or even the thought of some other man tasting her lips, feeling her full breasts against his chest as he could feel them now.

He wiped the tears on her face. "Go back to your party.

You had better go in the house and wash your face first. Tell them Byron got sick from too much whiskey and decided to go home. Tomorrow I will come to see you. When is a good time?"

She dropped her eyes, confused by the new desires he stirred in her. "You'd better come after five, when Uncle Terrence is there. He'd be angry if you came earlier."

"It is hard to talk with your uncle around."

She met his eyes again. "It's better than not seeing you at all. Maybe if he gets to know you better, he'd at least consider the idea of you and I . . ." She blushed and pulled away slightly. "You and I going somewhere together, to ranch or farm or something. I'm sure he wants me to be happy." She sighed and shook her head. "What am I saying? Uncle Terrence would never allow it." She looked at him pleadingly. "Maybe you can at least make him understand how much I hate Byron, Caleb. If he would just stop pushing Byron Clawson on me life wouldn't be so unbearable. And I would so love to go live in the country again, and maybe have some animals and . . . and I would love to see your little boy, Caleb."

He smiled reassuringly. "I will talk to him. He does not own you, Sarah. He is only your uncle. He was supposed to watch over you and give you protection until you were of age. But all that is over now, and I am just as capable of caring for you and protecting you as anyone. All I have to do is get myself settled somewhere. Go on back to the house now."

He took her arm again, and she looked up at him. "Thank you so much, Caleb. You took a chance. Byron won't forget this, and he has a lot of influence in this city, or at least his father does."

Caleb's eyes turned icy again. "He knows what will happen if he makes trouble, for me or you." He led her closer to the house. "You should not be seen with me, not today. I will leave you here."

He hesitated, then could not resist bending down and kissing her cheek. "I will see you tomorrow."

He left quickly, and she stared after him, her heart suddenly lighter. She had no idea what either of them would do or how she would ever convince her uncle to let her go on her own. She only knew she suddenly didn't care about Saint Louis or the riches Terrence Sax could give her. She cared only about a warm little cabin surrounded by plowed fields and grazing animals, and a strong but gentle man who would love her and take care of her.

Caleb arrived on time the next day, dressed in cotton pants and a clean white shirt topped with a leather jacket, white man's clothing he had purchased with some of his pay for volunteering at New Orleans. None of the men had expected compensation, but the citizens of New Orleans had contributed what they could in gratitude, and the till had added up to quite a bit of money, enough to keep a man going for a couple of months if he was frugal.

Sarah smiled warmly when she opened the door, impressed and surprised by his appearance, thinking him the most handsome man in all of Saint Louis. She was glad he had not cut his hair, for she liked it just the way it was, long and thick and beautiful. Caleb would not be Caleb without long hair. She gave him a sly smile as she pretended to be surprised to see him.

"Caleb!" She turned away, calling back into the house, "Uncle Terrence, Caleb Sax has come back."

She ushered him inside and closed the door as Terrence Sax came out of the parlor. The older man looked Caleb over suspiciously before smiling stiffly.

"Well, you made it through, I see. I heard some pretty exciting stories about New Orleans. Did you get to meet Andrew Jackson?"

The man put his hand out and Caleb shook it. "Yes, sir. He is quite a leader. And my ears still ring from all the guns exploding around me. It is something I will remember for a long time."

"I can imagine." Sax looked from Caleb to Sarah's eager face, then back to Caleb. "So, you've come to see Sarah once more before going back out into the wilds?"

Caleb held the man's eyes steadily. "Yes. But I may stay in Saint Louis a little while longer than I had planned. Sarah and I were great friends at Fort Dearborn, and I love her like a sister. I would like your permission to visit her as often as I can until I leave. I feel it is my responsibility to Tom Sax to make very sure she is happy before I leave."

Sax's eyes hardened and his jaw flexed in repressed anger. "Why shouldn't she be happy? She has everything."

"I did not mean to offend you, Mr. Sax. I did not even mean that I thought she was not happy. It's just that we hardly had a chance to talk the last time I was here. I fully intend to go back to my son, but after so many years apart, I would simply like to talk to Sarah a little more before I go. We share many good memories as well as some bad ones. Cora and Tom were her parents, and they were like parents to me."

Their eyes held challengingly, and Terrence Sax quickly surmised that the surest way to make Sarah more interested in this man would be to insult him and throw him out in front of her. He would tell Caleb Sax just what he thought, but he would tell him without Sarah present. He would make sure Caleb Sax left Saint Louis soon.

"I understand," he said cooly. "And because you were once close as children, I don't see why you can't visit while you're here. Just how long *do* you intend to stay in town, Caleb?"

Caleb forced a friendly smile. "I do not even know. I am anxious to get back to my son."

The man breathed a sigh of relief. "Of course. Well, do come into the parlor. I'll have Joline set an extra place and you shall have supper with us again."

"I really should not. You do not need—"

"Nonsense. Think no more about it."

The man walked toward the kitchen, and Sarah led Caleb quickly into the parlor. "I do not think we will have much chance to talk," he told her quietly.

"I know." Her beautiful green eyes danced with the teasing excitement he remembered seeing there when she was a little girl. "But at least you're here, and he's agreed to let you visit. You can tell us all about New Orleans, Caleb, and I want to know more about your life with the Cheyenne. You can at least talk about those things."

Their eyes held and he smiled. It felt so good to be near her.

Sarah was restless and unable to sleep, her mind filled with thoughts of Caleb Sax. She tried to envision him riding against the Crow, fighting wild Indians. How strong and fearless he was. It was exciting to think of the kind of life he had led, to realize the young man she called friend had truly lived with the Cheyenne and had married an Indian, going through the horrible Sun Dance sacrifice to prove his worth.

Yet the thought of Caleb with a pretty Indian maiden brought forth a jealousy so fierce it surprised her. Why did it bother her to think of Caleb holding and kissing an Indian woman, a woman who bore his child? The idea of making love frightened and fascinated her. Sarah had always thought it would be terribly humiliating, and yet the idea of doing something like that with Caleb made her whole body tingle. Somehow she could picture it, for Caleb would be so gentle and kind, and afterward she would truly belong to him.

She gasped at her own thoughts, sitting up and shaking her head in an effort to clear her mind. How terrible to envision herself with Caleb that way, and yet the picture came so easily. The way he had looked at her tonight had made her blush and stirred wonderful feelings deep in her soul. Was it possible she was in love with Caleb, the way a woman loved a man she married? Perhaps she had always loved him, even when they first met as children. Perhaps she just hadn't recognized it because she was so young.

She put a hand to her stomach and got up, walking to a window to look out at the moon. It was wrong to feel this way, not just because she should be thinking of him as a brother, but because he would leave in a short time. She knew by her uncle's attitude that he would not even consider letting her leave with Caleb, no matter how honorable Caleb's intentions. She could not bear the thought of his leaving, perhaps never to return this time. The idea made her feel like crying. Perhaps Caleb would go back and marry another Indian woman. Somehow that hurt more than anything, and again she felt filled with love for him as she stood looking out at the stars.

Just the thought of Caleb brought a warmth to her blood and a flutter to her heart. The Caleb who had returned was not the Caleb she had left at Fort Dearborn. He was mature, a man in every way, so much more manly than someone like Byron Clawson could ever be. The thought of Byron made her shudder. She had not seen him since the birthday party, but he lurked in the shadows of her life like a monster ready to pounce. Sarah feared that if and when Caleb left, Byron would spring, insisting on being permitted to marry her. Surely Caleb would not let that happen. Surely he felt for her the way she was beginning to feel for him, more than brother and sister, much more than friends. So much more.

Down the hall from Sarah's room her uncle angrily tossed his slippers and sat down on the edge of the bed.

"He'll be gone before long," Mary assured him.

"He'll be gone, all right," Terrence Sax grumbled. "I'll make sure of it."

"Oh, Terrence, how do you intend to do that?"

"I'll go and talk to him, that's what. I'll find out where he's staying and go talk to him." He stood up and paced. "That half-breed bastard can't come here and walk right into Sarah's life like he owns her. I'll not allow it. Did you see the look in her eyes tonight?"

"I saw. But he's practically a wild Indian, Terrence, not the settling type. Stop worrying. He has a son living with the Indians. That will pull him away eventually. If you interfere you'll only make matters worse."

"Oh no I won't. I'm going to prevent this situation from getting worse! I'll—"

"You'll do what?" His wife's eyes narrowed angrily. "You're awfully good at sticking your nose in people's lives and ruining them, Terrence Sax. You did it to Tom and Cora. Wasn't that enough?"

He turned and glowered at her, his face red with anger. He wanted to hit her, tell her to shut up. But his own guilt and the knowledge that Mary was right always kept him from doing so. She turned over in bed, and Terrence left the room.

He hesitated at Sarah's bedroom door. Perhaps he should tell her everything, talk to her, make her understand why he wanted the best for her. But she would never understand. He walked down the stairs to the library and poured himself a drink, contemplating how to approach Caleb Sax and make him leave town.

Chapter
Sixteen

CALEB had never felt so confused. Considering the opportunities Sarah had in Saint Louis, perhaps it was best he simply leave her to her uncle. It would not be so difficult but for Byron Clawson, who he had no doubt would try his way with Sarah again once Caleb was gone. But leaving Sarah had become more than a matter of worrying about Byron Clawson. Her angelic face continued to haunt him in the night, old needs combining with a startling awareness of her beauty and womanhood to make sleep impossible.

He sat up and lit an oil lamp. He had rented a small room in a boarding house, the woman who ran it eyeing him warily as though she feared she would be scalped. She had promptly warned him that she had no use for Indians and he'd better watch himself or she'd have the law on him. The idea of staying in such a bigoted place didn't appeal to him, but he had to stay until he decided what to do about Sarah. But what could he do? He was one young, poor Indian against a very powerful, wealthy white man, and in Caleb's mind Sarah was like a lamb surrounded by wolves. Terrence Sax apparently wanted the best for her, so much so that not even her own happiness mattered.

He rose and lit a pipe, puffing it a moment, the four walls of the room bringing on the suffocating feeling such places often did to his restless spirit.

He had to figure out what his true feelings were for Sarah. When he had first come to see her, he had not thought of her as a beautiful young woman with a heart and spirit any man could love. When he contemplated it, it seemed she'd be a perfect mother for Tom, the perfect solution to his own confused life. Caleb wasn't a man who could settle in a city, surrounded by civilization. Sarah would be willing to settle on a ranch or farm in the country. An Indian woman would consider nothing other than staying with her people. Sarah seemed liked the answer to his questions about how to live out his life, how to raise young Tom. They could have a little of both worlds, live where he could feel free, yet with enough civilization to suit Sarah.

"My God," he whispered, taking the pipe from his mouth. "What am I thinking?"

Again he was envisioning Sarah as his wife. There had been moments when he even allowed the fantasy of what it would be like to make love to her take over, and more than once the raging jealousy and anger had returned at the thought of some other man doing that to her.

A knock at the door interrupted his thoughts and he set his pipe aside, pulling out his hunting knife from the weapons belt that hung on a hook.

"Who is it?" he asked.

"Terrence Sax," came the reply.

Caleb frowned, amazed the man was still up at this late hour. He opened the door cautiously, not fully trusting the man. Sax stood outside looking anxious. "What do you want?"

"I want to talk to you. May I come inside?"

Caleb looked past the man but saw no one. He opened the door and let Sax inside, then closed the door and bolted it. He turned to see Sax looking around the small, plain room with disdain. The man faced Caleb then, looking him over. Caleb wore only his leggings. Sax studied the scars left from the Sun Dance, and the deep, white scar in Caleb's side where the Crow warrior had slashed him with his tomahawk. His eyes moved to Caleb's face, handsome but still bearing the thin white scar left by Kyle Wiggins.

"Your many scars say it all, Caleb," the man finally said.

"I do not understand."

"They only show the kind of man you are, wild and untrustworthy." The man sighed deeply. "I've come to ask you to leave Saint Louis right away—tomorrow if possible. I am willing to pay you."

Caleb's deep blue eyes turned cold and calculating. "I want none of your money. Is that what you think I came here for?"

The man's eyebrows arched. "Isn't it?"

Caleb sneered. "You white men are all alike. You think only in terms of money. I do not understand how you and Tom Sax could have been brothers. You are alike in looks, but inside you are very different."

Sax's eyes narrowed angrily. "Forget about Tom. He's dead. And I'm asking you to forget about Sarah. I want you to leave, Caleb, before the girl gets . . . ideas."

"Ideas?"

"You know what I'm talking about. I saw how she looked at you earlier this evening. You're like a God to her." The man stepped closer. "All right, let's say I believe you when you say you aren't here for money. God knows Indians have about as much sense about money as an ape. But Indian or white, you're a man, and I've seen you watch her. I know what you're thinking, and you'd best get it out of your mind, understand?"

Caleb looked him over, folding his powerful arms across his chest. "What do you fear, Mr. Sax? Sarah is as dear to me as if she were my own sister. I mean her no harm."

"No harm?" The man turned and walked to the window, staring out a moment before turning back to face Caleb. "If you stay around, Caleb, it will involve more than brother and sister. We both know it, so forget trying to avoid the issue. You're bad for her, just like Tom was bad for Cora.

If you take Sarah away from here you'll destroy her. She'll die young in a wild land, just like her mother."

Caleb frowned. "You speak of Cora Sax as though she was special to you. You seem to mourn her, but not your own brother. Why does what happened to Cora bother you so?"

The man reddened slightly, then turned away again. "I'll tell you this much, Caleb, but never tell Sarah. You're part Indian. Indians are supposed to keep their word, right?"

"I will not tell her."

Sax hesitated, but finally decided the truth might convince Caleb he himself knew what was best for Sarah. "Cora was once engaged to me," the man started. "Her name was Cora Dade then." He swallowed. "I . . . loved her very much. I was the son who got an education, planned, intended to be very successful—which I am. I had everything to offer her. Then Tom came home from one of his visits to the wilds. He . . . filled her with stories about his adventures, and with every story her eyes got bigger with excitement and admiration. Before I knew it, something was happening between them. She looked at him with that . . . that sick look of love, like Sarah looked at you tonight. He swept her off her feet with his damn buckskins and wild tales. The next thing I knew she was breaking our engagement, telling me she was in love with Tom and was going away with him." The man's fists clenched. "He stole her from me! But I showed him! I—" Sax broke off abruptly, and when he turned around there was bitter hatred in his eyes.

Caleb finally understood the hard feelings between the brothers, but he suspected Terrence Sax was not so hurt by losing Cora as he was at losing to Tom, at being shown all his wealth could not buy the love of a good woman. It was obvious he was trying to buy Sarah's love now, but Caleb wondered if the man even realized it.

Sax breathed deeply, trying to stay in control. "He took Cora off to Fort Dearborn, where she died young. She could have had everything, but instead she ran off with a man who could give her nothing."

"She was very happy. He gave her love, and that was all she wanted. Sarah is very much like her."

The man glowered at him, stepping closer. "Yes, she is. And she is very impressionable like Cora. I took Sarah in because she was Cora's daughter, and for me it was a way of having Cora back, a way of showing Tom up after all. The man couldn't take care of his own daughter, so he sent her to me."

"He took fine care of her," Caleb retorted angrily. "Tom loved her very much. But Cora had died, and there was a threat of Indian or British attack. He did not intend that you keep her forever, just until he could do it himself again. And he would have if he had not been killed."

"I have my doubts about that," he sneered. "He was wild and free—probably glad to be rid of Cora and the girl so he could—"

Caleb grasped the lapels of the man's woolen coat, yanking him close. "Never smear the name of Tom Sax or accuse him of not loving his wife and daughter or I will cut out your tongue." He shoved the man hard so that he fell onto the bed. "You white-bellied bastard! I do not doubt Cora began to see you for what you are: a selfish man who thinks all that is important is money and power. Before now I was not sure if I should leave Sarah here with you. Now I know I cannot!"

Sax rose from the bed, afraid of Caleb but not wanting to show it. "You try to take her away and I'll have you arrested and hung for kidnapping," he warned.

Caleb looked down at him haughtily. "Threaten me if you wish. But I will do what is best for Sarah. She is a good, sweet girl, and if you truly loved her you would want only what makes her happy. You cannot make her live her life the way you want. She must live her own life. You have taken good care of her, and Tom would be grateful. But he would say she must choose what she wants to do. She is eighteen and a woman."

"Yes," the man sneered. "She's a woman—that's what you're seeing. I'm telling you, Caleb Sax, that if you take Sarah away it will be to an early death, just like Cora. I won't let that happen again, and I have a lot of power in this town. Do you understand what I'm telling you?"

Caleb grinned. "I am not afraid of you, Terrence Sax. I will do what is best for Sarah, what she wants."

"Which is exactly what I intend to do," Terrence returned. He looked Caleb over once more. "The offer is still good. I'll pay you well to leave by tomorrow. You know where my office is. Go there for the money."

Caleb glared at him. "I choose to stay."

Sax stiffened, his knuckles turning white on the door-knob. "Go ahead, boy. Just don't try coming around to visit Sarah again or I'll have the law on you!"

The man went out, slamming the door so hard that moments later the woman who ran the boarding house came and chided Caleb for having company so late at night. "You keep it quiet or I'll get the sheriff," she warned.

"I am sorry," he told her. "It was not my fault."

She sniffed and marched back to her room.

Caleb closed his door again, softly this time. Terrence Sax had made up his mind for him. He would stay in Saint Louis—for a while at least. He would make sure of Sarah's feelings for him, and if they were what he suspected, he would take her away. But something must be decided soon. Tom was waiting for his father to return for him. Caleb had never realized how much he would miss his son, but he could not abandon Sarah.

Sarah left the clothing store, carrying the dress her aunt had insisted she buy for the upcoming St. Patrick's Day dance. The Saxes wanted Byron Clawson to escort her, but Sarah had objected vehemently, and finally her aunt and uncle had given in. She would go with them and be allowed to dance with whomever she chose.

"At least we know it won't be with that half-breed," her uncle had muttered. "He's gone back to the wilds where he belongs."

Sarah could not believe Caleb had left. Surely he wouldn't do that to her. But he had not visited for three days, and she had daringly checked at the rooming house where he had been staying, only to find he was no longer there. Never had she been so unhappy or felt so lost.

Caleb had quickly become everything to her, not just safety from Byron and a way to go back to a life she preferred, but as a man, a beautiful, wonderful man she loved. It didn't matter that he wasn't wealthy and educated like Byron. He was more man in all the ways that counted. He had made such brief appearances in her life yet he meant so much to her.

She passed an alley and heard someone call her name. She turned, and her heart quickened with joy and relief. "Caleb!"

He put a finger to his lips and signaled for her to come to him. She looked around, then quickly darted into the alley, moving with him around the corner of a building.

"Uncle Terrence told me you'd left," she said. She put her package on a nearby barrel and hugged him. "Oh, Caleb, I was so unhappy."

"I only wanted him to think I left, so he would not be watching you." Caleb replied. "Your uncle paid me a visit the other night."

She looked up at him. "Why?"

"He asked me to leave Saint Louis quickly."

She frowned. "I don't understand."

Their eyes held, and he could not resist drawing her closer. "He thinks that—" he swallowed, suddenly nervous. "He is afraid you and I might have feelings for each other." He felt her shake as the tears came.

"He would be right," she sniffed, hugging him tighter.

His heart quickened and he bent his head to kiss her hair. "Sarah," he whispered, unable to stop himself. Over and over he kissed her, her hair, her forehead. Slowly she turned her face up to his, wanting more, wanting to know. His lips moved over her eyes, her temples, her cheeks, then finally finding her mouth, her sweet, delicious, innocent mouth. He wanted her even more than he had wanted Walking Grass, for Sarah had been a part of his life for so much longer. He searched her mouth hungrily, unable to move away from it, wanting to linger there forever.

She flung her arms around his neck, returning the kiss with fervor. Though innocent of physical love, Sarah knew it felt right and wonderful and magic to have Caleb kissing her, wanting her, holding her. Fire spread through her body, and she knew instinctively that to be his woman would mean great joy and ecstasy. How could two men be so different? She could hardly stand Byron even looking at her, but with Caleb she wanted so much more.

His lips finally left her mouth and he held her close, trembling almost as much as she. "My God, Sarah," he groaned. "I have tried to stop these feelings."

"I tried, too," she whispered. "But the moment you returned I knew I loved you. I think I've always loved you, Caleb, since I was a little girl."

"And I have loved you," he replied. "Sarah, my darling Sarah."

Their lips met again in youthful passion, and she was breathless from being held so tightly—or was it just from his kiss?

The pain of wanting her was sharp and real for Caleb. If they were alone it would be so easy to lay her down and claim her, and he knew he must possess her soon. He must be the first and only man to hold this treasure, to lead her gently to womanhood.

He finally broke his kiss, his body aching with desire. He had never felt quite such an intense passion before. "We must meet somewhere alone where we can talk," he said.

She pulled away slightly, the fire still burning in her heart and body, her face crimson at the realization of her boldness. "Yes," she answered. "There is a carriage and driver waiting for me just up the street. I must go soon." She dared to meet his eyes, eyes that were glassy with desire. He smiled at her, the handsome, provocative smile that only made him more beautiful.

"I don't know what will happen, Sarah. I only know that I love you," he told her. "And it feels so good to finally say it."

How many times had she dreamed of belonging to Caleb Sax? "And I love you," she replied. "Where are you staying? I looked for you."

"I am camped in the woods behind the livery on Saint James Street. I wanted your uncle to think I had left town. Is there any way you can make it there?"

"Tomorrow. I'll have the driver bring me to town and tell him I intend to shop most of the day. I'll tell him to come back for me at a certain time. Then I'll walk to your camp. My aunt and uncle won't know. I do have a lot of shopping to do. I'll come back in time to buy a few things before I meet the driver."

He frowned. "I do not like making you sneak around. It is not right. But your uncle must think I am gone or he will try to stop us. We must talk and plan so we can get away. He tried to pay me to leave, and he threatened me. I am not afraid of him, but I think he is the type who would get many men to do his bidding. There is only so much one man can do to defend himself."

Her heart tightened with dread. "Oh, Caleb, Uncle Terrence wouldn't do that. He wouldn't hire men to hurt you!"

He caressed her hair. "You did not see the look on his face when he came to see me. We must go away in secret or we will not be able to go at all. I know you do not like deceiving him, nor do I. But with his money and power he will find a way to keep us apart if we go to him and say we wish to be together."

She hugged him tightly. "Oh, Caleb, he's been so good to me. Surely he would let us be together if he knew that's what I really wanted. I can't believe he'd hurt me that way."

He kissed her hair and ran his hands over her back. "I am afraid I can, Sarah. I know he has been good to you. But he—" He saw no gain in telling Sarah about the man's love for Cora Sax. It would only hurt her. "Believe me, Sarah, when I tell you he is very determined. Meet me tomorrow and we will talk. What time will you come?"

"Around one o'clock?"

"Fine. I will be waiting."

Their eyes held in love and happiness. They would be together. Surely God meant it to be. They had shared so much together, loved and lost together.

"Go now. And be careful tomorrow that no one sees you." He bent down and kissed her lightly. "I am so happy, Sarah. I was not sure you had the same feelings, but I could not leave until I knew. At first I came only to see you once more, but I knew when I did see you that I could not let you out of my life again. I have been so lonely. You bring new joy to my heart." He reached over and picked up her package, placing it in her hands. "You must go."

"I'm scared to be away from you, Caleb."

"It is only for another day. I will be waiting."

She reached out and squeezed his hand, then hurried back out to the street. Caleb watched her, studying the lovely little bounce to her walk, the roundness of her firm hips, her slender waist. Who would ever have imagined his little Sarah would grow into a woman he would want the way he wanted her now? The hours until he saw her again would be long indeed.

Caleb looked up from the small fire in front of the tent he had made from his buffalo robes. He smiled when he saw her, feeling relieved. Sarah looked beautiful in a dark blue velvet dress and cape, a muff over her hands, a dark blue velvet and fur hat over her red-gold hair. She walked faster when she was sure it was he, and in the next moment she was in his arms.

"Oh, Caleb, I'm so scared. I've never done anything like this before."

"You will not have to do it much longer. We will go away soon, when we know we can get far away before anyone can follow us." He turned. "Here. Come inside. There is not much room, but it is warmer. It is cold again." He took her arm and they ducked inside the large tent, where he had blankets spread on the ground. Just getting out of the cool wind made all the difference.

They sat down beside each other and their eyes met. In the small confines of the tent, that was all that was needed. Neither could deny passion. Caleb pulled off her hat and gently lay her back. He could not get enough of her, he thought as his mouth met hers. He wanted to consume her, invade her. But he realized how new it was to her, how careful he must be. There would be time for claiming her later. For now he would hold her, gently show her the lovely little things that could bring pleasure.

"Sarah, I ache for you," he whispered, moving his lips to her throat, running a hand over her flat stomach and up to gently caress one breast through the thick cloth of her dress.

Sarah gasped with the ecstasy of his touch. How glorious it was to be in his arms this way. It seemed that as soon as he touched her she was filled with burning passion, and both of them suffered the intense needs of youth, needs magnified by the fear that something would happen to keep them apart. She never wanted to be apart from him again.

His mouth met hers again, his long, dark hair shrouding her face, his broad frame hovering over her. She was at his mercy but didn't care, trusting him implicitly. This was Caleb, her dear friend, now her lover. He would never deceive her. She had often thought about love, but never dreamed it could be this wonderful.

He moved his lips over the dress, kissing at her breasts

and rubbing his face against them. She whimpered his name, touching his hair, wondering what it must be like to lie this way naked, to have a man actually taste her breasts. She knew she could only let Caleb do such a thing, no one else.

He kissed her throat again, then her lips, then raised up on one elbow, smiling almost bashfully as he looked down at her. "I did not mean to do that so quickly. I meant to talk first." He put a hand to the side of her face. "But when I am near you . . ."

She sighed. "I know," she whispered. "It's the same for me." She turned her face and kissed the palm of his hand. "What are we going to do, Caleb? My aunt and uncle want me to go to a special dance Saturday. Byron will be there, and I talked them into letting me go with them and not him. But I don't want to go at all." She met his eyes. "I just want to be with you. Yet I hate the thought of hurting them."

"I know, but it cannot be helped, Sarah. If your uncle even knows I am still around he will do something to separate us. And you must think of your father and mother. They would have wanted us to be together. Terrence is nothing like Tom. It is Tom we must think about, his wishes. Terrence took care of you, but he does not own you. You are old enough to make your own decisions. If you wish to go away with me and be my wife, which is what I want very much in my own heart, then I will find a way. Will you be my wife, Sarah?"

Her eyes teared. "You know I will," she whispered.

He smiled, his own eyes watery. "I can think of nothing more wonderful than us living together, raising Tom and having more babies of our own."

She reddened again and buried her face in his shoulder. He moved on top of her, kissing her hair. ''Do not be afraid of it, Sarah. I would never hurt you or hurry you. It will be so beautiful. You will see. We will be so happy."

"I know," she said softly. "It's all so beautiful. I'm just so scared it can never be."

"Of course it can be. We are meant to be together. I will take care of you always. I will never leave you again."

"How, Caleb? When?"

"We will wait, two weeks perhaps, until Terrence Sax is very sure I have gone and does not watch you closely or wonder where you are. You will tell him you are going to a friend's house for the day, but you will come here instead and we will leave. If we can get a day's start, we can do it. I know of no other way. I would rather go to him and face him, but he would find a way to stop us." He kissed her eyes. "It will be like riding into an enemy Indian camp and stealing a woman away. Clawson thinks you are his, but you are mine. He will not have you."

Joy rushed through her at his words. Yes, she belonged to Caleb Sax. She had always belonged to Caleb Sax, always known he would come back. His hypnotic blue eyes held her green ones, saying all that needed to be said. She was going to be his wife and they were going to be so happy together. He would gently show her how to be a woman, and she would give him more sons, and they would share a little cabin somewhere on the wild frontier.

Chapter
Seventeen

A week passed, a week of enjoying the sweetness of newfound love. They met three more times, and Sarah was hardly able to leave him each time. Her body and heart and soul were alive for him. Each meeting was filled with passion and love, the joy of being together, the wonder of realizing their feelings of kinship had turned into something so perfect and beautiful.

Each became more anxious to make it real and lasting. Caleb wanted her totally, wanted to be one in body, and knew she wanted the same. Denying the consummation of their love was painful, but it only seemed right they should first be married.

It was easy to imagine them living together in a cabin west of the Mississippi, raising little Tom, and Caleb was becoming anxious to get back to his son. Finally the hurt of losing Walking Grass was bearable. He could even live with the sorrow of losing Tom Sax, for now he had Sarah. He wanted to treasure her the rest of his life.

They discussed the possibility of simply telling Terrence Sax and getting it over with, but always decided against it. Caleb knew all too well the look Terrence Sax had given him the night he had told him to leave Saint Louis. Men like Terrence Sax did not appreciate the honest approach. Going against him was not the same as going against a band of Crow. This was a white man's game, and white men like

Terrence Sax did not wage their battles openly; they used underhanded deceptions at every opportunity.

Sarah did not want to believe Terrence Sax was capable of bringing harm to Caleb, or that the man could possibly be so cruel as to deny her the man she really loved. But as time passed she had to believe it. Terrence spent too much time at the supper table every night insulting Caleb, blustering that it was best for them all that Caleb was gone. She wasn't sure how to approach the man without getting Caleb in trouble, and she was certain her uncle would have Caleb run out of town before he would settle down and listen to her personal wishes. Each time she thought she had the courage to face him with her love for Caleb, he would say something about the upcoming dance or taking her on a trip East, and always he rambled on about how lucky she was to be living in Saint Louis, where "a woman can be a woman and not a plow horse."

How could she explain about Caleb? How could anyone like her uncle understand? It was so special and beautiful. Every time his lips touched hers, the magic started again. Just the thought of being loved and touched by Caleb brought a joy unlike anything she had ever experienced. It seemed as if they had never been children, that it had always been like this. She had always loved him, always known Caleb Sax would be the man she would one day love and marry. Nothing must separate them now. Nothing. Somehow they would find a way to be together forever. But in her joy and eagerness to see Caleb each time, she grew careless.

Terrence Sax looked up with a friendly grin as Byron Clawson entered his office, which was as elegant as his home. It was located above one of the several supply stores he owned, which together were called Sax Enterprises. Terrence reached out across the oak desk and shook Byron's hand.

"Well, young man, what can I do for you today?" he asked, leaning back in his padded leather chair.

Byron took a seat across from him, his face serious. "I'm afraid I have some troublesome news, sir."

"Oh?" Terrence's eyebrows arched. "And what might a bright young man like yourself have to tell me that is troublesome?"

Byron sighed deeply, feigning genuine concern. "It's Sarah, sir." He shook his head and frowned. "You know how I feel about her. I love her. I want to marry her. But, well . . . I'm afraid I've discovered something, quite by accident."

Terrence's heart quickened. "What are you talking about?"

Byron took out a thin cigar and lit it. "Well, sir, I saw her get out of her carriage in town yesterday and started to catch up to her when she headed toward Sixth Street. I thought that strange, since none of the best shops are there. I am afraid I couldn't help but follow, out of concern and curiosity." He puffed his cigar. "When she got to the livery, she walked behind it and into the forest, looking around first as though to make sure no one saw her. I waited awhile, then moved as quietly as possible in that direction. I saw a camp, a tent and two horses. I waited quite a bit longer until Sarah came out of the tent—with Caleb Sax."

Terrence paled. "Caleb Sax? But he left town. He checked out of his room."

Byron grinned pompously. "Out of his room, perhaps, but not out of Saint Louis, or out of our Sarah's life. Needless to say, I am very upset, Mr. Sax. I dearly hope the man has not stolen what I always considered would be mine on my wedding night, if you know what I mean. I never thought Sarah would do something like this."

Terrence felt the palms of his hands grow sweaty. Not Sarah. Cora had been bad enough, but Sarah? How could he tell this young man—or anyone—the truth about her? Only Mary knew now, for Tom and Cora Sax were dead. He swallowed, feeling suddenly weak and beaten. "The bastard," he whispered.

SAVAGE HORIZONS   (243)

"My sentiments exactly. What would you like to do about it, Mr. Sax?"

Terrence met the young man's cool gray eyes. "How do you even know Caleb Sax?" he asked. "I didn't know you'd ever met him."

Byron colored slightly, scrambling to think quickly. "I, uh . . . I met him the day of Sarah's birthday party. When I took her for that walk, the Indian had the audacity to appear out of the nowhere and threaten me, telling me I had no right being with Sarah." He snorted with disdain. "I needn't tell you that the man can be quite frightening when he wants to be. After all, he is a savage. He had a knife and I was alone, so I chose the best solution for the moment. I never said anything to you because I didn't want to make trouble for Sarah. But I do have a score to settle with him, and I would ike your permission to do so. Of course, considering the kind of man he is, it would take several men to persuade him to really leave this time."

Terrence leaned forward in his chair, seeming to age before Byron's eyes. "Are you asking my permission?"

"I thought it wise. He does, after all, have some kind of association with your family."

"My brother's, not mine," he retorted. "Do what you wish, but I don't want him killed or in some way mutilated, understand? I won't be party to anything like that. But a good licking with a threat of death might do it. As far as Sarah, I don't know what to do. You still love her?"

"By all means. I understand that she is still very much a child. She simply doesn't understand that she's acting foolishly, but I'm willing to be patient. She's a good girl. I'm sure she's done nothing . . . sinful. At least we must hope so. Once this young man is gone she'll come around soon enough." He puffed the cigar once more and leaned forward. "I would like your permission to marry her as soon as possible, Mr. Sax. Father is setting me up with a very good job in Washington, and I'd like to get married and move there in the near future. I'm sure once Sarah is there, surrounded by elegant ladies, the latest fashions and the powerful and elite of our capital, she'll wonder why she was ever interested in a worthless half-breed with nothing to offer."

Terrence nodded. "I think it's a wonderful idea. Right now I'm going home to make sure Sarah is there and stays there for three or four days."

Byron rose, putting out his cigar in an ashtray. "I'll need a couple of days to round up the kind of men who are willing to do the job and keep their mouths shut about it." He fully intended to go after Caleb Sax much sooner, perhaps even today, but he didn't want Terrence Sax to know the details. It was Clawson's personal vendetta. He hated Caleb Sax for humiliating him as he had done the day of the party.

"Just keep my name out of it."

"Naturally." Byron put out his hand and Terrence took it again. "For the love of Sarah," Byron told him.

Sax's eyes actually teared. "Yes. For the love of Sarah."

Sarah straightened her hat as she descended the stairs and headed toward the door. She was stopped by her uncle, whose face reddened with anger when he saw her.

"Where are you going?" he asked.

She had never seen him look at her as he was now, and it confused and frightened her. "Just shopping," she answered, feeling her cheeks warm.

"You have everything you need. What would you be shopping for?"

She swallowed. "Oh, Uncle Terrence, you know how women are."

He stepped closer. "Yes, I know—all too well. Get upstairs to your room. You'll not go out today. Or tomorrow or the next day."

She blinked, struggling against tears. "Why?"

"Because I say so."

Her brows knit together in confusion. "Uncle Terrence, you've never behaved toward me this way before. What have I done to upset you?" Did he know? Yes, she realized, somehow he had found out.

"You know what you've done, Sarah Sax. I've given you everything, yet you have gone behind my back and done something you knew I would never approve of."

Her love for Caleb gave her courage, and she managed to rise above her fear to defend that love. "Why not, Uncle Terrence? I love Caleb. I love you, too. It isn't that I don't appreciate all the wonderful things you've done for me, but can't you understand that I just want a very simple life with Caleb? What is so terrible about that? Caleb is good and kind. He's—"

"I told you to go to your room," Sax interrupted, his face stony and cold.

He suddenly was not the Terrence Sax she had always known, although the man had never been good-natured like his brother had. Still, he had always been friendly to her.

She met his eyes boldly. "And then what? You can't stop me from loving him, Uncle Terrence."

"He's only using you, an Indian panting after a pretty little white girl."

"It isn't that way at all!" she exclaimed, her eyes tearing. "I—I don't understand you. Why can't you just let me be happy?"

Cora Sax had once said the same thing to him. If not for Cora, perhaps he could be more patient with this girl.

"I am going to talk to your Caleb Sax," he lied. "And this time he will leave. A man will do anything for enough money. I'll prove to you that your Caleb is no different."

"He is different! He'd never take money to leave me."

"We'll soon know."

"And if he doesn't?"

He smiled sarcastically. "If he doesn't, then I'll interfere no more. Now go to your room."

She was tempted to run past him, run to Caleb—run and run and run. But perhaps it was best for the moment to simply do as she was told. Perhaps it was best her uncle knew. Once he talked to Caleb, he would see Caleb's good intentions, and maybe they could be together with Uncle Terrence's blessings. She turned and hurried to her room, flinging herself on the bed and weeping bitterly.

Caleb stirred the rabbit stew he had made especially for Sarah. He could barely contain his growing eagerness to see her.

Her uncle was going East on a business trip in a few days, and that was when they would leave. It was all planned and everything was ready. Soon they would go away, find a preacher, and be married, then they would get little Tom. By the time anyone found them they would be happily settled and there would be nothing Terrence Sax or anyone else could do about it. It went against Caleb's nature to have to sneak away with Sarah, but they had little choice. Here he could not fight a white man's battle in a white man's city, but once he and Sarah were in his own territory and she was his wife, no one could take her from him.

He stirred the stew once more, then stopped, sensing a presence, his Indian instincts suddenly alert. He rose and slowly walked toward his musket.

"Don't do it, Indian," someone yelled. "Move one more inch and eight musket balls will be rolling around your innards."

Caleb stood still, trying to think clearly. These were white men out to get him. Perhaps if he didn't move too suddenly he could get away with his life. That was the only important thing at the moment, to live, for Sarah and his son.

Eight men stepped toward him from behind the trees, all holding long muskets on him. One of them was Byron Clawson. Caleb faced him squarely.

"So you are too much of a coward to face me alone. You need seven other men to help you."

Clawson reddened with anger. "Call me what you wish. It won't matter when we're through with you, breed. Scum like you has no business taking something that's mine."

"She was never yours."

Byron's lips curled in a sneer. "She soon will be. We're going to be married, and we won't be stopped by the likes of you, coming here and taking advantage of my Sarah's youth and ignorance."

"I have brought her no harm," Caleb retorted, his eyes moving around the others, who all looked ready to pounce. "I love Sarah, and she loves me."

There were several snickers. "In love with her white tits, maybe," Byron sneered. "You filled her with stories about your wild adventures, didn't you? How long did it take you to get under her dress, Indian?" He spit on Caleb, but Caleb continued to hold himself in check. Byron would like nothing more than for him to fight back. Indians hung easily enough.

Caleb held the man's eyes challengingly. "Why don't you tell these friends of yours what you were trying to do to Sarah the day of her birthday? If I had not come along it is you who would have forced yourself on her. She would never have you any other way. I have never touched her that way, but if I did, it would be because she wanted me to."

Byron turned beet red, then quickly swung his musket hard, trying to hit the side of Caleb's head. But Caleb was quick. His hand moved up and grabbed the musket, but then something hit him hard in the middle of his back and he went to his knees, reeling with pain, trying to keep his thoughts clear. He wore no weapons since he had expected only Sarah. Everything was on his horse, and he could not get to them now.

"Consider this a friendly warning, Indian," he heard Byron say as he struggled to rise again.

Everything was suddenly clear. These men would not shoot him. Someone had told them not to. They intended to beat him into leaving Saint Louis. Whatever they had in store for him, he would not go down easily, and he would give Byron Clawson his due.

He felt them moving closer but sensed they were being hesitant, somewhat afraid of the Indian. Caleb used the moment to rise, feigning dizziness until he was sure it was Byron Clawson directly in front of him. He kicked out hard, catching Clawson in the groin so he doubled over. Then he brought up his knee, smashing it into Clawson's face. There was an odd crunching sound, and Byron went sprawling backward, his face a mass of blood.

Caleb whirled as another man approached him from behind. He swung out hard with his fist and caught someone in the side of the neck. There was a grunt, and then four more men were on him. Kicks, punches and blows seemed to be coming down on Caleb from everywhere, but he kicked out once more, catching a third man hard in the chin. The butt of a musket was again rammed into his back, and his knees buckled a second time as a horrible pain ripped through his body.

In the next moment he was on the ground, dirt in his mouth. Kicks from booted feet seemed to come down on him like rain until he was so battered he felt nothing. This was the white man's way of fighting, several men on one, none of them brave enough to take him on alone. But even with their great number, if he could have gotten to his weapons. . . .

"Rip down that tent," someone ordered.

"Jesus, he's some fighter," someone else swore.

To Caleb's horror he felt someone grab his hair. His mind swirled with visions of Indian scalpings.

"Cut it off," someone said, the voice sounding far, far away. "It's the worst humiliation you can give an Indian." Caleb felt the hair at the back of the neck being cut but could do nothing about it. Inside he screamed, but outside the kicks continued to be administered in all the right places until he saw and heard nothing at all. His last thoughts were of Sarah.

* * *

Sarah lay staring into the darkness, wondering what had happened to Caleb. Two days had gone by since her uncle had ordered her not to go out. She had only obeyed because she was so sure Caleb would come. But he had not. Her uncle had told her Caleb had taken the money and gone, but she didn't believe it.

She sat up, knowing she had to do something. Something was terribly wrong—not just with Caleb, but with her uncle as well. He was acting so strange lately. Why was he so set that she have nothing to do with Caleb? Should she try to sneak out and find Caleb? The only way to do that would be in the night. Was she brave enough?

She walked barefoot to the door, then opened it a crack and peered into the hallway. She saw no light in her aunt and uncle's bedroom, but she heard voices. If she was to sneak out, she must wait until they were asleep.

"I'll see she doesn't..."

It was her uncle's voice. Were they talking about Caleb? Perhaps if she listened, she would find out what had really happened to him.

"Well, she's not happy this way," her aunt said.

Sarah crept to the doorway, standing against the wall and listening.

"You might as well face the fact that if you hadn't raped Cora Dade after she told you she was leaving with Tom none of this would be happening," her Aunt Mary continued. "Sarah wouldn't be your daughter and you wouldn't be acting this way. How can she understand your anger when she thinks you're only her uncle?"

Sarah's eyes widened as the horror of the statement moved through her.

"You ruined Cora Dade's life, and now you're going to destroy your own daughter's."

"Shut up," Terrence growled. "Do you think it's easy living with the guilt of what I did? Why do you think I took Sarah in and gave her a home? I love her. She's mine. And

Cora was mine until Tom came along and stole her from me. But I was one up on him. I took her first."

Sarah put a hand to her stomach. Her mother, her beautiful, good, precious mother was raped by Terrence Sax? She could not think of him as her father—never! What kind of horrible man was he? She had been raised to think of him as uncle, not father, and to picture him forcing himself on her mother ... Hate swept through her like a great wave and she felt sick.

"You sound like a child fighting over a toy," Mary said in disgust. "It wasn't easy living with you after you told me, and it wasn't easy for me to take in Sarah, knowing she was yours. But she's a darling, sweet girl, and I have come to love her, too. But I can't stand watching you make her so unhappy. You never should have let them hurt that young man. You're jealous of him, that's what. You're jealous because he reminds you of Tom, and you're still jealous of him, even after death. May God forgive you, Terrence Sax!"

It was all Sarah could do to keep from crying out in her shock. It all made so much sense now, Uncle Terrence's possessiveness, and the mutual dislike between the brothers. She hurried back to her room, feeling numb and removed from herself. She quietly closed her door, trying to think. Her aunt had said something about Uncle Terrence letting someone hurt a young man. Did she mean Caleb?

"My God," she whispered as it fell into place. She closed her eyes and breathed deeply. She could not break down now. She had to be strong and smart, like an Indian woman, for that was the kind of woman Caleb needed now. She could not stay in this house a moment longer, and the thought of setting eyes on Terrence Sax again made her want to scream.

She padded silently to her dresser, opening a drawer and taking out clean clothes. She could not go to any of her friends, for their parents would tell. She had no choice but to try to get to Caleb's campsite in the dark, try to find him and hope he was still alive. If he was, she would help him and they would run away. Her young mind could think of no other answer, and youthful energy and determination convinced her it could be done.

She retrieved her carpetbag from under her bed and stuffed the clothes inside, then went to her closet and pulled out two cotton dresses, folding and stuffing them in as well. She removed her nightgown and put it in, then put on a plain blue cotton dress and pulled on long stockings and her bloomers. She went to the washbasin and wrapped a bar of soap into a washcloth, putting it and a towel inside the carpetbag. Then she brushed out her hair and tied it behind her neck and packed the brush. She picked up her warmest cape and tied it around her neck. It had a hood. With Caleb's warm buffalo robes there should be no worry about the cold nights to come. The days were pleasant because spring had come early.

She took one last look around the room she had lived in for over four years. She had learned much here and been given the things any girl would want. But she wanted none of it now, not this way. She moved to the door and quietly slid shut the lock. They would think she locked herself in out of anger and would not investigate right away. She had a little time.

She picked up her high-button shoes, deciding not to put them on until she got outside. She went to the window and carefully set her carpetbag and shoes on the balcony, then climbed through the window herself. As a young girl she had climbed down the rose trellis many times, out of sheer daring, pretending she was running from pirates, always giggling to herself when she knew her aunt and uncle didn't even know she'd been gone.

Sarah slipped the handle of the carpetbag over her arm, then leaned over the railing and threw down her shoes. They landed almost soundlessly in the soft grass. She pulled up her dress and moved her foot over the edge, placing it carefully on the first rung of the trellis. She pulled her dress

over the railing and carefully climbed down. She found her
shoes and slipped them on without buttoning them. There
was not time.

She ran off into the darkness, forcing herself not to be
afraid of the night. She had to think of Caleb.

Chapter Eighteen

"CALEB?" Sarah made her way through the dark
trees toward the small campfire. She had never
dreamed she would be brave enough to walk alone
through the back alleys of Saint Louis at night or into the
shadowy forest. But she had to forget her fear for herself.
She had to think of Caleb. What had they done to him?

She walked closer, finally seeing him lying on what appeared to be the robes that had once made his tent. The
small fire was nearly out. "Caleb," she called again.

He moved, slowly sitting up and reaching for his pistol.

"Caleb, it's me, Sarah." She hurried closer and set down
her carpetbag. By the light of the dim fire she saw that his
hair was cut short. She gasped, her heart filling with pain,
her throat constricting so that it took her a moment to find
her voice. "Caleb . . . what did they do to you?"

"Go away," he mumbled. "It is bad for you here. Go
home, Sarah."

She moved to stand above him, but his back was still to
her. "I'm never going back," she told him a shaky voice.
"We're going away together, Caleb. I waited for you to

come for me, and then I heard them arguing. They said something about you being hurt. I had to come, Caleb. I had to know what happened to you."

"I was going to come for you. But I was waiting until I was stronger. And my hair . . . I could not face you."

She knelt down behind him. "Caleb," she whispered, touching his hair. She gasped when he jerked away, putting a hand to his head. "Do not touch it."

"Caleb, it doesn't matter. Let me help you if you're hurt. What did they do?"

He rubbed his short hair. "Byron Clawson came with seven others. If I'd had my weapons I could have stopped them. I could not fight all eight of them, not one man against muskets used like clubs . . . and kicking feet." He shuddered. "I would like to kill them all . . . the Indian way. I would like to make them sorry for what they've done."

"No, Caleb. It's just what they want. It would give them an excuse to hang you." Tears ran down her face, and she rested her head against his back. "Oh, Caleb, I'm so sorry. I feel responsible for all of this. You should have gone back to your son and left me here."

He turned then, pulling her into his arms, ignoring the lingering pain in his bruised body.

"Caleb, take me away," she sobbed. "Let's just go away— right now, tonight. I can't stay in that house. I—I heard them talking." She put a hand to her face and trembled. "Oh, Caleb, Uncle Terrence isn't my uncle. He's my father!"

She cried harder for a time while Caleb gently rubbed her back.

"What are you talking about?" he asked when her sobs subsided a bit.

"I heard them arguing . . . my aunt and uncle. Aunt Mary said if he hadn't raped Cora, I wouldn't be here. Uncle Terrence took me in because I'm his daughter, Caleb. He raped my mother because he was jealous that she loved Tom more and wanted to go away with him." She clung to Caleb. "I hate him! I hate him! I'll never think of him as my father.

Tom Sax is my father, and I want to get away from Saint Louis."

Caleb closed his eyes against his own hatred. It was no wonder Tom Sax had nothing good to say about his brother. It all made so much sense. Terrence Sax had once loved Cora, and she chose Tom instead. Terrence had raped her out of spite, a jealous brother determined to have her before Tom did. Sarah was the man's daughter.

His heart ached for Sarah. What a terrible thing for her to learn. He had to protect her, take her away, but how?

"We cannot stay here long," he finally spoke. "You are a brave woman, Sarah, coming here this way. No matter what they did I would not have left without you. I was just not well enough to ride."

She sniffed and looked at him, seeing even in the glow of the small fire how badly his face was battered. "Oh, Caleb!" She gently kissed his bruised puffy lips. "My darling Caleb."

"They will look for you soon, and this is the first place they will come," he told her. "They have been watching me, coming every morning to see if I have gone."

"We'll leave tonight," she said quietly, sniffing and wiping her eyes with the sleeve of her dress. "And we won't leave any tracks."

Caleb frowned. "What do you mean?"

"We'll go by the river. I know where there's a raft. We can go far downstream before getting off and heading west. They'd never find the place where we got off. They'd never know where to start looking. By the time they find us—if they find us at all—we'll be married, and they'll have to give up."

His heart swelled with pride at her courage and determination. "Where is this raft?"

"Uncle Terrence used to forbid me to go near the river, but when I first got here two friends and I found a raft that doesn't seem to belong to anyone. We used to float it up and down the river, using poles to guide it, pretending we were pirates. It's farther up the river. I could go and get it, Caleb. Uncle Terrence would never figure out how we got away. Are you well enough to pack everything while I go and get the raft?"

He rubbed bruised ribs. "I think so. Will it hold two horses?"She frowned. "I don't think so. It might hold one, though."

He sighed, looking up at the fine Appaloosa. "The gray was given to me by Tom, but he is getting old." He swallowed back his sorrow. Again he must give up something he loved, but, after all, there was not time to consider other alternatives. "I will leave the gray and take the Appaloosa. He is younger and stronger."

"Good. I'll leave my carpetbag here." She started to rise, but he grasped her arms.

"Sarah." She stayed on her knees. "I do not like you going through the forest alone. I do not like any of this. You could be hurt."

She tossed her hair. "I'm as strong and brave as any of your Indian women, Caleb Sax. Would they do any less?"

He managed a slight grin through his sore mouth. "Tom Sax once said the Irish are stubborn, bull-headed and determined. You are all of that, Sarah Sax." He caressed her cheek. "No matter what happens, we belong to each other," he told her. "Nothing can change that."

She gently kissed his swollen knuckles. "I love you, Caleb. I'm so sorry for what they did to you." She leaned forward and kissed his cheek. "I want to be with you forever and ever," she whispered. "After tonight we'll never be apart again." She stood up. "Get everything together and go down to the riverbank. It's only a short walk from here. I'll be back soon and call out to you from the river until I hear you answer. It will be hard to tell in the dark just where this spot is, so listen for me."

She ran off. He started to object again, but she was already lost in the shadows. He got to his feet, ignoring his pain. There was no time to lose now. Never had he loved her more, for this night Sarah Sax showed the courage Tom Sax had raised her to have. Yes, she truly was Tom's daughter, not Terrence's, and she was unlike any white woman Caleb had ever met.

Every movement was an effort, but Caleb managed to pack the most important things onto the Appaloosa. He walked to the gray gelding and untied him, slipping the bridle from the animal's head. He reached around its neck then, hugging it. Saying good-bye to the gray was like saying good-bye to Tom Sax again. He prayed to the spirits that the horse would stumble upon a kind man who would keep it and be good to it.

"I am sorry to desert you, boy," he said quietly. "We have been together for a long time."

The animal whinnied and nuzzled his neck, and Caleb turned away, the pain of parting coursing through him. He picked up the Appaloosa's reins and led it toward the river. The gray started to follow. Caleb turned. "Go," he said in a loud whisper. "Go away!"

The horse whinnied again and tossed its head. Caleb walked up to it, then picked up a stone. "Go on! Go!" He tossed the stone and the gray jerked back, then turned and trotted off.

"Damn," he hissed. "Damn them all!" He turned and began walking, his gait not the usual long, easy strides, but a slow limp. He was not ready for this, but there was no choice. He must draw on all his inner strength. He must heal, and what was not healed must be ignored. He had been through the Sun Dance for Walking Grass. He would survive this for Sarah.

He moved through trees and thick underbrush to the edge of the river, then waited for what seemed an eternity before finally catching sight of one person on a small raft. Farther upstream the bell of a steamboat clanged, and somewhere far in the distance the music of a fiddle floated through the night air. Caleb smiled ruefully. He had been through much in his short life, moving back and forth between two worlds, but who ever would have though there would come a time when he would be sneaking away in the dead off night with Sarah, the woman he loved?

The raft came closer and he heard her call out softly.

"Here," he answered. It did not take much to be heard. Voices carried far over open water at night. He smiled again at the thought of Terrence Sax sound asleep, thinking his Sarah was nestled in her own room nearby, thinking a beating or the offer of money could make Caleb Sax leave Saint Louis and the precious woman he loved.

Sarah maneuvered a pole and got the raft close enough to shore for Caleb to step aboard. She helped him pull the Appaloosa on also. The horse balked at first, but Caleb spoke to it in Cheyenne, and the animal seemed to relax. Caleb tied a rope around the animal's leg, then kneeled, grunting with pain, and tied the other end of the rope around one of the raft's logs. He spoke soothingly to the horse more as Sarah pushed with the pole to get them back into the river's current.

"The river is calm for a long way," she said quietly. "We shouldn't have any trouble. We can be far downstream by morning, then get off and head west."

He walked around the other side of the horse, picking up another pole and pushing himself. He turned to look at her, so proud of her courage and daring. When she shivered he reached out to touch her shoulder encouragingly.

"You are wet."

"I'm all right. I slipped and fell into the water pushing the raft out."

He retrieved a robe from the horse. "Get those clothes off," he ordered.

"I can't. Not now, Caleb. There isn't time."

"You will get sick."

"No I won't. Just put the robe around me. Please, Caleb. We can't stop for anything."

Their eyes held in the moonlight and he bent down and lightly kissed her lips."I should not have come back here.

If it were not for that Byron Clawson I would have left you here where you belong."

He put the robe around her shoulders.

"But I don't belong here," she replied. "I never did. I belong with you, Caleb." She handed back his pole. "Can you push? Between us and the current, we'll make good time."

He took the pole. "I will do what I can."

A terrible dread came over him, the black feeling he had experienced before he lost Walking Grass. In his twenty years Caleb had never been able to hang on to anyone he loved. Now there was Sarah, and if they could get away, they would go and get little Tom. Was it possible he could have such happiness, possible he could have them both?

The weather turned suddenly hot, and the trees and underbrush hung limp and quiet. They had gone south on the Mississippi rather than west on the Missouri, hoping any trackers would search the Missouri first, knowing Caleb Sax would head west. In the early morning they left the river and moved onto land, making their way through the thickly forested parts of Missouri so as not to be seen, heading west toward Unorganized Territory. Caleb knew that once he was in Indian country they could make good time. But the heat, the heavy woods and his own injuries were slowing them up for now.

Sarah rode in front of him on the Appaloosa. She had refused to stop and change the night before. Now she removed the buffalo robe because of the morning heat, and her clothes were drying but still damp, clinging uncomfortably to her body. Caleb was worried about her, and by mid-morning he stopped the horse and dismounted, ignoring his own pain and pulling her down from the horse.

"You are getting out of that dress and everything else," he told her. He opened her carpetbag, pulling out another dress and a pair of bloomers. "Put these on."

"Caleb, there isn't time."

"There is less time for you to be sick. We will never get away if you are too ill to travel." He turned her around and unbuttoned the back of her dress, pulling it off her shoulders.

She folded her arms over her breasts and hung her head, stepping out of the dress, her high shoes still unbuttoned and soggy. Caleb stooped down.

"Pull," he told her, grabbing a shoe. She pulled her foot out of first one, then the other. He pulled her stockings off next, trying to ignore her slender thighs and calves, her milky white skin. This was the first time he had seen her this way, but his pain and the gravity of their situation left little time for lingering on her beauty. He yanked down her bloomers.

"Caleb, don't—"

"Don't be silly," he told her, rolling up the clothes and tying them while she stood there naked. To her relief he did not stare at her, and she loved him more than ever, almost wanting him to look, yet devastated at the idea of being stripped in front of him in the bright morning light. He picked up the dry bloomers and she stepped into them. Only then did he glance at her secret place as he pulled them on.

A certain tension hung in the air for a moment. Then both of them began to relax slightly and realize what they had done, that they were alone together and could do whatever they wanted. All they needed was a little more time, time for healing and time to get farther away.

Caleb grasped her wrists, and she hung her head but did not resist when he gently pulled her arms away so he could look upon her breasts, full and white, her pink nipples erect from the stimulation of his gaze.

He leaned down and lightly kissed each nipple, making her gasp and whimper his name, her cheeks turning crimson with a mixture of embarrassment and pleasure. He pulled her close, running a hand over her bare back and kissing her damp hair. "You are beautiful, Sarah," he groaned. "I love you so. You are so brave . . . so good."

She leaned against him, realizing he could do anything

to her and she would be loved and respected and would never have to be afraid. She belonged to him, and when the time was right, she would let him claim her. It felt so right to be in his arms, and she would let him take his pleasure in her when he wanted. She wanted to please him the way his Indian wife had.

"We must get going," he told her, pulling away and picking up the clean dress. He slipped it over her head. This one buttoned in front, and his big hands fumbled with the tiny buttons. "You should wear a tunic like the Indian women," he told her. "They are lighter and cooler, and you have only to tie them at the shoulders." He stopped at her breasts, then took her chin and lifted it, giving her a teasing smile. "Or untie them," he added.

She reddened but smiled, her heart aching at the bruises and cuts on his face, his shorn hair. Yet to her the injuries did nothing to detract from his handsomeness. "Caleb, I . . . I don't want to wait." She looked down. "I mean, I don't want to wait till we find someone who will marry us. That could be days, even weeks. We might get caught. Who knows what will happen? I just, I want it to be with you, Caleb, the first time."

He brushed her breasts lightly with the backs of his hands, then continued buttoning the dress. "The time will be right soon, and it will not be wrong. For the Indian, when a man takes a virgin she is his, they are man and wife. It will be that way with us. Your God and mine—and who knows that they are not the same?—know of our love for each other and want us to be together. It is not bad for us to mate and be one and enjoy our love. No one, not even Terrence Sax, can change that love, Sarah—even if we are caught. In our own hearts we will be man and wife forever."

She raised her eyes and he leaned down to lightly kiss her lips. "*Ne-mehotatse*," he whispered. "We must go," he told her.

She nodded and turned, getting back up on the horse. Caleb stood there a moment, sniffing the air, studying the shadows, his keen ears listening. To her he seemed as much a part of the forest as the birds and the rabbits, sometimes blending right in with the shadows and leaves in his buckskin clothing and dark skin.

"So far no one follows," he told her. "We will keep going well after dark before making camp."

They slept without a campfire that second night, wrapped in each other's arms. Sarah felt achy but attributed it to the sudden change from the kind of life to which she had grown accustomed. She had not lived this ruggedly for many years, and she had also lost a lot of sleep. In the morning they ate meager strips of beef jerky before going on. By the third night they reached a refreshingly lovely place where the grass was thick and green, and a small waterfall spilled into a shallow stream that danced over rocks. The banks of the stream were littered with spring wildflowers, and not far away Caleb found a cave in the side of a rocky hill. He hurried back to Sarah, who was unloading the horse. His gait was faster now as his body was healing.

"We will stay here and rest," he told her. "This is a good place. There is a cave not far from here. We will make a fire there and sleep inside it."

"Oh, Caleb, do we dare stay here a day or two? I would love to stop for awhile."

He smiled, kissing her cheek. "So far I do not think anyone follows. We will stay. It is better to rest and be well to travel than to get sick and perhaps not be able to go on at all." He took down her carpetbag. "Do you have soap and a towel in here?"

"Yes."

"Good. You stay here and bathe in the stream and change your clothes again. You will feel much better. I will make you some moccasins so you can stop wearing those tight shoes. And I will try to get us something to eat. I will use my bow so that I make no noise."

He was off then, leading the Appaloosa up the hill. Sarah

turned and began undressing, more aware now of her body than at any time in her life. Perhaps it would happen here, tonight or tomorrow, here where they could relax and eat and be alone together in the cave. She shivered at the chill of the stream, yet it felt good on her sweaty body. Again it seemed she was hot from the inside out, and it irritated her that perhaps she had taken cold. She did not want anything to happen to slow them down.

She quickly bathed and washed her hair, then put on a clean dress and proceeded to wash the two dirty ones and hang them over limbs to dry, along with her bloomers and stockings. She set her shoes on a rock in the sun, laying her towel and the soap beside them, then hurried up the hill to where she saw the horse tied. Caleb was bent over cleaning two rabbits.

"Oh, Caleb, they look wonderful. That didn't take you very long."

"I caught sight of them earlier, running under that dead stump over there. I simply waited for them to come back out, but it was not easy to keep an eye on them, not when all I had to do was look the other way to see you lying naked in the stream."

"Caleb Sax! You weren't supposed to look."

He laughed lightly. "That is a cruel request of a man who has not been with a woman in over two years and is now alone with one he loves—and one so beautiful." He looked up at her, his expression serious. "Besides, you can always pay me back. I still have to bathe."

"I would never—"

"Oh, yes you will," he interrupted. "Maybe not today, but you will." He stood up and laughed lightly again. "Here. You cook these over the fire I have started. I am going to take my turn in the stream, and later I will make you some moccasins out of an old buckskin shirt I have. We will sleep well tonight, Sarah, and with full bellies." He raised his arms and threw back his head. "We have made it. We are free. Thank you, *Maheo.*"

Sarah watched him, her love in her eyes. He was shirtless, and his ribs and back bore many bruises from the beating. Her heart ached at the thought of how horrible that day must have been for him. And standing there with arms upraised, he seemed to her the epitome of all she could ever want in a man. The shorn hair and bruised body could not detract from his beauty, and she felt the prickly desire to watch him undress at the stream. But when he walked off and began unlacing his buckskin leggings she looked away, tending to the rabbits.

She watched the outer fat just under the skin begin to sizzle and drip, wiping her damp brow and wondering if she should tell Caleb how feverish she felt. No. He might become alarmed and stay longer for her sake. It was peaceful here, and no one seemed to be following, but they dared not stay too long. They must go on. She would be fine once she was rested and had eaten.

Chapter Nineteen

FOR that night and another day they did nothing but eat and sleep, and Sarah's fever seemed to subside. She said nothing to Caleb about it and ignored the continued aching in her bones and muscles. It was enough to be safe. At least she had time to rest, and Caleb had time to heal. There was time to talk, to laugh, to share their deepest thoughts and fears and love. Neither of them wanted to ask if it could last. They must believe it would.

The evening of the second night in the cave, Caleb came back from tending to the horse to find Sarah already snuggled under the robes of their bed. He laughed.

"So, already you are becoming a lazy woman," he teased. "If I had known I was marrying a woman who goes to sleep before supper I would have left you back in Saint Louis." He put more wood on the campfire just outside the cave, then came inside, kneeling beside her. "Are you all right?"

She smiled, moving one arm out from under the robes to reveal a bare shoulder. "I'm fine. Why don't you come to bed, too, Caleb?" His smile faded, and her face turned crimson at her own boldness. She pushed the covers down to her waist, revealing naked breasts, and his eyes rested on them lovingly before meeting her provocative green eyes.

"Sarah, you don't have to."

"Yes, I do. I want to," she replied.

She looked like a wide-eyed little girl and he felt almost guilty. But he reminded himself she was not truly related, and she was eighteen years old, in Indian terms well beyond the marrying age. She was a woman, but not completely. It was up to him to apply the finishing touches, and he loved her as dearly as his own life.

Her eyes suddenly teared. "I'm scared, Caleb. Scared I'll never have you this way again. Please . . . if you're well enough. We can be married right here and now in God's eyes. You said so."

He bent over and kissed a warm, pink cheek, thinking she must be flushed from her embarrassment and excitement. He never considered it could be anything else. "If you are sure," he said softly.

She was lost in his intense blue eyes. "I am."

He gently smoothed back the hair from her face. "Then we shall be one, *Ishiomiists*. That is my Indian name for you, Rising Sun. Like the sun you bring me new life." His eyes teared. "When Walking Grass died, I also died. Now I am alive again because of you."

He stood up, removing his moccasins and leggings. He

stood before her, a magnificent man. Even her virgin eyes knew that, and when he untied his loincloth and cast it aside all fear left her at the sight of his proud beauty. He was her Caleb. He would teach her, be patient with her. She decided that no matter how much it hurt, she would not be afraid or make him stop. She wanted nothing more than to give him pleasure.

His eyes never left hers as he knelt again to move in beside her under the robes. She sighed when he pressed himself against her flat belly, then his mouth covered hers, and she gloried in the sensation of skin against skin. Caleb, magnificent, wild Caleb was hers, catching his fingers in her long, red-gold hair, pushing his tongue into her mouth enticingly so that she felt like a wanton woman. She was suddenly wicked and passionate, not sure what to do yet knowing he would bring it all out of her naturally, with the right words, the right touch, the right movements.

He groaned with his own pleasure, his mouth leaving hers to trail over her throat. His hand massaged her back and bottom, moving around to touch that most private place never touched by a man, sending waves of ecstasy through secret places finally being awakened to womanly desires. His fingers moved in a circle, making her whimper and grasp his hair as his lips lingered on her taut nipples. He could feel the silken moistness that told him her womanly passions had been aroused and her virgin body was preparing for him.

Sarah! At last he would have her, but he reminded himself to move carefully. He had been a long time without a woman. He wanted to devour her, invade her, explore every curve and claim every secret place for himself so that she would belong only to him. But he must not move too quickly or be too demanding this first time. Still, her own eager desire was as great as his. She seemed to respond with the same desperation he felt, and soon their heated bodies were damp from passion, and whimpers and whispered words of love were spoken breathlessly between kisses.

He seemed to be everywhere, her mouth, her breasts, her stomach, her most private places, touching, tasting, ravaging in ways she never dreamed possible. But with Caleb it was all right and natural. She felt herself melting, being led along a road to ecstasy. He made her want to do everything, broke down her resistance, wiped away bashfulness and inhibitions. He touched and explored and possessed, seeing, claiming, changing her from girl to woman.

His mouth trailed back to her own, lingering on different parts of her body until he met her lips again and his broad, beautiful frame moved up on top of her. He pushed with his knees to part her slender legs and move between them, and her heart pounded furiously with anticipation and apprehension.

"Caleb?"

He felt her trembling and nuzzled her neck. "*Ho-shuh*," he said softly, moving gently, pressing his manliness against her. "Do not be afraid. It does not hurt for long." He kept rubbing against her until she felt a wonderful explosion, and she arched up to him brazenly, her body pulsing with the most wonderful feeling she had ever known. He knew she was ready then, and it must be done quickly. He pushed deep. There was no other way.

She gasped in surprise at the pain, and her nails dug into his arms. "Hang on, *Ishiomiists*," he whispered. "It will be over soon." He grasped her hips and pushed, gasping himself at the ecstasy of the moment. He was one with Sarah, claiming her, loving her, branding her, taking her virginity. Now no one else could have it. It belonged to Caleb Sax.

She screamed his name in a mixture of pain and ecstasy, and his life spilled into her in lingering surges. He finally breathed a long sigh and lay down beside her, pulling the blankets over them and holding her close. She was crying, and he kissed her hair.

"I am sorry it has to be that way," he told her. "It does not last. I hurried. You brought me so much pleasure, I could not hold back my life." He kissed her over and over, caressing her and murmuring words of love. "I will bathe you and you will sleep," he told her. He moved a big hand to her abdomen, massaging it gently. "It will be better next time. This is a promise."

She kissed his chest. "It was beautiful," she whispered. "I just didn't know it could hurt that much. But I don't care, Caleb. I belong to you now. Nothing can change that, can it?"

He kissed her eyes. "No. Nothing can change that. *Nemehotatse, Ishiomiists.*"

"*Ne-mehotatse,*" she whispered.

They fell asleep then, exhausted from the agony and ecstasy of newfound love.

For two more days they stayed in the cave. It was against Caleb's better judgment, yet it seem unlikely they would ever be found in this place. And to be with Sarah, to love her in all the ways humanly possible, was more temptation than he could fight. He couldn't get enough of the woman he loved.

Those were precious hours, precious days, and they both prayed they would not become just precious memories. Together they rose to glorious heights of ecstasy, explored, tasted, shared, enjoyed. Sarah cared little that she had left behind the luxuries of a rich girl. Being with Caleb was true wealth, loving and being loved, being a woman in every sense.

But all too soon they both had to face the reality that they must leave. Someone might track them or stumble upon them. And there was little Tom to think of now. Caleb was more anxious than ever to get back to his son.

"We'll make it," he told Sarah, kicking at the dying embers of the fire. He looked at her. She stood there watching him, then ran to him, crying. He swept her into his arms. "It will be all right," he told her.

"Oh, Caleb, I don't want to leave. So much happened here. It's—it's like this place belongs only to us."

He held her tightly. "I know. Maybe some day we can come back, and we'll be long married and bring our children with us. He squeezed her tightly. "I love you, Sarah. I've never loved another so much. I'd die to keep you with me."

She clung tightly to him while he kissed her hair, her cheek. She turned her face to meet his lips then, kissing him with all the knowledge of an awakened woman, glorying in the pleasant things he had taught her.

"We must go," he said, letting go of her. She met his eyes and saw that his, too, were watery. He forced a smile for her. His face was almost normal again, and she had grown accustomed to the short hair, which after much cajoling he had agreed to let her cut so that it looked like a normal haircut and would look nicer as it grew out.

He led her reluctantly out of the cave, a place that had come to represent happiness and security. He helped her up onto the horse, then moved up behind her with ease. Everything about him was sleek and provocative, and she dearly loved the Indian in him, from the lovely Cheyenne words he whispered to her during their lovemaking to the scars he bore from the Sun Dance and the bravery it must have taken to participate.

She turned and looked at him, and he grew somewhat alarmed at the circles under her eyes and the thin, pale look about her. He told himself it was the hard journey and the traumatic events that had taken place in her life.

"Do you feel well?" he asked, concern in his eyes.

She looked away, a poor liar. "I'm fine. I've never felt more wonderful," she said, pretending the awful ache in her lower back was better now.

Caleb nudged the horse into motion and they rode away from the special place where Sarah Sax had become a woman. Neither of them looked back. It hurt too much.

The next day the fever that had been trying to build in Sarah broke loose. She awoke in a sweat, throwing off her covers, but Caleb was immediately there putting them back over her.

"You will take a worse chill," he told her.

He had been watching her all morning as he made them some breakfast. The heat from her body was so intense it had actually awakened him. Now he was filled with dread. Why hadn't he seen the signs for what they were instead of avoiding the truth? She was sick, probably had been since she fell in the water the night they left. She had been trying to hide it.

She opened glazed eyes, meeting his own. "I've ruined everything, haven't I?"

He bent down and kissed her forehead. "No. It is I who have ruined everything. I never should have come back into your life, Sarah." His eyes grew dark with worry. "What have I done? We are far from help and you are very sick."

"I'll be all right," she whispered, forcing a smile. "We have to keep going, Caleb."

He rose and looked around. "Sarah, we are miles from nowhere and going to a place where doctors are unheard of. I fear you need a doctor."

"No," she protested. "You can take care of me. You must have some Indian remedy."

He desperately fought an urge to cry out. Why? The awful dread enveloped him again. Not Sarah! His mind whirled with indecision. Sometimes when Indian children had a fever their mothers immersed them in cool water to bring it down.

"We'll go on a ways," he told her. "I smell water. If we find a stream or a river, I will put you in it to cool your body. A fever is dangerous. I have seen men go mad from it."

Caleb could not eat. He was too worried about Sarah. He managed to get some tea down her throat, and Sarah wondered how she swallowed it at all. There seemed to be hardly enough room in her throat for air to go through. In her mind she was screaming, screaming with terror and disappointment.

Caleb packed their gear, then helped her rise, but she couldn't get all the way to her feet. He held on to her as she lay back down. "Oh, Caleb," she whispered. "What's wrong with me?"

"I do not know. That is what frightens me. I will build a travois and take you back."

"No," she groaned. "We can't go back!"

"We have no choice. I could not live with myself if you ... if something happened to you out here. This is all my fault."

"No. We had to try, Caleb. It isn't your fault." Her chest heaved in a sob. "What will we do?"

He knelt down beside her. "Try not to get upset." He leaned down and kissed her fevered forehead, agonizing over what to do. She needed a doctor's help. Her breathing was dangerously labored and she felt like fire. How would he ever forgive himself if she died out here, running off with a man who could offer her nothing? He could not gamble with her life by taking the chance on going forward and hoping she would get better.

"Don't go back, Caleb. Please don't go back," she wept. "Uncle Terrence will do something terrible. I know it! I'd rather die out here than go back."

Caleb struggled against his own tears. "I will never let that happen, Sarah." He reached behind his neck and removed his blue quill necklace. Leaning down, he laid it across her breasts. "We must take our chances, Sarah. I will wait one day. If you are not better, we will go back. I do not know what will happen, but no matter what, I give you this necklace as a love gift, a vow of my total devotion. I gave this gift only once, to Walking Grass. Now I give it to you. May it protect you from death and all harm. Keep it forever, Sarah, no matter what happens to me."

She held his eyes, moving her hand up to grasp the necklace, understanding how important it was to him and how much he loved her to give it to her. It was all he had of his own mother.

"Caleb," she whispered lovingly. "Tell me everything will be all right . . . that we'll always be together."

A tear slipped down his cheek. He put a hand to his heart, then laid it against her own. "Here. We will always be together here, in spirit."

Sarah closed her eyes. She loved him so much, she thought, it couldn't end this way.

"I will make you a travois," he said dejectedly. "We will go to the water. It is not far. We are only three days from Saint Louis. If we hadn't stopped at the cave . . ." His words choked. Was that all he would have of her? Just those few days at the cave? He rose and took two robes off the horse to use for a travois. "It is probably good that we stopped here. Otherwise we would be much farther from help. This way there is a chance to get you to a doctor."

"No, Caleb. If we were already farther away . . . I would die out there." She grasped her throat. "This is . . . no different."

"Yes it is," he snapped, taking a small hatchet from his gear. "Out there there would be no help. But here we are still close enough." Their eyes held a moment, then he turned away to find some slender young saplings to cut for poles.

As he worked Caleb realized that one of Terrence Sax's predictions could come true after all. Perhaps Sarah would die, just like Cora. Perhaps it was true such women should not go to the wilds. But Sarah was stronger than Cora had been, more spirited. Surely she was strong enough. What had happened could happen to anyone. It was just another cruel twist of fate that seemed to plague him. Everyone he loved seemed to be taken from him. Would little Tom be waiting there for him when he returned?

He chopped wildly at a sapling, taking out his anger and frustration on the little tree. He cut another and dragged them both back, sitting down to remove the branches. Caleb wanted nothing more than to hold Sarah, for she lay weeping from pain and fear, but he must get the travois ready. He began tying the buffalo robes to the poles, stretching the skins and tying them with rawhide until the structure was ready.

He threw down the hatchet and secured the two poles on either side of the Appaloosa. When it was secure he walked over to her, bending down to pick her up. But he could not stop his own grief and fear. He lay down beside her and pulled her into his arms. Both of them wept.

The water did not bring down her fever, and Caleb realized he had no choice. He would take her back, and if she lived he would find a way to take her again. Her life was most important, and she was only getting worse. She lapsed into fits of delirium as her fever raged and her breathing became more labored. Caleb moved swiftly, and with each day's ride Sarah slipped farther away from him.

During a moment of cognizance she asked him to put the blue quill necklace in the lining of her carpetbag, fearing that if her father found it on her he would destroy it. Both knew the chance they were taking by going back, but they also knew the greater risk of not returning. It was amazing that a person could be so happy one day and so devastated the next. Their days in the cave had been like a dream, a sweet, wonderful dream. But reality had struck hard. The gods had not smiled on them after all, except to keep them close enough to Saint Louis to get help for Sarah. The dream had turned into a nightmare.

Caleb paid a ferryman to take them back across the Mississippi, having no idea where the raft was. The man eyed him warily, and Caleb wondered how many people in the area had been warned to be on the lookout for them. Yet it was too late to go back, and he wouldn't if he could. Sarah was worse than ever, hardly aware most of the time of where she was or who she was with. That made everything worse.

He could not even talk to her, tell her he loved her, tell her good-bye or that he would come back.

They left the ferry and headed north toward Saint Louis. Was it only days before that they had left, so happy and excited and alive with love? Caleb stopped when the city came into view. He knelt down beside Sarah.

"Sarah," he said softly. *"Ishiomiists. Ne-mehotatse."*

She said nothing. She looked still as death, and his heart tightened. "Sarah?" He closed his eyes and shuddered, taking her hand and bending his head down to kiss it. She was dying. Tom and Walking Grass he had learned to bear . . . but not Sarah. His body jerked in a sob.

"Sarah," he screamed. "Speak to me. I love you, Sarah. I love you! God, forgive me. I have killed you!"

Her lips moved slightly, and she gave a little gasping noise, but that was all. Caleb stood up, sobbing openly. He stumbled to the Appaloosa and grasped the reins, heading blindly toward Saint Louis. His mind was reeling with the horror of the possibility of Sarah's death. How would he bear such a thing? Was he bad? What was there about him that brought disaster to those he loved most?

He got to the outskirts of town, wondering if he would be shot down on sight. A few people stared at his Indian garb and the travois, but no one said anything. He stopped and asked a passerby for the nearest physician, then headed in that direction, coming to a sign that read WILLIAM NEDERER, M.D.

Caleb walked to the door and knocked, and a few moments later a balding man answered.

"Yes?"

"I am Caleb Sax. There is a girl on my travois. She is very sick."

The doctor frowned, looking out the doorway at the travois, then looking up at Caleb. "Get her off there and bring her on in," he said.

Caleb quickly went to get Sarah, carrying her limp body

through the doorway and laying her on a padded table the doctor indicated.

The doctor quickly closed a curtain around it so that Caleb failed to notice someone hurrying out of the office. The doctor came inside. "What's wrong with her?" he asked.

"She got wet one night. I told her to get into dry clothes, but she refused. A few days later she got sick ... a bad fever. I did not know what to do for her."

The doctor raised Sarah's eyelids, then felt her throat. He frowned, quickly opening her dress and putting a stethescope to her chest. He sighed as he pulled a sheet over her face. "She's dead," he said matter-of-factly.

"No!" Caleb stared at him, shaking his head, his heart filled with aching sorrow. He looked at Sarah's covered body, then bent over and pulled the sheet off her face, unaware of anything around him. She couldn't be dead. Only days before he had held her warm, beautiful body close to his own, made love to her, shared the pleasures of lovemaking with her. They had talked and laughed and loved. How could this happen. Why?

"Sarah," he wept, his face against her own, his hands clinging to the sheet. "You can't leave me. I need you!"

A moment later he felt cold steel against his neck. He choked back a sob and slowly stood up. The doctor was pointing a musket at him.

"I know who you are, Caleb Sax. This girl is Sarah, Terrence Sax's niece. You're in a lot of trouble, boy. She's dead, and you're going to hang. I've sent for help."

In spite of Caleb's sorrow he knew he had to act quickly. If it were only Sarah he would stand there and let the man shoot him, for he would have nothing left to live for. But somewhere in the wilds a little boy waited for his father to return, and as hopeless as life seemed now, he had to get to little Tom. Tom was his only life, his only hope for happiness. He would not die in this hated city and never see his son again. Sarah would want him to get away and return to his son.

In a flash he grabbed the musket and pushed upward. The gun went off and plaster fell from the ceiling. Caleb dove through the curtains and hurried out the front door, leaping off the porch railing onto the Appaloosa and getting the animal into a gallop just as several men came running toward the doctor's office.

"*Hopo! Hopo!*" Caleb urged the Appaloosa to run faster. He charged around a corner, deliberately slamming the travois into a fence to try to break it loose. The carpetbag and other gear went flying, but the sapling poles were too green to break easily. He slowed long enough to take out his hatchet and chop the rawhide strips that held the poles in place. He saw the men who had been running toward the doctor's office grab other peoples' horses, and Caleb urged the Appaloosa on.

He charged into the thick trees, unaware that when the doctor's musket was fired Sarah Sax had stirred at the loud noise.

Chapter Twenty

THE Appaloosa galloped through underbrush and splashed through creeks; but the animal was tired from being driven for long hours when Caleb hurried Sarah back to Saint Louis. It was quickly winded and Caleb knew that the men following were closing in, since their horses were fresher.

He tried not to think of Sarah; the agony was too great.

He thought instead of Tom, his little Tom. He had to get to his son. Tom was all he had left.

If his pursuers were Crow, he could fight them. But Crow Indians didn't carry muskets, and he knew his one musket would be no defense against several. White men did not fight hand-to-hand. They used their guns, and he knew that even if they didn't kill him, he would find no justice in Saint Louis, not against a man like Terrence Sax. Everyone would be ready to believe that Caleb had kidnapped and raped Sarah, then killed her, and Sarah was not alive to tell anyone otherwise.

Caleb and the Appaloosa charged down the river embankment, but the Appaloosa's front legs buckled, sending animal and man tumbling. The horse landed on Caleb, and he felt his breath knocked out as pain seared through his right shoulder. The Appaloosa rolled off, struggling and whinnying, but it could not get to its feet. Caleb crawled away from the horse, using his left arm for support and holding his right arm tight against his chest, unable to move it at all.

He scrambled toward an old log, hoping he could hide in it, but he was too big to fit. He searched desperately for another place to hide, hearing horses crashing through the forest nearby.

"Look, his horse," someone shouted.

"He's down! He's down someplace. Spread out!"

The horse whinnied in pain, and then Caleb heard a gunshot. The animal made no more sound. He curled up against a tree. Gone. Everything was gone. He bent over, pain overwhelming him, both from a broken shoulder and a broken heart.

"Over here," someone shouted close by.

Caleb's first instinct was to run. In his mind he thought he was up and running very fast, but in reality he was stumbling. There was another gunshot, and a new pain enveloped him in the center of his back. He fell forward, hearing voices from a great distance.

"Should I kill him?"

"No. Wait for Sax. He'll be here in a few minutes. He stopped at the doc's first."

Someone kicked him. "He's still alive." The voice sounded like Byron Clawson's. "Apparently my bullet is taking its time finishing him off."

"Don't look to me like he'll live for long. Dirty son of a bitch. I wonder what he did to that poor girl."

"Well, Sax wants it kept quiet, don't want the girl's reputation ruined."

There was general laughter and conversation then, and every once in a while someone else would kick Caleb to see if he was still alive. Then there was the sound of more horses.

"Over here, Mr. Sax!"

Moments later Caleb was kicked several times. "Bastard! Bastard," someone snarled. "She's dead! My Sarah is dead because of this no-good!"

"He ain't dead yet, Mr. Sax. You want us to finish him off?"

"No! I want him to suffer." There was a moment of silence. "I don't want the law in on this, understand? Any of you let this out and I'll have your jobs. I don't want my Sarah involved in any slander, even after death."

"Yes, sir."

"Any of you know how to contact some river pirates? Maybe someone on the docks who would deal in selling men to oar slave ships?"

"I might be able to make a contact," someone answered.

"All right. Take this heathen and hide him somewhere until you do. Tell whoever you talk to that I will pay very well to have the body taken away. I don't want it to be around here, understand? I want it done downriver. If he lives, they're welcome to sell him for what they can get. If he dies, I want the body dumped off as far south as possible—New Orleans wouldn't be too far."

"He don't look to me like he's gonna make it."

"All the more reason for none of you to say a thing. We're all in this together, and we've taken the law into our own hands. It ends right here. Understood?"

There was a round of agreements. Caleb felt himself being lifted, and to his horror he could not seem to move or speak. Someone slung him over a horse. That was the last he remembered of the men in the forest.

Sarah stirred, only able to open her eyes. She wet her dry parched lips as she stared at a white ceiling. She swallowed, her throat aching, and tried to think where she might be. The last she knew she was with Caleb, and he had her on a travois. He had been bringing her back to Saint Louis. She opened her mouth to call for him, but only a small whimper came out. She tried again, and the noise brought a stout woman to her bedside.

"Well now, the child is finally comin' around," the woman said with a strong Irish accent. "Sure 'n her uncle will be happy. A whole week she's been layin' here lookin' like death."

A man came and bent over her, looking into her eyes, feeling her throat, opening her gown and putting something cold to her chest. "She just might make it after all," he said. "I never thought such a thing could be possible. She had all the appearances of being dead when she was brought in. I couldn't even find a heartbeat."

"Ca . . . leb," Sarah whispered.

"What's that, child?" The woman bent closer.

"Caleb."

The woman looked at the man. "She's askin' for that young man you told me not to talk about, doctor, the one you said brought her in."

"Do me a favor and send someone for Terrence Sax, will you?"

"Sure 'n I will, doctor."

The stout woman left, and the doctor leaned closer. "Your

uncle will be here shortly, Miss Sax. You just lie still. I'll get you some water."

Sarah didn't want her uncle. She wanted Caleb. She tried to tell him, but the words would not come. She closed her eyes, thinking. The woman had said she'd been there a whole week. Where was Caleb? What had happened to him?

The doctor returned with a cup, lifting her slightly and letting her drink a little water.

"There we are," he told her. "You're much stronger than I thought, Sarah Sax," he continued, laying her back down and setting the cup aside. "We all thought you dead when you came here, even that Caleb Sax. But it doesn't much matter what he thought, does it? You'll get well eventually, and you'll see the foolishness of your ways. It's all over now. You're home safe and sound, and you've learned a lot, I expect. It's a hard life out there in the wilds." He stood and left Sarah.

Minutes later she heard a familiar, hated voice. Terrence Sax stepped into the room looking at her with a mixture of anger and love, then stepped closer and leaned over her.

"Why'd you do it, Sarah? Why'd you run off on me after all I've done for you?"

Her eyes held all the hatred she had for him. "Heard you," she whispered. "You're . . . my father."

The man paled, seeming to wilt as he pulled a chair close to the bed and sat down. "It's true," he said quietly. "But it was so long ago, Sarah, and I truly did love Cora. I've lived with the terrible guilt of it ever since, but something good came of it." He looked at her again. "You. You're the most precious thing I've ever had, far more precious than my most expensive material possession. I want what I know is best for you. You're so beautiful, Sarah. You belong in a grand house with a respectable man, not in some cabin with a half-breed who doesn't know the first thing about providing you with the comfort you deserve. He'd have you pregnant and worn out in no time. Why, you nearly died just trying to run away with him. How do you think you would have survived out there in the wilderness?"

A tear slipped out of one of her eyes and trickled down the side of her face. "Caleb," she whispered. "Where is he?"

Sax sighed deeply, realizing he must do this right so that she believed him. "Caleb is dead, Sarah."

She let out a little cry, her head moving from side to side in denial. Sax rose, grasping her face between his hands.

"Listen to me, Sarah. I didn't mean for him to be killed. You must believe me. If he had just waited and talked to me. After running off with you, I would have listened, tried to understand for your sake. But the kid ran, Sarah. He ran, thinking he'd be in trouble. He had already been told you were dead, and for all appearances you were when he got you here. Even the doctor thought at first you were dead. He couldn't even find a heartbeat. Caleb panicked and ran. I and some of my friends went after him. I just wanted to get it all straight, Sarah. But Caleb must have thought I meant to hurt him. Then his horse fell, and it landed right on top of him, crushed him."

She kept shaking her head. It couldn't be true.

He held her face more firmly between his hands. "Sarah, he's dead, and quite by accident, I swear to God. I can take you and show you his grave if you want. We dug one for him right there. Even the horse's carcass is still there. Damn it, Sarah, I'd put up with the smell of that stinking carcass to take you there and show you the animal's broken leg. It's God's truth, Sarah. He shouldn't have run. I'm damned sorry. I never would have hurt him. My God, he brought you back here, took that risk because he loved you. I couldn't have hurt him after that. You must believe me."

Her body shuddered with sobs of horror and sorrow. Caleb. Her beautiful Caleb. Those precious moments of joy and ecstasy in the cave were gone forever. She closed her eyes against a pain so deep it seemed to tear her soul in two.

"You can come home pretty soon, Sarah, and this will

all be over. We'll talk about the other—about what happened years ago. I want you to understand, Sarah, how much I loved your mother . . . and how much I love you. We'll talk. Everything will be all right now. You're safe."

But Sarah didn't hear him. The shock of Caleb's death overwhelmed her until her body shook violently. Terrence yelled for the doctor, who made her drink something that soon put her back into a blessed sleep.

Caleb opened his eyes to darkness. A strong, rancid smell entered his nostrils and he curled his nose at the odor. But almost instantly he realized that curling his nose was apparently all he could do. When he tried to move anything else, nothing happened.

A door opened above him and he squinted when sunlight came through the opening. He scrambled to think as a man came down some wooden steps. With the sun at the man's back and being momentarily blinded from looking up too quickly at the bright light he could not see who it was that approached, but Caleb could make out that he wore high boots.

"Well, mate, you able yet to pull your own weight?" He kicked Caleb and Caleb grunted with pain. The man sighed. "We dug out the musket ball and fixed up the shoulder as best we could, Indian. But you don't seem to be able to move a muscle. Paralyzed and useless, that's what you are." The man kicked him again. "Too bad, mate. A man your size would have brought a fine price. A fine price. That's me damned luck, ain't it?" The man paced a moment, then lit an oil lamp. Caleb gazed around at damp wood, stacked barrels, and several men chained together, none of them looking too healthy. "Well, laddy, I've got me orders. I was paid well to bring you this far, and could have sold you for even more if you'd got well. But you're a burden to me now and I'm gettin' rid of you. This is as far as you go. The river will finish you off, and you'll die a far distance from Saint Louis, just as intended."

The man looked up at the hole above. "Blade! Henderson! Get your scummy butts down here!"

"Yo, sir!" Two men came down the wooden steps.

"Take this one and throw him in the river. He can't swim. He can't even move. He'll drown and no one will know where he came from."

"Aye, sir."

Caleb groaned with excruciating pain when they picked him up carelessly and dragged his large frame up the steps. He tried to struggle as they carried him to the side of the boat, but movement was impossible. In the next moment cold water hit him, enveloped him. He readied himself for a peaceful death by drowning, and visions of Walking Grass and Sarah moved through his mind. They were both dead now. Memories of bringing Sarah to Saint Louis returned, and a terrible sadness for all he had lost filled him.

He sank lower, feeling his body being pulled by the current to a blissful death. But then he realized that for some reason he could move slightly. Whether it was the way he landed, perhaps awakening some injured nerve; or the cold water; or perhaps only its buoyancy; he could move his arms and legs to some extent. His own stubborn determination took hold then. Fate had tried again and again to destroy him, but he would win, he would not be beaten this way. He would live to see his son again and nothing and no one would ever take the boy away from him.

His body caught on a fallen tree and he grasped desperately for a hold, finding a branch with first one hand and then the other. He was shocked to realize how weak he was, and the pain was almost unbearable, but he managed to pull himself along enough to get his head out of water. He gasped for breath, shivering with the cold and his injuries, not even sure how badly he was hurt. He managed to pull himself slightly farther up the tree to a point where a good share of his body was out of the water, but as soon as the buoyancy of the water left him, so did his strength and his ability to move.

How long he lay there he couldn't be sure. He heard the
sounds of a town or city not far away, and a few boats
passed by, clanging their bells, voices talking on board. But
none of them noticed him. Finally a raft floated by, the two
old men on it fishing.

"Look there, Ben. Somebody's snagged on that there
tree."

"I'll be damned."

There was a moment of silence, and then Caleb felt someone grabbing him. He groaned with the awful pain.

"He's bad injured. Look at the bloodstains on his back."

He was dragged aboard the raft, groaning desperately with
every touch until at last he lay facedown on the raft. Someone lifted his buckskin shirt.

"Look here, Ben. They's bandages wrapped around him,
all dirty and bloody. And up here he's all purple. You can
see it, even with that dark skin. What kind of Indian do
you suppose he is?"

"Who knows? Probably some theivin' renegade that
somebody shot," the man called Ben replied. "Looks about
dead to me. Maybe we should just throw him back in."

"We can't do that. The man is alive. He looks mighty
young to boot." The man leaned close then. "Who are you,
boy? Is there someplace we can take you?"

Caleb forced himself to talk, but it was a great effort.
"Where . . . am I?"

"Don't you know?"

"No."

"New Orleans, boy. You're in New Orleans."

New Orleans. Was the war over? Had he volunteered
again? New Orleans. Emily was in New Orleans. He needed
help. Maybe these men would take him to Emily. Surely
Emily would help him. She owed him. He had to get help
or he would die and never see Tom again.

"Stoner."

"What's that?"

"Emily . . . Stoner. Marie's place."

"Marie's?"

"Brothel . . . Marie's . . . Emily Stoner."

The man frowned and looked at Ben. "You know anybody named Marie who runs a brothel, Ben?"

The one called Ben grinned. "Do I know Marie's? Do I know how to breathe? Hell, I took you there once, Jake. Don't tell me you've forgot Jeannette."

Jake snickered. "Oh, yeah, now I recall. I reckon he wants to go there, but I didn't think the whores would take Indians."

"Some of them will take anything for the right money. Let's float back home and load him up. Maybe that there Marie or whoever will pay us for bringin' him in. Hell, this here might be a wanted man."

Jake's eyes brightened. "I never thought of that."

Caleb lay quiet and helpless as the raft was guided to the docks. It seemed hours before he was again being moved. He cried out with the horrible pain, blacking out from it as soon as he was thrown into the back of a wagon filled with hay.

The wagon lumbered away, and Caleb slowly came around again, hearing voices and laughter and city noises.

"What you got there?" someone called out.

"Don't know yet," came the reply. "Found him in the river."

"Pretty big fish you got there, Jake."

There was more laughter. The wagon jolted and bounced, and Caleb groaned. Finally the vehicle came to a halt. He lay waiting, and for a few minutes there was only the sound of wagons passing and people talking. Then he heard Jake again.

"Here. He's here in the wagon, Miss Stoner. He said your name and mentioned Marie's. You know him?"

Someone climbed into the wagon, and he smelled cheap perfume, but this time it was a welcome smell.

"Caleb," Emily gasped. "My God, what happened to you?"

He could not reply.

"Get him inside and up to my room," he heard her saying. "I'll have someone get a doctor." Her hand gently stroked his hair. "You'll be all right, Caleb. I suppose I owe you this one, don't I?" Her fingers moved through his hair. "They've even cut off your hair. Where in God's name have you been?"

"Found him in the river, miss. Somebody tossed him in expectin' him to drown, most likely."

"Most likely," she mumbled as she straightened. "Be careful with him."

Again he was moved, and again he cried out with the pain. It seemed to take hours for the men to get him inside and up the stairs to Emily's room. They laid him facedown on a soft bed.

"Here," Emily said. "It's a ten-dollar gold piece for your kindness in bringing him here."

"Thank you, ma'am. Most obliged," Jake replied.

Caleb heard footsteps and a door closing. In the next moment Emily was stroking his hair again. "You'll be all right now, Caleb. I've sent for a doctor. You just rest. Don't even try to talk. You can tell me what happened when you're stronger."

She traced a finger along the thin scar on his cheek. Her life as a near prisoner in her father's house at Fort Dearborn seemed a lifetime ago, as did the nights of sexual pleasures with Caleb Sax. Such a boy he was then, full of curiosity and innocence. She ran a hand over his muscular shoulder and arm, remembering how he had fascinated her then, a time when she was certain she had been partially insane.

That was over now. She was not the crazed child she had been, but she still plied her trade by selling her body to men. Yet she had certainly never planned on seeing this one again. How strange that he seemed to keep reappearing in her life, in spite of the separate paths they followed.

"Well, Caleb Sax, what kind of trouble have you gotten yourself into this time?" she asked softly, smiling as she stroked his hair. "Trouble seems to follow you like a plague, doesn't it?" Her smile faded. "I hope it isn't all because you had to run away from Fort Dearborn that night."

She stood up and walked to a table, taking out a pair of scissors and returning to carefully cut through the center of his buckskin shirt, not wanting to move him. She pulled it open, then cut along the sleeves, grimacing at the ugly wounds on his back and shoulder. She managed to pull the shirt from under him. It was then she realized he wasn't wearing his blue quill necklace.

"Now what happened to that precious necklace of yours, Caleb Sax? As a boy you wouldn't take that thing off it it meant your life."

The necklace. Caleb remembered giving it to Sarah, putting it in the lining of her carpetbag. Even the necklace was gone now. The carpetbag had fallen off the travois when he fled Saint Louis. Sarah. The necklace. He could not stop his tears.

Emily touched his tears, surprised by them. "My God," she whispered.

Chapter
Twenty-One

THE agony that followed for Caleb Sax was worse than the agony of the Sun Dance. At the Sun Dance, he had been young and happy and in love. Now he was beaten and paralyzed, those he loved dead. The doctor did all he could for Caleb, cleaning out and cauterizing bad infections in his back and shoulder, but unable to do anything about the damage to his spine. The musket ball had been removed carelessly from his body, doing even more harm. That kind of healing took time and patience, and a lot of hope, for there was no guarantee that Caleb Sax would ever have use of his limbs again.

Emily Stoner found a new purpose to her life. Helping Caleb became her goal. She hoped that helping him would somehow vindicate the cruel trick she had played on him years earlier, and it felt good to do something decent after groveling in bed with strangers and having nothing else to do with her life. Marie insisted Caleb be moved out of Emily's room because he was interfering with business. Emily arranged a room for Caleb at a nearby hotel whose proprietor insisted she enter and exit by a back door so others did not see her frequenting his establishment. Because of Caleb's condition, however, Emily was given permission to go to his room whenever she chose, and stay the nights when he needed extra care.

Emily began dividing her time between Caleb's room and the brothel, continuing her prostitution in order to pay for Caleb's room and medications. She nursed him herself, cleaned up after him, fed him, and sometimes held him, especially in the deep of the night when he could not sleep because of his pain and sorrow. Even Emily Stoner, cold and calculating as she had become, was touched by his grief. The normally proud, strong and determined Caleb Sax seemed to be a broken man. She could help him physically, but she could not heal the inner wounds or change the things that had happened to him. And she knew that if not for the knowledge that he still had a son, Caleb Sax would not will himself to live at all.

Little Tom was all that kept him going, the only thing that made Caleb try vainly every day to move. Watching him tore at Emily's heart, but each day she placed his hands on the railing over his head. Then he would try in vain to make his arms work, to pull his body upward and build the strength back into his muscles. But he could not do it. Whenever Caleb seemed to be giving up completely, Emily reminded him again of little Tom.

"The water," he told her after two months of lying helplessly in the bed.

"What?" Emily turned, a tray of food in her hands.

"The water. I remember now. When they threw me in the river, for some reason I could move." He met her eyes. "Something about feeling lighter, I think, being able to float. Maybe if you could get me to water I could at least move a little bit. Maybe I could slowly build up my muscles that way."

She sighed and sat down on the edge of the bed. "All right. I'll get a wagon and have some men bring you to the river." She buttered a biscuit. "Just don't drown on me, Caleb Sax. Not after all I've gone through to keep you alive. What a trick that would be to play on me."

She met his eyes, smiling, but sobered at the serious look on his face.

"Thank you, Emily, for all your help. I probably would have died."

Her eyebrows arched. "If memory serves me right, you *wanted* to die at first." She winked. "You just keep Tom in mind. I don't doubt your little boy and your own damn stubbornness will get you walking again. We can't have a fine specimen like you lying around helpless." She gave him a sly grin. "I can think of better things we could be doing."

He smiled sadly. "I am afraid a woman is the last thing on my mind," he said. His smile faded. "After Sarah, I'm not sure I'd ever even desire another woman, let alone fall in love again."

She looked away, stirring his soup. "Well, God knows I'm not talking about love, not the likes of Emily Stoner. But if you ever get well and want to know if you're recovered in every possible way, I'll be glad to help you out. I taught you the first time around. I'll just teach you again."

He finally grinned then, thinking what a waste it was for her to end up as she had.

"If I get the need, I'll let you know."

She kept staring at the soup. "I hope this . . . I hope I've made up for some of it, Caleb. As a girl I was almost insane. I didn't know what I was doing. Now it's too late for any of it."

Caleb closed his eyes, tired from the short conversation. "You keep telling me it's not too late for anything. Why don't you believe it yourself?"

"We're like night and day, Caleb Sax, and you know it. Now eat up. Tomorrow we're going to the river. You'll need your strength."

She held a spoonful of soup to his mouth. He took the soup, swallowing and meeting her eyes again. "I should go back to Saint Louis if I ever get out of this bed. I should visit Sarah's grave."

Her eyes narrowed. "You'll do no such thing, Caleb Sax. Do you want to hang? You're damn lucky you got away with your life. You have a son waiting for you. As soon as you're well—and you *will* get well—you're going west to get your little boy. If you're smart you'll stay there, anyplace west of the Mississippi. Your luck isn't too good this side of the muddy waters, in case you haven't noticed."

He sighed, his eyes suddenly tearing. Why did this weakness seem to make him weak on the inside, too? "My God, Emily, I as much as killed her," he whispered, putting his head back again. One tear slipped out of the corner of his eye. "She was so good, so sweet and beautiful and trusting. With all the battles I've faced in my life you would think I'd be able to protect those I loved. But I failed Walking Grass and then I failed Sarah."

"You didn't fail anyone," she replied, taking one of his hands. "You're a victim of society, Caleb, a half-breed too white to live forever with the Indians, and too Indian to live in total civilization. Life has handed you a bowl of skunk stew, just like me. But unlike me, you fought it. You've

kept your dignity and pride. You've done nothing wrong,
and you loved Sarah Sax as much as any man can love a
woman. But for some reason it wasn't meant to be. At least
you're left with something. You have a little boy. Now stop
thinking about Sarah and think about Tom—and eat this
soup before I bring some men in here to force it down your
throat. I have to get back to Marie's before she tells me I'm
through. Her girls make more than any prostitutes in this
city, and I'm not about to go someplace else. I work at the
cleanest, most respectable brothel and I don't care to lower
myself by leaving it."

He looked at her and laughed lightly. At least she had a
sense of humor about her life. She reached out and wiped
away the tear with her fingers, then pulled on his hair. "It's
getting much longer. By the time you're walking again this
hair will be right back where it was, long and beautiful.
You'll be the old Caleb Sax again—or should I say Blue
Hawk?"

He shook his head, grinning his handsome grin. "I do
not know myself. I guess in some ways I have never decided."

She held another spoon of soup to his lips and he took
it. She was right. He had to keep up his strength. Why
hadn't he thought of the river before? He began to think of
recovering with the same determination he had taken his
vengeance against the Crow. This life would not beat him.
He would beat it, and he would go and get his son. Perhaps
when he held his little boy in his arms again he would finally
begin to truly heal. His physical wounds were nothing compared to losing Sarah. Never would he find anything that
precious again. Never would he love that way again. But
maybe Tom would help ease the pain.

Sarah sat on the loveseat, looking at her hands in her lap.
She was still much too thin after her illness; the horror of
learning Caleb was dead had not helped the healing process,
nor had the realization that she was pregnant.

In one respect the pregnancy was beautiful, wonderful. It was Caleb's child, and the only thing she had that made her want to live again. The life that was beginning to make faint stirrings in her belly was the precious product of the love she had shared with Caleb Sax. Every time she felt the faint flutterings she thanked God for being given Caleb's seed, a part of his wild and free spirit that she could keep forever.

She would have this baby no matter what it took, no matter how much shame it brought her family. It was hers and Caleb's, and it was nothing short of a miracle that she had clung to the tiny bit of life through her terrible illness. The doctor could not imagine how she had lived at all, yet to Sarah that was even more reason to believe that God meant for her to have Caleb's baby.

But now came the confrontation. It had not been so difficult to tell her aunt, who had been sympathetic about her running off with Caleb and was still upset about the way her husband had handled the entire incident. During Sarah's recovery her uncle had been patient and loving. She could not think of him as father and never would, and she even continued to call him uncle. He had accepted that, and had been rather humble since learning she had heard the conversation about Cora Sax. More than once he had tried to explain, trying to compare his love for Cora with her own for Caleb. But Sarah could not forgive him. If she had loved another man, Caleb would never have raped her for spite. The thought of it was ugly and horrible, and to think of Terrence Sax doing such a thing made her hate him.

Her hatred was strengthened because it was Terrence who had killed Caleb and nearly killed her by forbidding them to be together. No matter how much he swore he had nothing to do with the way Caleb had died, that he would gladly have talked with them about their love, Sarah could not believe him. How could she believe a rapist? How could she believe a man who would condone sending ruffians out to brutalize Caleb and cut off his hair?

Life in the Sax household had been civil, bearable, but nothing would ever again be the same. Because of her illness, Sarah had had no choice but to go back to her aunt and uncle. And now, because of her pregnancy, she feared she might not be able to leave at all. Taking a deep breath, Sarah looked up and told her uncle about her condition. His humility and forgiving attitude vanished.

"I actually let myself believe nothing had happened between you and that Indian," he raged. "I didn't even let the doctor examine you for such a thing because I trusted your goodness and decency!"

"I loved him," she replied boldly. "If you had let us be together and get married none of it would have happened the way it did!"

"That is no excuse for a girl who's been brought up as you have! Even Cora would have abhorred such a thing!"

"What do you know about what my mother would have approved or disapproved? Is what you did to her any less sinful than what Caleb and I did? At least I loved him. At least I was willing, not forced. At least it was an act of love, not one of lust!"

The man looked ready to hit her, but Sarah did not flinch. Terrence turned and left the house, and all Sarah and Mary could do was await his return. Sarah dreaded what he might say or do. At the moment she was still at their mercy, with no money of her own and no place to go.

She closed her eyes, thinking of Caleb and the beautiful days at the cave, moments she would never experience again. She thought back farther, to the days of their childhood when they had played and learned together. She thought of her mother's beautiful face and serene nature. Sarah understood now the hint of sorrow that was always in her eyes, understood why Tom Sax seemed overly protective of her feelings. And she thought of Tom himself, a kind, joyful, loving man who had never given one hint that he was not her father. How carefully he had guarded her from the truth. He had loved her as much as any real father could, more than the man who she had discovered really was her father.

It hurt to think back. But looking back seemed easier than looking forward, for the future seemed to hold little for her, except that she would have Caleb's baby. No matter what, she would have Caleb's baby.

An hour later the front door opened and Sarah looked at her aunt. There were voices in the hallway, and in the next moment Terrence stepped into the parlor, his face stern and determined. Behind him stood Byron Clawson, so much uglier with his crooked nose which had never healed right after Caleb broke it.

Sarah looked away, her face reddening, her heart pounding. What was Byron Clawson doing here? She refused to look at either of them when Terrence spoke.

"The decision has been made," he told her. "And you shall abide by it, Sarah. I'll not have you running around Saint Louis with a big belly and no husband. You have ignored Byron long enough, and he loves you enough to be willing to marry you in spite of the pregnancy. Byron understands that you simply made the mistake of a young, foolish girl—a mistake you deeply regret."

"I don't regret anything," Sarah said cooly, turning to look at her uncle. "Not one thing." She stood up. "How much did you pay Byron to marry me . . . Uncle?" She emphasized the word deliberately, enjoying the way he flinched when she used it.

Terrence reddened, but Byron smiled cooly. "Don't be silly, Sarah, dear. He didn't have to pay me anything," he said. His eyes moved over her as though she were naked. "I simply love you. I've wanted to marry you for a long time and you know it. You can no longer protest that you are too young or not ready. Considering the circumstances, I think you are more than ready." He stepped closer, and her stomach churned at the sweet smelling perfume he wore. "I am prepared to make a respectable woman of you, Sarah. You obviously can't have a baby without being married,

and no one else would have you now. I will take you to
Washington, D.C. with me, where I am to start a very good
job in a few weeks. No one around Saint Louis will know
exactly when you had the baby, and when we get to Washington we will simply lie about how long we have been
married." He watched her carefully, hoping she believed his
words. It wouldn't do to let any of them know it was her
inheritance he was after—and always had been. Combined
with the wealth he would one day receive from his father,
Sarah's inheritance would make him a very wealthy, powerful man.

Sarah looked at her uncle. "I will not marry this man.
You know I hate him!"

Terrence stepped closer so that both men towered over
Sarah threateningly. "You will marry him, Sarah. You will
learn to love him. Many people marry without love and the
love comes later. You will learn to love Byron simply for
the grand thing he is doing at this moment. His future looks
very bright. You will be a rich, important woman, as well
as respectable. You will have a home and a name for your
child. No one but those of us in this room will know. Byron
is making a great sacrifice, and you should appreciate what
he is doing. Don't shame me any further, Sarah."

"*Me* shame *you*?" She turned away. "I won't marry him."

"You will—or I will have the baby aborted. It's a simple
matter, we need only give you something that renders you
helpless and have Dr. Nederer take the baby. He's done it
for whores; he can do it to you."

A horrible chill swept through her at the realization that
he was serious. And was he comparing her to a whore?

"Terrence, how can you—" Mary started to protest, but
was quickly interrupted by her husband.

"Shut up! You have interfered enough. You will either
support me in this or pay dearly later," he said harshly.

The woman looked at her lap. She had always considered
it an honor to be married to Terrence Sax, at least for the
first few years. She had been plain, her family poor. In her

youth a man like Terrence had been a wonderful catch indeed. Little did she know then he was only marrying her because he needed someone submissive, someone who would accept what he had done to Cora and not turn on him for it. He liked being domineering, important. Mary Whittaker had been the perfect choice, for she had worshipped him those first few years, until she came to really understand Terrence Sax. Still, she was living a life of wealth and prominence she never dreamed possible, and nothing, not even Sarah, could make her give that up. She rose and left the room, and Sarah felt like a rabbit surrounded by wolves.

"You can't take my baby," she said in a shaky voice, her back still to them.

"I can do whatever I feel is for your own good. I have done many things for you, Sarah. You owe it to me to have a husband when your child is born. Is that so much to ask?"

"I . . . I don't love Byron."

"Love will come with time. After all, the man is overlooking what you did and is even willing to take in your baby—another man's child. I'd say that is very big of him, Sarah, something you should be grateful for."

Sarah turned, seeing the sick humor in Byron Clawson's eyes. He was not doing anything big, she thought, he was simply winning his own little victory. It made her ill, but she had to think of the baby, Caleb's baby. She would do anything to keep it. Anything. She met his eyes boldly.

"You agree to keep my baby and raise him as his father?"

He nodded. "I've wanted you a long time, Sarah Sax. If this is the only way I can have you, I accept. But I will expect my conjugal rights."

She colored deeply, the thought of him touching her turning her stomach. But she knew without asking again that Terrence Sax was serious about forcing an abortion if she did not get married. And that was the worst possible threat. She *must* have this baby. It was Caleb's. Perhaps if she could get through this and have the child, making it all respectable, she could divorce Byron later and get away from him. But for now she had to find a way for her baby to survive.

She swallowed. "I have been ill. I would expect some respect for that," she answered. "I need some time . . . to adjust. I've been through a lot, Byron. And I'm not completely well yet. I'll marry you, but I will not be a wife to you in the full sense . . . for a time." Her face flushed again at the horror of it. "However, I will not deny you for long. I only ask for a little patience on your part and some respect for the fact that I do not love you. I do respect the fact that you are willing to marry me, and I accept—if you promise to give me a little time."

His eyes moved over her again. "I will give you until we reach Washington. That will be roughly one month from now."

Her eyes teared at the horror of it. Byron Clawson, the very man Caleb hated most and tried to protect her from. Now he would be father to Caleb's child. What a strange, cruel blow fate was dealing her. But at least she could keep the baby, and if Byron was cruel to her, she would divorce him just as fast as she could. There was shame in divorce also, but not nearly the shame of having a baby out of wedlock. She did not want her child called a bastard. She owed Byron some small bit of gratitude for at least relieving her of that worry. She would try to be civil, try to at least like him.

"When are we to be married?" she asked coldly, feeling as if this were all an awful nightmare.

"Considering the circumstances, I would say tomorrow would be none too soon," Byron answered. His eyes fell to her waist. "At least you don't show yet. We will explain to our friends that because I'm due in Washington soon we decided to get married right away to give you time to 'adjust' before going off with your new husband," he sneered. "After all, young ladies sometimes find marriage rather a shock— young ladies, that is, who are still virgins."

She struggled not to cry, refusing to let him make her buckle.

"No one but the men who chased Caleb know about this, and all have been paid well to keep their mouths shut," Byron continued. "You are still young and probably the most beautiful woman in Saint Louis. I will be content with that. You will make a fine looking wife on the arm of a senator or governor some day—which is what I plan to be. Be a decent wife, Sarah, and you will never want for anything, nor will your child."

She nodded. "Very well. Tomorrow we will be married and we will come back here to stay until we leave for Washington. I do not want to be alone with you until then. And we will have separate rooms while we are here."

His lips curled in an ugly smile. "As you wish." He stepped closer and kissed her cheek, then turned to look at Terrence. Sarah unconsciously rubbed her cheek with her fingers.

"I'll make arrangements with the church, sir," Byron said. "My father will be delighted. He's always favored Sarah. He, of course, doesn't know about the baby. I don't intend to tell him."

Sax nodded. "Fine. We'll go into town today and pick out a dress for Sarah. And I will remind you that I love her," his eyes moved to Sarah, "like a daughter. The two of you have made a bargain, and she has been very sick. I expect you to adhere to her request to wait until you get to Washington."

Byron put out his hand. "You have my word, sir."

Terrence shook it firmly. "Thank you, Byron. You're a fine young man, a fine young man. This means very much to me. I'll help you all I can with your career. If you ever need a loan or anything—"

"Thank you, but you have no cause for concern. Father keeps me supplied." He turned and looked at Sarah again, bowing slightly. "Good-bye, Sarah dear."

She glared at him. Byron sighed and shook his head. "I

apparently have my work cut out for me, sir," he said to Terrence. "But I love her. We'll manage."

"Of course you will."

The two of them left the room, and Sarah sank back into the loveseat, grasping her stomach and bending over. "Caleb," she whispered. "Oh Caleb. I have to do this ... for our baby."

She hung her head and wept, her devastation overwhelming. Caleb would never let this happen if he were alive. But he was dead. For a while she had hoped the grave she had been shown was just a trick, but there had been the dead horse, and for over three months there had been no Caleb. If he were alive he would have come for her. What choice did she have now? She could not even run away, not with a baby growing in her womb. All hope was gone. The last bit of beauty and love she had left was Caleb's child, the seed of their love. Whatever she had to suffer to keep it, she would suffer—even to marrying Byron Clawson.

She would be brave now, for Caleb. She would go to her room and take out the blue quill necklace and hold it while she prayed for strength, and she would feel Caleb's spirit and power with her. Thank God her carpetbag had been retrieved that awful day Caleb had fled Saint Louis. The necklace was still inside when she had finally been able to look. It was the most joy she had known in many weeks. When she held the necklace in her hand she felt safe and loved. It had been Caleb's most sacred treasure, and now it was hers. No one would take it from her, just as no one would take Caleb's baby.

Emily took Caleb to the river as often as possible. With the help of men she hired, Caleb was supported in the water and able to exercise his limbs, his body lighter in water. Eventually his muscles strengthened enough that he could start moving his limbs out of the water, but Emily suspected it was due not so much to actual physical recovery as Caleb's determination to be whole again. Slowly the damage to the nerves in his back began to right itself, and Caleb's spirit improved with each day of hope that he could go to his son.

Emily would often watch him struggle with the painful exercise, seeing an inner strength in him that few men possessed, a part, she was sure, of his Indian heritage. She admired his spirit, his determination, his closeness to a world from which he drew strength. As often as he tried to explain the Indian religion, the belief in the earth and animal spirits, an attitude that was so vastly different from the white man's, Emily simply could not grasp it all. Yet she often wished she could find that other world in which Caleb sometimes got lost, a world of intense concentration and a connection with spirits that gave him power and courage and pride.

To his great relief, Caleb found he didn't need the sacred articles that normally helped him pray and grow close to the spirits. He had left his medicine bag with his son to keep forever should Caleb not return, hoping the bag would protect the boy from harm while he was gone. The only thing he had kept with him was the blue quill necklace, but now that was gone, too. He was determined that its loss would not destroy his strength and spirit. By concentrating very hard he was able to feel close to the spirits.

Emily saw an improvement every day, saw his muscles begin to firm up again, until finally the day came when she arrived at his room to find him standing at the window.

Standing turned to walking, then slow running, then riding a horse again. By autumn of 1815, Caleb Sax was well enough to return to his son. He was not totally recovered, but he would wait no longer. He needed his son more than ever now, needed the reassurance that life went on, that at least one good thing had come from his own life. And he needed to get back to the land he loved best, away from places that brought him so much sorrow.

Emily dreaded the day he would leave. For the first time in her life she had found a true friend, one who cared about her as a person. It was understood between them that this was as far as they would go, that they had their own lives that were worlds apart. Yet they had shared intimate feelings, had come to an understanding over the past, and she was satisfied that at least Caleb Sax no longer hated her. She had made up to some extent for what she had done to him, but would always regret that nearly everything that had happened to him had been because he had had to flee Fort Dearborn.

She helped him pack the horse she bought for him, loading the animal with clothes and gear, a pistol and musket, and a new knife, all things he had lost in Saint Louis.

"Sorry I couldn't supply you with buckskins, but I wouldn't know how to shop for something like that," she told him. She looked him over with admiration. He wore fine new boots and dark cotton pants, with a blue calico shirt that enhanced his provocative blue eyes. A new leather hat was perched on his thick, lengthening hair, which was tied at the back of his neck. He wore the new knife on a wide leather belt. "My God, you're beautiful," she sighed. "You're all man again, Caleb Sax."

He smiled bashfully, stirring her with the grin that made her feel weak. If only he had let her make him a whole man again, had let her have him that way for just one night. But she knew his mind and heart were too full of someone else, and would be for a long time to come. "Promise me you won't do something stupid like go back to Saint Louis," she warned.

"I promise." He turned and grasped her arms. "And I promise to send you money as soon as I get my life straightened out and earn some. I owe you so much, Emily, but what I have left I might need for now."

"You owe me nothing. What else would I spend it on? I have no family."

"I don't care. It is not right and I feel indebted. I am sending you money as soon as I can. It might take me a year or two, but I will send it."

"No. If you really care, Caleb, do this for me. Let me

have the satisfaction of feeling I truly made up for what I did to you. I have little to fall back on to keep me out of hell when I die. Let me have this." Her eyes teared. "Besides, if you don't mind, I'd prefer not to hear from you again. It would be easier to pretend you don't exist anymore. To hear from you and be reminded again would be too hard."

He swallowed back a lump in his throat. "Emily, if I could feel that way for you, I would. It has nothing to do with you. It has to do with being unable to love at all for a long time."

"Oh, Caleb," she said chidingly, forcing a smile through her tears. "Do you think for one minute that if you thought you loved me that way I'd let you do something as foolish as taking on a woman like me?" She pretended to laugh. "You're made for much better things, you and that little boy of yours. I'm used up already, Caleb. There's not much left for any man to care about. I wouldn't dream of destroying someone like you. And I'm not about to give up this life. I think I was always meant to be what I am."

She had done so much for him. He pushed back her hair from the scarred side of her face and bent down to kiss the scar. "What else can I say or do, Emily?" he whispered.

She grasped his wrists as her tears fell. "You can go. And you can promise me—the word of an Indian—that you will not contact me again unless you're in bad trouble. Go away and forget me, Caleb. That's your problem, you know. Your heart is much too soft for your own good."

"But Emily—"

"Promise me, damn it!"

He nodded. "All right. I promise."

She sniffed and held up her chin. "Now. Go. If I never hear from you again I'll be glad. It will only mean you've found some happiness at last. I know that little boy is just fine and waiting for his father to get the hell out there to him, so get going. But ride easy, Caleb. You're still healing, you know."

He nodded. "I'll be careful."

Their eyes held. "Good-bye, Caleb Sax. God be with you. I don't know if he listens to people like me, but I will pray for you."

He bent down and kissed her lips lightly. "And I will pray for you," he said softly.

She turned away. "Go on."

Caleb stood awkwardly for a moment, hating to leave her, but knowing he must. He turned and mounted the shiny black mare. It was a fine animal. "*Tonoeva* means autumn in Cheyenne, and leaving such a good friend makes me feel the sadness of autumn, which is almost upon us. I will call the horse Tonoeva."

She nodded, refusing to turn back and look at him again, smiling through tears at his words. "That's fine," she muttered. "Please go now, Caleb, and keep your promise to me."

There was a moment of hesitation. "Good-bye, Emily," he finally said. "I love you for the good person you truly are. You will not go to hell, Emily Stoner."

She heard the horse trot away, then move into a canter. She waited until she could hear it no more, refusing to watch him go.

Chapter
Twenty-Two

THE rain poured down as if the heavens had opened the gates to an ocean above. Caleb drew his poncho closer and pulled his leather hat farther down on his forehead. It was still daylight and in spite of the rain he wanted to keep going. Now that he was headed west an anxiety to see Tom and get away from the horrors civilization seemed to bring him made him keep a relentless pace, more than he should be doing in his condition. But he paid no heed to his weary bones. Tonoeva proved to be a strong obedient animal that never balked at his orders. The horse seemed to sense the urgent mood of its master, and the mare pranced delicately through red, slippery mud at the base of a high mountain.

Caleb had chosen to go north through Arkansas Territory, then he would veer northwest into Unorganized Territory. To take the river north would have kept him too far east, and he had no need to go to Fort Dearborn. He also had no desire to go near Saint Louis again. There was nothing left for him in either place, and only danger in Saint Louis, where a vengeful Terrence Sax could have him arrested and keep him from his son.

Thunder seemed to shake the very earth, and lightning occasionally lit the countryside. To Caleb the storm seemed to epitomize the storm that raged in his soul, a soul that still hadn't found a home, a soul that was still restless, thundering, raging. He fought the constant temptation to think about Sarah, to remember the beautiful little girl who had taken his hand at Fort Dearborn and had helped him learn the white' man's ways; the budding young woman who had left Fort Dearborn to go to a new life; the ravishing young woman he had found in Saint Louis. Those thoughts inevitably led to their time together in the cave, to her silken skin rubbing against his own, the glory of hearing her whisper his name in ecstasy, the wonder and joy of being inside of her, of pleasing her.

He groaned aloud, shaking his head and urging Tonoeva ahead, gritting his teeth against the gnawing pain that often plagued his middle and lower back. He supposed he would always be troubled by it, but it was better than the awful paralysis. It had seemed there was nothing to live for then, but he had, and surely he had recovered because God meant him to go and get his son. He still had not made any decisions about what he would do then. He could not think about it, for to think about it meant realizing he must go on without Sarah. It still seemed impossible that she was gone, but he had seen the look of death on her face that day, had seen the doctor declare her dead and cover her.

Tonoeva slipped on a smooth rock and faltered. "Easy, girl," he soothed. "You don't have to hurry in this mess." The words were meant to calm the animal, but they had to be shouted above the pounding rain. He reined in Tonoeva to let the animal rest a moment, looking around for a cave he could use for shelter. He saw nothing, although the terrain was rocky and mountainous. It was then he thought he heard voices. He frowned, straining to listen above the pouring rain and rolling thunder.

There it was again, someone shouting. He urged Tonoeva forward curiously, coming upon a clearing around the bend of a jagged mountainside to see deep ruts in the ground apparently left by a heavy wagon. He looked ahead and heard voices again, but could see nothing.

The wagon tracks curved around yet another bend and

Caleb followed, finally coming upon a flatbed wagon loaded down with bulky objects covered with canvas and blankets and tied with an abundance of rope. Six mules were hitched to the wagon, apparently having decided not to go any farther. A woman stood to one side, holding a rope tied to the bridles of four horses, one of which was saddled. The woman was heavyset and wore an Indian tunic. Three cows and a sorry looking bull stood grazing nearby, their heads hanging in the rain. A man who looked dark like an Indian but who wore white man's clothing was swearing at the mules, trying to make them go. A young girl and a little boy, also dressed like whites, stood at the back of the wagon knee-deep in mud, pushing the wagon and trying to help get it out of mud that oozed right up to the bed.

The man shouted at the mules again, and the girl and boy pushed. Caleb noticed that just above them the side of the mountain gaped an ugly brown. Apparently there had been a small mudslide, and somehow these people had been caught in it. They pushed again and the wagon gave slightly, but then the little boy slipped under a wheel and the wagon rocked back again, pinning him.

"Father! Father, make them go! Make them go!" the girl screamed. "Lee is caught under the wheel!"

The woman holding the horses yelled something in a language Caleb had never heard and went to help push.

Caleb charged Tonoeva forward at a gallop, jumping off the animal before it even came to a halt and slopping through the mud. There was no time for any of them to wonder who he was or where he had come from. They had help.

"Try to get them moving again," he shouted to the man, putting his shoulder against the back of the wagon. Caleb grabbed a wheel spoke. "Get ready to pull him out quickly if I can help move this," he told the woman. She nodded and knelt by the boy while the man cussed the mules again, whipping them until they finally struggled forward slightly.

Caleb pushed with everything he had, pain ripping through his back. He shuddered with the strain, finally relaxing when the woman managed to pull the boy from beneath the wheel. Caleb's legs buckled and he fell to his knees with a groan.

"Lee," the man shouted, coming around to the back of the wagon and helping the woman lay the little boy on firmer ground. They felt his body, and the boy said something in the same strange language the woman had used, then grinned. The woman pulled him close and hugged him.

The young girl knelt beside Caleb then, putting a hand on his shoulder. "Are you all right, mister?"

Caleb rocked with the pain. "I will be. I have a bad back injury. It was not good for me to push the wagon." He didn't even look at her he was so lost in his pain.

"Father, he's hurt," the girl yelled through the rain. "He cannot get up."

The man was instantly at Caleb's side. "Can I help you? You helped save my son. I am sorry you are hurt."

Caleb shook his head. "I have a bad back." He shivered with fear of the paralysis returning.

"Stay with him," the man ordered the girl. "I will find shelter."

The man left and Caleb stayed on his knees, unable to even get out of the mud at first. The girl stayed right beside him. "I am Marie. Marie Whitestone. Thank you for helping us."

Caleb just nodded, the pain subsiding slightly.

"We are Cherokee," the girl added, not sure what else to say to him.

He turned to look at her then. Though her face was covered with mud, he could see that she was pretty. Her eyes widened slightly, and in her eager youth it was impossible for her to hide her pleasure in what she saw: a very handsome young man who was as dark as she. "You are Indian too?" She asked the question with the bright smile of a curious little girl, but Caleb guessed her to be fourteen or fifteen.

"I am Indian, too," he answered, wincing with pain. "I am . . . part Cheyenne." He looked away again, bending over, daring to move slightly just to make sure he could.

SAVAGE HORIZONS   (307)

"Cheyenne? I have never seen a Cheyenne! There are no Cheyenne in Georgia. That is where we are from. We are going to Unorganized Territory. My father has bought land from the government."

Caleb nodded, glancing at her father. The man was pounding stakes into the ground near a rocky cliff that provided some shelter from the wind and rain. The woman walked slowly over to her husband, leading the little boy by the hand and watching him walk to make sure he was all right. Caleb was relieved to see the little boy appeared to be fine, then noticed that the man was building a tent from canvas and blankets.

"Is the little boy your brother?" he asked.

"Yes. He is only four."

Caleb tried to straighten, but the pain was too great. He moaned, bending over again. "The mud . . . probably saved him," he told the girl, suddenly wanting to keep talking. "The wheel just pushed him deeper into the mud and it cushioned him. If the ground had been hard he would have been crushed."

"God was with us this day then. And he sent you to help us. We are very grateful."

He nodded. "Help me . . . try to get out of this mud," he said, trying to straighten again.

She took hold of his arm. "I will try, but I am small and you are a grown man. I am not sure I can help much."

"Just let me hang on to you while I pull myself up with my other hand. I'll grab the wagon wheel."

"All right." She stood up, taking hold of his right arm while he grasped the wagon wheel with his left. Caleb gritted his teeth against the pain as he slowly pulled himself to his feet. He leaned against the wagon, panting from the effort, then managed to get one foot ahead of the other and make it to firmer ground before collapsing again and rolling onto his side.

"Father, Mother!" the girl shouted. "He is badly hurt! Hurry!"

The woman came running, bending over Caleb. "We will help you," she said in English. "Do not fear."

The tent was finally ready, although at the same time the rain finally stopped.

"Get the feather mattress out of the wagon," the man told his daughter. "I have put dry blankets over the ground inside the tent. Put the mattress on top of them and we will let him rest inside and try to find some dry wood for a fire. We will all rest here, and everyone should get into something dry quickly." He turned to his wife. "Go get his horse and find some dry clothing. We must get these wet things off him right away, then the rest of us will change."

Marie rummaged under the canvas of the wagon, glad to discover the rolled up feather mattress was dry. She tugged at it and finally yanked it loose. It was heavy with down and goose feathers, and it would not be easy to carry it to the tent. When she turned with it in her arms she could not help staring at the Cheyenne. His shirt had been removed to reveal a magnificent build, but he had many scars, and there was one in the middle of his back that was white and indented, as though there had been a hole in his back. Her heart immediately went out to him. Where had this young man gotten all the scars? And why was he traveling alone?

She looked away as her father helped the man take off his pants. She wanted very much to look, for he was beautiful, and she had been curious lately about men and how they might look naked. But it was bad to look, and she held the mattress to one side so she could not see as she walked past him.

Caleb caught sight of her as she went by, and for the first time he noticed that she limped because one foot was bent outward. But she walked gamely toward the tent, carrying the heavy feather mattress.

Caleb awoke to the smell of bacon frying. He stirred, thinking of the cave and Sarah. He spoke her name before opening his eyes and fully awakening. He was inside a tent, lying naked under soft blankets. His gaze fell on a pretty, dark-haired girl whose bosom seemed too large for her small, young body. She gave him a bright smile.

"Hello, mister," she said, her bright dark eyes dancing. "How do you feel?"

He remembered then. "Marie?"

She nodded. "You fell asleep soon after my mother and father put you in here. You slept all afternoon and all night. You must have been very tired. Have you not been resting?"

He sighed and stretched, reaching bare arms out from under the blankets. "Not much," he answered.

"Who is Sarah? Are you in a hurry to go someplace? Are you going to see her?"

Caleb looked at her again. "No. Sarah is . . . someone I knew once. She's gone now. I have a son living with the Cheyenne. He's about three years old. I haven't seen him for a year or more. I was going to get him."

Her heart tightened some. A son meant a wife. "Were you going to live in the wilds with your son and his mother? Why did you leave there?"

Caleb lay back and stared at the top of the tent. Oh, how all the memories hurt. "His mother is dead," he said quietly. "And why I left there is a very long story." He met her eyes and saw deep sorrow and concern.

"I am sorry his mother is dead. Was she the one called Sarah?"

Caleb held her eyes, but she felt he was looking through her rather than at her. "No. Sarah isn't his mother."

"Your eyes have much sadness, but they are nice eyes. I never saw such blue ones."

He smiled. "Thank you."

"How do you feel? Can you move now?"

He sighed deeply, stretching a little again, then slowly sitting up. "I feel a lot better," he answered. "I think I'm all right."

She stared at his powerful shoulders and broad chest

where the blankets had fallen away. "What is wrong with you? How did you get all those scars?" she asked curiously.

She reddened when his eyes fell on her abundant bosom for a moment before he lay back down with another weary sigh. She was self-conscious of her breasts, which had somehow matured before the rest of her. She was sure he must think her oddly shaped, with her big bust and crooked foot, and she had never thought of herself as pretty. She was suddenly embarrassed and felt like crying. "I . . . I ask too many questions," she said quietly, turning to crawl out of the tent.

"Wait," he told her. "It's all right."

She darted out of the tent to tell her mother he was awake, and moments later the older woman brought him a plate with bacon and biscuits on it.

"My daughter says you are better. I suppose she was asking you many questions. You must forgive her. She is only fifteen and asks whatever comes to her mind."

"I do not mind." Caleb sat up again, managing to get to a full sitting position so he could put the plate in his lap. The woman moved to the back of the tent as the man came inside with a cup of coffee for Caleb.

"How are you feeling?" he asked.

"Much better. Your daughter tells me I slept all afternoon and all night. I hope I have not slowed you down."

The man smiled. "No more than the rain. And our son might be badly hurt if not for you. Who knows how long the mud would have protected him?"

Caleb took a bite of a biscuit. "Mmm. I'm hungrier than I realized. I have been traveling hard and haven't stopped to eat much."

"You should slow down and take care of yourself or you will never get where you are going," the man told him. He held out his hand. "I am James Whitestone and this is my wife Ellen. My family and I are headed for Unorganized Territory. I have a piece of paper that shows where there is land I can farm for a small price to the government. We have left Georgia to go there."

Caleb shook his hand, quickly swallowing the biscuit. "My name is Caleb Sax. I am part Cheyenne and am headed back to my people. I have a little boy living with them. He is three summers and his mother is dead. I was going to get him." He frowned. "It is wild country where you are going. Why do you go?"

Whitestone nodded. "I am aware it is dangerous land. But some of our Cherokee friends have already gone there."

"Why have you left Georgia? I heard the Cherokee Nation is strong there."

The man nodded. "It is, but there is trouble coming. One day the Cherokee will be forced to leave their beloved homeland, just as other Indians farther east have had to leave theirs. Some think us foolish to go, and they laugh when I say that some day terrible things will come to the Cherokee in Georgia. I do not want my family to suffer. So we leave now. We will join some friends on the Canadian River. We will farm."

Caleb sipped some coffee before asking, "Farm? Out there?"

The man nodded. "A good man can farm any land. I have grown up farming. As a boy I worked for a white man who owned much property. I learned to speak English then. My woman, she learned from white missionaries. Our children speak both Cherokee and English, and they can read. When we join our friends we will form a small Cherokee community in Unorganized Territory. We will be among the first settlers there, and some day, when the Cherokee are forced to leave Georgia, we will already be settled and can help the new ones who come."

Caleb finished his biscuit and ate a piece of bacon as the man talked. He glanced out of the tent opening as Marie went by, and he grinned, realizing she was listening. He looked back at James Whitestone. "You take a big chance traveling alone."

The man nodded again. "We are aware of that. But we could not get anyone else to come with us, and I was told in a dream I must leave. Perhaps there is a reason you happened upon us. You are Cheyenne. Marie told us. You must know this land where we go. And you are traveling alone and in the same direction. You have trouble with your back. We could help each other. You could guide us and be an extra hand to help protect my family. And we would be there to help you if you had trouble with your illness again. We would be company for you in your travels, and when we reach our destination, you could go on to the Cheyenne and get your son."

Caleb frowned, surprised at the offer from a man who hardly knew him. Their eyes held a moment, and Caleb realized James Whitestone was half begging him to help. He was probably somewhat lost, Caleb thought, and afraid his family would come to harm from his decision. But he was also too proud to go back.

"We have plenty of food," the man added. "And I can even pay you."

Caleb looked at Ellen Whitestone. Her eyes asked him not to damage her husband's pride. They were pleasant people, and they were, after all, heading in the same direction as he. Again he felt strangely led by fate, happening upon these Cherokee in a land where he had expected to see no one at all. He could get into dangerous trouble if his back brought on the paralysis and he had no help. The important thing was Tom. He had to get to Tom, and these people could help make sure that he did.

He frowned. "But you know nothing about me."

James Whitestone smiled. "We know that you have a good heart, that you risked great pain to help save our little boy. That is all we need to know. If you choose to tell us more about yourself we will be glad to share your joys and your sorrows." He looked toward the open end of the tent with a grin. "Especially our Marie," he said louder.

They heard a rustling nearby as the girl hurried away,

and the girl's father laughed lightly. Caleb grinned, feeling comfortable and welcome with them. "All right. I will guide you," he told the man. "But as soon as I get you where you are going I must go on. It has been a long time since I have seen my son."

The man nodded. "I understand. And I am grateful, Caleb Sax. The spirits have brought us together, I believe. I prayed for help and you came."

Caleb drank more coffee, wondering if Emily had been right when she said his heart was too soft. He hoped he was not getting himself into some kind of new trouble. He had had all the trouble he ever wanted to see for the rest of his life, but he was only twenty-one. And like Bo Sanders had once told him, his life would probably take many more turns before it was over. He wondered where it would go next. Cherokee. He had never known Cherokee before, and now he would be leading a whole family of them into Unorganized Territory. But at least it would give him some company on his journey, something to help keep him from thinking about the past, about Sarah.

Caleb rode forward to greet five Indian braves. They were nearly naked, riding painted ponies, wearing feathers in their hair and bedecked with assorted weapons. Caleb wished he had his blue quill necklace to prove his Indian heritage, but he had only his dark skin and long hair. He guessed the braves to be Arapaho, friends of the Cheyenne, but they could be Pawnee or Kiowa in these parts.

He moved closer, eyeing them squarely, noticing tufts of horse hair at the tops of the feathers in their hair, a custom of the Arapaho. When he lived with the Cheyenne they had begun associating heavily with the Arapaho, and he remembered some of their language. He made the sign for Arapaho and pointed at them. One of them nodded. Then Caleb made a snakelike sign indicating Cheyenne, and pointed to himself.

From the wagon Marie watched in fascination. As the

weeks had passed she had become totally and helplessly in love with the handsome Cheyenne man who had befriended and guided them. Caleb Sax was a god to her, strong and beautiful and brave. He had killed a grizzly that had threatened their camp one night, bringing it down with a shot from his musket, then finishing it off with his knife when it stirred. They had greatly enjoyed the sweet meat, and made a blanket out of the bear skin. Later, Caleb had brought down a buffalo cow with bow and arrow. He had patiently shown Marie and her mother how to skin and clean the carcass of the great beast, how to carve out the meat, use the bones and skin and intestines, smoke and cure the meat. The Plains Indians lived very differently from the Cherokee, and it was obvious that the lifestyle of the Cherokee in this new land would be very different from what it had been in Georgia.

Marie watched Caleb talk to the five braves who had appeared seemingly from nowhere, looming up out of the tall prairie grass to face them as they moved toward the endless horizon that would be home. Marie's heart swelled with pride as she watched Caleb use a mixture of words and sign language to communicate with them.

Slowly but surely they had learned his story, and she wanted so much to tell him everything was all right, that she loved him desperately and would take care of him and be his companion if he would only ask.

But Caleb Sax seemed to have no desire for her. She knew his heart was full of one called Sarah, that he still grieved and would for a long time to come. But she wondered if, even when he was ready to love again, he could ever look at her that way. Surely such a handsome, virile man would want someone much more beautiful than she, and she could tell he looked at her as though she were a child. Sometimes she wondered if he truly noticed her at all, if he ever saw the love in her eyes, understood what a good wife she would gladly be to him if he would let her.

He rode back. "Arapaho," he told her father. "I think I

can please them with a little tobacco if you have any. They mean us no harm. They're just curious. I have told them we are peaceful, that we just want to go through this land to our new home on the river. They say the river you search for is not many miles ahead."

Marie's heart tightened at the information. It meant they were almost to their destination and Caleb would be leaving them soon, going on to find his son. He would probably never come back. She had to think of something to make him stay.

Her father transferred some tobacco from a tin to a leather pouch Caleb handed him. Caleb rode back to the Arapaho, speaking with them a few minutes longer. Marie knew that if they attacked Caleb would fight valiantly. She could just picture him riding against the Crow when he told them about his vengeful raids after his Cheyenne wife was killed. A woman would never have to be afraid in this land with a man like Caleb Sax at her side.

The Arapaho stared at Marie as she drove the wagon past. Caleb watched, thinking what a strong good-hearted girl she was. Marie drove the wagon every day while her mother rode alongside with Lee. The extra horses were tied to the back, and Mr. Whitestone rode the fourth horse, herding the cattle. Caleb rode ahead, keeping watch for Indians or other dangers.

Marie turned and smiled at him, and he smiled back, aware of the youthful crush she had on him. He sometimes felt awkward about it, for he couldn't return her feelings. He wanted nothing now but his son and some peace in his life. He could not love again, he was sure; even if he could, Marie was very young. Fifteen was not so young to the Indian, but Marie seemed even younger than fifteen sometimes, especially when she smiled. She was like a curious little girl, and now a lovesick one. Caleb had no idea what to do about it, other than to be himself and be patient with her. He would be gone soon anyway, and she would soon forget him.

Still, he did not truly look forward to leaving the White-stones. He liked them and would worry about them once he left. They had been good to him, and welcome company. Teaching them about living in this land had been an experience, an Indian teaching Indians. It seemed strange to Caleb that there could be so many different tribes in one country, people that were so different yet one in spirit at the same time.

The wagon rattled over one rolling hill, then another, a great sea of prairie grass and undulating lifts and falls, until finally they stopped to make camp. Marie worked hard at preparing a good supper, hoping to impress Caleb.

"I'm sure you will be at your destination in a day or two," Caleb told James Whitestone. "You can finally rest and get settled. Will there be many others there?"

"A few," the man replied. He smiled. "We are very grateful, Caleb. You have helped us in so many ways."

Caleb nodded. "I am also grateful. It has been good not to have to travel alone."

"And you seem stronger than when you first came to us."

"I feel stronger." He glanced at Marie. "Thanks in part to your wife and daughter's fine cooking," he added.

The women both smiled, and Marie blushed. Caleb walked off to tend to Tonoeva, taking a brush from his saddle bag and walking over to the unsaddled animal. He curried the horse briskly, stopping when he sensed someone near. He turned to see Marie watching him, the love in her eyes so evident it made him feel sorry for her.

"We'll be there soon," she said.

"Yes."

"You will leave us then?"

Caleb turned and continued brushing Tonoeva. "I will. The weather is getting colder. I must get to the Cheyenne before winter sets in."

She struggled desperately not to cry. "I . . . I hope you find him well."

"Thank you."

She watched him, trying to memorize every detail about him so she would remember his beauty always.

"Your son will need a home. Will you stay with the Cheyenne?"

"I do not know," Caleb answered. "I really have no other place to go."

She breathed deeply for courage. "You could . . . come back here. We are your friends now. You would always have a home here."

Caleb stopped brushing and turned to face her, their eyes holding for a moment. "Thank you, Marie."

"We need help. And you need a home. You . . . you speak of not knowing where you belong. Here we live between the white man's world and the wilder Indians. Perhaps this is where you belong, too, Caleb."

The hope in her eyes was almost pitiful. He knew she desperately wanted him to give her some kind of sign that he could be interested in her.

"Perhaps," he answered. "I will think about it. If I return, it will probably not be until the spring. I will miss you, Marie—all of you. It has been good to find new friends."

Her lips quivered slightly, and she gazed into his hypnotic blue eyes. "Will you . . . miss me the most?"

He smiled, again feeling pity for her youthful devotion. "Yes. I will miss you the most."

She smiled at his words, looking as though she wanted to run up and hug him. "I will miss you, too, Caleb. We have all been together many weeks, and you have shared your sorrows with us. You have taught us many things, helped us. God sent you to us, and I know you will come back here. I know it. I will pray for you—and your son."

"Thank you."

She turned and ran off, as though to prove that even with a club foot she could run. He knew her well enough by now to look beyond the deformity to her inner beauty. He hardly noticed her limp anymore, and he saw behind her frail body and childlike face the makings of a very pretty woman. He

knew he could have her if he wanted, that in her youth she
would give herself to him willingly enough. But he did not
want to use her that way, and he would be doing just that.
He had no feelings of love for her, not the kind of love a
man should have for a woman he wanted to marry. All he
had right now were tiny pricklings of manly desires long
buried, desires he did not want reawakened. It was too soon.
To awaken that part of him would be to open the wounds
of lost love, to relive the painful memories of those days
in the cave with Sarah.

No. He wanted none of those things. Soon he would leave
the Whitestones. Soon he would be back with the Cheyenne,
with his son.

Chapter
Twenty-Three

THE early winter winds raged across the prairie as Caleb
made his way to the place where the Cheyenne usually
gathered for the winter. Finding nomadic Indians in
such vast territory was not easy, even for one who had lived
with them. He knew only the general area in which to look,
and it had taken longer to track them than he had anticipated.
He was low on supplies, and the harsh winter was taking
its toll on his spirit.

His loneliness was keen in the great emptiness of the
land. Sometimes it seemed he was the last man on earth,
and he found himself wondering if there really would be a
son waiting for him when he reached the Cheyenne.

Tonoeva struggled through deepening drifts, and Caleb knew he could soon be in trouble if he couldn't find shelter. In open land the snow blew with uncontrolled fury, and the snows could drift as deep as a man stood. He kept pushing Tonoeva, desperate to find some kind of shelter, sure that not far ahead lay *Hinta-Nagi*, the place of thick timbers where the Cheyenne usually made winter camp. But the winds blew with such force that he could not listen for the sounds of people or horses, and the snow blinded him, making it impossible to look for campfire smoke.

He finally came upon a hill big enough to shelter him from the wind. He would nestle into the bank and try to wait out the storm. He forced Tonoeva as close against the side of the hill as possible. He pulled off the buffalo robe he had kept from the kill he had made when he was with the Whitestones. He had taken it knowing winter would set in soon and he would need the warmth. Caleb threw down the robe and rolled into it, tying Tonoeva's reins to his wrist so the horse could not wander away. He pushed away the snow so the horse could get to the grass beneath it.

Caleb pulled his hat down and closed his eyes to rest, fighting a small panicky feeling that he might die in this place, buried in the snow. He tried not to let his thoughts go to Sarah, as they were prone to do when he stopped. He concentrated on Marie and the small Cherokee village he had left behind. They would have a hard time in this violent land. Already many of the other Cherokee had died from disease, accidents or Indian raids. He had to admire their courage and determination, though. James Whitestone was a man of vision. Caleb did not doubt he was right about what the future held for Cherokee in Georgia. It had already happened to too many Indians in too many other states farther east. At least out here a man like Whitestone—and himself—could be free.

In his mind he saw Marie as she had looked when he left, like an abandoned fawn. He was sorry to hurt her, but he could do nothing about her childish love. Caleb was sure that after he was gone a while she would get over him. He wanted nothing to do with love again, even if he were to go back to the settlement. He just wanted his son and some peace in his life.

Caleb knew he would consider returning to the Cherokee. They had all seemed lost when he had left, looking to him as though he had the skills to show them how to survive in the strange new land. At least if he lived with the Whitestones and helped them get their farm going he would have some purpose to his life, something to keep him busy and keep his mind off the things that brought him such deep pain.

If it were not for little Tom, none of it would matter. But Caleb had to keep going for the boy's sake, and that meant getting over Sarah. The way the Cherokee were living seemed like a happy medium, a world between white and Indian. That's what he was, a man living on the border, torn between two worlds.

As much as Caleb loved his people and their way of life, he had been in the white man's world enough to know that James was probably right. There was no future at all for the wild Indians, and only a slim hope of survival for those who would choose to live the white man's way. The survivors would be those who adjusted early and quickly. And Caleb realized that after all he had been through, he was a survivor. His son made that survival instinct stronger. He fell asleep thinking about little Tom, wondering what he looked like.

The rising sun shone brightly on the side of the hill, waking Caleb with its orange glow. The sky was clear and blue, the air calm. The first blast of winter had moved further east across the vast land. Caleb sat up, throwing heavy snow from the buffalo robe. He stood up, sure he'd heard voices. Wading through the knee-deep snow, he made his way to the top of the small hill. He let out a whoop when he saw tipis amid a thick stand of trees that bordered a partially frozen river. There was no mistaking the paintings on the tipis; they were Cheyenne.

He smiled with excitement, then hurried back to Tonoeva, half falling in the deep snow, laughing at himself for being so close to the village and not even knowing it.

It was a huge settlement, surely the greatest share of Cheyenne anywhere around. He picked up his robe and threw it over the horse, then climbed onto the animal. Tonoeva tossed her head, her nostrils flaring as she realized there were horses not far away. She turned willingly at his command and pushed her way through the deep snow toward the village.

Caleb called out in Cheyenne when he drew close, laughing when he saw some familiar faces as women stood up from campfires and men came out from the tipis. Snowdrifts piled gracefully in odd shapes over the sides of some of the tipis, and the trees were weighted down with snow. Dogs ran and barked, snow flying over their bodies as they came out to chase him. Caleb put up his hand in a sign of peace and asked the first woman he saw if she knew Three Feathers and where he could find him.

The woman shook her head, her brown eyes looking tired. "Three Feathers died," she told him in Cheyenne. "There has been much disease. Many have died."

Caleb's heart tightened. "When?"

"Three, four moons ago."

"Is this Three Feathers' band?"

The woman nodded. Others gathered closer, some of them recognizing him.

"Blue Hawk! It is Blue Hawk, the great warrior who killed many Crow!"

"My son," Caleb asked the woman, ignoring the others. "I left him with my aunt, Sweet Seed Woman. Is she here? Are they all right?"

The woman shook her head. "Sweet Seed Woman is dead, too. And her sister. Buffalo Man gave your son to Many

Seeds, wife of Gray Dog. All have wondered if you would return to—"

"Take me to Many Seeds," he interrupted as relief washed over him. Little Tom was alive. He had a son and he was alive. It seemed a good sign to Caleb, that there was a reason to go on living after all.

He dismounted, walking with Tonoeva and following the woman, who led him far into the village to a large tipi painted with dogs. She rattled the buffalo hooves that hung at the entrance, then waited with an impatient Caleb until a man pushed aside the flap and stepped outside. He stared at Caleb a moment, then nodded, and the woman left discreetly.

"So, Blue Hawk, finally you have come for your son. He is like a son to us now."

Caleb's eyes were watery. "I would have come much sooner, but I was wounded by white men and I was many moons recovering."

Gray Dog looked him over. He was a stern, discerning man, with a long sharp nose and thin lips, a man who seldom smiled, even when he felt like it. "Your son is playing a game with my own two sons. Come."

Caleb eagerly ducked inside. The atmosphere was warm and loving. A woman sat to one side mending some moccasins, and when she saw Caleb her face fell. She knew who it was and why he had come, but she loved little Tom and would hate to see him leave. How could anyone not love him? He was plump and beautiful, with a ready, dimpled smile and sparkling brown eyes that could charm prized eagle feathers off the proudest warrior. He was a sweet, obedient child, and Caleb knew instantly which child was his, even though one of the others was nearly the same age. In the sparkling eyes of his son he could see Walking Grass.

The likeness stabbed him like a sword, and the memory of her death overwhelmed him. He hurried over to Tom and lifted the boy, hugging him desperately, not caring if Gray Dog and his wife knew he was crying. How could he not cry? He had lost so much, yet here was someone he still had, a part of him that lived and breathed. All else was gone, even Three Feathers and Sweet Seed Woman. He would never see them again. And he knew in that instant, as he held his son in the middle of a Cheyenne camp in the wilds of the Unorganized Territory, what he must do. He could not stay here. It had all changed too much, or perhaps it was he who had changed too much. Caleb would take his child to the Canadian River, to the Cherokee settlement.

He rubbed his face against the velvet softness of his son's cheek, breathed deeply of the boy's sweet scent, ran his hand over the sleek gloss of the boy's blue-black hair. How could there have been a time when he did not want this child? How could he have been full of that much hatred and revenge, that he would leave this son to others? He had always thought it would hurt too much to be near the child— but now as he held him, he realized what a healing effect the boy had on him. If only Sarah could . . .

Oh, the hurt of it! They were going to live together in a little cabin, and Sarah was going to be a mother to little Tom. What a wonderful mother she would have made! But there was no Sarah now—and no Walking Grass. Sometimes it seemed he had no past at all. The only proof was this precious little boy, who pulled back and looked at him now with puckered lips and a scowl, looking as if he were trying to determine just who this man was who had so suddenly picked him up and interrupted his game.

"Father," Gray Dog told the boy in the Cheyenne tongue. "He speaks no English," the man told Caleb.

Caleb smiled broadly, tears on his cheeks. "I'll teach him."

Tom traced a fat brown finger along the scar on Caleb's cheek. *"Ne-hoeehe?"*

Caleb laughed lightly and kissed the boy's chubby cheek. *"Ai,* little one. I am your father."

* * *

Sarah turned away as Byron walked into the bedroom. She was glad that she was big with child now, for it meant he would leave her alone. The first few months after arriving in Washington had been hell, and she knew she could not survive a lifetime with this man. She was determined to divorce him as soon as the baby was born. It would be easy enough to prove his infidelity. After all, everyone knew that as soon as her condition made her undesirable Byron Clawson had started seeing other women of their social circle openly. It mattered little to her, for it only gave her grounds to leave him as soon as she could. He had even begun frequenting brothels, bragging about how much the whores looked forward to his visits and how she could benefit by taking lessons from them.

Sarah wondered how she had managed to stay sane this long. If not for the child she could not have done it. She trembled at the memory of his clammy hands, the way he deliberately took his time with her, drawing out her agony, knowing full well she detested his touch. She had made a bargain and was living in hell for it. But she kept to her part of the agreement, despite the fact that she had never enjoyed even being with Byron Clawson, and being bedded by him was worse than she had imagined. He always grinned while he took her in vile sex acts, his small penis darting into her in quick jabs. She wondered what the other women he escorted around town would do if they knew he was only half a man. She knew now that his bragging about all his experience with women had been lies. He didn't know the first thing about how to please a woman, and even if he had, he was not man enough to follow through.

When he sat on the bed and began removing his clothes she could smell the liquor on him. His drinking had increased since their marriage, but it did not seem to affect his social image. How clever he was at putting on a refined facade. None of his colleagues seemed to mind that he was a bit of a ladies' man. After all, his wife was big with child, and a man had his needs.

His drinking hadn't seemed to affect his career, either. Byron was political and legal advisor to a senator, with political ambitions of his own, and in that capacity he was successful. But none of it impressed Sarah. She longed for the life she could have had with Caleb, a little cabin in a peaceful land, lying in a deep feather mattress with Caleb Sax beside her, curled up against his virile body, safe in his strong arms. How could two men be so different? Wanting to live had been a delicate choice for her, for losing Caleb was like losing her life's blood. There was only the baby now.

Byron eased into bed beside her and she feigned sleep, then chilled when he pressed against her back, reaching around and fumbling with her breast. What was he doing? He had promised to leave her alone now that she was so big. He began kissing her shoulder and neck, his hand moving down to pull up her gown. Drunk! The fool was drunk and wanted her!

She moved farther away. "You've been with the whores. I can smell their perfume," she told him. "Leave me alone."

He grabbed her arm, jerking her onto her back and crawling on top of her swollen stomach.

"I don't want the whores. I want my lovely wife." His breath nauseated her.

"Get off of me," she said. "You'll hurt the baby!"

"So what? It's not my brat. And who are you to speak against whores, Mrs. Byron Clawson? You're a whore yourself, spreading your legs for that Indian scum."

She pushed him and tried to get out from under him, but he suddenly punched her in the jaw. Her heart raced with panic. He had beat her before, but he had not touched her since she was so big. All she could think of was the baby.

He began ripping her gown and slapped her across her cheek. Sarah tasted blood in her moth and struggled against him in a daze, feeling her gown torn free. His cold hands moved over her swollen stomach, terrorizing her as he pushed.

"Bastard," he sneered. "Bastard seed! Why doesn't the thing come so I can have my woman back?" He pushed harder and she screamed, kicking at him and turning to get away, but he grabbed her and slammed her back onto the bed. "Get the thing born, woman! I'm sick of looking at your fat belly and knowing it belongs to that half-breed son of a bitch!"

"Leave me alone," she pleaded. "I won't fight you, Byron, if you don't hurt me."

He laughed like a madman. "Won't fight me?" He rose and jerked her off the bed, then slapped her face again, sending her flying across the room. Her naked body crashed against a dresser and she fell to the floor. Byron looked at her for a moment in the dim light of an oil lamp, always left burning low.

"You don't need to worry about fighting me, Mrs. Clawson. I don't want your body with its bloated belly anyway."

He stumbled to the door, taking a robe from a hook and pulling it on. When he flung open the door a maid gasped and darted back. Byron grinned. "Hello, Tilly. Did you enjoy listening?"

The young girl just blinked. He stood there with his robe open, so drunk he didn't even realize he was fully exposed. He stepped closer. "There's still extra pay in it if I can come see you in your room later," he said, leering drunkenly.

She straightened, looking him over. He was her boss and paid well but she was afraid of him. He was a cruel man. The only reason Tilly stayed was because she felt sorry for Mrs. Clawson.

"I'll think about it, sir," she said, hoping she sounded convincing. "But maybe I'd better see to Mrs. Clawson first."

He shrugged. "Go ahead. I'm going to get another drink."

He stumbled down the stairs of the elegant brownstone he had purchased, running his hand along the polished walnut railing. He went to the buffet and poured himself a

drink, waiting for Tilly. Moments later she came hurrying
down the stairs.

"Mr. Clawson, you'd better send for the doctor! Your
wife is having her baby."

His eyebrows arched. "Really? How nice for her." He
swallowed the drink. "Send the stable boy."

"Yes, sir. Do you want me to go up and stay with her
once I've done that, sir?"

Byron stared at the bedroom door at the top of the stairs.
"No. Let her suffer alone until the doctor comes."

Tilly frowned. After all, it was the man's own child.
"Aren't—aren't you going to sit with her, sir?"

He glared at her strangely. "You are perfectly aware that
I just beat the hell out of my wife. Why would I want to
sit with her? For reasons of my own I don't care if the child
lives or dies—or my wife, for that matter. I'm sure you'll
understand the need to keep our secrets. You *do* understand
what will happen if you say a word of this to anyone?"

She paled. "I understand."

"Good. Now go and get the damn stable boy. And make
sure he gets Dr. Zajac."

"Yes, sir." She hurried away. Byron looked up the stairs
again, smiling when he heard a scream. He hoped she suffered plenty delivering the bastard.

The pain was beyond anything Sarah had expected. Perhaps if she had not been beaten first, perhaps if the labor
had not been forced by Byron's abuse the delivery would
not have been so miserable. The labor lingered for hours,
and the doctor did not seem to be helping. She had never
liked this doctor, but he was the one Byron insisted she
have, claiming he was one of the best.

She was consumed by clawing pains, helpless to stop
what would happen. The doctor left for a moment, and she
managed to turn on her side, moving her hand under the
mattress. Sarah retrieved the blue quill necklace she kept
hidden there, where she could take it out and cling to it in

the night, drawing on its power for courage and strength.
She rolled onto her back again, gasping as another con-
traction began. She clung to the necklace, wishing Caleb
could be with her. If he were, he would be right by her
side, coaching her, helping her, loving her, anxious to see
his child.

"I'm . . . doing it for you," she whispered.

The door opened and she moved the necklace under the
blankets, still clinging to it. The doctor came back to the
bed. "I have a little something for the pain," he said. "The
baby will come on its own now. You don't have to be fully
awake if you don't want to."

"I don't want anything." She groaned. "I want to be
awake."

"Now, now. I insist you take it. I might have to turn the
baby, Mrs. Clawson. I think it might be breech."

"Breech?" She whimpered, already weak from hours of
labor and the shock of Byron's attack. "Don't let anything
happen to my baby!"

"Nothing is going to happen. Come now. Take the medicine." He poured some into a small glass and held her head,
putting it to her lips and coaxing her to drink the milky
liquid. Sarah was too weak to object. The doctor studied
her bruised and battered face. "That's quite a fall you took,
Mrs. Clawson. I'm sure that's what brought this on."

"Fall?" She started to tell him she had not fallen, that
Byron had beaten her. But suddenly her mouth would not
work, and then the room was spinning. Voices sounded far
away. She heard screams, but had no idea they were her
own. She heard Byron's voice then. She didn't want Byron
there.

"What's this?" A damn Indian necklace! I'll bet it was
his!"

Sarah wanted to protest when Byron tore the necklace
from her hand, but she was powerless.

Her legs were parted and she felt strange movements
through her abdomen . . . hands, words, screams, a baby's

cry . . . then all was blackness. She had no idea how long she lay there before awakening to a quiet room, clean and covered, the sun lighting up one wall. She was so weak that just opening her eyes seemed an effort. The first thing she saw was the doctor.

"Baby," she moaned.

Dr. Zajac was instantly at her bedside. "Well now, Mrs. Clawson, I was beginning to wonder if you would ever wake up."

She stared at him with dull green eyes, feeling strangely heavy. She spoke with slurred words. "Baby," she repeated. "My baby."

The man frowned, sitting on the edge of the bed. "I'm sorry, Mrs. Clawson. I'm afraid I couldn't save her."

What did he mean? she wondered.

"It was a little girl, Mrs. Clawson. She lived only seconds before turning blue and choking to death. Who knows what causes these things? If we knew we could save so many."

Sarah made a choking sound in an effort to scream. It couldn't be true. How could she have lost Caleb's baby? It was all she had to keep her going. Sarah felt as if what little was left of her heart was being crushed. "Baby," she wailed.

"Calm down, Mrs. Clawson. I'm so sorry. I did my best. But you can have more children."

She didn't want more. She wanted Caleb's baby.

The door opened and Byron came into the room. Byron. It was his fault. He killed the baby, killed it just the same as if he had put a gun to its head. He saw the look in her eyes and moved closer.

"Well, dear, I see you're awake," Byron told her, bending down and kissing her forehead. "I'm sorry about the baby, I truly am. We had to bury her right away, of course. You've been sleeping for two days now."

She wanted to lash out at him, to kill him. But she couldn't even move. All she could do was stare at him and shake with wrenching sobs that tore her soul apart.

"By the way," Byron added. "You were holding an Indian

necklace in your hand during the birth. I supposed it was something special to you, so I took it and buried it with the child. I thought you might like to know that."

Sarah saw the victory in his eyes. Caleb Sax was dead, now his child was dead, and Byron had removed her only other link to the man, the blue quill necklace. She began shaking violently, and the doctor was there immediately with more medicine. They were making her drink it. She didn't want to drink it. But she was helpless. She coughed and choked as it went down, and seconds later all was black again.

"That will keep her quiet for a good long time," the doctor told Byron. "If you keep her drugged long enough, she'll eventually become very weak, and as a result very submissive and dependent on you. That is what you requested, isn't it?"

"Yes. I want to keep her quiet for awhile, until I'm sure she's given up and is convinced the baby is dead." He smiled wryly at the doctor. "I guess I'm not a total villain," he said to the man. "I could have had you kill the baby. But in all good conscience I couldn't quite go that far."

The doctor grinned and shook his head. "You'd be surprised what I can do for enough money," he answered. "But I only do what I'm paid for, and you paid for a cover up, Mr. Clawson."

Byron watched the man put away his instruments. "If the damn brat hadn't been so dark I might have let her keep it. If it had been fair like her I could have stood it. But that one was all Indian. How would I have explained that to my associates?"

"I understand. My lips are sealed." The doctor turned and they shook hands. "Keep giving her that medicine I've left on the table, two tablespoons every time she wakes. When the medicine is gone, let me know and we'll see how she's progressing." He walked to the door. "Call on me if you need anything else."

Byron nodded, turning to Sarah as soon as the man left.

"Now you are totally mine, Sarah Sax Clawson," he said. "I'll not share you with some other man's brat. And I'll not have you mooning over that damn Indian trinket either. It's with that bastard child where it belongs. Let the child wonder where the hell it came from."

"All right! All right!" The stout woman who ran the Pennsylvania orphanage pulled her robe tight as she lumbered to the kitchen door. The pounding continued.

"This is an ungodly hour to be comin' to call," she hollered. She flung open the door to see a carriage rattling off into the darkness. A crate sat on the back step.

The woman bent down to check the contents. Her eyes widened when she peeled back the blankets and found a baby.

"Well, I might have known," she muttered. She leaned farther out the door, shaking her fist in the direction the buggy had gone. "Cowards! Bring me another bastard, will you? Can't own up to your own mistakes?"

She bent down and picked up the crate, carrying it inside to a table and setting it down. When she picked up the baby something fell back into the crate. The woman frowned, hoisting the baby into the crook of one arm and reaching into the crate with the other. She pulled out a blue quill necklace. She looked from the necklace to the baby, a beautiful child with dark skin and a shock of jet black hair.

"Indian, are you? I've never had an Indian child in this place before." She examined the necklace. "I suppose somebody wants you to have this—a gift from someone you'll never know now, little one. We'll hang on to it for you." She shook her head. "Now what would an Indian be doing in these parts? And Indians don't drive fancy carriages." She unwrapped the blanket to see that the baby was a girl. "Well, I guess we'll have to pick out a name for you and hope you're lucky enough to get adopted soon. You're too pretty to be slaving away in a factory all day."

The baby opened her eyes, eyes as blue as the sky. The

woman's eyebrows arched. "Well, well! Now I think I understand. A little half-breed, are you? And which one had the blue eyes, hmm? Your mama or your papa?" She laid the necklace across the baby's chest. It was almost as big as the baby. "Looks like this was made for a man," she mused. "Is that it? Is your papa the Indian?"

She turned and headed up the stairs. "I guess that's something we'll never know, will we, child?"

Chapter
Twenty-Four

IT was hard work, clearing the land, planting, weeding, harvesting. And Caleb worked harder than any of them, because he wanted to keep busy. Tom was at his side every minute of every day, toddling through the fields or riding in the wagon with him when Caleb made trips to a trading post on the Arkansas River.

Caleb and Tom were so close that the Cherokee joked about it. "I think there is an invisible cord tied between them," one would say. "The boy can go only so far and then the father pulls him back."

"Have you seen Caleb and the boy today?" they would ask, never, "Have you seen Caleb?"

Marie Whitestone had been ecstatic the day she saw Caleb Sax ride into the settlement. It was the spring of 1816 when he came, and the prairie was alive with wildflowers. It was a time when a young girl's heart is softest, her hope the greatest, her love the most painful. Caleb had returned and she was sick with love for him. She had dreamed of him all that winter, praying daily that he would come back.

But her joy was short-lived, for she soon realized Caleb's whole world was his son. She could not blame him, knowing what he had been through and what the boy meant to him. And she certainly couldn't blame the child, a sweet and beautiful four-year-old. She only blamed herself, sure he did not find her attractive because she was crippled. She wished that she would get taller, but she only grew stronger and more stout, beginning to develop the solid build of her Cherokee mother. She could imagine how beautiful the one called Sarah must have been, with her red-gold hair and green eyes. And it seemed most white women were more slender than Indian women. Surely after loving one like that Caleb Sax could never find someone like Marie Whitestone desirable.

And so her heart loved secretly, painfully. Caleb paid little more attention to her than he did to any of the other settlers. He built his own cabin and shared it with his son. He began taking the child with him into the mountains to the east to search for wild horses, and by the end of that summer he had a corral full of mustangs.

"I am not so interested in farming," he told the White-stones one night. He had been invited for supper, and Marie had cooked the entire meal, hoping to impress him. She brought him a large piece of berry pie, and he hoisted Tom onto his lap and let the child poke at it and eat some while he talked. Marie's heart fell. Caleb did not even take a bite of it.

"Horses," he continued. "That's my kind of crop. I will break them, and sell them to new settlers, maybe herd some to the trading post. Soon more people will come here and they will need horses. I love the animals, love raising them. I think I can do well."

James Whitestone nodded. "Each man must do what he does best. For me it is farming." He laid some pods in front of Caleb. "Try these."

Caleb frowned, turning one of them over in his fingers. Tom picked one up and put it in his mouth to suck on it and Whitestone laughed. "You must break the shell," he told Caleb. "Then eat the nut inside."

Caleb urged the boy to spit out the pod. He broke it open then, tasted one of the nuts inside and gave the other one to Tom. "This is very good," he told Whitestone. "I've never seen a nut like this before. What do you call it?"

"Some call them groundnuts, some goober peas or ground peas. I call them peanuts. The Cherokee grow them in Georgia. They grow under the ground and have to be roasted after they are harvested."

Caleb ate another one, giving part of it to Tom again. The boy grinned brightly, poking at the piece of pie and sticking some gooey berries into his mouth.

"Do you not like the pie, Caleb?" Marie finally asked. "I baked it especially for you."

Caleb glanced at her, and when he saw the hope on her face he felt suddenly cruel. He had seen that same look whenever he was around her. He had avoided it, deliberately ignored it. He had no use for loving again, but he knew perhaps she misunderstood his reasons.

He gave her a wink. "The meal was the best I have had in a long time. And I intend to eat the pie, more than one piece if I can have it."

She brightened, visibly reddening under her dark skin. He noticed she wore a pretty yellow dress, appreciating the way she filled out the bodice. Marie Whitestone was most certainly well endowed, and although a bit stout, she had a very pretty face, a face full of love and sweetness. She would obviously make a very good wife some day. But that day was far away for him, if it ever came at all.

Caleb politely finished two pieces of pie, more for Marie than because he was hungry. Lee, now five, took four-year-old Tom aside to play a game with beads, and Caleb stretched and rubbed his stomach. He lit a pipe. "I'm so full, I think

I'll walk outside for a few minutes and smoke my pipe," he told James. "Do you mind if Marie walks with me?"

The girl met his eyes, then blushed, feeling flustered.

"By my guest," James replied, aware of his daughter's crush on Caleb.

Marie hurriedly found a sweater, wondering how she kept her legs from folding beneath her. She walked to the door and Caleb followed her out, taking her trembling arm.

"Let's walk over here," he said, leading her to a bench made from two stumps and a log laid between them. "Sit down, Marie." She did so gladly, and Caleb sat down beside her. He puffed his pipe for a moment, then set it aside, leaning forward and resting his elbows on his knees. "Marie, I wish . . . I wish we could somehow remove the awkward feelings between us. I mean, I see the way you look at me, and it hurts me to not be able to return that look. You're a young woman with a good heart, full of love to give unselfishly, and there are many fine young Cherokee men in this settlement."

Marie felt tears fill her eyes at his hesitant speech. She sniffed. She had lost him without ever having him.

"Don't cry, Marie. I did not bring you out here to make you cry."

"I can't help it," she blurted. This was her only chance to tell him. "I love you, Caleb. If I could make myself stop, I would. I—I try to. I know I am plain and crippled and you don't care about me that way, but I can't stop how I feel." She started to run off, but Caleb grabbed her arm, forcing her back down to the bench. He faced her, grasping both her arms.

"Is that what you think? That I don't like the way you look . . . or that I find you undesirable because of your foot?"

She couldn't reply.

He leaned closer. "Marie, listen to me. I do not look at you the way you think. In you I see a great beauty, a goodness that can make a man feel the way he should feel about a woman he cares for. I treat you as I do because . . .

because inside I am terrified. I do not fear Indians or outlaws
or the elements or wild animals. There is only one thing
that I fear, and that is to love again. I do not let my son out
of my sight because I'm so afraid of losing him. Death
stalks me like a spirit. It has taken all those I have ever
loved—" His voice broke and he swallowed to stay in control. "You have to understand, Marie. You have to let me
heal. But that does not mean we cannot be good friends.
And it doesn't mean that I could never look at you as a
woman I would want. It only means that I do not want you
pining away for me. If some Cherokee man takes a liking
to you, you should think about him. Do not wait for me. I
have no desire to love a woman again—not for a long time."

His face was so close, so beautiful. "You . . . you really
think I am pretty?"

He gave her a handsome grin. "Of course you are pretty."

"And if not for your sorrow you could . . . want me?"

He studied her for several moments. "Yes," he answered
in a near whisper. "I could want you."

A tear slipped down her cheek. "Would you kiss me,
Caleb? Just once? I promise I will never bother you again."

He smiled, his eyes sparkling in the moonlight. "You are
not a bother. I only want you to understand so you do not
feel bad. Do you understand?"

She sniffed. "I understand. Can I help you take care of
your horses sometimes, and watch little Tom for you? He
is such a beautiful boy. You have to let go of him, Caleb.
You will smother him."

He frowned, then nodded. "You are wise for sixteen,
Marie Whitestone. I know you are right. I am just afraid."

"You should not be afraid. Everything will be good now.
And one day you will love again, be happy again."

A warm breeze ruffled her long hair. He leaned forward
then, meeting her lips tenderly, surprised at how quickly
just touching her mouth awakened feelings he preferred to
keep buried. Every nerve seemed to tingle painfully, and he
knew he was not ready for this. It still hurt far too much.

Marie felt herself melting under his kiss, sure in that quick moment that Caleb Sax must be everything she imagined as a husband and lover. She would never be afraid with Caleb. She longed to be the one to please him in the night again, to give him more sons. How wonderful it would be to be Caleb Sax's woman.

He left her mouth, kissing her cheek then before pulling back. "No more sad eyes," he told her. "And no more thinking it has something to do with you. Promise?"

She nodded, unable to find her voice.

"Good. Now let's go back inside. I want some more of that good pie."

She stood up on shaking legs and he put an arm around her as he walked her back. "Right now what I really need are friends, Marie. Be my friend."

"I will always be your friend," she answered, finding her voice. Surely there was hope. He had kissed her, and he wanted to be her friend, and he walked with his arm around her. He could tell her to pay attention to the Cherokee boys, but she would not. Caleb Sax was all she wanted. She licked her lips, trying to grasp the lingering taste of his mouth on her own. She would remember the magic of it forever.

"What the hell is wrong with her, doctor?" Byron paced beside the bed while the doctor examined Sarah. "She hasn't come around in weeks. She's an absolute invalid. I've had to hire a nurse to clean up after her."

Dr. Zajac straightened, looking over his spectacles at Byron. "I'd say she's had some kind of reaction to the drug you've been giving her. I told you not to give her more until she was fully awake. Yet the whole bottle is gone. That combined with the heavy bleeding Tilly told me about must have done this to her."

Byron frowned. "Damn it, I didn't want her to get like this."

"Are you suffering from guilt, Mr. Clawson?"

Byron's gray eyes turned glassy. "I have nothing to be

guilty about. *She* does! I just can't stand the way she'd look
at me, with those knowing green eyes. I wanted to make
sure she was weak enough not to put up a fuss. I want this
whole thing over with, and I want to mold her into the right
kind of wife for Byron Clawson. She's beautiful. I want her
on my arm at social events, and I want her to need me—
for the drug or whatever—just so she needs *me*. The baby
is gone now and that damn Indian is dead. It's time she
started living a normal life with me. I'm still willing now
that the bastard child is gone."

"Well I'd say that won't happen for a long time, Mr.
Clawson. She's had a reaction to the drug and she's slipped
into some kind of coma. I don't have any idea what to do
about it or how long it might last."

Byron paled. "No idea? What are you saying?"

"I'm saying it could be two weeks or two years."

"Two years!" He glanced at Sarah's limp, thinning body.
"I'm not going to put up with that . . . that thing in my house
and my bed for two years! You've got to do something!
What will I tell her aunt and uncle?"

"Calm down. You can simply tell them she bled heavily
after the baby and slipped into a coma. It does happen,
although we don't know just why. If you want her out of
your bed, then send her back home. Let her aunt and uncle
take care of her."

Byron turned to look at Sarah again. He had gotten his
way with her, although it hadn't lasted as long as he had
hoped it would. Terrence and Mary Sax certainly couldn't
blame him if he wanted a divorce from this useless creature.
If only she had cooperated he could have given her a grand
life. It wasn't easy finding someone as beautiful as Sarah
Sax, but she wasn't worth the hardship of caring for her the
way she was now. He had done Terrance Sax a favor by
marrying her. It wasn't his fault the baby had "died" and
Sarah Sax had gone into a coma. He nodded.

"Yes. That's an idea. I'll just send her back home. I'll
pay for the best ambulance wagon and driver. In fact, I'll

go along. They should see how distraught I am." He turned to the doctor. "I needn't tell you what I'll do if any of this gets out—the drug and baby and all."

The doctor met his eyes squarely. "You needn't tell me. That's what you paid me for, remember? I'm sorry she's slipped off on you, but you didn't follow my directions." He turned, putting away his instruments. "So, you'll ship her off to Saint Louis and you'll be free as a bird here in Washington, free to pursue your own career without the burden of an invalid wife." He closed his bag. "Do you intend to divorce her?"

Byron shrugged. "I'll have to think about it." There was, after all, Sarah's inheritance to consider.

"Of course. You're a brilliant young man, Mr. Clawson, with a promising future. Should the time come, I know some eligible young ladies who might interest you and who could help you in Washington. You could hardly be blamed for a divorce, and there are some very wealthy ladies here in town."

Their eyes held in mutual understanding. "You will remember me some day when you're a senator or something of the sort, won't you?" the doctor continued. "I might need a few, shall we say, favors?"

"I'll remember," Byron answered. "Can she be moved without harming her any further?"

"Oh, I think so. Have a good trip. Let me know when you return how she did."

"I will."

The doctor left, and Byron turned his eyes back to Sarah. None of this had worked out as he had planned. He had so much more to offer her than that penniless half-breed, he could hardly believe she wouldn't prefer her life here in Washington.

"You'll regret it some day, you haughty bitch," he sneered. "The day will come when you'll wish you were still Mrs. Clawson. It looks like someone else might share the inheritance after all, but by God, I had you, and there's nothing of that damned Indian left for you."

He left the room. Sick people irritated him. He would have a drink and then hire someone to help him take her back to Saint Louis. Once there he would make his final decision about Sarah.

Marie sat by the river, trying her hand at fishing with a stick and a string, while Tom built variously shaped mounds from river mud. Marie had agreed to watch the boy while Caleb broke in some mustangs. Caleb always worried that Tom would somehow get in the way of the bucking horses. Someday he would teach his boy to help him, but Tom was still much too young.

Marie agreed, but sometimes she wondered if Caleb would ever think the boy old enough for anything, he was so protective of the child.

It was spring, 1818, and Caleb had been with them for two years. Marie was more relaxed around him, loving him quietly but maturing enough to be able to keep up a friendship without the lovesick look in her eyes that made him uncomfortable. She was eighteen and had become more patient, more accepting. She even allowed herself to be visited by a couple of Cherokee boys, but deep inside there was only one man she loved.

Marie and Caleb talked often, and she was sure she knew Caleb Sax better than he knew himself, how confused he was over his mixed blood, how gentle he was and yet how capable of extreme violence when someone he loved was threatened or taken from him. And he was so afraid to love again. She couldn't blame him. She could only wait and hope.

She looked up to see Tom piling up more mud. He would soon be six, and he was growing like a weed, slimming out and looking as though he would turn out to be tall and broad like his father. He jumped on a mud house he had built to smash it, then laughed at his action, his dark eyes sparkling. Marie laughed too, but her smile faded when she suddenly heard yips and calls. At first she wasn't sure, but after a moment she realized it was Indians. They had never had trouble with the Plains Indians before, and often traded with them. Thanks to Caleb they could converse with most of them, and the Cherokee, Kiowa and Pawnee had gotten along well. After all, there was not enough settlement in these parts to be any kind of threat to the Indians.

But Marie saw warriors riding over a ridge on the other side of the river. They were not like any Indians she had ever seen. They were painted and held lances or tomahawks in their hands. Her eyes widened when they rode down the bank and into the river.

She screamed Caleb's name as loudly as she could, hoping he would hear her. His cabin and corals were quite a distance from the river. Her own father and mother would be out plowing for the spring planting, and her seven-year-old brother Lee would be helping them. There was really no one else nearby, and there were at least five or six warriors heading across the river.

Marie got to little Tom just before the Indians crossed the shallow water. Tom was standing and staring at the painted ponies splashing toward him, completely fascinated. Marie lifted him and started running as fast as she could, but a moment later a warrior rode up beside her, grabbing for Tom. She hung on tight, screaming again for Caleb. Something hit her back and she tumbled forward, refusing to let go of Tom even though one warrior hit her over and over again with his quirt. The stinging leather tore through her dress and bit into her back, but still Marie held on. She had heard there were some Indians who stole little children. She would not let them have Tom.

The warriors continued their attack until she thought she might faint. The man striking her laughed, apparently thinking it quite a game to see how many lashes it would take to make the woman let go. The six other men circled the group on their ponies. She went to her knees, hovering over little Tom and clinging to him as tightly as possible amid the blows, while all around her there was more yipping and hollering.

Then she heard two gunshots and another warcry, this one slightly different. A black horse thundered up and there was a thud. One of the raiders landed hard on the ground right beside Marie, his chest split open and squirting blood. She screamed and managed to get to her feet, realizing they had stopped beating her. She pulled Tom with her and scrambled away, turning to see Caleb leap from his horse into the second warrior, both men crashing to the ground. A third warrior lay nearby, apparently from the shot Caleb had fired from his musket.

For a moment it was difficult to tell Caleb from the Indian with whom he fought, for Caleb had begun wearing buckskins again, and his hair was long and loose. He was as much Indian as the rest of them. Marie watched in wide-eyed terror as the two men wrestled for the tomahawk Caleb held, rolling over and over. Finally the raiding warrior got Caleb on his back and grabbed the arm that held the tomahawk with both of his own hands, pushing Caleb's arm up over his head. Caleb used his other hand to strike the warrior's face, digging his nails into the man's eyes and skin until the warrior screamed out and let go. In an instant Caleb's tomahawk smashed into his skull.

Caleb quickly threw him off, barely managing to get to his feet before a fourth warrior rode hard toward him. The raiders had chosen to take on Caleb one by one, a common Indian custom, a game of bravery and skill. Caleb pulled a pistol from his belt and fired. A red hole appeared in his attacker's throat and the man fell backward off his horse.

The remaining two warriors backed off, glaring at Caleb, who stood panting, his knife pulled out and his body bent and tense, ready for more action. His eyes blazed, and he exuded the fierce vengeance he had once exacted in his days of warring against the Crow.

The two Comanche warriors remaining smelled death at the thought of taking their turn at this strange Indian who fought far better than they had expected. This was no soft white settler, and instinct told them this was not a man who would go down easily. Indian stared at Indian, and the one who had single-handedly killed four of the Comanches had earned their respect and the right to live.

One of the Comanche nodded and grinned at Caleb, then whirled his horse and rode off, yipping and laughing. The sixth man stared at Caleb a moment longer, looking as though he was considering combat. But then he, too, turned and rode off.

Caleb watched until they were out of sight, then stumbled to Marie, blood streaming from a wound to his forehead. "Tom!" he cried anxiously, grabbing the boy from her.

"He is all right," Marie said. "They tried to steal him. I would not let go. I wouldn't have let them take him, Caleb."

He hugged the boy tightly.

"Father, you hurt," Tom said, tears in his eyes.

"I'm all right, son." It was only then he noticed Marie's bloody back. She sat hunched against the pain. "Marie!"

"I wouldn't . . . let them," she repeated as she began to cry.

Caleb's heart ached for her, realizing what she had been through and how she had suffered to save Tom.

"My God, Marie," he said, bending over her and caressing her hair. He quickly examined Tom, seeing that the boy was all right.

"They tried to get me, Father, but Marie wouldn't let them," the boy said, sniffling with concern for both Marie and his father.

"Yes, I see that, son." Caleb knelt by Marie again. "I will help you to the house, Marie. Can you walk?"

"I'm not sure," she answered, wiping at her tears. She did not want to cry in front of him. She wanted to be strong.

Caleb took hold of her arm and helped her stand. She stumbled against him, and he held her arm, putting an arm around her waist, trying to avoid the deep gashes made from the thick rawhide quirt. She began to shake from shock, and finally he picked her up in his arms. "Sit high," he told her. "Put your arms around my neck so I don't have to touch your back."

She did so gladly, feeling instantly safe and protected. Caleb had saved her from the warriors. Perhaps it was only Tom he was thinking of, but she preferred to pretend it was her. She inhaled his manly scent, and his long hair brushed against her face as he walked with her, carrying her as though she weighed nothing, even though she was a solidly built young woman.

Young Tom ran alongside them. "Father, you fought good! You got them, didn't you, Father?"

"Not soon enough," Caleb answered, hugging Marie closer.

"You will not let Marie die, will you? I do not want her to die."

"Marie is not going to die. She is hurt, but she will be all right."

Ellen and James were running from the field then. They reached the house just as Caleb got there with Marie. Ellen directed Caleb to lay Marie on a feather bed in the corner of the small two-room cabin. Caleb took out his knife and quickly sliced off the remnants of her plain blue dress, exposing her bare back, and her mother wet a cloth, laying it gently over the cuts. Marie moaned and struggled against the tears.

"Damn," James Whitestone muttered. He turned to Caleb. "We heard the gunshots, but it all happened so fast. Was it Indians?"

"Comanche, I think," Caleb replied, his heart aching at the sight of Marie's back. "They don't usually come this far north. They often steal children and either use them for slaves or adopt them into a family as their own." He faced James. "We are Indians fighting Indians. It is strange living in this border country."

James nodded. "Do you think they will come back?"

Caleb looked at Marie. "I hope not. We had better keep watch."

"You should tend to the cut on your head," James said.

"I will in a minute." Caleb leaned close to Marie, gently brushing the hair back from her face. "Thank you, Marie," he said. And then he whispered, "I love you."

He kissed her cheek, and Marie Whitestone felt no pain after that. There was too much joy in her heart. He had spoken the beautiful, magical words.

Chapter
Twenty-Five

THE Comanches did not return. Caleb visited Marie every day, and Tom brought wildflowers. Caleb began watching them together, for the first time realizing how close they were. How many times had he pictured Sarah raising his son? He had to stop fantasizing and face reality. He was only twenty-four years old and most likely had many years ahead of him. He watched Marie and Tom hugging, amazed he had never before noticed the genuine love between them. He thought about the day the Comanches had attacked, remembered seeing them beating Marie viciously as she bent protectively over little Tom.

"Is your back healed enough to picnic by the river tomorrow?" he asked.

Her face brightened. "Yes. It is just red scars now. It hurts a little, but it is not so bad."

He leaned forward, his elbows on his knees. "We will go alone. Tom can stay here with your mother and father."

Her eyes widened and her heart pounded furiously. Alone? He had never done anything with her alone. She had not forgotten the beautiful words he spoke to her the day of the raid. He had not spoken to her like that since, but was this invitation a sign that he was finally learning how to love again? Was it possible he could love *her* that way?

"I will make the food," she said.

"A berry pie? You have to bring a pie or I will not go," he teased.

She smiled, her dark eyes sparkling. "I will make you two pies."

Caleb arrived the next day leading a buckskin colored mare that Marie had always admired. The horse had been young when he brought her in with a group of mustangs, and she had been easy to break, with a gentle nature that made her safe for anyone to ride.

Marie told herself to stay calm. If anything was to develop between them it must come from Caleb. He was so afraid to care. She must not make him feel pushed or he might run from her again. She must be the friend she had been to him all this time and not behave any differently. Yet deep down she hoped something was different. She carried out a basket of food and Caleb lifted Tom down from the mare.

"I want to go with you, Father," the boy complained.

"Not this time. You stay with Mrs. Whitestone."

They boy's lips puckered. His father seldom went anywhere without him.

Marie gave the boy a hug and patted his behind. "Don't give your father trouble," she said. "Be a good little Indian. Lee is behind the house shooting arrows. Why don't you go and practice with him?"

The boy's face lit up and he ran off, and Marie handed the basket to Caleb.

"He obeys you better than me," Caleb commented as he hooked the basket to his saddle.

"That's because you are not firm with him," she answered. "Being firm is also a sign of love, Caleb. You are so close you do not even discipline him."

She looked up at him, sitting tall and beautiful on the gray and white spotted gelding he rode. Tonoeva was aging, and he seldom rode her now. There was something in Caleb's eyes, something Marie could not quite read. He nodded toward the buckskin mare, then dismounted, saying, "I will help you up." He walked around his own horse and lifted her easily, the feel of his hands on her waist making her pulse accelerate.

As she straddled the horse her yellow dress caught under her and exposed one leg to the thigh. Marie started to pull it down, but Caleb reached it first, and as he adjusted it for her the touch of his fingers on her thigh made her shiver.

Caleb felt his own aching needs awake at the sight of her smooth dark skin and the firm muscles of her leg. She was a big girl, but not soft and fat. She was strong, and he was beginning to realize she was also brave, patient and loving. He didn't even notice that the exposed leg was the one with the club foot.

He gently pulled down the dress, looking up into her dark eyes. "The horse is yours," he told her. "It is my gift to you for saving Tom."

Her mouth dropped open and she speechlessly stared as he remounted his own horse. The gift of a horse from an Indian man to an Indian woman was a great honor, usually a sign of love.

"Caleb," she finally managed, "I do not know what to say. She is so beautiful. You know I have always loved this horse."

His lovely blue eyes held her spellbound. "That is why I'm giving her to you. If a man is going to show his gratitude the best way possible, he does not give a small gift."

They rode to the river, and he led her to a place where

the trees were thick and the grass was green. For a while
they ate and talked, sharing the same friendship they had
shared for months now. Caleb kept his musket and tomahawk nearby and wore a knife at his waist, so she knew
she was safe. They talked mostly about Tom. He suddenly
wanted to know her true opinion. Was he raising the boy
wrong? Was he really too lenient? Was he too protective?

He watched her as she talked. She was wise for an
eighteen-year-old. And she was beautiful in all the ways a
good woman was beautiful to a man. Her heart was good.

After they ate, he smoked a pipe while she fished, and
he struggled between the terror of loving again and the
desires that burned inside him, as well as what he knew
was a growing love for Marie Whitestone.

When his pipe was cold he stood and removed his weapons belt, moccasins, buckskin shirt and leggings. Her back
was to him. He walked to the river, standing near her wearing only his loincloth.

"Do you want to go swimming, Marie?" he asked. "It's
warm."

She looked up at him, her breath catching at the sight of
him standing there nearly naked. She set aside her fishing
pole. "I—I would get my dress wet."

He stepped closer, touching the side of her face. "Take
it off then."

With that he untied his loincloth and threw it aside. She
knew what he had done, yet could not bring herself to look
at him. She kept her eyes on his, wondering, hoping, trembling with love.

His eyes suddenly teared and he drew her close so that
her face rested against his bare chest. "Help me, Marie,"
he whispered. "I am so afraid."

She hugged him tightly and kissed his chest. "I love you,
Caleb," she said. "I love you so. You should not be afraid."
She looked up at him and he bent to kiss her mouth gently.
She didn't care if he was using her or really loved her. She
wanted only to give him his pleasure.

He pulled back and began unbuttoning her dress. She stood still, on fire for him, unsure what to do but knowing she didn't need to know. Caleb would teach her. He peeled down the dress, exposing her large bosom that had never been touched or tasted by any man. He pulled off the rest of her clothes, then lifted her in his arms. She embraced him and let him nestle his face into her full breasts, kissing them, tasting her taught nipples and sending flames of passion through her entire body. She whispered his name as he carried her to the river and lowered her into the water.

After that she wasn't sure if things were real or if she was dreaming. They swam and played in the water. Sometimes Caleb would pull her under the water and kiss her, sometimes he would swim up under her, kissing her thighs, her private place, her stomach, her breasts, her throat, until he came out of the water and met her mouth, covering her lips with his own, sending shivers of ecstasy through her virgin body. Finally he carried her out of the water and placed her on the blanket near the bank. He pulled another blanket from his horse and returned to her with it, using it to dry her off.

She lay still, enjoying every touch, watching his own firm muscle as he massaged her with the blanket. She dared to let her eyes rest on his full nakedness, and what she saw was as big and powerful looking as the rest of him. It was both fascinating and frightening to her.

He bent over her, resting on his elbows, his hardness pushing against her belly. "There is no one out here to marry us," he told her. "We will be married the Indian way. We will simply be one and you will be my wife."

A tear of joy slipped down the side of her face. She reached up to touch the thin white scar on his handsome face. "I know of no greater honor than to be the wife of Caleb Sax," she whispered. "I will love you forever, Caleb."

He bent closer, nibbling at her lips. "And I love you, Marie," he whispered.

His lips kissed her throat, her breasts again, and he took

pleasure in their fullness, feeling somehow comforted when he nuzzled into them. Then he seemed to be everywhere, touching, kissing, his fingers moving into private places and setting her on fire, working some kind of magic that made her lose any remaining inhibition, making her want him as she had never wanted anything in her life. He began probing her until suddenly the pain hit her as he entered, pushing hard. It had been a long time for him. It was difficult to be gentle, and she cried out with pain, but he surged into her over and over, partly out of love, partly out of need, partly from pure anger over all the loss he had known. Soon his life was pouring into her and he was suddenly spent.

He held her close, relaxing beside her and laying his face against her soft breasts. To his surprise his tears came suddenly, tears he should have shed years before but had not. Caleb realized he had finally faced the fact that Sarah was gone and he had to go on with life. He wept.

Marie cradled him against her and stroked his hair, saying nothing. She understood.

Sarah looked up as her aunt walked into her room, using a cane for support. The woman was suffering from a crippling pain in her joints that made it difficult for her to walk or bend her fingers. Sarah stared at her coldly as she moved closer, dressed completely in black, the taffeta rustling in the otherwise silent room. It was the spring of 1819 and Terrence Sax had just been buried.

"How are you feeling today, Sarah?"

Sarah looked down at her own thin white hand. "If I could stop shaking every time I get up I would be able to walk."

"In time, dear. You've improved so much."

Sarah looked away. It was difficult to be kind these days. She felt only cold and empty.

"Perhaps in time you will be strong enough to visit your father's grave. It's only proper—"

"I'll never visit his grave," Sarah snapped. "And don't call him my father. Tom Sax was my father!"

The woman sighed deeply, blinking back tears and turning away. "I may need your help, Sarah. It seems many banks are closing and several of your father's —your uncle's— businesses folded before he died. I suppose that's partly what killed him, on top of seeing what forcing you to marry Byron did to you." She sniffed and dabbed her eyes. "At any rate, there's not all that much money left, and I'm not very good at handling such things. The house is ours free and clear, thank the Lord. You are, of course, welcome to stay here as long as you like."

Sarah laid her head back against the pillow. "I don't see that I have much choice, Aunt Mary. I'm still not well enough to do otherwise, and even if I were, where would I go? What would I do? I have nothing left to live for. Caleb Sax was all I wanted, and you and Uncle Terrence took him from me."

The woman sobbed. "I disagreed. I've told you that so many times." She wiped her eyes again. "Oh, Sarah, what's happened to you? You were always so sweet."

Sarah kept her eyes closed. "Sweet? It did me a lot of good to be sweet. How can you expect me not to be changed, Aunt Mary? You let me marry that animal. He killed my baby, Caleb's baby. I can't prove it, but I know he did. And he destroyed Caleb's necklace. I nearly died having the baby, and that—that doctor he hired gave me something that only made me sicker." She opened her eyes and looked at the old woman. "Do you know what it's like to fall asleep and wake up two years later? To find you've aged two years, your husband has divorced you because you no longer have enough money for him, and remember the horrors that got you into the situation to begin with? Then I was in bed for another year struggling to even get out of that bed." She smiled bitterly. "I don't even know why I'm trying to get better. What in God's name do I have to get well for? Tell me, Aunt Mary. Why should I ever get out of this bed?"

The woman took a deep breath, then exhaled as though exhausted. "For yourself, Sarah, and for Caleb Sax. If he truly loved you he would not have wanted to see you this way. This is not the Sarah he loved."

"Well he isn't here to love me, so it doesn't much matter, does it?"

Mary was once again tempted to tell her that Caleb Sax had not been killed that fateful day, that there was a remote chance he was still alive. But Sarah was bitter enough, and Mary needed the girl, especially now that her joint disease was getting worse. If she angered Sarah further she might leave when she was well enough and Mary would be alone.

"It does matter, Sarah. To yourself, to God, to Caleb's memory—and your mother's. Do it for them if nothing else."

"Just go away, Aunt Mary. I can never mourn Uncle Terrence. Don't ever ask me to visit his grave again."

Sarah watched the woman slowly walk from the room, a tiny spark of pity flaring deep in her soul. What must life have been like for the woman, married to a man she knew never loved her as much as he had loved someone else, a man who had raped for that love and then expected the woman he married to live with and accept what he had done? Mary Sax must surely have loved Terrence very much to put up with the pompous, hyprocritical man. Sarah could not imagine why, but whatever the reason, Mary had remained devoted to him.

The door closed and Sarah turned on her side. She was only twenty-two but felt old beyond her years. What lay ahead for her now? The only good thing that had happened was that she was rid of Byron Clawson. He had divorced her quickly when he learned Terrence Sax had nothing left to offer. He was nearly broke at his death. The country's economy had crumbled and so had Terrence Sax. Nothing had come of his plans for a wonderful life for his daughter who would always despise him.

* * *

It took more than a year after the Panic of 1819 for the news to reach the frontier settlements. It was early in 1821 when several white men rode into the Cherokee settlement, stopping at each farm with the news. When they reached the Whitestone farm Caleb hurried to his own cabin to get his musket. Marie sat in a rocker nursing their three-week-old son, John, born in early March. She watched Caleb pick up his musket.

"What is it?"

"I'm not sure. Several men are coming. You stay in the house."

She watched him go, knowing that whatever happened her husband would protect them all. She got up from the rocker with some effort, still heavy from the pregnancy. She went to the door, opening it slightly to look out and listen. John sucked at her breast, oblivious to any trouble, and Caleb walked out to greet the men.

"You James Whitestone?" one of them asked.

"No. I am Caleb Sax, his son-in-law. James is out in the fields."

The man who had spoken looked around, assessing the cabins and outbuilding and fine horses in Caleb's corrals. "Those mustangs for sale?"

"Some. You need horses?"

The man scratched his chin, looking down at Caleb haughtily. His clothes were obviously well made, rugged clothes designed for this land but bought in more civilized places.

"I only thought they might help pay off your father-in-law's debt."

"Debt?"

"To the government." The man put out his hand. "I'm Philip Rand, official representative for Howard McKenzie, one of the few businessmen in Saint Louis who has managed to survive the Panic."

Caleb felt a stab of pain at the mention of Saint Louis.

"Panic? What do you mean?" He slowly reached up and shook the man's hand.

"I mean that most of the banks have fallen, Mr. Sax, and many wealthy men have gone out of business. Those who have survived are doing their best to bail out people like your father-in-law. Mr. Whitestone signed a paper when he left Georgia promising to settle out here and give up his citizenship in Georgia."

"I understand none of this. Wait here and I will get James." He eyed them warily, then walked back to the house, handing his musket to Marie. "Stay inside," he told her. "If they do anything threatening, fire this so I hear you. I don't think they are dangerous, but I'm not certain why they are here."

She took the gun, looking worried. He leaned down and kissed her cheek. "Do not worry. Whatever it is, we will manage."

He turned and walked over to mount his horse and rode out to find James, wondering what this new trouble might be. For once he had found some peace. He was happy here with the Cherokee, happy with Marie, who loved him devotedly, never turning him away in the night, never failing to set a good meal on the table or be there when he needed her. Life had taken on meaning for him again. At twenty-seven he had finally found some purpose to life. His back seldom bothered him anymore, and the inner scars were healing. Nine-year-old Tom was healthy and growing, becoming a friend besides a son, and now he had a second son whom he loved dearly. What more could a man want? There was a time when it had seemed he had nothing left at all to live for, but he hoped those times were behind him.

As he rode up to James, Tom and Lee stopped their hoeing.

"Some men are here," Caleb told James, "saying something about owing the government money and banks folding. They want to talk to you."

He put out his hand and James took it, climbing up onto the back of Caleb's horse. Caleb headed back, while Tom and Lee ran behind him to see what was happening. When Caleb and James reached the strangers, they introduced themselves and dismounted. Philip Rand also dismounted, shaking James' hand.

"Like I told Mr. Sax here, I'm representative for Howard McKenzie of Saint Louis. There has been a panic, Mr. Whitestone. A great many people have gone out of business, banks have folded, and the government is calling in money due on land loans like yours. You left Georgia with an understanding that you would settle the land and buy it for two dollars an acre. You had ten years to start paying on it. I believe you asked for, uh . . ." He took out a piece of paper and unfolded it. "One thousand acres. Have you claimed that much, Mr. Whitestone?"

James Whitestone blinked. "Yes. But I do not farm it all. I have only been here a few years—"

"That would come to two thousand dollars. The government is asking that all monies be paid within six months. Do you have two thousand dollars, Mr. Whitestone?"

James looked helplessly at Caleb, who frowned angrily at Rand.

"Of course he does not have that kind of money. You said yourself that the government agreed he could start paying for the land in ten years. Even then it is to be in payments, not two thousand dollars at once."

Rand sighed as though irritated by their ignorance. "I'm afraid Mr. Whitestone failed to read the fine print of his agreement," he replied, "as did many others. The fine print says the government can demand the money after five years if there is a need. Times are bad, Mr. Sax. Now Mr. McKenzie understands that most of you frontier settlers would never have that kind of money, so he's willing to help you out by paying the debt himself. Of course, the land would be his then."

Caleb's blue eyes turned icy. This was another of the white man's many tricks. They had not changed. "And where does that leave us?" he demanded.

"Well, McKenzie would be happy to let you stay here and farm the land just like you have been doing—for a share of the profits, of course. He would set up a trade line, send wagons for the crops and sell them or horses for you, give you a share of—"

"We would be his slaves, in other words," Caleb interrupted.

Rand bristled. "Certainly not."

"It is the same thing. Do not try to twist things, Mr. Rand. We understand exactly what you are telling us. We may stay here as slaves if we sell to his man McKenzie, or we can just get out and hope to survive someplace else."

Rand had to look up at Caleb, who towered over him. "What is your interest in this, Mr. Sax? You don't look like a Cherokee, you aren't even all Indian. I never saw a blue-eyed Indian before."

"I am part Cheyenne, not Cherokee. But I am married to a Cherokee woman and these people are family to me now."

Rand sniffed pompously. "Well, McKenzie is very kindly helping your 'family' out. You people are lucky the government gave you such a good deal in the first place, considering the fact that some argue whether Indians should be allowed to own land at all. The government's intentions were generous and sympathetic when they contracted with the Cherokee who chose to leave Georgia. They had no idea the economy would fall."

"And what about the Cherokee who stayed?" James asked with concern. "How is it now for them?"

Rand reddened slightly, swallowing. "Not good," he answered. "Some are already heading into land farther west of here. Those who refuse to leave and fight removal through the courts will lose in the end, Mr. Whitestone. If they don't leave Georgia peacefully they'll be forced out."

"The land west of here is not worth much. It will be hard for them."

"That is no concern of mine. At least it will be free."

"And you are telling us to go there?"

The man shrugged. "If you choose to leave here I think it is a good suggestion. Several of the other settlers have expressed a desire to do just that."

Caleb quelled a temptation to hit the man. "Well, we will have to discuss what we want to do."

"Will this Mr. Mckenzie pay us for the land?"

Rand smiled mockingly. "Pay you? He is paying off your debt, Mr. Whitestone, a debt you haven't paid a dime against. Why should he pay you?"

"We have worked hard here, broken the ground for him, spent money on supplies to get out here, cut trees for the cabins and buildings, put much sweat and toil into the earth. It will be easier for the next man. Surely that is worth something."

"You're being offered completely free land farther west, Mr. Whitestone. That's your payment. However, Mister McKenzie did say to tell you people that a man named Moses Austin was in Missouri not long ago looking for people to settle in Texas. It's a province of Mexico, and anyone who lives there must abide by the Mexican laws. But the land is free, and you would be living among fellow Americans. Austin went there after being bankrupted by the Panic, but when he returned to ask people to go back with him, he died. His son, Stephen, carried on his father's plans and has taken a number of people to Texas with him to a settlement on the Brazos River called San Felipe de Austin. There's a regular little city built up there, I hear, and it's the central meeting place for Americans who want to settle there. They're mostly whites, but considering the circumstances and the needs, I'm sure anyone would be welcome."

Caleb sighed disgustedly, turning and looking back toward the cabin, catching the sadness in Marie's eyes. She did not want to leave either. He looked back at Rand. "How soon does this McKenzie want us off the land?"

"As soon as possible. Of course, considering the time element out here it would be several months before he could resell the land or do whatever else he wishes with it."

"How do we even know he will pay off the debt?" Caleb asked. "Or that anything you tell us is true?"

Rand turned to his horse and took several papers from his saddlebags. He handed Caleb newspapers with headlines about the panic, as well as public notices posted by the government and banks notifying people that all land loans were due immediately. He also handed him a paper signed by McKenzie stating that he would in good faith pay off the money owed by James Whitestone. "Is that enough proof? You do read, don't you?"

Caleb rolled up the papers and shoved them back at Rand. "I can read. We are not ignorant savages, Mr. Rand. Some of us can even spell our names." He turned and walked away. "We will leave, Rand. Tell your Mister McKenzie he can find someone else to be his slaves."

The Whitestones and Saxes sat around the table studying crude maps.

"This is not such a good map Rand left us," Caleb told them. "But it looks as though San Felipe de Austin is directly south, perhaps five hundred miles."

"That's a long way, Caleb, through hostile country. Comanche are in that land."

"A little farther west than south. I don't think there are so many directly south." He looked at Marie. "What do you think?"

"I go wherever my husband goes. I am not afraid." Their eyes held, and she knew his fear that he would lose loved ones again.

Caleb looked back at James. "I want to go to this new land. I feel drawn there. Wherever the government sends Indians you can bet the land is not good, so I do not think we should go west. Cherokee are not the only ones they will send. There will be Choctaw, Creek and other eastern Indians being pushed out here. Eventually the Plains Indians may even be forced somewhere. I love my people, not just the Cheyenne but also the Cherokee. Even the Indians we call enemy will one day be called friend in a common cause. But I also love my wife and my sons, and being free to do what I wish with my life. Indian removal by the white man's government will bring trouble, more government problems and tricks, and more men like Howard McKenzie. With the Indians will come the whiskey peddlers and cheating traders. I have had enough trouble in my life. I want to go to Texas, to this new settlement where the land is free and good and we can do what we please without worrying about it being taken from us."

"What about the Mexican government? Could they take the land from us?"

Caleb leaned back in his chair, taking a puff from the pipe he had lit. Earlier, after his temper had cooled, he had gone back out to talk to Rand more about the land in Texas, at which time he was given the crudely drawn maps. He looked at the map again. Marie watched her husband, trusting any decision he would make.

"They probably could. But Rand said Mexico recently won its independence from Spain. They need money and welcome American settlers to help increase trade with the United States. I think it is worth the chance. Is it any different than the risk we took settling here? We do not want to go farther west, and we all know we cannot go back East."

James nodded. "All right. We will try this place called Texas. But it is like going to a foreign land."

Caleb leaned forward and studied the map again. "For people like us, any place is a foreign land now. You cannot go back to Georgia, and I have been away from the Cheyenne too long to rejoin them. We will see if any other families want to join us in going south."

His eyes scanned the large territory called Texas, a province of Mexico. They would join the Americans there. Again his life had been uprooted, but this time he had Marie and his sons. Perhaps he was destined for Texas. Perhaps there he would find total peace, for its name came from the Indian word *tejas*, meaning friends, allies.

He leaned back again, smiling at Marie. "Texas it is then. We will leave as soon as we have enough supplies for the trip."

Chapter
Twenty-Six

SARAH carefully basted the material, then pulled the thread to create the fullest ruffle possible. Left with little money from Terrence Sax's estate, she had opened a dress shop in the Sax house. From the time Cora Sax had first given her a needle and thread to help make their clothes in Fort Dearborn, Sarah had always had a talent for sewing and enjoyed it. To earn money to help care for her ailing aunt, and out of a need to have some purpose to her life, Sarah had taken up the thing she knew how to do best.

Her aunt called out for her. Mary was no longer able to get out of bed. For the first three years after Sarah's return from Washington, it was Mary who had cared for her constantly. Now Sarah was finally well, except for spells of weakness and shaking, and she felt duty bound to nurse Mary, though her own bitterness was growing over her situation. She had few friends and her time was spent almost entirely in taking care of her aunt and sewing. There was no room in her life and no desire for frivolities, including men.

It was 1822. She was twenty-five years old and divorced,

with no desire to be touched by a man again. There was only one man she wanted, and she could not have him. He was gone, and with him had gone all her love, all her joy. It had been seven years since those precious moments of incredible joy in Caleb's arms, ecstasy she would never forget, and six years since her precious daughter was born. Her only memory of that event was hearing the baby cry for one brief moment. Sarah had never even seen her. After that had been the hell of struggling to come back from the darkness and gaining her mobility again.

Mary called for her again, and she set aside the sewing, sighing deeply. She was tired.

"Just a minute, Aunt Mary," she called out.

Now there was only this—existing. There was just enough softness left in her to have some pity for Mary, some small feeling of indebtedness. If her aunt had had any spine she never would have allowed her uncle to force her to marry Byron Clawson. But Mary never went against her husband's wishes. Now she was an old crippled woman. Sometimes when Sarah looked at her she wondered if she too would age before her time, alone and lonely. And if and when she did, who would take care of her? There was no one now.

She got up from the chair. She dared not dream about other times, about her happy childhood at Fort Dearborn, about her precious mother, about Caleb. There were no dreams left for her, only the reality of her situation. She walked down the hall. She had put her aunt in the guest room downstairs so she did not have to go up and down the stairs every time the woman needed something, which was often. She went to the door.

"What is it?"

"Could you get me some tea, Sarah? Everything aches so. I'm sure tea would make me feel better." Mary's voice was weak, and she looked extremely frail.

"I'll get it." She turned and went to the kitchen, putting some tea leaves into a strainer and setting it inside a cup.

She poured water into the cup from a kettle she kept warm over the kitchen hearth.

She stared at the teacup as the leaves steeped, thinking again about the visit she had had earlier in the day from Byron's father. Byron had remarried. Why had he come to tell her? What did she care? He also said Byron was returning to Saint Louis with his new wife, and since he was retiring he would make Byron president of his bank. Sarah knew Byron might one day run for senator or congressman in Missouri. Let him, she thought. As long as Byron never stepped foot on her doorstep, she didn't care what he did. She was sure his father was hinting that she make no trouble for him, afraid she might tell the world what life had been like with Byron Clawson. He wanted to keep the divorce as quiet as possible, wanted Byron to make a good appearance with his new wife.

She lifted the tea leaves from the hot water and set the strainer aside, carrying the tea in to her aunt.

"Oh, thank you, dear. How sweet of you." Mary took the cup and saucer. "Who was here earlier, Sarah?" She sipped some of the tea.

"John Clawson," Sarah answered, walking to the window to gaze at still another new building going up near the house. Saint Louis was becoming the center for travel to the west, which was beginning to pick up. "Gateway to the West" some were calling it, predicting that soon thousands would emigrate westward, and the businessmen of Saint Louis would reap a fortune. She thought about Caleb's Cheyenne people. What would happen to them?

"What did John want?"

Sarah turned away from the window, bending down and straightening the blankets at the foot of the bed. "Just to tell me Byron has remarried and is coming back to Saint Louis to take over the bank. He might run for congress or some such thing. I don't know why he bothered to tell me. I couldn't care less."

The woman sighed. "Don't you have any feelings for him, dear? After all, he was your husband."

Sarah's face darkened with anger. "Don't be a fool, Aunt Mary. He was an animal I was forced to marry just to give my baby a name. Now there is no baby and the hell he put me through was for nothing."

The woman shook her head. "Oh, if not for that Caleb none of this would have happened. If only he had never come here. I hope he died a slow death, all the trouble he gave you. Even your uncle changed after that boy showed up. He never would have been so cruel. He just didn't want you to end up like Cora. He wanted the best for you, Sarah. I wish you could understand that."

"He never understood what I really wanted. He—" She straightened, realizing what Mary had said. "What do you mean you hope he died a slow death? You know how he died. He was crushed under his horse. Uncle Terrence buried him along the river."

Mary colored, her hand shaking slightly. "I only meant ... I hope when that horse fell on him he suffered before drawing his last breath." She took another sip of tea, refusing to look at Sarah.

Sarah felt her entire body shiver with apprehension.

"That's a lie, Aunt Mary, isn't it? You're lying, and I want the truth! What really happened to Caleb?"

"We told you what happened. If it was any different he would have come for you, wouldn't he?"

Sarah began to shake, as she always did when she was upset since coming out of her coma. She leaned closer to her aunt, jerking the tea out of her hands so that some of it spilled onto the blankets. She threw the cup to the floor, grasping Mary by her arms then and shaking her slightly.

"Tell me the truth," she exclaimed.

The woman looked at her wide-eyed, frightened at the almost demented look in Sarah's green eyes. "I promised Terrence—"

"Terrence is dead," Sarah screamed. "My God, Aunt Mary, tell me the truth! What happened to Caleb?"

The woman trembled and started to cry. "You're hurting me, Sarah."

Sarah's eyes widened and she suddenly let go, surprised herself at how cold she had become. She turned away. "Please. Tell me, Aunt Mary." She rubbed her hands together, trying to stop her shaking.

"I . . . I don't want to anger you. I need you, Sarah. Please don't leave me all alone."

Sarah closed her eyes, feeling ill. "I won't leave you, Aunt Mary. I promise. Just tell me the truth."

The woman sniffed. "Caleb really was injured that day when his horse fell. When he tried to run . . . someone shot him in the back. But he didn't die. They kept it a secret. The law never knew about it. And Terrence . . . Terrence sold him down the river."

Sarah closed her eyes and put her face in her hands.

"He told them . . . if Caleb lived they could sell him to a slave ship. If he died, he was to be . . . dumped farther downriver so no one would connect him with Saint Louis. Even if he went to a slave ship, Sarah, he would be dead now. Men don't live long on those ships, I'm told. No matter how you look at it he's still dead. He . . . he never came for you, so he couldn't possibly still be alive."

Alive. Could he be? "Did Byron have a part in it?"

The woman hesitated. "He was there. That's all I know."

"I wouldn't doubt he was the one who shot Caleb in the back," Sarah said disgustedly. She started to pick up the teacup, then hesitated. She looked at her aunt. "You told me that I was very sick when Caleb brought me back, so sick that even the doctor thought I was dead. Wouldn't he have told Caleb I was dead?"

The woman blinked, wiping her tears. "I suppose."

"Then Caleb must have thought me dead. Even if he lived, he wouldn't have come back to Saint Louis because he knew he might be wanted. After all, he'd have been lucky to get out alive the first time. And with me dead, there would be no purpose. He could still be alive, Aunt Mary, alive and thinking me dead."

"Oh, Sarah, give it up. He can't possibly be alive."

Sarah's heart lifted. For the first time in years she had a small bit of hope to hold on to. "But what if he is, Aunt Mary? What if he is?"

It was the first time Mary had seen any resemblance of happiness in Sarah's eyes since she had come out of the coma, the first time there was any sign of the old Sarah there. "Sarah, even if he was alive, he's gone on to his own life now. Perhaps he's even married. And how would you ever go about finding him?"

Sarah began to wring her hands. "I'm not sure. I just need to know. Don't you understand, Aunt Mary? I need to know whether Caleb lived. I can't go through life not knowing."

"And how would you prove otherwise, go to the wharves and ask for pirates? It would be far too dangerous."

"There has to be a way to at least try to find out. If he lived, he's out there somewhere. Maybe . . . maybe he went back to Fort Dearborn for some reason. It's a city now, Chicago they call it. Maybe he went for his son and returned to Fort Dearborn, or maybe he went west. There has to be a way to get word—" She walked to the window again, watching a boy hawking newspapers on the street outside. "The newspaper," she muttered. "I could place ads in every newspaper in every city along the Mississippi and the Missouri, and any they might have out west. I could hire a man to do nothing but travel out there to place an ad saying I'm looking for a man named Caleb Sax—that I'm in Saint Louis. I could just sign it Sarah and leave a post office address so no strange men would come here. If Caleb saw the ad he'd know who it was and he'd come." Her face lit up like a child's. "Yes, he'd come. I know he would."

"Sarah, that's crazy. It would never work."

She bent down to pick up the broken teacup. "Of course

it would. It's all I have, Aunt Mary. I'll find Caleb if it takes every penny of my savings." She looked at Mary, so frail and pitiful. "You should have told me sooner, Aunt Mary."

The woman sniffed, dabbing at her eyes again. "He . . . would have divorced me. He always threatened me with that. I never dreamed I could be married to someone as important as Terrence. I worshipped him, Sarah. I didn't want to lose him."

Sarah felt her anger return. "It was that important to you?" She felt sick again. She carried the cup out of the room, returning to change the blankets, angry but burning inside with hope. She couldn't control her wild thoughts. Caleb might be alive and she might even find him. Caleb! There was no proof of his death. "I'll find him, Aunt Mary. I'll find him," she kept repeating. "I'll place ads in a hundred newspapers—a thousand."

Mary did not answer, and when Sarah tucked a blanket closer, the woman's gnarled hand flopped down oddly. Sarah's heart froze and her skin tingled.

"Aunt Mary?" She drew in her breath and looked closer. There were still tears on her cheeks, but Sarah knew instinctively the woman was dead.

"Oh, Aunt Mary," she groaned. She sat down beside the woman, drawing her into her arms and rocking her, weeping as she had not wept in years. She cried for Mary, for Tom Sax, her mother, Caleb, her dead baby. Her agony knew no bounds.

But at least now she had a tiny bit of hope. Caleb had left Saint Louis alive.

In that same year, Antonio López de Santa Anna conspired with the revolutionary generals who had achieved Mexican independence to oust Emperor Agustin I, exiling him from Mexico. They formed a new National Congress and set up a federal republic, with plans for a Mexican Constitution. Santa Anna, ruthless and ambitious, and only twenty-nine at the time, already had it in mind to one day govern Mexico.

The journey south was not an easy one for Caleb, Marie and the rest of the Whitestones. Only one other family had come along, and the trip was long, hot and dusty. They had two wagons, several head of cattle, mules, and Caleb's mustangs, which he herded behind the small parade. Marie drove one of the wagons, and James herded the cattle.

But James Whitestone was never to make it to his new home. He collapsed and died on the way, and they had to leave his grave somewhere in northeast Texas, sure they would never see it again. Marie's grief was great, as was her mother's and Lee's. Young Tom felt as though he had lost a grandfather, and Caleb mourned because John would never know his grandfather at all.

The procession continued sadly, leaving the lonely, rock-covered grave behind. Caleb longed to stay by Marie's side in the wagon, but he had to take care of the horses, and now the only other man along had to herd the cattle. Tom and Lee were both excellent riders and did their best to help. Caleb prayed every step of the way that he had made the right decision.

But once they reached Texas they found life was not easy. They settled near the Austin colony amid a varied group of people, some good, some running from the law, a few wealthy men but mostly poor farmers and frontiersmen. In 1823 another son was born to Marie and Caleb. He was named David, and the boy survived a bitterly cold winter that left his mother and everyone else thinner. They had little to eat, and Caleb went out often to hunt buffalo, deer, and anything else that meant meat on the table. There was no bread, for the corn seeds had to be saved for the spring plant.

Still, they all shared one thing in common: freedom. There was plenty of free land, and friendships spawned from mutual needs and problems. Others nearby were in the same predicament, and many graves were dug that year. But that only brought the community closer. Marie and Caleb began to feel that perhaps they really had found a home. At the same time their love had mellowed and grown richer as both matured. Marie knew deep inside that there was only one true, passionate love in Caleb's life. Walking Grass had been the love of his youth, that sweet first love that no one forgets. But Sarah Sax was his true love, the one he had loved since his boyhood, and most surely the most beautiful. He had never spoken of her after that day he took Marie at the river. But Marie knew Sarah Sax still lived deep in his soul, in his dreams.

But no woman could ask to be loved and cared for more than she was by Caleb. It was all she wanted or needed, and the joy in his eyes when she gave birth to their second son, David, made her proud. Caleb's three sons were all fine, healthy boys, the children of his seed who gave him something to live for. And because he wanted successful futures for his sons, and for Marie and her brother Lee, he laid claim to twenty thousand acres that very first year.

Here a man had only to say what was his, with a limit of forty-nine thousand acres to an individual settler. The next spring, taking Lee and Tom along, he rode the perimeter of another twenty-nine thousand acres, marking rocks and trees and using any means he could to stake his claim. It was a dangerous undertaking, riding that far from the settlement, for the wilder Indians moved freely through the land, stealing horses and weapons and food. Caleb had built their cabin at the leading edge of the property he claimed, which was closest to Austin's settlement. He knew that he and the others who had come early would benefit the most and retain the most rights if there were any squabbles with the Mexican government.

"We won't light a fire tonight," he told Tom and Lee one night when they were far out in the hills. "I saw signs of Indians a ways back. We don't want to announce our presence." They had found a beautiful valley surrounded by low mountains, which by day was a startling array of colors, the deep green of the valley grass playing against the purple and red of the surrounding hills. "A perfect spot for horses," Caleb had exclaimed. "This has to be part of our land. I will name it Blue Valley because of how blue the hills look at dusk."

"Father." Tom spoke in a near whisper, moving his bedroll closer to Caleb's.

"What is it?"

"I do not understand sometimes. We are Indians, and you have spoken of how you worry that some day the white man will settle all this land and all the Indians will be gone. But we settle the land, too."

Caleb stared up at the stars. "Well, Tom, you have to learn how to survive without betraying your own people. If I make a promise, I keep it. Most white men do not. If Indians wish to move across my land to camp on it I will not stop them, as long as they don't steal my horses or harm my family. I could never be a part of forcing them to live as white men, or forcing them onto little pieces of land where they would die in shame. I understand how those Indians must live. But I know the white man will not allow them that life forever, just as James could see that. He did not want his family to suffer what was to come, nor did I. We both understood the white man's ways better than most Indians, and I am half white. So we decided to use that knowledge to protect our sons and grandchildren. To survive, the Indian will have to learn to live the white man's way, but you must be careful to never be like the white man on the inside."

"How is that, father? Why is he different?"

Caleb felt a piercing pain at the memories of Terrence Sax and Kyle Wiggins, the contempt he had seen in their eyes.

"They judge men by the color of their skin, for one thing. And they think money is worth killing people for. They put money above all else. But a man must be judged by what is inside, by his courage and honesty. Many white men lie. They tell you one thing but mean another, like the men who tricked James into settling that land and then took it back from him. A man should say what he means."

"Do you think Stephen Austin is an honest white man?" Lee asked. Lee was eleven, a solid boy who was obviously going to be very big when he got older. He was handsome, by Cherokee standards or any other, with a bright smile and compelling dark eyes. He had the strength of older boys, and he and Tom were becoming the new "men" of the family. They were a great help to Caleb.

"Yes. I do see honesty in Mr. Austin's eyes. You can tell a lot by a man's eyes. His father was a dedicated man who believed in freedom and loved this land he wanted to settle. He died before he could do so, and Stephen Austin brought people here because it was his father's wish. He is a good man. He did not have to do it, but he loved his father and has honored his memory. For me that is a sign of a good man."

"I feel good here, father, even though it is hard and dangerous," Tom said. "It's exciting, and so much will be ours. I hope the Mexicans let us stay forever. I feel like . . . like it's mine now. If the Mexicans tried to take it away, and if I were old enough, I think I would fight to keep it."

The statement hung in the night air, and Caleb ignored the uncomfortable premonition the words stirred in him. There had been no trouble with the Mexicans. They welcomed American settlers, deliberately opened up their land to them. He had never even met any of the Mexican leaders, including the one called Santa Anna that a few people talked about. They were far away and had not bothered the settlers. Their biggest worry was Indians, not Mexicans, and Caleb tried, whenever possible, to befriend the Indians, not be their enemy. But the Comanche was not easily befriended, and there had been many attacks on the settlement. When he was gone, Caleb insisted that Marie and Ellen and the two babies stay with others closer to the settlement.

He wanted to lose no more loved ones. He wondered if he would ever really get over losing Sarah, but knew instinctively he would not. He would simply have to live with the pain of it. He could sometimes see her as vividly as if she were standing right in front of him. Sometimes it seemed she was not dead at all. But she was, and now he had Marie and his sons, and he was in Mexico, far away from Saint Louis and all that went with that world. Occasionally he thought about Emily, wondered if she even still lived. He had kept his vow to never contact her, for it had been her wish. But sometimes he felt guilty about it. Perhaps he should write her, tell her of his marriage to Marie and his life in Texas.

The pain moved through his heart again. No. Emily was a part of a past he had been struggling to forget. He would put it all behind him and think only of Texas and how he would protect all the land he had claimed. Life would be good now, in spite of the fact that it had been a dry spring and it looked as though it would be another hard year. But spring also brought more settlers to San Felipe de Austin. The tiny community was growing, while Santa Anna's power also grew, or so they heard. He would be the next man to govern Mexico. But no one worried about who headed the Mexican government. The American settlers had enough worries just staying alive and keeping food on the table.

Sarah sewed as the mantel clock ticked quietly. Sometimes she wondered if she would go crazy with the silence. Mary was long buried and she was alone now, with only the dress shop to keep her going. The sudden hope she had felt when she first learned Caleb might be alive had dwindled when time had passed and there were no replies to any of her ads. She had even paid a scout to go into Indian country to try to find Caleb, but to no avail. She had to face the fact that perhaps he was dead after all.

When someone knocked on the door she rose wearily and set the sewing aside. It was dark out and she picked up a pistol. Saint Louis was growing rapidly, and one never knew what to expect from the many strangers passing through. A lady friend had advised her to get someone to live with her, but Sarah liked living alone. For the first time in her life she was on her own, making her own decisions.

She moved to the door. "Who is it?"

"Emily Stoner," a woman's voice answered.

Sarah frowned, trying to remember where she had heard the name.

"We knew each other at Fort Dearborn when we were young," the voice added.

Sarah's eyes widened. Of course, the preacher's strange daughter. The last Sarah knew the girl had been taken prisoner by Potawatomi Indians and had never been heard from again. Sarah opened the door, and for a moment their eyes just held.

Emily looked Sarah over, her smile warm. "May I come inside?"

Sarah stepped back, realizing instantly what Emily was, though Emily had tried to dress more demurely. Her eyes and lips were too painted, and she had a hard, used look about her that gave away her profession. Her perfume smelled cheap, and her pale blue eyes were dull. Sarah closed the door.

"Emily! I . . . I heard the Indians took you—"

She stopped and gasped when Emily pulled back her hood, revealing the scar on the side of her face. "Yes, they took me." She held her chin proudly. "I will be quick about this, Sarah. I can see by the look in your eyes what you're thinking, and you're right. I sleep with men for money— in New Orleans. And if I took the time to explain all the reasons we would be all night. I hope no one saw me come into your house. I wouldn't want to ruin your reputation. I only came—" She swallowed. "I came because I saw your ad in a newspaper. I came to tell you I saw Caleb. I nursed him back to health in New Orleans. He's alive, but I have no idea where he is now. He went to get his son, and that was the last I saw of him."

She saw Sarah grow pale. She took hold of her, helping her to a chair.

"I guess I threw all that at you awfully fast, didn't I? But what's going on here? I thought *you* were supposed to be dead. That's what Caleb told me."

She helped Sarah to a loveseat. Sarah grasped her forearm so tightly that it hurt, forcing Emily to sit down beside her. "Tell me. Tell me all of it. He was alive? Caleb was alive? Truly?"

Emily took hold of her other hand. "He was when he left me. He had been shot, paralyzed. I wasn't sure he'd live at all. He was dumped in the river and some men found him. He muttered my name and they brought him to the place where I work. He'd been there before."

Sarah blinked, her eyes tearing.

"Oh, it wasn't what you think. Caleb saw me in the street when he was in New Orleans for that thing with the British. We talked, that's all. He was surprised to see I'd survived the Indian attack and was glad to see someone from Fort Dearborn, just like I was." She studied the trace of innocent trust that still dwelled deep inside Sarah Sax's eyes. She decided not to mention the reason Caleb had fled Fort Dearborn. Perhaps Sarah didn't know. What was the use of telling her? "At any rate, we talked and he left. And the next thing I know he shows up on my doorstep badly wounded, muttering about you being dead." She squeezed Sarah's hand. "He was in a bad way, Sarah. At first I thought the wound would kill him, then I thought maybe his sorrow over you would do it. The only thing that kept him going was the thought of returning to his son. He finally got well enough and he left. That was the last I ever saw of him. I wish I had better news—"

"Better?" Sarah hung her head, crying quietly. "My God, he's alive. At least I know that much. Caleb is alive!" She bent over and broke into deep sobs.

Emily felt sorry for her, realizing from talking to Caleb how much they had loved each other. If only Caleb knew

Sarah was still alive. But he could be anywhere. He could be all the way out in California for all they knew, or up in Canada. He was a wandering man who had had little purpose left in life but to keep his son and protect him.

"Stay," Sarah muttered. "Stay the night. Talk to me."

Emily looked around to see if all the shades were drawn. "I don't know. If anyone knew I was here . . . I walked the last two blocks from the carriage because I didn't want anyone to see where I was going. That's why I came after dark. When I saw the ad, I knew it was you. When I arrived I asked a couple of people if they had ever heard of you and one had. I don't think in the dark he could see how I really look—"

"Oh, Emily, don't. It doesn't matter. Nothing matters but Caleb." She straightened and suddenly hugged Emily, weeping with joy. "Oh, thank you. Thank you for coming all the way from New Orleans. Just knowing Caleb is alive helps. I might never find him, but the important thing is knowing he lived." She pulled away, wiping her eyes. "Take off your cape, Emily. I'll make some tea and we'll talk. We'll talk all night if necessary. I want to know everything, about your own terrible ordeal, about the first time Caleb visited you, and what happened when you found him wounded. Everything." She rose from the loveseat. "Stay right there and relax. Please say you'll stay, Emily."

The woman studied the terrible loneliness in Sarah's eyes. She was so beautiful, but already so defeated.

"All right. But only if you promise to tell me what the hell happened to you. You were pronounced dead right in front of Caleb—by a doctor."

Sarah clasped her hands together, trying to stop the shaking she felt coming on. "It's a long story, Emily. I'll get the tea first."

Emily saw her shaking and rose, putting an arm around her waist. "Sarah, is something the matter with you?"

"Just a little problem I have sometimes when I get excited. I lost Caleb's baby, and I've not been well since."

Emily felt a chill. "Caleb's baby? You were pregnant?" Sarah nodded. "Caleb never knew."

Emily closed her eyes. "My god," she whispered. "You poor thing. Come on. I'll go to the kitchen with you. We can talk there while you make the tea. I'll stay, but just the night. I must leave before anyone realizes I'm here."

Emily helped Sarah to the kitchen, chilled by the fact that all that had happened could in a way be blamed on her. But how could an almost insane young girl driven by her father's abuse have known? How different she was from Sarah, yet they had both loved the same man. Emily had never admitted it aloud and never would. What was the use? But she could not help wondering what her life might have been like if her father had allowed her a normal childhood, if he had not beat her and made her a prisoner in her own home. Life at Fort Dearborn seemed a hundred years away, and their lives had taken so many different directions, three young people growing up together, yet growing so far apart, their dreams never realized.

Chapter
Twenty-Seven

CALEB, sixteen-year-old Tom and seventeen-year-old Lee lay hidden amid the rocks overlooking Blue Valley, where Caleb's horses grazed. After years of struggling against starvation, Indian attacks, drought, hurricanes and sicknesses without doctors, Caleb Sax's horse ranch in San Felipe de Austin was developing into a profitable enterprise. Ships came to the gulf from a number of eastern ports and Mexico, sending buyers up the Brazos River to the American settlement to trade for or buy the goods settlers had to offer. Caleb's ware was his fine horses, which were such good quality that their reputation was spreading. He could ask top dollar for the carefully bred steeds, and all the hardships they had encountered over the years in Texas were beginning to pay off. His cattle were also a benefit, but his horses were his most valuable asset.

But new problems had developed recently. Although Indians continued to be the major problem to all the settlers, they also had to contend with squatters, theives, and outlaws. The Mexican government was centered much too far away to protect the settlers, and in this area of Texas there were not even a great number of Mexicans, since more and more Americans were coming in.

Caleb's immediate problem was a band of rustlers he and Tom and Lee were now watching. Below they could see the dead bodies of two men Caleb had hired to help watch the animals.

"I count seven of the bastards," Caleb said quietly. "Do either of you see any others?"

Tom and Lee, both strong, sturdy boys, watched quietly.

"No," Tom replied.

"We'll go down to the north outlet. That's the way they'll go, across the Brazos and on into the States. They are too far away for us to get them from here. Shoot to kill when you get close enough."

"If they're caught they get hung anyway," Tom said as they crawled down the hill to their horses, standing up as soon as they were out of sight. "Might as well save the government the trouble." He mounted his horse excitedly. As tall as his father now, he was broad shouldered and slim, looking every bit like Caleb except for his mother's dark eyes.

Lee was shorter, with broad shoulders and a more solid build. Both were handsome and energetic. The two young men made quite a pair, sometimes troublesome in their antics, but they always pulled through in the end.

"I'll race you, 'Uncle' Lee," Tom teased. He thought the term amusing, since Lee was only a year older than he. But Lee was, after all, Tom's stepmother's brother.

The whole family often laughed about the grand mixture they were with their different mixtures of Indian and white blood, joking about which Indian blood was the bravest or strongest or smartest. Tom kidded that John and David had the best advantage: the intelligence of the white man, the bravery of the Cheyenne and the strength of the Cherokee. Then he would add that all Lee had was the strength, but not enough intelligence to know how to use it, and not enough bravery to use it to its fullest advantage. Then would come the wrestling to prove who was truly the stronger, with neither knowing for sure because they never wanted to hurt each other. All of it was in fun, and watching his sons and wife and brother-in-law gave Caleb a feeling of warmth, of finally belonging.

They mounted and rode hard, hoping to get to the valley's narrow outlet before the rustlers. They were three big men on three big horses, sod and rocks flying as they rode. They were fine horsemen who knew their animals and knew the land, and they fit the wild territory as well as the bobcats. They spread out when they neared their destination, each knowing what to do. Each dismounted and lay down to wait.

Tom thought about his father and tales Caleb had told of the days he warred against the Crow in revenge for Walking Grass' death. The boy often wished he could have known her, and it seemed ironic that Caleb had never known his own mother either. He wondered sometimes about the blue quill necklace. Caleb spoke of it occasionally, over night campfires when they were alone and Caleb would talk about the woman called Sarah. He blamed himself for her death, and Tom knew his father had loved the woman very much by the way he spoke of her.

At sixteen it was difficult for Tom to fully understand how a man could love more than one woman, but his father had. Tom sometimes wondered, had Walking Grass not been killed, if all three of them would still be living with the Cheyenne. There were times when he longed to live with the Cheyenne again, to know that side of himself. But those feelings were overshadowed by his love for his father, a man he worshipped. His father had chosen this place called Texas, and Tom had grown to love the land. They had suffered many deprivations to stay here and make it work. Nothing and no one would take it from them now, and no rustlers were going to steal Caleb Sax's valuable horses.

He heard the whistles and shots of the rustlers and readied himself, praying quickly to *Maheo* that his father would not be hurt. As part of their permission to settle in Mexico, Caleb and the family had taken a vow to abide by Mexican law and convert to Catholicism. But in his own heart and Caleb's, the Catholic God was no different from the Cheyenne God *Maheo*, and Caleb still secretly worshipped his own way, still smoked the prayer pipe, still drew on his own Indian spirit for strength and guidance, as Tom was learning to do. Lee and Marie had taken up the Catholic faith, but there were no arguments over religion. To Caleb, each must have his own belief, and their gods were the same God.

Tom rested his musket on a rock, shouldering the butt. He was to take the man in the lead, Caleb the second man who appeared, Lee the third, so that no shots would be wasted. Having no time to reload their muskets, they would ride down on the rest.

The first man appeared and Tom took careful aim. His musket exploded and a moment later the man flew back off his horse, immediately trampled by the Sax horses he was in the process of stealing. Almost simultaneously second and third shots were fired, and two more rustlers fell from their saddles. The ambush was working. Tom quickly mounted his horse, as did Caleb and Lee, and all three let out war whoops, yipping as they rode down on the other four men, who took off in startled flight.

Tom aimed his pistol at one but missed. Lee got a man, leaving three. Caleb fired, grazing one across the shoulder, then rode his horse into the side of the rustler's horse, swinging his tomahawk and knocking the man off his mount. The man fell under the thundering hooves of the stampeding horses, and Caleb kicked his own horse into a faster gallop to move out of the herd. He circled around the herd and saw through the billowing dust that Tom was wrestling on the ground with one of the rustlers. Lee came riding back through the dust, and both had nearly reached Tom when Tom thrust a knife into the rustler's chest.

The boy stumbled back, his arm bleeding badly. Caleb quelled his panic, the panic that always crept up on him when he feared something might happen to Tom. It was the one thing he knew he could not bear, and allowing the boy freedom to be his own man had been difficult for Caleb. He rode up to the boy, dismounting before the horse even came to a halt.

"He pulled a knife on me." Tom grimaced and held his arm.

Caleb quickly untied a scarf he wore around his neck and tied it tightly above the cut.

"Bastards," he muttered. "You get back to Marie right away and have her clean it and wrap it tightly. It doesn't take much for a man to bleed to death. Take the regular trail. Lee and I will herd the horses back the same way, and if anything happens to you, we'll see you." He met the boy's eyes. "Can you make it?"

Tom grinned. "Father, it's only a cut. I did not lose my arm."

"You just do what I said. Out here a cut can turn into much more if it isn't treated."

The boy shook his head and mounted his horse, easing up in one leap, preferring to ride without a saddle like his father. "You worry too much, Father. But I will do what you say."

"I have plenty of reason to worry. Now get going. Lee and I will not be far behind you."

Tom turned his horse. "Yes, Father." He turned to Lee. "Hey, how come you let one get away, 'Uncle'? Not enough bravery or brains?"

"Get going, 'Nephew', before I add to your wounds."

Tom laughed and rode off. Caleb watched after him before mounting his own horse and riding over to Lee. "Let's get the horses." He looked down at the man Tom had stabbed, then around at the other fallen theives. "We have to do something. It's like Austin says. The Mexicans don't care much about protecting the Americans here. They're too far away to be of any use and we need more protection. Things like this are only going to get worse."

Lee sighed, looking at the dead thieves. "What we need is more strength, more power," he replied. "Maybe this part of Mexico should belong to the Americans. The Mexicans don't seem to care about it anyway. We have settled it for them. They profit by it but do not help us."

Their eyes held. "What you say may be true, but do you know what it means?"

Lee nodded. "I know. It is the same thing many others are saying. We are tiring of Mexican rule."

"Watch what you say and to whom you say it," Caleb warned. "It could be dangerous talk. If it is spoken too often, the Mexicans might decide they do not want us here any longer."

"And would you leave if they told you to go?"

There was a long silence. Caleb looked around at the beauty of his land. His Cheyenne side argued that no man should own land at all. But his white side told him that was the only way a man was going to survive in these changing times. He had his family to think about.

"No," he answered.

"And if the Mexicans tried to force you out?"

Caleb straightened, jerking his horse around. "I will worry about that when and if it happens." He rode off, his long hair flying behind him, the fringes of his buckskins dancing. Lee grinned and shook his head. He knew Caleb Sax would fight to keep this land.

Chapter Twenty-Eight

LYNDA tried to keep her eyes open as she sewed on yet another button. The Philadelphia clothing factory in which she worked sixteen hours a day was hot and airless, and her neck ached from sitting so long in the same position. She hardly saw sunshine six days out of the week since she was up and at work by six A.M. and stayed there until ten at night. But she had no choice. It was required by the orphanage that every girl over twelve begin earning her own keep or leave. Lynda knew next to nothing about the outside world, but she had considered leaving at times, especially when she grew so weary she was sure she would die right in her chair, button in hand. But she was also afraid of it. How would a thirteen-year-old girl survive? The orphanage had been her whole world.

She sighed when she saw McKenzie Webster approaching. Webster was the foreman she dreaded seeing, for he always stopped by her work station to watch, bending too closely, his liquored breath making her wince. Lately he was in the habit of casually putting his hands on her, moving them close to her breasts, sometimes over them, sending shivers of horror through her blood. But to resist could mean losing her job, which meant losing her security.

The man stopped beside her, studying the way she rapidly sewed on the button. "You work very fast, Lynda," he said with a grin.

She did not reply. She could feel his steely gray eyes on her, and she felt ill.

Webster studied her exquisitely beautiful face, which was too mature for a girl her age. She was tall, with a firm body, her hair a long cascade of dark waves, her eyes large and startlingly blue, enticingly provocative. Her skin was dark and satiny, and the thought of how she must look naked brought out Webster's animal instincts, especially when he considered her vulnerable position. She was at his mercy, and he knew it. He put his hand on her shoulder.

Lynda tensed, wanting to scream as his hand moved down to gently squeeze a breast.

"You are the prettiest girl here. Do you know that, Lynda?"

She refused to look at his pinched, red face and the balding head, his thick waist and wrinkled hands. "I've decided to take you out of this hot, uncomfortable place, away from the long hard hours. I'm taking you to a beautiful home, where it's cool and there will be little for you to do but care for my invalid wife."

She jerked away, shuddering. "What do you mean?"

Webster smiled. "It's all arranged, child. Out of the kindness of my heart, I am adopting you. I need someone to care for my wife, and the orphanage is more than happy to find a home for you. Quite grateful, in fact. You're getting too old to be taking up space there and eating their food. Tomorrow morning, instead of coming to the factory, you will be going to live with me. You'll ride in a fine carriage and have a room all your own. Won't that be nice?"

Tears stung at her eyes. "No," she answered in a shaking voice. "I'll keep working here. I don't mind."

"You really have no choice, no say in the decision." He wound his fingers into her thick hair. "And you could show

more gratitude. You'll even be paid to care for my wife."
He rubbed her neck. "There are several ways you could
show your gratitude, Lynda—and ways you could make
even more money. All you have to do is not lock your
bedroom door at night." He moved down to fondle a breast
again. "My wife has been sick for a long time. I'm a lonely
man."

She stood abruptly, knocking over her chair. Others turned
to stare and Webster's eyes narrowed angrily. Lynda glared
back at him, her blue eyes cold. "Don't you touch me
again." Her cheeks were crimson, and she could feel the
others looking at her, all of them understanding but none
of them courageous enough to talk back to McKenzie Webster.

"We will discuss it tomorrow when I pick you up at the
orphanage. Be ready." He smiled cunningly. "The orphanage says you are probably part Indian. You certainly look
as proud and wild as one right now. But I'll quickly tame
that stubborn side of you." His eyes moved over her appreciatively.

"You'll wait a long time," she sneered.

Webster only smiled again. "You think about what it's
like out in the streets, girl. You'll be waiting for me." He
turned and left, and moments later it was quitting time.
Lynda choked back hot tears, saying nothing to anyone as
she put down her sewing and ran from the factory. Her tears
nearly blinded her as she hurried back to the orphanage, not
even waiting for the two other older girls who worked with
her.

How could she tell the people who ran the orphanage that
she did not want to work for Mr. Webster? They thought
he was kind to provide jobs for the girls. They would never
believe her side of the story, they would simply think her
ungrateful. It would be the word of a bastard child with
Indian blood against a prominent businessman who was
known for his "charitable" deeds. She had nothing, no money,
no family. All she had was the blue quill necklace that had

been left with her, her only clue, her only link to her parentage.

All her young life she had wondered about the necklace, wondered why it had been left with her. And whenever she touched it, she felt a presence, a warm, sweet feeling of love. It was obviously an Indian necklace, and because of her own dark skin and hair she was certain she had Indian blood. But was it through her father or her mother? The necklace was her secret treasure, and she often fantasized about her real parents, picturing them as beautiful and loving people, for that was what she would have wanted them to be.

She would probably never know. She was an orphan, scorned by outsiders, treated like a slave and loved by no one.

She hurried into the orphanage and ran up the stairs to her cot, taking the quill necklace from under the mattress. She lay down and started crying into her pillow. What should she do? Where would she go? She had to decide by morning, or they would make her go home with Mr. Webster. Going off alone and risking the consequences had to be better than that.

She clutched the necklace to her breast, wishing her parents were there to protect her and give her a home like normal children. Had they loved her and wanted her but been forced to give her up? Or had she simply been an unwanted child to begin with? Perhaps she was the result of some Indian warrior raping a pretty white woman. She wondered what it was like for children whose parents loved and wanted them.

She thought about Mr. Webster again and her stomach churned. No. She would not go with him. She would take her chances out there and make her own way. If there was one thing she had inherited from her Indian side it was pride and courage, a stubborn pride that told her she was worth just as much as the next person and courage to fight those who would destroy her.

She sat up, wiping her eyes and pressing her lips together in determination. She pulled open her drawer in the large dresser she shared with others. She threw her few belongings onto the bed, then pulled up the top blanket and tied it around them, making a bundle that she could carry. She would leave this place. She would do it tonight after everyone was asleep, and she would never come back.

Maybe, just maybe, she would even find her parents.

Lynda stayed in the trees as much as possible, making sure those who passed on the nearby road did not see her. Perhaps the orphanage or Mr. Webster would send people looking for her. Her stomach growled with hunger, and she stopped to eat some wild berries, wishing she knew more about her Indian heritage and how those people survived. She hoped she could reach another city, or a smaller town where no one would know her and get a job so she could rent her own room.

At least it was warm, so she wouldn't be cold. And there was plenty of foliage on the trees and underbrush to hide in. She ducked again as a fancy carriage came into view. She watched, waiting for it to go past, but it made a funny scraping sound and stopped.

A dark handsome man stepped out of it, muttering something under his breath and looking upset. She stared, for she had never seen quite such an elegant man before. His hair was neatly combed and topped with a black velvet hat. He wore a dark blue velvet waistcoat, with gilt buttons and tight, dark blue breeches and shiny black boots. His white shirt was ruffled, with a dark blue bow tied at the throat. If there was one thing she knew from her work, it was clothes, and his were very expensive.

From where she watched the man appeared to be as handsome as his apparel. He knelt beside a front wheel of the carriage and seemed to be trying to fix something, then yelled out. He kept yelling, pushing on the wheel rim at the same time. Lynda hesitated. He appeared to need help, but she was frightened of strangers. Her cautious side told her not to go to him, but her softer side compelled her to approach warily. As she got closer it was obvious he was in intense pain. She set down her bundle and approached him, staying at a distance.

"What's wrong, mister?"

He looked over at her, in too much pain at the moment to appreciate her youthful beauty. "Help me," he groaned. "The wheel. My fingers are caught in the hub." He winced with pain, closing his eyes and pushing again. "Please . . . Push on it so the center ring moves away from the hub."

She hurried over, unable to watch him suffer. She took hold of the rim and shoved with all her might, her girlish strength just enough to move the wheel a bit so he could get his fingers out. He groaned and grasped his wrist, sitting down beside the wheel. She knelt close to him.

"Is there anything I can do?"

He leaned his head back, breathing deeply. "I don't think so. I just have to wait for the pain to go away . . . and hope I didn't break something."

Lynda waited until he finally opened his eyes and looked at her. He frowned, looking her over with a touch of humor in his eyes.

"Thank you, young lady," he said in a smoother voice. "Where on earth did you come from way out here?"

She reddened slightly, thinking how raggedy she must look to such a fine gentleman. "I—I am on my way north, to find work."

He squinted, studying her more closely. "Work? A pretty little thing like you has to work? Don't you have a home?"

She swallowed, afraid to tell him about the orphanage. "My—my mother is very sick. I have to find a job to help pay for a doctor and all. My sister is staying with her while I try to find a way to earn some money."

He smiled inwardly, not believing a word she said. He began to notice her unusual beauty. She was very young. But perhaps she was alone and needed help. He was never one to pass up a chance to help a pretty girl, although this one might be a bit too young for the payment he usually got. Then again, maybe not. And if she was grateful enough ... After all, she could certainly use some pretty new clothes.

"You must let me repay you for helping me," he said, giving her a handsome grin that made her heart flutter. "How about a ride to wherever you're going? As soon as my hand feels better I can fix the wheel."

She studied him closely. His eyes were kind—a little mischievous, but kind. And he was the most beautiful man she had ever met. "I ... I don't know your name."

He got to his feet then and bowed. "A thousand pardons. The name is Luke. Luke Corey. Lucky Luke, some call me. I have a way with cards, if you get my meaning."

She frowned. "No sir."

He straightened. "Oh. Well, I'll explain on the way. I'm headed west myself." He studied her, sure she had lied to him so far. "I don't suppose you'd consider going west instead of north?"

His eyes hypnotized her they were so dark, so full of joy and humor. "I ... I suppose I could try that direction. You'll let me off whenever I say?"

"Of course. And your name?"

She reddened. She'd best make up a last name. Maybe he'd heard she'd run away—heard the last name the orphanage had given her ... Brown. "Lynda," she answered. "Lynda Webster." It was the first name that came to mind, for she'd had McKenzie Webster on her mind all morning.

"Well, Lynda Webster, that is a very pretty necklace you're wearing, though somewhat large for your pretty young neck. Is it an Indian necklace?"

"I ..." She put her fingers to the blue quills. "Yes. An old Indian gave it to me."

He suppressed an urge to laugh. There were few Indians left in these parts, and she looked Indian herself. Surely it was some relative of hers and she was afraid to tell him.

"Well, it looks very interesting. Why don't you pick up

your bundle and climb into the carriage? I think I can fix it and we can be on our way."

She studied him another moment, then hurried back to get her clothes. There was something about him that made her trust him. At least it was a quicker way of leaving Philadelphia behind her. No one would look for her in such a fancy carriage. He worked on the wheel a moment, then they both climbed up into the fine leather seat. He released the brake and the shiny black horse that pulled the carriage moved on.

"Do you like my carriage?" Luke asked.

"Yes. It's beautiful."

"Just one of Lucky Luke's many winnings," he told her. "I picked this up last night. Three aces did it for me."

"Three aces?"

He laughed as though delighted with her ignorance. "I see you have a lot to learn. You must let me teach you, Miss Lynda Webster." He smiled to himself. He could teach her many things. This beauty could help him if she would stay with him. His guess was she had no place else to go. All he had to do was make her feel comfortable and safe. Perhaps a new dress would help. He would take her to the closest city and buy her a new dress, and everything she needed to go with it. He would leave her someplace where she could bathe, buy her some food . . . yes, by Jove, she was a looker, and by his guess completely alone.

"You ever drive a carriage before, Miss Webster?" he asked.

"No."

"Well now, that's the first thing I will teach you. Here." He handed her the reins, gently putting them into her small hands. He reached around her and wrapped his strong hands over hers, pulling her close and showing her how to drive.

Lynda did not mind his closeness. He was nothing like McKenzie Webster, nothing like him at all.

Chapter
Twenty-Nine

THE outlaws used the dark of night as cover. There were ten of them, well-armed men who stalked untamed and lawless lands, looting, taking women of their choosing and living off the brave settlers who struggled so hard to survive on the frontier. An outlaw life was an easy one in Texas. There were no marshals to come after them, no protection for the settlers. Everything was there for the taking, although most of the settlers had very little of value. As much as the settlers complained about the outlaws' raids, the Mexican government never kept its promise to help protect them.

"Why are we bothering with this place, Reem?" one of the men asked. "They're all Indians. I don't want no Indian squaw."

Reem patted his horse's neck. "There are some fine horses down there. We're after them this time, not women. We can get gold from the Apaches for those horses, probably more gold than those mounts are even worth if we bargain right."

"Yeah," another man said. "Injuns don't know much about the value of money, do they?"

Reem adjusted his hat. He was their leader, though leadership among such men tended to change hands often since each thought himself just as good as the next man and jealousy was rampant. But for now none of the other nine men cared to challenge Reem. So far two had tried and lost their lives for it.

"Be careful, boys," Reem said. "There are only a few of them, but you know how fiercely some of these settlers will fight for their women and belongings. Stu?"

"Yeah, boss?"

"Make sure that dynamite takes care of the bunkhouse. If we eliminate the hired hands we don't have much else to worry about."

"I'll do it right."

"Get the main house, too. There might be men in there."

"Okay, Reem."

Reem watched the ranch below, which lay basked in bright moonlight. The only lantern light came from one window in the main house. He gave the signal and they quietly moved in.

Caleb lay with an arm around Marie, exhaustion from a long day of branding making him sleep harder than usual. It seemed like he was dreaming when he heard someone shout. Then there was a gunshot. Caleb jerked away and was almost instantly out of bed, wearing only his loincloth.

"Caleb?" Marie rubbed her eyes and tried to see him by the dim light from the outer room. He was reaching for his musket in the corner. He grabbed his knife and shoved it into the waist of the loincloth, then grabbed his tomahawk.

"Trouble," he said. "Stay here with the boys and keep low."

He disappeared outside and Marie got up, pulling a robe on over her heavy frame. She was pregnant again and had gained considerable weight with the pregnancy now that food was more plentiful. She hurried to John and David's room. Both boys were awake now. They were big boys for eight and six, John more lanky like his father, David more stocky like his mother, both with dark Cherokee eyes.

"Who's shooting?" John asked sleepily.

"We're not sure. Pull on your pants in case we have to run."

Her own heart beat with fear. Every time something like this happened she worried she would lose Caleb. How would she live without the man she worshipped? Life had been so good, and no woman could ask for more pleasure in the night than to lie with Caleb Sax. She had grown heavier, and in her mind plainer, but Caleb never seemed to notice. He needed her in ways that went beyond physical attraction, and in his arms at night she was always beautiful. Being with Caleb had been eleven years of ecstasy, in spite of the hardships. But she had loved him longer than that, loved him since that day he helped free Lee from under the wagon wheel.

She took the boys out to the main room where her mother got up from her cot by the hearth.

"What is it, Marie?" Ellen asked.

"I'm not sure. Caleb went to get Lee and Tom."

Just then they heard a great explosion outside. They ran to a window to see the small bunkhouse where the few Cherokee men who lived with them as hired hands slept. Pieces of splintered wood were still falling down on the pile of rubble that was left. The men inside couldn't have survived. Marie groaned Caleb's name as she bolted the door and lay down on the floor, ordering the children and her mother to do the same. She began praying desperately for Caleb, Lee and Tom. It couldn't be Indians. They didn't have the means to blow things up. She could hear thundering horses and several shots were fired.

Outside two outlaws already lay dead. Lee and Tom had awakened before Caleb and had headed for the corral where the best horses were kept, sure Apache or Comanche had come to steal them. But in the moonlight they could see these were white men.

The outlaws were everywhere, one opening a gate, more circling inside the corral. Suddenly a big Indian pounced on the one at the gate, letting out a war whoop that put fear in the hearts of some of the others. A tomahawk landed in the outlaw's back as they went down.

It was Caleb. He got off his victim as Lee and Tom ran after more men.

Caleb glanced at the burning bunkhouse. There would be no help from those men, and there was no time to mourn the loss of friends. There was not even time to help Lee and Tom, who were fighting desperately. Four men rode toward the main cabin. For a brief second Caleb stood torn. His precious son could die fighting at the corral, but men were headed for the house, headed for Marie and David and John.

He started running. His spent musket was useless except as a club. He crouched as another man headed his way, then rose at the last minute, swinging the weapon hard. It landed with a loud crack against the rider, and Caleb wondered if it was the gun that had shattered or the man's ribs. The man flew back off his horse, landing with a thud on the ground, and Caleb quickly took out his knife and rammed it into the man's chest. He yanked the weapon out and ran toward the cabin. Marie would bolt the door and pull the wooden shutters over the windows. The men wouldn't get in easily, and if he had anything to do with it, not at all. He had to save Marie.

Caleb's heart froze when he saw one of the outlaws on the roof, standing near the chimney. He took out his knife again and threw it hard. It hit its mark, landing in the man's back. The outlaw screamed out and fell, rolling from the rooftop, but just before hitting the ground there was another explosion. Caleb watched in horror as the cabin disintegrated into a ball of flames.

The rest of that horrible night was just a vague, confused memory to Caleb. He did not even remember running toward the burning rubble, trying desperately to find Marie and his sons, reaching into flames with his bare hands. His mind completely shut out the sight of Marie's charred body, as well as that of her mother and David. Somehow John had survived. He had been thrown from the cabin by the force of the explosion and landed far enough away that he wasn't burned, though he had a dislocated shoulder.

Caleb had no memory of the men riding off into the night, leaving behind seven of their own. Four had died at the hands of Lee and Tom, who suffered only cuts and bruises; three had died at the hands of Caleb Sax. But Caleb's fierce fighting had not been enough.

He sat staring at Marie's grave, which he had dug into the side of a lovely green hill not far from the charred remains of their cabin. She lay beside her son and her mother. Caleb had buried with them what he could find of their most precious belongings, but there was little left. He wrapped their feet in buckskin from one of his own shirts, for they needed shoes for the long walk along *Ekutsihimmiyo*, the Hanging Road to heaven. He was sure Marie's Catholic God would not mind.

Caleb felt desolation wash over him. He had not loved Marie the way he had loved Walking Grass or Sarah. But he had loved her just the same, and he had been with her longest. In their years together she had become his strength, his friend, his comfort, his steadfast wife. He could depend on Marie. He needed her now. How was he to bear the loss of his precious David without Marie? And his unborn child? How was he to withstand the loss of all of them? The agony seemed to move through him in endless waves. Why was he destined to lose those he loved?

He sat by the graves for three days, speaking to no one, eating nothing, obeying the Cheyenne custom of letting blood for loved ones by cutting a gash in each arm. He was barely aware that his hands were burned or his shoulder and elbow were bruised from falling with the first man he had attacked. He didn't care that the horses had been saved. It was Marie, their unborn child and his son who should have been saved.

It was his third night by the graves that it happened. He

felt a strange presence surround him. It had been a long time since his Indian spirit had stretched beyond the limits of the real world and moved into the spiritual world. He was sure he could hear shaking rattles and beating drums, soft chanting and tiny bells jingling rhythmically, carried on the wind. He closed his eyes and heard Black Antelope telling him he must be strong and brave no matter what he faced. Then he could see Tom Sax, hear his voice telling him almost the same thing. Next Bo Sanders was explaining that his life would take many directions. The chanting and drumming grew louder and he saw the blue hawk again. It divided and flew in two directions, one red and one white, then joined and was blue again, as a woman's voice told him to be strong. Be strong. Be strong. Always he had to be strong. Then he was in Walking Grass' arms, and she was his strength. But then she was gone. Next came Sarah . . . sweet, beautiful Sarah, his most cherished love. She faded, but did not leave him as Three Feathers appeared. "You have a son," he said. "He needs you." His face faded away. Then Marie was holding him, comforting him, before she too left. They all disappeared, but then Sarah's face came into view again, as vivid as life.

"Sarah," he whispered.

"I am here," she answered. "I have always been here, if you would but look for me."

"Sarah," he cried out. "I need you!"

Someone was shaking him. "Father."

Caleb opened his eyes and sat straight up. "Sarah!"

"Father, it's me. Tom."

Caleb sat grasping the boy's arm as reality returned. It was dark. Sarah was not there and never would be. Now Marie was gone, too, and his son. He put his head against Tom's arm. "It is too much this time, Tom."

Tom rested his head against his father's, rubbing a hand across the man's shoulders. "You will survive, Father. You are strong. My mother would not want you to lose your spirit like this. Nor would the woman Sarah or my step-

mother. You are Blue Hawk. You went through the Sun
Dance. You survived the Crow wars and the British war.
You lived through a wound that left you paralyzed, and you
have fought many times for this land Marie helped settle.
Now you must continue to fight for it, Father, for her—for
those of us who still live." The boy's voice broke. "Come
back to us, Father," he whispered. "We need you, John and
I. You still have us. And Lee ... he has lost much also."

They hugged tightly. How long they sat there, neither
could be sure. Caleb finally rose to his feet, the voices of
those who had spoken to him still sounding in his ears. He
stared at the graves, feeling the presence of spirits in the
bright moonlight, feeling surrounded by all those he had
loved.

Tom put a hand on his arm. "I love you, Father. I need
you, and so does John. He is lost without his mother and
David."

Caleb sighed, rubbing his eyes. "My God," he whispered.
"Poor John."

"Please come back with me, Father. Leave this place for
awhile. We should all be together."

Caleb's eyes rested on the graves, the stone markers glow-
ing in the mixture of lingering moonlight and dawn. "Yes.
Marie would not want me to leave John alone like that. She
would scold me for it." His eyes teared again at the memory
of how she would sometimes gently chide him without really
nagging. Marie was so good. If only he could have told her
good-bye, that he loved her. If only he could have held her
once more.

He looked at Tom. "Our blood is in this ground now,
Tom. Marie, her father and mother, my son David and my
unborn child. All died on this land—for this land."

Tom sensed the same determination that must have been
there when his father rode against the Crow, and when Caleb
forced himself to walk again, or even when he was just a
small boy and killed two Chippewa warriors.

"You are looking at the worst kind of enemy a man can

have," Caleb continued, "a man with the instincts of an Indian, and the love of his own land and determination to defend it that comes from the white man in me."

"The love of land is Indian, too, Father. They will fight for all of it. You will fight for just a piece of it. You love it for what it is, a part of the great circle of life. It has spirit, just like the animals, and you draw strength from it."

Dawn broke then, and the sun struggled to rise, casting a pink glow on the gravestones.

"Life's struggles never end, Tom," Caleb said. "It has taken me thirty-five years to understand that. I am many men on the inside, fighting, struggling. I never had true purpose before. Now this land will be my purpose."

He turned and headed down the hill toward the blackened cabin, already deciding the next house would be made of stucco, like most buildings in this land. Stucco was cooler and didn't burn so readily.

Chapter Thirty

JANUARY of 1831 was cool on the Mississippi, but bearable and even warm on the section between New Orleans and Saint Louis. The steamboat trade was flourishing and many of them provided gambling and entertainment for the passengers. Lynda had never dreamed life could be so glamorous. She studied her hair in the mirror, the way the sides were drawn up in a beautiful coif and the rest of her long, wavy locks cascaded down the center of her back.

Fresh flowers decorated the curls, and she wore just the right touch of color on her eyes and cheeks. The skin of her bare shoulders glowed from expensive creams, and her blue eyes were enhanced by a rich blue silk dress that dipped across her generous bosom just enough to be enticing to any man. But she didn't care about other men. She cared only about Luke Corey, her first man, her only man, the love of her life.

Luke pampered her like a doll. He had since that first day they met and had become friends. He had bought her all new clothes, fed her well, gave her the best rooms in hotels, and never asked a thing in return. Lynda had fallen in love, quickly and totally. He had never mentioned marriage, and she understood. Luke was not the marrying type. But it didn't matter. He was true to her, good to her.

Within three months after they met she had been sharing his bed willingly. How could she have resisted his generosity, the loneliness in his eyes, the way he touched her and made her feel? He had been so gentle and kind. He had even stayed by her when she lost the baby. She was too young, he had said. He left her alone at night for a long time after that. Now they were sharing passion again, but were still not married. That was all right. Luke loved her. She knew he did, even though he didn't say it. He didn't have to say it. He had done so much for her. And he had promised that once he had enough money he would help her find her parents.

Lynda lived for that promise, loved him because of it, worshipped him for offering to help her. They had done nothing about it yet, but Luke was waiting until he had enough money and enough time. He earned that money by gambling, and sometimes the money came, then went again. That was the way it was for men like Luke, and she understood. Luke was Luke, and a woman either loved him the way he was or didn't love him at all. There were times when she felt tiny pangs of misgivings, little desires to be a wife, a mother, live in a real house and have all the things she had missed as a child growing up in an orphanage. But Luke was so good to her she didn't have the heart to nag him about it.

Luke walked into the cabin and stood behind her to place a diamond necklace around her throat.

"Luke, it's beautiful."

"Worthy enough for your sixteenth birthday?" he asked.

"More than enough! Oh, Luke, you shouldn't have. I—I don't even know for sure which day is my birthday. The orphanage told me I was found in January. That's all I know."

"That's enough. You were apparently born in January. Between that and the blue quill necklace, perhaps we'll find your parents one day."

"Luke, you will help me find them, won't you?"

He smiled, kissing her shoulder, then the fullness of her breasts revealed by the low-cut gown. "Of course I will, love."

She looked at him and their lips met in a gentle kiss. His dark eyes fell to her bosom. "This dress and your ravishing beauty should keep the other players off guard tonight," he said, kissing her before straightening. "You are a great help, Lynda dear. All you have to do is float around my table like usual, hang on me so that you're . . . uh, generously exposed, and the men I play cards with will be so distracted they won't know what hand they've got. You make a perfect partner, my little Indian beauty."

She smiled, taking one last look at herself before rising. She was not vain, but she was pleased with what she saw, grateful to her mysterious parents for at least blessing her with a rare, dark beauty. That and her Luke were all she had, except for the strength she derived from the blue quill necklace. She wore it rarely now, for Luke kept her in magnificent jewelry. But she would never let the necklace go. She treasured it beyond all the lovely things Luke could get her, and she kept it faithfully in her carpetbag, wrapped in a cloth to protect it, sometimes taking it out and just holding it, studying it, trying to picture its owner.

They walked out of their cabin on the elegant *Suzanna*, a fine steamboat with live entertainment and a good deal of gambling on board. Luke had taken a liking to the riverboats, where a man could meet many different people and gamble against many different men. He could stay on one boat and wait for passengers to come and go at each city. It was a grand, elegant life they led, constantly moving between New Orleans and Saint Louis.

They were headed toward Saint Louis on this trip, a city still primitive compared to some farther east, but it was raw and exciting and bulging with people. They would get off the boat there and Luke would take her dining and to the new theater, if it was finished yet.

They entered the gambling room and made their usual rounds until Luke decided which table he would occupy for the night. A few times he had been accused of cheating, but Lynda never believed it. Luke would never cheat. He was a gambler, but an honest one. She never dreamed that her efforts at distracting other men from the game only gave Luke an easier chance to sneak in an extra card here and there. She only thought it helped the other men lose their concentration. Luke played for big money, and any help she could give him was certainly worth it. After all, he had done so much for her.

Luke introduced her as his companion, an introduction that always brought stares and subtle smiles. Lynda didn't mind. It was part of the game. But there was one man at the table that made her uneasy. His dark eyes were too discerning, and he didn't seem to respond to her charms when she laughed and talked between hands, flirting at just the right times. She sometimes had to argue with her conscience when guilt would nudge her, urging her to consider if what she was doing might be wrong. But she always convinced herself it was not. After all, she was only helping Luke. How else was she to pay him back for all his kindness?

The men played for two hours, and Luke won much more often than the others. The man with the dark, piercing eyes kept looking from Lynda to Luke, and Lynda felt alarmed by the intensity of his gaze.

Suddenly the man threw down his cards and drew a pistol, accusing Luke of cheating.

Lynda's heart raced and her eyes widened with fear. "Luke," she whispered. There had been accusations before, but never a gun.

"You'd better go back to the cabin, Lynda," Luke told her.

"Sure," the man with the dark eyes sneered. "So she can pretend she ain't a part of this."

"A part of what?" Luke asked boldly. "I've done nothing wrong."

"Haven't you?" Luke's accuser growled. "Take off that fancy jacket and roll up your shirtsleeves."

Luke didn't make a move at first. Lynda stared at him. Why didn't he do it? Why didn't he prove he wasn't cheating?

"Roll 'em up," the man ordered louder, cocking his pistol.

People around them whispered and backed away. Luke removed his jacket and threw it on the table. He glanced at Lynda then with a sorrowful look on this face. Then he turned and bolted away. The pistol went off as he reached the door and Luke fell forward, a bloody hole in his back.

Lynda screamed and stumbled to his side, collapsing beside him to cradle his head in her lap. She bent over him, sobbing with grief and horror. Luke was her life, her support, her refuge from the world that frightened her so. Now he was gone. It had all happened so quickly, and on her birthday of all days.

Suddenly someone jerked her away. She screamed and fought, but a man held her arms while another man yanked up Luke's sleeves. Several cards fell from each sleeve, mostly aces. The room was silent for a moment as everyone stared at the cards. Lynda was as surprised as the rest, and her heart ached with the disappointment of realizing Luke really did cheat. Yet it did nothing to ease her grief or lessen the love she felt for him.

She was distracted from her misery when she realized that all eyes had suddenly turned to her. The man who had shot Luke stepped closer.

"You'd best get off this boat at the next stop, missy," he warned. "Run and keep goin', else you'll find yourself sittin' in the poke." His eyes fell to her generous bosom. "Lots of things ken happen to a purty little thing like you with the law after her."

"But I didn't know! I didn't!"

"Come now, you little hussy," the man holding her said. "Why else would you bat them pretty eyes and bare your bosom for the other men, huh?" He moved a hand up over her shoulder and she jerked away, suddenly feeling cheap. She had never meant it to be that way, had never thought of it that way until now. But she would do it again. She would do it again for Luke.

She took a last look at his dead body. She could not go to him now; these men meant business. What if they made her go to jail? What would happen to her there? McKenzie Webster had often told her things that happen to girls in the streets or in prison, trying to discourage her from ever leaving the orphanage or the factory. As she faced the leering, threatening men, she realized Webster's stories might be true.

She turned and ran when more men crowded around her. She hurried to their cabin, the lovely room she had shared with Luke. They had made love only hours before. Now he would never hold her again. He was gone, and with him had gone all her security.

She packed everything she could into a carpetbag, including the precious blue quill necklace and a money pouch Luke had hidden in the room. She knew he had more money on his body in a money belt, but she would never get to that now.

She ran back to the door and bolted it, then moved back to sit on the bed and wait for the boat to dock at Saint Louis. She wanted nothing more than to get off the steamboat, although she had no idea what she would do when she did. At the moment she was too frightened to even cry over Luke, but inside she screamed in sorrow, and shook in the terror of being alone again.

The rain poured down in torrents and Lynda shivered under her cape, which was soaked through. The girl struggled against tears of sorrow and terror. It had been a long time since she felt this loneliness, this abandonment. Not since McKenzie Webster's threats had she felt this way. Luke had saved her then, but he could no longer protect her. The men on the boat had been threatening, and she was worried that they might follow her.

Suddenly Saint Louis had become a frightful place, where people refused to answer knocks in he middle of the night and everyone was a stranger. She trudged through a muddy street, looking up at a sign and reading it quickly as lightning lit it. It was a boarding house.

She hurried to the door and pounded on it. When no one answered she pounded again. Finally she saw the movement of a lamp inside and a woman opened the door a crack. "Yes?"

"I—I need a room. I have money."

"Got no rooms."

"Please. I'll sleep in the kitchen, anywhere. I just have to get out of the rain."

The woman opened the door farther, holding up the lamp. "You look a might young to be roamin' the streets this time of night. You a whore?"

Lynda's eyes widened and at first she couldn't find her voice. Was that what this woman would call her for living with a gambler? She shook her head, stuttering. "N—no! I—my husband was killed . . . on a steamboat. They shot him. I was afraid. I had to get off."

"They? They who? Why was he shot?"

Lynda just blinked, unsure what to say.

"I don't like this business, young lady. The law after you?"

Lynda shook her head and the woman held the lantern even closer. "You're dark. You look Indian."

Lynda put a hand to her face, struggling not to cry. "I am. At least I think I am."

"You *think*? You don't know?"

"I—"

"Go on with you. I'll have no whoring Indians staying here."

The woman started to slam the door, but Lynda caught it. "Please! Can you at least tell me where I can try to find a room? Or where I might find work?"

The woman scowled. "What kind of work?"

"Sewing. I can do seamstress work. I worked at a clothing factory back East."

The woman looked her over as though summing her up. "Not sure. There's a woman lives two streets over. Sarah Sax is her name. You'll see it on a sign hangin' outside her house, Sarah's Stitchery. She makes clothes for people. Maybe she could use some help."

"Thank you," Lynda answered gratefully.

"Look young lady, if any harm comes to that nice lady I'll know who to send the law after, won't I?"

Lynda's eyes hardened. "No harm will come to her. I just hope she's kinder than you." She whirled and ran into the darkness.

Thunder rolled outside, making the house shake. Sarah turned up the oil lamps. She had never liked storms, especially at night. She remembered how Caleb used to tease her about screaming at thunder and lightning as a little girl, telling her it was only the spirits talking and showing their power.

Caleb. She had resigned herself to the fact that she would

most likely never find him. She had exhausted all her options. He had vanished just as surely as if he really was dead, and for all she knew he was by now. Anything could happen to a man living in the wilds, and that was surely where Caleb had gone. It would be like him. Her only consolation was that at least he had lived through the ordeal Terrence and the others had put him through.

That thought made her think of Byron. She had not seen him since he returned to Saint Louis, in spite of the fact that it was not such a big city. She had simply avoided him, and Byron, apparently not wanting to be linked to her and what he had done, had avoided her in return. That was fine with Sarah Sax, who refused to even use his last name. She had gone back to her maiden name when she came out of her coma, and she wanted no more link to Byron than he wanted to her, even though it was tempting to consider how she could ruin him if she wanted. But what would be the use now? It was all over. She would never tell him Caleb had lived. Perhaps it was best he didn't know. She was tired of bitterness and hatred.

Thunder boomed again, and she jumped, sure she had heard a knock at the door at the same time. The knock came again, and as always she quickly took her pistol from the stand beside her before going to the door.

"Yes?" she called out.

"Miss Sax?"

"Yes."

"My name is Lynda, Lynda Webster. I'm looking for work. I—I'm good a sewing. I worked in a clothing factory in Philadelphia. A woman who runs a boarding house told me to ask at your place. Do you need help, Miss Sax?"

The voice was very young, and then Sarah heard a cough. She unlatched the door, staring out at a drenched young girl. She couldn't see her well but realized she was alone.

"I don't really need help, but come in, Lynda," she told the girl. "You're soaking wet. What on earth are you doing out on a night like this?"

The girl ducked inside and Sarah closed the door, turning to look at her in the full light as Lynda pulled off the hood of her cape. Sarah's eyes widened at the girl's soaked condition and the circles under her blue eyes.

"I don't understand—"

"Please. I need shelter for awhile. I can work. Really I can. You make clothes, don't you? I can sew," Lynda repeated. "The woman told me you have a clothing shop here."

Sarah studied her a moment, confused and unsure what to do about this sudden intrusion. "Come over by the fire," she told the girl, leading her to the hearth where a brighter lamp was lit.

Lynda set down her carpetbag and followed Sarah. She removed her cape and sat down in a rocking chair, shivering as she pushed back her long, tangled hair and looked up at Sarah. What a beautiful, kind looking lady she was, Lynda thought.

"I'll get you some—" Sarah stopped to take a good look at the girl.

Lynda reddened. "I know I look a mess, but—"

"No. It isn't that," Sarah assured her. "You just . . . your eyes. They remind me of someone." It was startling. The girl was so dark she looked Indian, yet had such blue eyes . . . just like Caleb. There was an unnerving likeness. Sarah blinked, gathering her thoughts. "Please tell me what's happened to you."

The girl suddenly broke down, begging for help and shelter, begging for a job, blubbering something about being alone, that the man she depended on to take care of her had been killed and his murderers had forced her off the steamboat.

Sarah's heart went out to her. "Dear God," she whispered, smoothing the girl's hair. "How old are you, Lynda?"

"Sixteen," she sniffed. "I don't know my real birthday. I don't even know my parents. We—Luke and I were on the *Suzanna*. Luke got shot. I had to leave the boat, and

I've been asking around town for a place to stay. It's so dark, and I was afraid in the streets. The woman at the boarding house said to come and see you about a job."

Sarah sighed. "You're confusing me. I don't know who this Luke is and I think you need some rest before you go any further. I can't say I'll give you a job, but I will at least put you up for the night." Sixteen. Her child would have been sixteen this month, had she lived. How could she turn this poor girl away? "I'll get you the tea," she told her. "You rest tonight and we'll talk in the morning."

"Oh, thank you. Thank you," Lynda said, breaking into more tears. Sarah took a lap robe from the davenport and draped it around the girl's shoulders, then walked over and picked up Lynda's carpetbag, carrying it to the guest room and setting it on the floor, unaware that a blue quill necklace was packed inside.

Chapter
Thirty-One

"WE must be careful in our loyalties," Stephen Austin warned. "When we settled here we pledged allegiance to Mexico. We gave our word. If we can just win our rights, trial by jury and religious freedom, there is no reason to talk of independence. Such talk will bring more problems than we are ready to handle."

Caleb watched the man, who appeared hardly older than himself. He still trusted him, and most of the settlers still looked to him for leadership. But the number of Americans in Texas had increased dramatically, and there were many more settlements similar to their own, all left unprotected, all without the full freedom they enjoyed in America, all without solid laws and the proper delegation of justice. They were twenty thousand or so Anglos practically forgotten by Mexico's eight million occupants further south.

"Something has to be done," Tom said. "Our family has suffered much loss. There will be more raids, more injustices. The American government needs to know what is happening here."

"That's right," someone else went on. "Some kind of decision has to be made. We can't go on like this, with one foot in Mexico and the other in the United States, not knowing anymore where our loyalties lie. And we must have religious freedom."

"Perhaps something will be worked out between the United States and Mexico," Austin said. "A messenger has told me that General Sam Houston is coming to Texas to make some surveys of his own, even to buy land. He will get word to President Jackson of the situation here. He is very close to the president."

"Houston," Lee whispered, looking at Caleb. "He is a great friend of the Cherokee. He even lived with them for a while and I have heard he now has a Cherokee wife."

"Then his friendship with Jackson is very odd," Caleb replied. "I fought with Jackson at New Orleans. He was a great man, but he is no friend to the Indians. It is Jackson who is helping send all the southern tribes to Indian Territory, including your Cherokee."

"It is difficult these days to say who is friend and who is not. Jackson is no friend to the Indians, yet he might help us as Texans," Tom said.

"Be careful how you use that word, Tom," Caleb answered. "You make Texans sound like a separate people."

"Aren't we?"

Their eyes held and Caleb gave him a chiding look.

"I need some volunteers," Austin said. "Someone who

will go to the States on our behalf, urge even more people to come here and settle. There is strength in numbers. If we remain loyal to Mexico, but have a strong voice in insisting we get get better laws and protection, perhaps we will get some action and avert any further problems."

"Like a war with Mexico?" The question was voiced farther back in the crowd, and everyone quieted.

"I prefer that word not be used," Austin answered. "We didn't come here for that."

"You can't keep Americans down forever," another man put in. "You step on an American too hard and he'll bite off your toe."

Laughter filled the room, but it was nervous laughter.

"That's true," Austin answered. "But in this case if you bite off the toe, a big foot will kick you back and kick hard. There are perhaps twenty thousand of us, and eight million Mexicans. Let's be rational. Who would like to go to some of the bigger cities in the States and do some politicking for us, get more people to come and make people aware of the situation here?"

A few raised their hands. Lee and Tom both looked excitedly at Caleb. "Let us go, Father," Tom said. "I have never seen a city."

Stinging memories washed over Caleb, memories of a young man going into the civilized world, curious, naive. "I don't know. I need your help."

"We have hired hands. And you could get more—just for a while."

"Maybe they don't want Indians as representatives."

"Sam Houston himself is a great friend of the Cherokee," Lee put in. He raised his hand without waiting for a reply.

"Good," Austin said. "A couple of our Indians will help show them we are a people who accept everyone, as long as each man pulls his own weight and abides by Mexican law." He turned to the crowd. "Our purpose is simply strength in numbers and a bigger say in governing ourselves. Remember: No one speaks of independence. That's very important. When you speak of independence, you speak of war, and if it comes to that you stand to lose everything you've worked hard for over the years. All those loved ones who have died helping settle this land will have died in vain and this territory will go back to Mexico. This is simply a place where a man can come, pick out his land and settle, and get rich off trade with the States. We don't want to look like land hungry mongers taking advantage of the new Mexican government."

"We won't take advantage of them if they don't take advantage of us," someone shouted.

There was general shouting then, and some raised fists.

"Where will we go, Mr. Austin?" someone shouted above the din.

Austin waved his arms for silence. "If we can get enough volunteers, you'll take a ship to New Orleans, then head north, perhaps split up and hit most major cities along the Mississippi, maybe all the way up to Saint Louis. Make the newspapers, if you can."

An odd pain moved through Caleb at the mention of Saint Louis. He looked at Lee and Tom, who were both excited, young men eager to see new places, eager to do what they could for their homeland. He could not blame them for wanting to go. But New Orleans—St. Louis. He wondered if Emily Stoner was even still alive, and if she was, if she was still in New Orleans. And Saint Louis. Would it be dangerous for Tom, bearing the name Sax? Surely not after all these years. Who would bother to come all the way to Texas to find him? And let them try if they wanted to. Caleb was a wealthy, powerful landowner now, harder, more determined. Surely Terrence Sax knew Caleb could in turn tarnish the Sax name if he chose to do so, could reveal what he and Byron Clawson had done. Did they both still live? Perhaps they were not even around Saint Louis any longer.

Watching Tom, Caleb could see there was no hope of changing the young man's mind. He and Lee were already talking about what they would say and do. Lee had been just a child when his father brought him west, so he remembered little about the States and more civilized places. Both were young and curious. They would go, and there would be no stopping them. But they were also Texans. Texans first. They would come back. Of that Caleb had no doubt.

Sarah sat by the hearth, again grappling with the strange feeling she could not quite put her finger on, the strange aura that had settled over the house with Lynda Webster's arrival. The girl had been with her for a month now, a very good worker and wonderful company. Sarah knew that the girl was an orphan from Philadelphia who had run away and taken up with a gambler named Luke, who was killed in a fight over a card game. She was sixteen, the same age Sarah's own daughter would be if she still lived, and her pitiful state had led Sarah to let the girl stay and work for her.

Sarah liked Lynda, even felt drawn to her. She was sure Luke had taken advantage of Lynda's youth and vulnerability, but she understood that Lynda had loved the man and was suffering her own grief. Sarah couldn't help feeling sorry for her, remembering some of the shocking, terrible moments of her own youth. Perhaps by helping this girl she would be helping heal some of her own remaining wounds.

What disturbed her was the girl's eyes and coloring. She looked so amazingly like Caleb that it was unnerving for Sarah to look at her. How could she explain her feelings to the girl? She didn't want her to leave, but she surely would if she knew the effect she had on Sarah. She was an excellent seamstress and a great help. Sarah was able to take in even more customers and her business was growing.

She settled back to watch the fire. It was February, 1832, and Saint Louis was booming. There was a lot of talk about a place called Texas, where a lot of Americans had apparently been settling, talk of perhaps annexing Texas to the United States. She had thought so many times about Caleb, wondering where he could be now. The territory west of the Mississippi was vast and wild. She had exhausted all efforts of finding him. It was over. To keep searching was to keep reawakening the pain of losing him.

The fire crackled and the rocker squeaked, and again the lump came to her throat. Just that morning she had turned down an invitation to go to the theater with a reputable gentleman. Why was she unable to respond to another man? Why was she so afraid to care again? The mixture of her profound love for Caleb and the horror of her marriage to Byron was the answer. She could never love that way again, nor could she take the risk of marrying another man who would turn out to be as cruel and sick as Byron Clawson. It was easier this way, answering only to herself. She had had her glorious passion with Caleb. In spite of all that had happened to her since she would not change that memory for anything.

She heard footsteps on the stairs and waited. She sighed and closed her eyes, rocking quietly as Lynda came into the room. The girl moved into the firelight and sat opposite Sarah.

"I can start the dress for Mrs. Preston tonight if you want," she said.

Sarah smiled, opening her eyes. "No." She sighed deeply. "I think I'd rather sit here and talk." She studied the girl, again overwhelmed by her resemblance to Caleb.

Lynda felt nervous, wondering what Sarah would want to talk about. Was she going to throw her out?

"I'm so glad you came along, Lynda," Sarah said, surprising and relieving the girl with the remark. "I didn't want to admit it, but I was getting so lonely. You're a pleasant companion, and being the same age as the child I lost makes it . . . I don't know, somehow comforting, as though by helping you I'm being a mother to the child I never knew."

Lynda smiled bashfully. "I'm glad you feel that way, Sarah." It had been difficult to call the woman by her first name, but Sarah Sax insisted on it within a few days. "I like it here. You're a very nice lady, very kind. In fact, you're the kindest person I've met in my whole life." Her smile faded and she looked at her lap. "Except for Luke."

Sarah pulled a quilt over her lap to help ward off the cold. "But Luke didn't really have your best interest in mind, Lynda. Surely you know that now."

The girl nodded. "I know. But he was never mean to me."

Sarah thought of Byron Clawson. It was no doubt better to be with a kind man and not married than to be married to someone like Byron. "Well, I'm glad of that," she said aloud. "You took a great risk going away with him."

"Anything was better than that man at the factory," the girl answered. She met Sarah's eyes. "We've talked so much about me. What about you? You've never really explained about the baby girl you lost or why you live alone. You're so beautiful, Sarah. You should be seeing men. You should be married."

Sarah's eyes hardened slightly. "I was once." She looked at the fireplace. "But he wasn't the man I loved. I never had the chance to marry the man I really loved." To her own surprise the story began spilling out of her. She realized she needed to talk about it, about Caleb. She needed to tell someone the story and share her great love with another human being who would understand. Lynda would understand. She had been in love. And she was young, still full of all the passion of youth.

Lynda listened, enraptured, trying to picture Caleb Sax, for Sarah described him as a very handsome man, strong and brave and sincere. Sarah surprised even herself when she was so bold as to tell the girl about her affair in the cave, sensing Lynda would not look down on her for it. Why was it suddenly so easy to talk this way? She had kept all these things to herself for so long. It felt wonderful to finally talk about them. Perhaps if Lynda understood just how much she had loved Caleb, and how cruel Byron Clawson had been, she would understand why it had been so difficult to ever care for another man.

Sarah went on, explaining how Caleb had been wounded, and that she had learned it was possible he was still alive somewhere.

"But that does me no good now. At the time I was convinced he was killed," she told Lynda. "And I found I was with child, Caleb's child. The child needed a father, and Byron Clawson cleverly volunteered to make the baby legitimate and save my reputation. I was so ill and weak that between Byron and my—my father," the word came hard, "I had no chance."

She went on with the story, and as she told it Lynda felt little pinpricks of familiarity, as though she had something to do with the story. Perhaps it was because it was so much the way she had pictured what might have happened to her own parents.

"Caleb had given me a necklace," Sarah went on, after describing the terrible birth. "It was a blue quill necklace his Cheyenne mother had made for him."

Lynda felt as though someone were draining the blood from her veins.

"He called it a love gift and told me to keep it. I clung to that necklace," Sarah said. "It seemed to help the pain. But then the doctor gave me something that made me groggy. I felt Byron tearing the necklace from my hand, and that was all I remembered until I woke up and was told my baby had died. Byron boastfully told me the child was already buried, and that he'd make sure I forgot Caleb. He said he'd buried the necklace with the baby so I'd never see it and think of Caleb again."

She had been staring at the fire the whole time and did not notice the strange look in Lynda's eyes. She heard the girl gasp quietly and turned to look at her. Lynda's eyes were wide, and she looked at Sarah with a mixture of shock and joy and even fear.

"What is it?" Sarah asked. "Are you ill?"

Lynda shook her head, swallowing. "Describe the neck-lace," she said in a near whisper.

Sarah felt a strange tingle, as she studied Lynda's in-credibly blue eyes. "It was an Indian necklace, made of painted blue quills. It was rather large. It had been made for a man, then given to Caleb's mother who in turn gave it to Caleb to remember her by. It was held together by rawhide strips. It was quite lovely."

Lynda began to shake slightly, blinking back tears.

"Child, what is it? What have I said?"

Lynda shook her head, closing her eyes and looking at her lap. "It's probably just a foolish notion . . . a coinci-dence. It couldn't possibly be the same necklace."

Sarah felt a numbness moving through her bones. "Neck-lace? What necklace?"

Lynda met her eyes, searching Sarah's almost lovingly. "The lady at the orphanage told me that a very fancy carriage dropped me off, as though someone wealthy had brought me there. I was left in a crate, along with a necklace. It was an Indian necklace made of blue quills."

Their eyes held, and suddenly Sarah was overwhelmed with the possibility her baby had not died at all! How many times had she felt it, doubted it, wondered about it? Byron Clawson was such a liar about so many things. This girl looked so Indian—except for her eyes.

"Where was this orphanage?" she managed to ask.

"Philadelphia."

Sarah began to shake. "My God," she whispered, looking down at her trembling hands. Philadelphia was close to Washington. Of course. It would all have been so simple for Byron. Get rid of the child and tell the mother it had died. Sarah had been so drugged she would never know the difference. And there would be no blood on Byron Claw-son's hands.

"Sarah, are you all right?" Lynda asked, rising from her chair. She bent over and grasped the woman's hands, then gasped when Sarah suddenly looked up at her and gripped her hands so tightly that it hurt.

"The necklace. Show me the necklace!"

Lynda's lips puckered and she shook her head.

"Show me the necklace, Lynda," Sarah begged, rising but still clinging to Lynda's hands as though she might fall if she let go.

"I'm . . . afraid to," the girl answered. "If it isn't the same one . . ." She sniffed.

Sarah's own eyes teared. "Don't be afraid, Lynda. For years I have prayed to find my Caleb again." she paused. "Perhaps I never will. But if I could find my child, could know she's alive, it would be all the comfort I could ask for the rest of my life. We have to know, Lynda. Please. Show me the necklace."

Lynda managed to free one hand and she wiped tears from her cheeks. Clinging together, they walked haltingly toward Lynda's room, each of them filled with compelling anticipation and dread that this sudden discovery would lead to nothing.

Lynda let go of Sarah's hand and took her carpetbag from a closet. She reached inside and took out the necklace, bringing it over to Sarah and holding it up.

Sarah stared at the necklace as though it were a ghost, her eyes widening more. She trembled violently, raising her eyes to meet Lynda's again. She could no longer deny those eyes. How could they look so much like Caleb and not belong to him?

"Your story . . . it's true?" she asked. "You didn't just find the necklace someplace?"

Lynda shook her head. "No. It was in the crate they left me in. I was a newborn. The woman who took me said they had a hard time finding a nursing mother who would agree to feed me because I looked Indian. I almost died."

Sarah was smiling while tears spilled down her cheeks. "But you survived," she said. "You survived because you're Caleb Sax's daughter. You're strong like him."

Lynda studied the woman with a wonderful new love growing in her heart. "Like him? After what you went through, I'm not so sure who was the stronger, Sarah."

Their eyes held a moment longer and then they suddenly embraced, both of them too full of tears for the next several minutes to say anything. How could it not be true? It made too much sense. Yet Sarah knew there was one way to be very sure. Byron Clawson. She detested the thought of seeing him, but she had no choice. She must face him again to find out for sure.

Yet in her heart she already knew. Instinct proved much more than physical evidence. This was surely her daughter, her beloved daughter, the seed of Caleb Sax. God had not abandoned her after all.

Byron looked up from his desk, stiffening when he saw Sarah Sax standing in the doorway of his office. She was more beautiful than ever, with a woman's firm roundness, a woman's maturity and wisdom. Her red-gold hair was piled into great swirls topped with a deep green velvet hat that matched her velvet dress, cape and gloves. She was pure elegance, and none of the old fear was in her eyes.

"Hello, Byron." She smiled almost victoriously at his shaken appearance. She could tell by his eyes and his sallow complexion that he still drank. She swallowed back the nausea it brought her to see him so close again, to remember the hideous nights she had spent in his bed. He was older now, with crows feet about his eyes and a little gray in his receding blond hair. His gray eyes were steely and wary as he rose from his chair.

"What are you doing here? I thought my father talked to you before I came back from Washington. You agreed—"

"I know what I agreed to, Byron," she interrupted in a silky voice. She turned and closed the door. "Don't be so upset. Half of Saint Louis knows we were once married. The city isn't that big, you know. What is the harm in a man's ex-wife visiting him to express her hopes that he does well in his congressional campaign?"

"Refreshing people's memories that I am a divorced man won't help," he grumbled. "I wanted to keep all that quiet."

Her eyes narrowed and he felt a chill at the hatred in them. "Yes. You are very good at keeping things quiet, aren't you, Byron?" She stepped closer, reminding herself she must be strong and demanding. "Like keeping it quiet that Caleb Sax was not dead when he left Saint Louis. And keeping it quiet that my own daughter did not die, but was shipped off to an orphanage."

She found pleasure in the way he paled, smiled at his attempt to keep his composure. "I—I don't know what you're talking about!"

"Yes, you do. I have found my daughter, Byron. Oh, don't worry. I don't intend to use what I know against you— unless you refuse to cooperate."

His eyes narrowed. "Cooperate?"

She met his eyes squarely. "I want a simple yes or no, Byron. That's all there is to it. I simply want to know if my baby girl was given away to an orphanage in Philadelphia and if Caleb's blue quill necklace was with her."

There was a long moment of silence, after which Byron swallowed, remaining on his feet with effort. "All right," he said quietly. "Yes. I gave her away. And don't think me so terrible. I could have had her killed, but I simply wasn't that evil. You might say you could thank me for that."

Her joy at his answer was overshadowed by the ridiculous remark that followed. "Oh yes. I have so much to thank you for, don't I?"

He folded his arms, trying to appear more masculine and overbearing. "How did you know? And what is this about Caleb still being alive?"

Sarah smiled sarcastically. "You shouldn't have thrown in the necklace, Byron. She kept it. I have found my daughter, but I won't give you the satisfaction of the details. Nor will I tell you how I know Caleb was not killed along the river like you told me." She smiled again. "But I would be careful if I were you, Byron. As I remember, Caleb was a vengeful man. If I should one day find him and he discovers what happened after he was shipped out of Saint Louis..." She shrugged. "Well, I wouldn't want to be in your shoes. It would be hard to sleep at night."

His eyes glittered. "Bitch! I'll—"

"You'll what? What will you do, Byron Clawson?" She struggled to control her shaking. Facing this man was the hardest thing she had done in a long time. She still feared him, but she dared not show it. She must be confident for Lynda's sake. "You know I could destroy you, Byron."

His eyes were cold and piercing. "What the hell do you want from me?"

"I simply want extra insurance that you will leave me alone and never bring harm to me or my daughter. I am giving you a simple promise to never harm your career, as long as you never harm me. All I wanted was an honest answer about Caleb and my daughter, and now I have it. It's that simple. I just wanted to be sure the girl I have found is really mine."

He gave her that victorious look he used to give her when he knew she would give up her pride and allow him his husbandly privileges. It sent shivers through her bones.

"All right. It appears we're at a stand-off. I won a victory of sorts, and so have you. We're even. We can each go our own way now."

She nodded. "Fine. And I thank you for being honest about the girl. I had little left to be happy about. You destroyed my life. Now I have something to live for again. I will even go so far as to introduce my daughter publicly as simply a girl who has come to work for me. The child has suffered untold grief and trauma because of what you did, but just being together is all either of us needs now. Knowing for certain we are mother and daughter is recompense enough." She looked at him haughtily. "Good luck in the political arena, Byron."

She turned to leave.

"Wait," he said.

She turned, her profile beautiful, her green eyes dancing with victory as she faced him more fully.

"What about Caleb?" he asked.

"What do you mean?"

"I mean . . ." He swallowed. "What if—just what if— he really is still alive and you should somehow find him?"

"So?"

"Well, what would he do? What would *you* do?"

She smiled at the worried look on his face. "I already told you what I would do. Nothing. I have given you my word. But I certainly can't speak for Caleb. Perhaps he suspects you were the one who put the bullet in his back. Were you?" His face reddened and she had her answer. Sarah turned and left, unable to look at him another moment. She wished she could get away with killing him.

Byron sank into his chair, opening a drawer and taking out a small vial of whiskey. He swallowed some, then leaned back and closed his eyes.

"We should have killed him," he muttered. "By God, we should have killed him outright that day. What idiots!" He glared at the closed door, then threw the small bottle against it, wishing the bottle were Caleb Sax. He had been haunted for years by what might have happened to the man, by the possibility he could have lived. It seemed so improbable. Apparently Sarah had never found him. And he had never shown up in Saint Louis again.

He got up from his chair and took a deep breath. It was a foolish worry after all these years. If Caleb Sax wanted him he would have come by now. Byron walked to the door and began picking up the glass. His secretary entered and her eyes widened.

"Mr. Clawson! What happened, sir?"

"Nothing. Just a little accident. Clean this up, will you? I have more important things to do."

He walked to a window and looked out at the street below,

where a newsboy was hawking papers, shouting about more political and social unrest in Texas. He wondered if it might not be a good time to buy considerable property in that province of Mexico. If it ever became a part of the States, land values would increase dramatically. He would have to talk to his brokers about that.

Chapter
Thirty-Two

EMILY Stoner approached the three men timidly, which was in a sense amusing, for she had spent years being around men, sleeping with strangers. But this was different. These men were not coming to her. She was going to them, and for a very different reason. These were brave, prominent men who might shun her. Perhaps she had no business approaching them at all, yet the possibility of starting a new life someplace else was too enticing. She had been shunned and scorned for years. What did she have to lose now?

The crowd was dispersing, talking among themselves about Texas and the land that could be had for free. Some wondered aloud if slavery was allowed there. But Emily Stoner didn't care about slaves, or whether Texas was part of Mexico or the United States. She cared only that it was someplace new, where there were perhaps lonely men who needed a woman to help keep house, to cook—maybe even marry. She had deliberately left the paint off her face and wore a plain blue cotton dress.

"Excuse me," she said to a burly, bearded man with ruddy skin and kind brown eyes.

The man turned, looking her over with a frown. She was thin and pale, and for some reason she held a shawl over one side of her face, a face that bore traces of youth too soon destroyed.

"Yes, ma'am? What can I help you with?"

Emily swallowed, her pale blue eyes darting about as though someone was going to point a finger and chase her away.

"I was just wondering . . . I listened to you talking about Texas. The newspaper said some men from Texas would be down at the docks to talk to people about settling there. I realize you speak mostly to men, telling them about free land and all. But what about women? Are women needed?"

A faint smile passed over the man's mouth and his eyes took inventory. Skinny, awfully skinny. Could be pretty, though. He pushed back his hat. "Ma'am, women are always needed in places like that. Some men go there alone, some go with wives who end up gettin' killed or die givin' birth, things like that. It would take a pretty brave lady, though, to go there alone. Is that what you're asking?"

She dropped her eyes. "Well, I have some money, enough perhaps to pay someone to build my own cabin. I could take in wash, mending—perhaps cook. I can do all those things."

He rubbed his chin. "Well, ma'am, let's just say in Viesca, where we come from, a nice little woman like you would be mighty popular. You might find more mendin' and washin' and cookin' on your hands than you could handle, along with several offers of matrimony. There's a lot of lonely men in them parts."

She smiled, raising her eyes almost bashfully. He apparently did not suspect what she was. Maybe none of them would. She could be a respected woman. "Viesca. Where is that?"

"About a hundred miles north of San Felipe. Most of our

men are from San Felipe, Austin's headquarters. They went on upriver. We come from all over the Anglo settlements, actually. Viesca is pretty rugged territory. There's a lot of dangers, ma'am. No doctors. Indian raids and such. But there's quite a few of us, and we'd see to it you'd be protected, if you wanted to settle there."

She nodded, holding the shawl close over her face. "Well, I'm alone. My family is all dead and my . . . my husband died recently. I have debtors who hound me," she lied. "I thought perhaps if I went to Texas—"

He laughed lightly. "Say no more. People have gone there for worse reasons. New Orleans is as far as we planned to go. We brought some goods to trade and agreed with Mr. Austin to say our piece about Texas, try to get some help and make people aware of what's happenin' there. We want good, honest men and women—no riff-raff and no squatters. We're hopin' that with enough numbers we can get a few more rights under the Mexican government."

"I see. Well, how would I go about getting there?" She widened her eyes for an innocent look, somewhat amused that he thought her respectable. Perhaps in someplace new that would be possible.

He shrugged. "We're headin' back in about three days. I'm Howard Cox." He turned and nudged the man next to him. "Look smart, you two. This here nice lady is thinkin' on goin' back with us." The two men turned and looked her over appreciatively, both grinning. "This here is Case Dressel," Cox told her, nodding to a blond man of perhaps thirty. The man flashed her a handsome smile. "Now Case here, he could use someone to wash and mend and such. Lost his wife about four years back."

Emily frowned. "Oh, I'm so sorry."

"Thank you, ma'am," he answered.

Cox turned to the third man, who was tall and looked weathered and worn. His hair was red but graying, his brown eyes rather hollow. "This is Milton McBride. He owns quite a bit of land in Viesca, has a wife and four sons."

McBride nodded and Emily smiled. "I am thinking of going to Texas," she told the man. "I can take in wash, mending. Perhaps your wife would need help."

"Possible," he answered curtly.

Emily turned her eyes back to Howard Cox's round, bearded face. "My name is Emily, Emily Stephens," she lied, afraid to use her real name in case someone had heard it. "I can pay you to take me back with you. I would need protection, and you all look like reputable gentlemen. Surely men brave enough to settle in a place like Texas are also reliable men who can be trusted."

Cox beamed. "Yes, ma'am. There are certain things you would need. Do you have a horse of your own?"

"No. But I can get one. I don't have much to take along. I'll get a packhorse for my belongings. Would that be too much?"

"No, ma'am. That would be fine. We have horses of our own to take back. We'll go by boat through the Gulf and then to the Brazos."

"Are there many others going with you?"

"A few. Most will wait to sell their land or businesses and all first. It's a big decision, ma'am. Maybe you'd best wait and do some thinkin' on it yourself."

"No, I don't have to wait. I already know what I want to do, and here are three men who could accompany me. I don't want to pass up the opportunity. When should I meet you, and where?"

"Well, this is Tuesday. Meet us right here Friday mornin'. Bring your belongin's, your horses and money. We won't charge you ourselves, but you'll have to pay your own passage."

"I can do that."

He smiled, lifting his hat a little. "Well then, we'll see you on Friday. Once you see how pretty Texas is, Mrs. Stephens, you'll be glad you went. It kind of grows on a person. You get there and you just don't want to leave again." He winked. "And those people your husband owed won't bother you there. If they do, we'll turn them over to the Comanche." He laughed, a deep laugh that made his stomach shake.

Emily smiled. "Thank you, Mr. Cox."

"You need any help getting your things together, ma'am?" Case Dressel asked.

She met his eyes, and felt stirred by his fine physique. But she was determined she would never betray her past life if she went to Texas. She would conduct herself properly and maybe even find a husband.

"No," she replied quickly. How could she take him to Marie's place and show him where she had been living? "No, I can take care of everything."

"Those people you owe won't give you any trouble, will they?" Cox asked.

"I don't think so." She backed away, keeping the shawl over her face. "Thank you, all of you. When I heard you talking you just made Texas sound so wonderful. I hope I can help somehow when I get there. I . . . I have a good education, too. I could teach children, if such things are needed."

Cox grinned more. "Why, that would be a welcome help indeed, ma'am. We surely do need fine women like yourself."

She nodded, then turned and disappeared into the crowd, finding it difficult not to break into a run. Texas. Perhaps something about her dreary, sordid life would change. Perhaps it was not too late after all to be someone special. She thought about Caleb, how he had tried to get her to change her life so long ago and how hopeless she thought it was to try. Now she would do it.

She would be a different person, Emily Stephens, widowed and homeless. She was going to Texas.

Sarah opened the door, surprised at the sight of Byron Clawson. In the years he had been back in Saint Louis, he had never set foot on her doorstep, and she had not heard from him since her visit to his office. He looked frightened, and he stood there holding a newspaper tightly in his hand.

"What are you doing here?" she asked calmly. "I told you never to bother me."

He held out the newspaper with a shaking hand, his lips curling when he spoke. "Have you seen this?"

She frowned. "No. Why?"

"You little liar. You thought I wouldn't notice. You thought you'd just sneak off to him and arrange for him to come kill me."

She shook her head. "Byron, I don't know what you're talking about, but I wish you would leave."

He studied her green eyes. "You really haven't seen it yet, have you?"

She glanced at the paper he held under her nose, a shiver coursing down her spine. "If it's today's, no, I haven't."

"Well, you'd know soon enough. You might as well hear it from—" He looked past her at a tall, beautiful young woman who came down the stairs to stand behind Sarah. "Is that the girl? Your daughter?"

Sarah turned, and Byron barged into the house, pulling the door from Sarah's hand and slamming it shut. Sarah stepped back as his eyes took inventory of Lynda.

"Yes," Sarah answered quietly. She turned to Lynda. "Lynda, this is Byron Clawson, the man who so kindly gave you away to an orphanage."

Byron reddened, and Lynda's blue eyes instantly took on the cold look Byron had once seen in her father's eyes. "Oh, yes, she is every bit his daughter, isn't she?" Byron sneered. "Caleb Sax's women. How sweet." He unrolled the newspaper and held it out. "I wonder how many more women he's got—in Texas."

Sarah's eyes widened as she took the paper with a shaking hand.

"Here," Byron said coldly, pointing to an article on the front page.

Sarah looked at the article, still bewildered. Lynda stepped

closer to her as she quietly scanned the paper. Byron took
a cigar from his pocket and lit it as Sarah read. He scanned
Lynda appreciatively, but she was Caleb Sax's daughter and
that made her loathsome. He should have had her killed.
Seeing her gave him chills.

"Oh, my God," Sarah finally murmured. She began to
shake and Lynda quickly put an arm about her waist.

"Mother, what is it?"

Sarah closed her eyes, holding the paper tightly in her
hands, momentarily speechless.

"Mother, come and sit down. You're shaking," Lynda
told her, urging Sarah to a chair in the entranceway. She
glared at Byron. "What have you done to upset my mother?"
she demanded.

Byron kept his cigar between his teeth and grabbed the
paper from Sarah's hands. "Here. Let me read part of this
article to you. It seems some delegates from Texas have
come to Saint Louis to encourage people to go back with
them. The Americans want bigger numbers, more rights in
Mexico, and they need help and strength in fighting Indians
and outlaws." He took the cigar from his mouth and held
it between his fingers, scanning through the article. "Well,
that isn't important. What is important is that some names
are mentioned. One of the delegates is a Mr. Tom Sax."
His steely gray eyes meet Lynda's blue ones. "Son of one
of the biggest landowners in the American settlement of
San Felipe de Austin, a man who is known for his quality
horses, Mr. Caleb Sax."

He watched Lynda pale. The girl pressed her hands tightly
on Sarah's shoulders. "My father?" she asked.

Byron threw the newspaper to the floor. "I'm afraid it
must be. The article says something about the Saxes being
part Indian." He threw his cigar into the fireplace and suddenly grabbed Sarah's wrist, jerking her out of the chair
and close to his face.

"Leave her alone," Lynda told him, grabbing Sarah's arm.
He shoved her hard, knocking her against a wall.

"You'll find out, won't you?" he sneered. "And when you do, if this is the Caleb Sax you whored with all those years ago, you had better warn him to stay in Texas. You keep him away from me, understand?"

Lynda ran past them into the parlor.

"No one tells Caleb Sax what to do," Sarah answered. "Not even his women."

"I should kill you," he hissed. "He already thinks you're dead."

"Get out," Lynda screamed. Byron turned to see her pointing a pistol at him, the gun Sarah always kept for protection. "Get out before I kill you myself!"

He saw in her eyes the wild, vengeful look he had seen once in Caleb's eyes. She meant business. He let go of Sarah, shoving her as he did so.

"You get out of here right now or there will be more headlines in the papers about Byron Clawson's sordid life and violent death." Lynda held the gun straight and steady, her blue eyes filled with bitter hatred.

Sarah clung to the arm of the chair, staring at the girl with alarm. "Lynda, put the gun down," she pleaded.

"Not until he's gone," Lynda answered firmly.

Byron backed toward the door. He glanced at Sarah again. "You remember what I said. As long as Caleb Sax stays in Texas, he's safe. Perhaps you should go to him and—"

"And get out of Saint Louis so you don't have to worry about her marring your good name?" Lynda sneered. "I don't know my father, Mr. Clawson, but I know enough about him to know you're the one who might not be safe. You're trying to scare us, but you're the one who's scared. You're a coward—a lying, cheating, repulsive excuse of a man. Now get out of my mother's house!"

Byron blinked. "Bastard," he hissed. "You illegitimate little whore!"

Lynda deliberately fired, hitting the door only inches from Byron's face. The man immediately whirled and flew out the door. Lynda hurried over to it to see him running down the street. She looked down at the gun, staring as though surprised it was even in her hand, then turned to her mother, who just looked at her in shock.

"Lynda," Sarah finally muttered. "You might have killed him!"

The girl swallowed and quickly set the pistol aside. "I hate him," she muttered, staring at the gun. "Now that I've seen him I hate him even more." She looked back at her mother. "And I'm not afraid of him. Neither should you be, mother. Especially not now. Not if Caleb Sax is alive. Even if he's married or something, he'd help you if that man gave you trouble. I know he would."

Sarah's eyes began to tear, and she sank into the chair, her legs suddenly weak. "Lynda, do you . . . do you think it could really be my Caleb?" she asked in a whisper.

Lynda smiled at the way her mother spoke as though Caleb Sax was a very precious object to be treasured. She bent down and picked up the newspaper, reading the article quietly, then meeting Sarah's eyes again. They were shining with love and hope, mixed with fear and apprehension.

"There's only one way to find out," Lynda told her. "We have to go and talk to Tom Sax."

Tears slipped from Sarah's eyes. "But what if—what if Caleb is married and has other children?" She wiped her tears with shaking hands. "Oh, Lynda, I can't just walk back into his life, not if he's found someone else. And yet he should know I'm alive. What should I do?"

Her heart pounded wildly with hope and dread, dread that if it really was her Caleb there would be no way they could be together again. She had tried so long to find him, and now without warning, after giving up her own efforts, he was back in her life again. She had struggled so long to get over him. Now it was all reawakened, and the pain was almost unbearable.

"Mother, we have to know. Remarried or not, I intend to find my father. We're going to see Tom Sax."

"I can't. I can't go, Lynda. I'm afraid. I'm afraid he'll

tell us that it isn't our Caleb or that he's got a wife. Maybe he wouldn't want me anymore."

"Oh, mother, don't be silly." The girl turned and went up the stairs. "I'm going to put on my prettiest dress and I'm going to the square where they're having that meeting this afternoon. I'll talk to Tom Sax and find out the truth." She stopped halfway up the stairs, her heart getting even lighter. "Mother!" She turned. "Mother, if it's true, then this Tom Sax would be my brother, wouldn't he? You said Caleb had a son by a Cheyenne woman and named him Tom. That makes him my half brother." She smiled and ran up the rest of the stairs. "It has to be the same one, Mother!"

Sarah stared after the girl as she disappeared into her bedroom, babbling about maybe finding a whole family, about Texas and what it might be like, then laughing about how fast Byron Clawson had run away from the house. But Sarah heard little. There was a Caleb Sax living in Texas, a man who was part Indian and had a son nàmed Tom. How could it be anyone but her Caleb?

She had searched for so long, yet the possibility of finding him frightened her. What would he be like? What would he think of her now? Would he even want to see her? He would be like a stranger after all these years. Was it better to leave it alone and not pursue the matter? No! She had to know. And even if she was afraid to find out, Lynda would not let it go. She was a determined girl, determined and stubborn and free spirited like her father.

Lynda rushed down the stairs wearing a deep red velvet dress and cape, looking beautiful. She leaned down and kissed her mother's cheek. "Good-bye, Mother. You change and get ready. I might be bringing Tom Sax home with me."

She flew to the door and went through it. Sarah wanted to tell her to stop and wait. It was all happening too fast. She was terrified to take hope in any of it. She finally found her feet and went to the door, but Lynda was already far down the street. She looked down at the pistol that lay on a table nearby.

"Yes," she muttered, "you *are* Caleb Sax's daughter."

Chapter
Thirty-Three

THEY reached the ledge of the rocky canyon wall while it was still morning since they had broken camp very early. The wall ran for miles, a barrier dividing what was on the other side from the rest of the world. They had been through some beautiful country, but the wall seemed to be the border between one world and another. Sarah caught her breath when they reached the ledge, and the four of them just stared for a quiet moment, Sarah, Lynda, Lee and Tom.

Before them lay a vast expanse of land unbroken by forest or mountain, yet it was startlingly beautiful in its nakedness. The morning sun cast purple pink and orange shadows across the endless horizon.

"My God," Sarah said softly. "What is it?"

"Texas," Tom replied. He breathed deeply, drawing strength from the air of this land.

"It's so big."

Tom grinned. "They say it would take a man a year or more to ride its border. Some people don't like such open spaces, but Father says this naked land is like looking at a beautiful woman without her clothes. Everything is there for the taking, and her full beauty is revealed."

Sarah reddened, old feelings reawakening. She had been that way once for Caleb Sax. Did he think of her when he spoke of the naked land he loved?

"Come," Tom said. "We'll show you the way down."

He turned his horse and rode ahead of them.

"Be careful," Lee told Lynda. "It's not easy going down."

"I think by now I'm as good a rider as you, Lee White-stone," she replied pertly. Their eyes held a moment, teasingly, suggestively, saying much.

"We'll see about that," Lee answered with a wink, turning his own horse. He wondered how long he could bear looking at Caleb Sax's beautiful daughter without grabbing her up and riding off with her so they could be alone. He had never seen anyone so beautiful in his entire young life, and anything she had done until she found her mother made little difference to him. He didn't care about the gambler she had told them about. During their long journey to Texas there had been plenty of time to talk, to get to know each other and become friends. And he knew Lynda Sax was strong and brave and stubborn and beautiful. He had watched her, guided her, helped her, taught her, fallen in love with her. But it was a love as yet unspoken.

The women followed, leading their own packhorses. It had been a long journey, slow at first because Lynda had to learn to ride and Sarah had not ridden in years. Tom was determined that nothing would happen to these two women. His excitement over the surprise he was bringing his father made him want to hurry, but he would not rush Sarah and Lynda. They were very special women, and he would die for them if necessary, for the most important thing was to get them to Caleb.

Caleb himself was probably worried by now. They had had to wait three extra weeks while Sarah and Lynda got their affairs in order and sold the Sax house. He and Lee had told the others that they had to stay for personal business. How could they explain the long story of Caleb and Sarah Sax? So the rest of their party had left without them.

And because Tom wanted to surprise his father, he sent no message.

While they waited in Saint Louis Sarah had fussed that perhaps they shouldn't go, perhaps they should wait in Saint Louis while Tom told Caleb he had found them, then let Caleb come for them if he wanted to. But Tom Sax would have none of it.

"Do you still love my father?" he had asked Sarah.

Her answer was in her bright green eyes.

"Father will want you there," he had told her then. "I have no doubt in my mind. Why waste so much time? Why not go right now? My father is very lonely. He needs you. Besides, he can't leave Texas. There's too much to do with so much land."

Lynda had left little choice. There would be no waiting for her. She wanted to see Texas and was determined to meet her father. She would most definitely go, and she would not leave her mother behind.

They headed down a narrow path, small rocks sliding in front of them. It was a dangerous trek, but soon the path widened and the women relaxed. Sarah watched Tom, such a handsome young man, with his father's build and spirit, but such dark eyes, surely the eyes of his Cheyenne mother. She smiled when she turned to watch Lee. He rode back to Lynda to make sure she was all right. He was so obviously doing all he could to prove his manliness and skill that it was almost humorous. The young man was openly enamored with Lynda Sax, and Lynda was no less enamored with the handsome young man. He was husky and strong, with shoulders "like a bear," Lynda had said aside to her mother once. He was not tall, barely taller than Lynda, but he was very strong and almost cuddly-looking, with his round, happy face and bright smile.

Sarah turned her attention to the land that stretched before them. Texas. Was she crazy to come here like this? Perhaps. But it felt wonderful to leave Saint Louis and the ugly past behind. Here she would be free of worry about what Byron might do to her, be a new woman, awaken all the feelings the old Sarah used to have. She could smile. And oh, how good it felt to smile.

She was thirty-five years old. It had been seventeen years since she last saw Caleb. Her most vivid memory was of their interlude in the cave, those glorious beautiful moments in his arms. Could it be that way again for them? Would he still want her that way? She hadn't changed all that much physically. Why, a lot of women her age even had babies. Perhaps she could have another child. It was not impossible, and how wonderful it would be to have a little baby that she could know from birth and raise herself.

Sarah reddened then at the thought. Before she could have a baby, she and Caleb would have to rediscover all they had lost. Maybe the magic would be gone now. She hoped not.

Tom rode back to her. "Are you all right? Do you need to rest?"

"I'm fine, Tom. You fuss too much over me."

He grinned. "I wouldn't want to have to answer to Father for letting something happen to you just when he has found you again."

She smiled in return, but her eyes teared and she looked away. "Tom, are you sure I should be doing this?"

"Of course I'm sure! Father spoke of you so many times. He never stopped loving you. I could see that. Even Marie knew it, I think. She never said anything, though. She just loved him. Marie was a good woman."

"Yes, I'm sure she was. I can tell by watching Lee."

Tom nudged his horse closer and leaned over. "Hey, I think that Lee is sick with love for Lynda. What do you think?"

Sarah laughed lightly. "I think you're right."

Tom nodded. "My sister is the prettiest girl in Texas." He gave her a wink. "Besides her mother."

Sarah blushed, feeling like a young girl herself again. She swallowed back a lump in her throat and quickly wiped her eyes. "Tell me again, Tom. What is he like? Are you absolutely sure he'll want me?"

Tom shook his head, adjusting his leather hat. He wore buckskins like his father, but Lee chose to wear white man's clothing.

"You shouldn't worry so about it. I guarantee that now that you're here you'll never leave Texas. Father won't let you. I don't think he has changed much over the years. He is still a big, strong man. I never saw a man with so many scars, though. When he tells me all the things he went through when he was young, I wonder if I could have done it. He got even more the night he tried to save Marie and David. He was like a crazy man that night."

Sarah's heart ached at the thought of it. "Poor Caleb," she said quietly. "He's suffered so."

Tom turned to look at her. From what he had learned, this woman had suffered terribly herself, yet she did not seem to be so concerned about that as she was about Caleb. Sarah Sax was the good woman his father had always said she was.

"It has been three years since Marie was killed. Father has been very lonely. He will be happy again when he sees you," the young man told her. "But it is not an easy life here, Sarah. It's dangerous, and now there are a lot of problems with the Mexican government."

"I don't care what the outside problems are. I can handle anything as long as I'm with Caleb. I've been through too much to be concerned about such things."

"I just wish we could have left with the others so we'd have more protection."

"God is with us this time, Tom. He didn't perform this miracle and bring us this far to let something happen before we reach Caleb. I'm not afraid."

He grinned. "Let's hope you are right."

Why should she be afraid? Sarah thought. God had helped her find Caleb Sax, and now she was going to him. Nothing would stop them from being together this time. Nothing.

* * *

They got to a river, and Tom and Lee helped show them the way across the shallowest part.

"This is the Brazos," Tom explained. "We are on Sax land now."

Sarah's heart tightened when she realized they were that close. She felt her nerves start to tingle and prayed the awful shaking would not overwhelm her. She followed the others almost in a trance then, hardly noticing the beautiful scenery around them as Tom explained first one landmark and then another. This particular spot was greener than the land they had been through, rockier, more hilly. They came upon a rise and looked out at a green valley.

"Those are some of father's horses," Tom said.

Sarah stared down at the herd, a mixture of beautiful mares, geldings and colts.

"They're beautiful," Lynda exclaimed.

"They sure are," Lee answered.

She turned, realizing he was looking at her, not the horses. She felt the color rising to her cheeks. Why did he make her feel like an inexperienced girl? She had lived and slept with a gambler for two years, had even lost his baby. But this Cherokee man made her feel like she had never been with a man. He was the sweetest, most virile man she had ever met, and she could not help wondering what it would be like to be held in his powerful arms. But he was also bashful. Perhaps he had never even been with a woman. After all, there were not many available women in these parts.

"Do you think you will like it here?" he asked.

Their eyes held. "I know I will," she answered. "You'll show me all of it, won't you? I want to ride every inch of my father's land, get to know it and help with all of it. I don't want to just stay in the house. I want to really be a part of it, Lee. I've never belonged anywhere before. I'm so happy. I have parents and a brother."

He grinned, reaching over and taking her hand. "And an uncle, right?"

She laughed and he squeezed her hand when a tear slipped down her lovely cheek.

"Hey, everything will be good now. I'll make sure of it. In fact, I can show you something else right now." He reached over with a powerful arm and grabbed her off her horse, pulling her onto his own. She let out a cry of surprise at his sudden boldness. "We'll be right back," Lee shouted to Tom and Sarah. He turned his horse and headed down an embankment to a cluster of trees several yards away. "Here it is," he told her.

Lynda looked around, seeing nothing but the cottonwood trees. She shivered at the feel of his powerful arm wrapped around her from behind.

"Here what is?" she asked, smiling nervously.

His hand moved up to brush at the trace of a tear still left on her cheek. "Turn around and I'll show you."

She felt her blood warm as wonderful stirrings moved through her body. She moved a leg over the horse's neck, sitting sideways and looking into Lee Whitestone's very dark eyes, paying no heed to the fact that part of her leg was exposed when she swung it around.

Lee felt like he was on fire, and he knew it was not the Texas heat. He had never been with a woman, yet all his manly instincts came naturally. He swallowed, drinking in her dark beauty, her splendid blue eyes. "I've been watching you, Lynda. For weeks we have traveled together, even slept together for warmth, treating each other like relatives. But we are not relatives. I do not want to be relatives—not that kind."

She studied the sincerity and honesty in his eyes, then turned away. "Even when you know about the man I lived with?"

"You could not help that. You just needed somebody strong and sure to love you, Lynda Sax. You are like a lost little girl. Now you have a family . . . and me, if you want me. I think you are the most beautiful woman I have ever set eyes on."

She turned back to meet his kind, brown eyes.

Lee's heart went out to her at her tears. "The past is over now, Lynda."

He leaned forward and cautiously met her lips. She moved her arms around his neck, and in that moment Lee White-stone had never known such absolute ecstasy. Nor had Lynda Sax. Here was a man who would love his woman for all that she was, marry her, give her a home and children, and be entirely devoted to her. Yes, life was going to be very good in Texas.

A few yards away Sarah and Tom continued to watch the horses. Then Tom straightened. "Hey! Father is down there!"

Sarah's heart raced wildly. "He is?"

"Yes. He just rode around the bend down there. We could not see him before."

Sarah watched. A rider appeared wearing buckskin pants and a vest, his long dark hair flying behind him as he chased a wandering mare back to the herd.

"Oh, dear God," she whispered. "It's him."

"Let's go."

"No," she almost yelled. She sat frozen in place. "I can't. I can't!"

Tom frowned, noticing she was begining to shake. "It is all right, Sarah."

She shook her head. "You . . . you go first and tell him. I'll wait here."

He reached over and squeezed her arm. "Are you all right?"

She nodded, watching Caleb in wide-eyed wonder.

"All right. You wait right here. I'll ride down and tell him."

The young man began the descent and Sarah watched. Caleb. It really was Caleb. She could tell even from here, and he didn't look so very different, at least not from a distance. Lee and Lynda rode back to where she sat.

"Where's Tom?" Lee asked.

Sarah swallowed and nodded toward the valley. "He's down there. Caleb is there."

Lynda gasped and looked down at the riders. "It's my father! Oh, Lee, let's go down there."

He kept an arm around her and squeezed her tighter. "No, Lynda, not yet. Look at your mother," he said quietly.

Lynda looked over at Sarah, who was visibly shaking, with tears on her face.

"Let them be alone first. It's a special time for them. And this will all be a shock to Caleb. Let's go back down to the trees and wait there. Give them a few minutes."

Lynda wiped away her own tears. "Yes. Yes, you're probably right."

He kissed her hair and turned back, disappearing again into the trees.

Sarah was hardly aware they had been there at all. Tom had reached Caleb. He called out to him, and they rode close and dismounted. They hugged for a very long time and then started talking. Caleb looked up, back at Tom, then up again. They talked more, and then Tom mounted his horse and moved through the herd Caleb had been tending, while Caleb remounted his horse and directed it toward the rise where Sarah sat watching. He kept looking up, even stopped once to stare as though unable to believe it, perhaps afraid to believe it. Then he kicked the horse into a gallop.

Sarah did not move. She half expected the man coming toward her to be a complete stranger. For a moment he disappeared below, then reappeared, closer now. Yes, it was Caleb. It was his handsome face, his beautiful blue eyes, his broad shoulders and strong arms, his long hair, his dark skin. He stopped on a wide, flat rock not far below, just staring up at her in his own disbelief. Time seemed to stop. She looked at him, a beautiful man perched on a grand stallion, with Texas sprawled out behind him, and for a moment he looked unreal.

But he was real. He moved again, galloping to the rise.

He reined the mount near her, his blue eyes looking at her as though he were seeing a ghost.

What could he say? He was speechless. It was Sarah. She had hardly changed and she was alive! He rode closer. She was shaking almost violently and he frowned. What had happened to her? What kind of hell had she been through? Tom had said she had a daughter, his own daughter.

She clung tightly to the saddle horn. "Help me, Caleb," she said quietly.

He quickly dismounted, walking to her horse and reaching up, his big hands grasping her about the waist and lifting her down. He said nothing at first, but merely pulled her into his warm, welcoming arms. He held her tight, very tight, wanting to stop her awful shaking. Her arms slowly moved around him, and he lay his cheek against the top of her head.

"Sarah, my Sarah," he groaned.

From the edge of the cottonwoods, Lee and Lynda watched.

"My God, it's really him," Lynda whispered, putting her fingers to the blue quill necklace she wore around her neck. She had put it on that morning, wanting her father to see it the first time he met his daughter, to know his love gift had brought his family together at last.

A hawk circled above and cried out, then flew off into the sun, the light reflecting on the bird in just the right way to make it appear blue. Its shadow moved over Caleb and Sarah Sax, but they were too lost in each other's arms to notice.

I hope you enjoyed my story. I love to hear from my readers. Please feel free to write me at 6013-A North Road, Coloma, MI, 49038. Send a self-addressed, stamped envelope and I will be happy to send you my latest newsletter regarding other novels I have written as well as forthcoming novels. Thank you for your interest and support.

F. Rosanne Bittner